PRAISE

"Bestselling authors Simon Gervais and Ryan Steck have teamed up to deliver an absolute knockout with *The Second Son*. This adrenaline-fueled thriller grabs you from page one and never lets up. Chase Burke is the kind of hero readers crave—flawed, fierce, and driven by loyalty and love. Filled with heart-pounding action, jaw-dropping twists, and ripped-from-the-headlines conspiracies that keep you guessing until the final page, add *The Second Son* to the top of your list TODAY! I devoured this one—and you will too! Get ready—*The Second Son* has arrived with a vengeance!"

—Jack Carr, #1 *New York Times* bestselling author of *Red Sky Mourning*

THE SECOND SON

A THRILLER

ALSO BY SIMON GERVAIS

Caspian Anderson Series

The Elias Network

The Elias Enigma

Clayton White Series

The Last Protector

The Last Sentinel

The Last Guardian

Pierce Hunt Series

Hunt Them Down

Trained to Hunt

Time to Hunt

Mike Walton Series

The Thin Black Line

A Red Dotted Line

A Thick Crimson Line

A Long Gray Line

Blackbriar

Robert Ludlum's The Blackbriar Genesis

ALSO BY RYAN STECK

Matthew Redd Series

Gone Dark

Out for Blood

Lethal Range

Fields of Fire

Alexander Hawke Series

Ted Bell's Monarch

THE SECOND SON

SIMON GERVAIS
RYAN STECK

A THRILLER

This is a work of fiction. Names, characters, organizations, places, events, and incidents are either products of the author's imagination or are used fictitiously. Otherwise, any resemblance to actual persons, living or dead, is purely coincidental.

Text copyright © 2025 by Simon Gervais Entertainment, Ltd. and Ryan Steck
All rights reserved.

No part of this book may be reproduced, or stored in a retrieval system, or transmitted in any form or by any means, electronic, mechanical, photocopying, recording, or otherwise, without express written permission of the publisher.

Published by Thomas & Mercer, Seattle
www.apub.com

Amazon, the Amazon logo, and Thomas & Mercer are trademarks of Amazon.com, Inc., or its affiliates.

EU product safety contact:
Amazon Media EU S. à r.l.
38, avenue John F. Kennedy, L-1855 Luxembourg
amazonpublishing-gpsr@amazon.com

ISBN-13: 9781662529290 (paperback)
ISBN-13: 9781662529276 (digital)

Cover design by Damon Freeman
Cover image: © prochasson Frederic, © Chipmunk131, © Fiqy / Shutterstock

Printed in the United States of America

THE SECOND SON

A THRILLER

PROLOGUE

Colombia

As the turbine engines of the Colombian Aerospace Force Sikorsky UH-60A Black Hawk began to spool up, Michael Burke closed his eyes and tried not to think about the list in his pocket.

Five names.

Two of them had already been crossed off, but neither of those were the one he most wanted to remove from consideration. Despite everything he'd done, officially or off the books, *that* name was still a glaring question mark. Had he made a mistake? Part of him hoped so. Because if he hadn't, then it could only mean one thing.

There's literally nobody left I can trust.

Michael shook his head in disgust.

My God. How has it come to this?

The whine of the turbines rose in pitch, accompanied by the steadily increasing beat of the rotor blades as they began to spin faster and faster.

Focus on the operation. That's all that matters right now.

In the jump seat opposite him, FBI Special Agent in Charge Jay Crawford, leader of the joint task force, nodded in his direction and held out a closed fist. He extended his thumb and waggled it up and down—a question.

You good?

Michael returned a solid thumbs-up.

Good to go.

He was in Colombia as part of an FBI joint operation with the Comando de Operaciones Especiales—an elite subdivision of the National Police of Colombia. The previous month, during a failed drug buy, two American backpackers had disappeared in Bogotá. As an analyst assigned to the Office of Analysis for Terrorism, Narcotics, and Crime—TNC—a division of the US State Department's Bureau of Intelligence and Research—INR—Michael had been working with the FBI and the Colombian National Police to locate and secure the release of the two Americans, who were now believed to be hostages of the oldest and one of the most powerful insurgent groups in Colombia: the terror organization known as Ejército de Liberacíon Nacional, or ELN for short.

Intel gathered from a variety of sources—signal intercepts, tips from informants, and drone overflights—put the hostages at one of half a dozen secret smuggling bases in the rugged Choco Department on the border with Panama. How long they would remain there was anyone's guess, which was why there was such a sense of urgency surrounding today's operation.

Michael's interest, however, extended beyond merely bringing back two American citizens who in all likelihood had been dipping their toes in the international drug trade and gotten burned for their trouble.

For nearly two years, Michael had been tracking criminal organizations across the Western Hemisphere, looking for connections that might indicate more than just partnerships of convenience. It was his belief—a gut feeling, really—that there was a single, unifying entity guiding or perhaps even controlling them all, a Pan-American criminal empire with tentacles stretching from the tar sands of Alberta to the secret coca fields of the Bolivian rainforest.

The organization—which, according to whispers on the dark web, might or might not be called FATHOM, if it existed at all—had become Michael's personal white whale. He'd volunteered for the joint op in Colombia in hopes of being able to interrogate any prisoners taken in the raid, with a view to extending his map of FATHOM's reach. What he had not anticipated was being asked to accompany the strike team.

And yet here I am, riding along.

Contrary to popular belief, INR analysts were not law enforcement agents. Most of them were academics—experts in international relations, political science, linguistics—but rarely had field experience.

Michael was an exception.

He had joined the FBI right out of college and excelled in his chosen career, eventually getting tapped to join the Hostage Rescue Team, the Bureau's elite tactical unit, where he'd worked for five years until being offered a senior position at INR. So, when three of the FBI Fly Team's SWAT operators had been sidelined at the last minute with an unexpected stomach bug, he'd been presented with a choice.

Gear up and ride along with the strike team . . .

Or see the operation postponed and risk losing track of the hostages.

Truth be told, it was an easy choice. While he did not regret leaving the Bureau to join the INR, there were times when he missed the adrenaline rush of field operations.

Still, proficiency in a tactical environment was a perishable skill. Unlike riding a bike, you couldn't just pick up a submachine gun and fall back into rhythm. His current job didn't require him to stay certified with weapons and, apart from his monthly two-hour sessions at a local shooting range, it had been a couple years since he'd truly sent lead downrange. Meanwhile, the SWAT guys were a team, training and rehearsing together, building an almost telepathic bond that allowed them to move with precision on an objective, often with a minimal amount of verbal communication. Michael wasn't part of that rhythm, and everyone knew it. That's why he'd been tasked to provide rear security for the rest of the team.

You won't get to be the tip of the spear, Crawford had joked. *You'll get the shaft.*

The turbines quickly reached max RPMs, and at a signal from the crew chief, the Black Hawk rocked a little and then was airborne, moving above the tarmac of the José María Córdova International Airport and slowly gaining altitude. There were five helicopters in the flight, four of them carrying Colombian police commandos and this one, the fifth, carrying the FBI SWAT team—or at least what was left of it—along with Michael and Jay Crawford.

The Colombians would take the lead—it was their country, after all. But since it was the FBI, with a ton of help from Michael, who had provided the intel and analysis that had given them the target location, the Colombian authorities had allowed them to join in on the raid.

It was about 160 miles from Rionegro, just south of Medellín, to the objective—not quite an hour's flight time. Because there was heavy vegetation around the target, the assault force would have to fast rope down and sweep across the objective on foot while the Black Hawks moved off to rendezvous with an air tanker flying over the Pacific Ocean. Once the area was secure, the commandos would have to work quickly to clear an LZ where the helicopters could set down and pick them all up.

Major Rojas, the senior officer of the commando unit and leading Chalk One, predicted a quick turnaround. "The moment they hear our choppers, they'll scatter like frightened rabbits. My bet is that we won't even need to engage them. They'll drop their weapons long before our boots touch the ground."

Michael wasn't quite as optimistic about the mission. His years with HRT had taught him the most basic rule of combat:

The plan is always the first casualty.

In some ways, Murphy's Law had already become manifest with the loss of the three SWAT operators, ostensibly to a stomach bug. It was more than a little suspicious, or at least Michael thought so, but Crawford had just shrugged it off.

Shit happens sometimes, Crawford had said. *Literally.*

During the first half hour of the journey, Michael was able to put aside his concerns. The view of the Cordillera Central and Cordillera Occidental—the northern extent of the Andes Mountain Range—passing by below, looking almost close enough to touch, was truly breathtaking. But as they left the mountains behind, dropping down to fly nap-of-the-earth above the lush and mostly undeveloped Pacific lowlands, his apprehension deepened. He found himself checking his Garmin almost compulsively, counting the miles and minutes to the objective.

Twenty minutes to showtime.

He began mentally reviewing his fast rope training. Unlike rappelling, which uses some kind of friction method—either a device or a coil around the body—to reduce the rate of descent, fast roping was more like sliding down a fire pole, with just your gloved hands and booted feet to keep the speed in check.

Most important rule—don't let go until your feet are on the ground!

Equipment check was next. Michael went through his gear again, making sure all his pouches were closed, nothing loose. His M4 carbine—clipped to his plate carrier for easy access—was equipped with a Trijicon ACOG sight. The weapon was loaded, and its selector switch was on Safe. Helmet, check. Eye protection, check. Gloves, on.

Good to go.

He looked at the Garmin again. They were still thirty miles out—at least ten minutes to go.

Plenty of time to go over it all again.

Pouches closed, nothing loose—

From the corner of his eye, he spied a sudden flash of light and a puff of smoke rising from the treetops below.

In an instant, everything changed.

Michael's blood ran cold as a finger of white vapor reached skyward. Warning alarms began blaring throughout the cabin. His stomach lurched as the helicopter pitched sideways, veering away from the formation. Through the side window, he saw an eruption of fireworks—flares bursting from the lead Black Hawk as it, too, initiated evasive maneuvers.

Too late.

The inbound rocket sliced through the brilliant pink-orange shower and then detonated in an expanding black cloud that engulfed the targeted aircraft. A secondary explosion followed a moment later, and then what was left of the helicopter, wreathed in flame and trailing black smoke, fell from the sky.

A sequence of facts, detached and clinical, unspooled in Michael's brain, even as the rest of him went into sphincter-puckering survival mode.

That was a surface-to-air missile . . . a man portable air defense weapon.

None of our intel indicated the ELN had access to MANPADs.

We're thirty miles from the objective . . .

This was an ambush, he realized.

They knew we were coming.

Somebody had warned them. A mole in the Colombian Police? Or . . .

Suddenly, the suspicious stomach bug that had sidelined three of the FBI SWAT operators seemed a lot more suspicious.

Nobody left to trust.

Another trail of smoke streaked up from the jungle. Michael tried to track its trajectory, but with his helo jinking to avoid being acquired by the incoming missile, the view through the cabin window was a blur of green.

A loud bang reverberated through the airframe. The Black Hawk shuddered and lurched, and then black smoke and the smell of burning metal filled the cabin.

That wasn't a missile strike, decided the analytical part of his brain. *Probably a piece of debris blown off the other helo got sucked into one of the intakes.*

The survival-oriented part of his brain reached for a fire extinguisher.

Strangely, he felt no fear. Just a cold anger burning like dry ice in his gut. Anger at whoever had betrayed them to the enemy—*Someone will pay,* he promised himself—but also at himself for having tipped his hand. He'd been so careful to avoid drawing attention to his investigation.

But not careful enough.

From his jump seat, a coughing Crawford managed to throw the side door open, venting the cabin. With the air cleared, Michael could see the pilots in the cockpit struggling to keep the aircraft on an even keel while they searched for a place to ditch. Ahead and growing smaller in the distance, the other three surviving Black Hawks were already regrouping to the west, well out of missile range, while below a smudge of black smoke marked the location of the crash.

Somehow, the helicopter stayed in the air, reeling like a punch-drunk fighter, but Michael knew it was only a matter of time before it went down. With only one working turbine engine, the best they could hope for was to stay aloft long enough to find a good place to set down.

It would be a hard landing—a euphemism for *crash*—and some of the men aboard would probably die.

But most of us will survive.

Provided nothing else goes wrong.

Then something else went wrong.

A series of rapid thumps shook the aircraft—ground fire. Sparks flew as rounds found their way in through the open door, shattering the acrylic viewports and perforating bulkheads.

He ducked reflexively, though his safety harness kept him from going far. Outside, tracer rounds zipped across the sky, slowly bending toward the critically wounded Black Hawk.

Almost without thinking, he brought his M4 to his shoulder and, following the line of tracers back to their source, set the selector to Burst and started firing. He wasn't the only one. Several of the SWAT operators had unbuckled and moved to the door to join him in returning fire. Spent brass fell all around Michael as he emptied the carbine's magazine in a series of quick trigger pulls. He didn't think they had a prayer of hitting something meaningful, not at that range—the machine gun was easily eight hundred yards away, never mind the altitude—and not with the helicopter lurching crazily in the sky. It was more of a symbolic response to the attack—*If I'm going down no matter what,* his brother Chase had always said, *I'm at least going to be fucking swinging*—but the incoming fire nonetheless tapered off.

Time to keep swinging.

"I'll be damned," he muttered and then shot a triumphant grin back at Crawford.

His smile fell when he saw the FBI agent slumped forward in his jump seat. Blood, pouring out from the wound underneath his body armor, was already saturating his uniform, the stain spreading across his thighs. There was a hole as big around as Michael's thumb in the center of Crawford's chest. The machine gun round—a .50 cal or something comparable—had punched right through the man's armor plate and into his heart.

Shit.

Another volley of heavy-caliber machine gun fire rose from the jungle, arcing toward the beleaguered helicopter. Michael barely had time to shout "Incoming!" before a storm of lead ripped through the aircraft and the men inside. The pilots were killed instantly, and without their hands on the controls the mortally wounded Black Hawk nosed over and began a final, meteoric plunge toward the earth. Michael saw the emerald vastness rising to embrace them. His fingers dug into the seat harness, but he knew there was nothing left to hold on to.

Nobody left to trust, he told himself again, closing his eyes to shut out the spinning chaos.

In the final moment before the helicopter hit the ground, Michael's last thought was of the person whose name he had quickly scribbled at the bottom of his list. The one person he'd long feared was secretly a part of FATHOM. He pictured their face as anger and rage—*not fear*—ran through his body.

And then there was nothing else.

PART I

Brothers are what best friends can never be.
-Unknown

CHAPTER ONE

New York

Chase Burke carefully drew the cork from the neck of the jet-black wine bottle and brought it close to his eyes, inspecting the wood for any signs of crumbling, rot, or mold. Finding none, he set it aside and poured a small amount of the bottle's contents into a large-bowled wineglass.

Chase set the bottle on the counter and picked up the glass, tilting it to a forty-five-degree angle against the plain white of a paper napkin. He assessed the wine's color intensity by looking at how far the color extended from the core of the glass—where the stem is attached the bowl—to where there was only the shallowest depth of wine left.

Intensely pigmented. Almost to the rim.

The wine, which Chase knew had been fermented from a blend of merlot, cabernet franc, and cabernet sauvignon grapes—with a small quantity of petit verdot added in for its spiciness—and aged in French oak barrels, was a deep ruby color.

He swirled the contents gently, noting the streaks that formed on the sides of the glass as the wine slid back down into the bowl. These legs, also sometimes called *tears*, were a good indicator of viscosity and, consequently, alcohol content, which in this instance was substantial.

But of course, in wine, as in all things, looks could be deceiving.

He swirled the wine again, this time to release the aromas into the glass, then placed his nose over the rim and took a long sniff.

If asked to describe this wine's aroma—and as the head sommelier of Chrysalis, a Michelin-starred restaurant, he often was—he would have compared it to the smell of fleshy red and black fruits and dry violets, with a hint of black pepper. Also present—the secondary aromas—were subtle notes of vanilla and charred wood from the oak barrels in which the wine had been aged.

It was, he would tell his customers, a complex experience. One to be savored.

An image of his old master gunnery sergeant, Enzo Bartoletti, staring at him like he had two heads popped into his mind. The thought of trying to explain his new career to the grizzled senior noncommissioned officer—or really, to any of the men he'd served with—made him want to laugh out loud.

You do what for a living? Smell wine?

But the smile faded quickly as that train of thought pulled into the inevitable station, reminding him, as it always did, of how his years of service had ended.

Ten long months at the Midwest Joint Regional Correctional Facility in Leavenworth, Kansas. Loss of rank. A bad conduct discharge, and with it the loss of any benefits to which he might have been entitled as a veteran.

There was a saying in the Army. *Once a soldier, always a soldier.*

But did it apply to men like him who had earned themselves a disciplinary discharge? Chase didn't think it did. He was an ex-soldier. A scandalous designation.

Yep. That's what I am. An ex-soldier.
And a former boxer.
And let's not forget: a family disappointment.
But at least I'm a decent sommelier. I think.

Chase shook his head. *Hell of a résumé,* he thought.

A far cry from his big brother's CV. Whereas Chase's life had been a complex experience, Michael, on the other hand, had always been the golden boy. And that was fine with Chase. There was no bad blood between the two, and in fact, he was proud of Michael and the honorable life he led.

Or had led.

The realization that he would now have to talk about Michael in the past tense had hit him hard, and he wasn't ready for it.

Shit.

He brought the wineglass to his lips and took a small sip. He swished the liquid around his mouth to evaluate its acidity and tannin levels, then, holding the wine on his tongue, Chase breathed in over the wine, using his mouth as a mini decanter.

The first thing you'll notice, he might tell restaurant patrons, *are the tannins. Firm but well integrated, providing a solid backbone. Now, let the flavor explode in your mouth. Dark cherries, black plums, cassis burst forth, and a touch of blueberry. Cinnamon, clove, and a dash of black pepper . . . Powerful, but elegant with a strong, lingering finish.*

Trying to put the experience into words was an essential part of his job, but to his way of thinking, words could not adequately convey smell or flavor. You had to experience it for yourself.

The wine, a 2019 Mission Hill Oculus from the Mission Hill vineyard in the Okanagan Valley of British Columbia, was somewhat expensive, especially when compared to other good wines made in North America. Owing to its limited supply, how hard it was to find, the award-winning wine was special to Chase for reasons that had nothing to do with its perceived value and only indirectly to its attributes.

The Oculus had always been Michael's favorite wine.

Satisfied with his tasting, Chase poured the content of the bottle into a crystal decanter. The Oculus was best enjoyed after being allowed to breathe for at least forty-five minutes, which was more than enough time for him to whip up a chimichurri with the rib eye he planned to grill for his dinner. Wine was best enjoyed when paired with the right food. It was also best enjoyed in the company of loved ones, but that wasn't going to happen. Tonight, he would drink the Oculus to honor the man who wasn't there . . . who would never be there, ever again.

The shock of the news from Colombia had yet to fully sink in, but he knew the worst of his emotions was yet to come. At first, the initial reports had been just ambiguous enough to allow for hope that Michael might be found alive, but the latest word from Michael's boss and friend of the family, Secretary of State Connor Williams, had left no room for hope.

Michael was gone. Forever. And Chase Burke had never felt more alone.

As he toasted his lost brother, his voice quivered.

"I love you, bro," he whispered to nobody.

Earlier that day, Chase had gone to Hartford to visit his mother at the private medical facility where she had been staying for the last two years.

Chase's relationship with Henrietta Enfield Burke had always been difficult.

Not bad. Just . . . *difficult.*

As the second son, his accomplishments were always held up against those of Michael, four years his senior. Growing up, Michael had been the star athlete, captain of every team, with a shelf full of trophies to attest to his prowess. Chase, while athletic, had only ever wanted to be a boxer, and the only way for him to pursue his passion was through an underfunded after-school program at the YMCA. He was good at it, but somehow, his matches never garnered the same degree of favorable attention as Michael's football and basketball games, and his victories failed to impress their mother. Their father, a former investment banker turned diplomat, privately applauded his younger son's ambitions, but between his career—which often kept him away from home—and his desire to maintain a level of domestic tranquility, he was never open with praise or support.

Michael always cheered me on, though.

Despite their obvious differences, both in age and temperament, the two boys remained close. As close as brothers four years apart could be, anyway.

And now he's gone...

Both Chase and Michael had been outstanding students, but somehow, Chase always fell short in Henrietta's estimation. No matter what he did, Michael had always done it first and done it better.

When are you gonna live up to your potential? Henrietta would often ask, usually following some form of troublemaking antics. A fight at school. A bar fight. There was usually fighting—because when you boil everything down, that's what Chase was.

A fighter.

Not that Chase had made any real effort to please his mother, or father, for that matter. Michael tried to, and it worked. Chase had a different take on the world and accepted his role early on. When he had first read Robert Frost's poem "The Road Not Taken" in freshman English, the closing line had resonated with him.

I took the one less traveled by, and that has made all the difference.

Things had come to a head when, upon earning his master of science in business analytics from MIT—an accomplishment that had everyone in his family believing he'd *finally* lived up to his potential—he'd promptly rejected a job offer from a top Wall Street investment firm and instead announced his intention to enlist in the Army.

You have a master's degree from one of the most prestigious universities on earth, and you want to be a soldier? Henrietta had raged. *What's wrong with you? With your degree, you could be earning six figures this year. Do you know how much a soldier makes?*

It's not about the money, he had told her.

Of course you would say that. You've never had to work for anything in your life.

This is what I want to do.

Why can't you do something useful for once? Join the FBI like your brother did, for fuck's sake!

Michael's decision to pursue a career in law enforcement hadn't exactly pleased Henrietta, either, but she'd quickly found a way to turn it into something to brag about at cocktail parties. *My son, the FBI agent, says . . .*

Chase had thought about trying to explain the career path he was going to follow. With his degree, he was a shoo-in to join a psychological operations—PSYOPS—unit, using his intuitive skills to influence both allies and adversaries in the name of national security, but ultimately knew that no matter what he said, she would disapprove.

This is what I want to do, Mother, he had repeated.

You're not actually lowering yourself to a common soldier, are you? At the very least, get a commission and save some shred of dignity.

His recruiter had urged him to take that track. With his degree, he could go directly to Officer Candidate School. But Chase had no interest in being an officer. PSYOPS didn't need officers; they needed skilled NCOs who would stay with the unit.

He knew better than to expect his mother to take pride in any of *his* accomplishments. Still, her next outburst had driven a wedge between them. *You're even dumber and lazier than I thought, Chase. What a shame. You had so much potential.*

It was nothing she hadn't told him before, in one form or another, but that day, he'd decided he'd had enough. He walked out the door, went back to the recruiter he'd been consulting with, signed on the dotted line, and chose the road less traveled.

You're even dumber and lazier than I thought.

He never would have believed those words would be the last coherent thing he would hear his mother say.

The guard at the main gate greeted him like an old friend—not surprising since he'd been making this trip every Monday for the last two years—and thumbed the button that rolled the wrought iron security gate out of the way to permit his entry.

Havenwood Retreat was no ordinary assisted living home. Billed as "an oasis of tranquility where residents can relive their cherished moments, even as the tides of memory ebb and flow," it catered exclusively to a wealthy clientele, and while ostensibly dedicated to preserving the dignity of once-influential men and women dying the slow death of dementia, its real function was to ease the consciences of their clients' family members, who now had to deal with the social stigma of having a relative who was no longer in their right mind.

Henrietta had first begun to exhibit signs of dementia two and a half years earlier. Chase had been in the Loire Valley at the time, well on the way to his advanced sommelier certification—another life choice that would doubtless have earned his mother's scorn had they been on speaking terms—and by the time he returned stateside, her symptoms had already worsened to the point where his father had made the decision to move her to Havenwood Retreat.

Realizing that his window of opportunity to reconcile with his mother was fast closing, Chase had begun making regular visits, taking the train from New York to Hartford three times a week at first, in hopes of finding her in one of her increasingly rare lucid moments so that he could . . . what, exactly? Forgive her?

Like that would go over well.

But he felt it was his duty to at least try because once she was gone . . . *really* gone, it would be too late.

Ultimately, it didn't matter because every time he came to visit, she looked at him like he was a stranger. Her nurse would introduce him always just as Chase, never "your son," because telling her that might have unpredictable consequences. Better, he'd been told, to simply sit with her and see if his mere presence could bring her back to herself.

It didn't.

He began to think that maybe she was just pretending not to recognize him, but he was assured that was not the case. Her lucid moments were few and far between. After several months, and on the recommendation of Curtis McGraw, the facility's managing director, Chase had scaled back to just one visit a week. Counterintuitively, McGraw told him, the frequency of his visits might be inhibiting the recovery of her memories of him. Chase had rationalized limiting his visits because his father and brother were also regularly checking in on her. Then, six months earlier, shortly after being confirmed as the next American ambassador to Czechia, Robert Burke, an experienced pilot, had perished, along with three other souls, when the Piper Cherokee Six he'd been piloting flew into the side of a mountain. The National Transportation Safety Board's thirteen-page preliminary report stated "The pilot's inattention to the plane's altitude and speed, combined with the pilot's inability to adequately respond to his airplane's entry into an aerodynamic stall by executing multiple abrupt control inputs, resulted in the plane impacting terrain."

Executing multiple abrupt control inputs?
That makes no sense.

His dad, an experienced pilot who had racked up more than 1,200 hours of flight time on that plane, always paid attention to his surroundings.

Especially when he was flying.

Chase was looking forward to reading the NTSB final report. He was confident the federal investigators would find a fault with the airplane. They had to. A mechanical failure was the only thing that made any sense to him.

And now, as if his family hadn't suffered enough, Michael was gone too.

Chase shook his head. Even in his wildest dreams, he never would have believed their family would be reduced to just him and his mother.

He pulled into the porte cochere, leaving his car, a Mercedes S-Class, running, and got out, allowing the valet to drive it away. The vehicle had belonged to his father, but Chase had been borrowing it for the trips to Hartford for so long that it sort of felt like his. He supposed it actually was, now. His father's will had divided the assets between Michael and him, along with establishing a trust to pay for Henrietta's care, but Michael, who had been named executor, had still been in the process of determining how the property should be apportioned. Now that he was dead, too, that role would fall to Chase, along with the bulk of the estate.

But he didn't want to think about that right now.

He didn't want the family money. And thanks to a few smart investments that were paying off handsomely, he didn't need it.

As for the car, owning one was more of a liability than an asset for him, living as he did on Manhattan's Upper East Side. It was easier and quicker to take the train out to the family home in Long Island and then drive to Connecticut than it was to ride the train to Hartford and then catch an Uber out to Havenwood.

Curtis McGraw was waiting for him just inside. "Mr. Burke, so good to see you today," the managing director said.

McGraw, a British national who'd lived in the United States for over eight years, had lost none of his East End accent. His speech pattern reminded Chase of the actor Michael Caine. "Your mother is in the Memory Garden. I can take you there if you're ready."

"Thanks, Curtis."

McGraw, Chase had learned, had been a detective inspector with the Metropolitan Police in London for many years before emigrating. While managing a high-end care facility like Havenwood was no doubt far more lucrative than working in law enforcement, Chase had more than once wondered how McGraw had found his way into the job.

The Memory Garden was one of Havenwood's therapeutic spaces—a sprawling garden with native flowers, shade trees, and a meandering path with several benches where residents could peacefully while away the hours, but always under the watchful eye of the nursing staff. As he followed McGraw outside and onto the path, Chase easily spotted his mother sitting at one of those benches.

Chase had gotten his dark hair, olive complexion, and startlingly green eyes from her. Alzheimer's might have taken her mind, but even in her late fifties, she remained strikingly beautiful. Chase, however, was more interested in the pretty blond woman in dark blue scrubs sitting beside her.

"Who's that with her?"

"That's Lucy Noonan," said McGraw. "She's a recent addition to our family, but she and your mother get along famously."

"Where's Shana?" Shana had been his mother's primary nurse for as long as Chase had been coming to visit her.

McGraw seemed taken aback. "Oh my. You haven't heard. Well, of course, how would you? Shana was in an accident while on holiday in Mexico."

"Is she okay?"

McGraw shook his head in a gentle, discreet way that said it all.

"Damn," muttered Chase. "Shana? That's awful. How did it happen?"

"A parasailing accident. We're all just gutted."

Chase hadn't known Shana all that well, but the mere fact that someone else within his family's sphere of influence had met with misfortune left him rattled.

"How's Mother taking it?"

Henrietta had always been "Mother" to him. Not "Mom," "Mama," "Mommy," or anything remotely affectionate.

McGraw smiled. "You know how she is."

That bad, huh?

Chase did know. A moment later, when he approached the bench, Henrietta Burke looked up at him, smiled, and in that impeccable mid-Atlantic accent that sounded like Katharine Hepburn in her prime, said, "My, aren't you a handsome young man. How do you do? I'm Henrietta."

CHAPTER TWO

The visit went pretty much like every other one before. Chase met his mother as if for the first time, exchanging pleasantries about the weather and the garden and what they planned to do with the rest of the day. Henrietta seemed fascinated by Chase's description of his chosen career, a sure sign that she was no longer the woman he remembered. Chase never thought that he would one day miss her customary vitriol.

After an hour or so, the nurse—Lucy—indicated that it was lunchtime. Henrietta invited Chase to join her, but he begged off. He had a long drive ahead of him. And no matter how long he stayed, five minutes after he left she would have forgotten him completely.

As he stepped outside, and before the valet could bring the Mercedes up, a black Lincoln Navigator pulled into the porte cochere. The rear window lowered, revealing the face of US Secretary of State Connor Williams.

Chase got an uneasy feeling in the pit of his stomach. In addition to being a longtime family friend, Williams had been Michael's boss. While it wasn't that unusual for him to be at Havenwood Retreat, paying a visit to the ailing widow of his deceased friend, Ambassador Burke, the timing was suspicious.

"Hello, Mr. Secretary. Here to see Mother?"

"I thought I might drop in and check on her," replied the diplomat. "How's she doing?"

Chase shrugged. "Same as ever. They say the diet regimen and therapy are slowing the deterioration, but it's not doing much to fix what's been lost."

Williams returned a nod of commiseration. "That's unfortunate." He paused a beat. "I was also hoping to have a word with you, Chase. Why don't you join me?"

How did he know I was here?

Chase nodded, and when the door of the Navigator swung open, he climbed inside. Williams's driver pulled through the porte cochere and began driving back down toward the lane.

To fill the awkward silence, Chase threw out a conversational softball. "How's Jerry doing?"

Jerry Williams was the SecState's favorite nephew. He had also, quite by coincidence, been deployed to Djibouti with his Ranger company at the same time Chase had been there as part of a four-man PSYOPS team supporting the 1st Special Forces Group. When Jerry's fire team had been pinned down by an overwhelming insurgent force, it was Chase who, against all odds, had single-handedly gotten them back alive.

But there had been no hero's welcome waiting for him in the aftermath of his efforts.

Instead of getting a medal for his actions that day, Chase, in a twist of events, was arrested for striking an officer after the young lieutenant had accidentally discharged his rifle, almost hitting one of Chase's team members in the leg. After serving his time in the stockade, Chase had been drummed out of the military.

Jerry, however, had done quite well for himself. After leaving the military, Jerry, alongside some of his old college buddies, had founded a tech start-up in an effort to create a quantum key distribution application for data encryption. Chase, who had an instinct about such things, had plunked $75,000 into their company. Three years later, Jerry and his partners took the company public and the IPO had netted Chase a return of just over three million dollars.

It wasn't quite fuck-you money, but as far as he was concerned, it beat the hell out of a medal.

"Jerry is very busy," Williams replied. "As I'm sure you can imagine."

"Sure."

Williams nodded, then clapped his hands against his thighs. "I suppose you've guessed why I wanted to speak with you."

Chase shrugged. "Michael?"

"The Colombian National Police have ended search operations."

Even though the news didn't come as a surprise, Chase stiffened. "That's it? They're just giving up?"

"Your brother's helicopter went down in some of the most rugged country on the planet. The crews of the other aircrafts involved in the operation all reported that Michael's helicopter was on fire when it went down and exploded shortly after impact. Nobody could have survived."

"Then where's his body?"

"Remains were recovered from the wreck, but Chase . . . that fire burned at over 2,500 degrees. There's not much left."

Chase knew that everything Williams was telling him was true but felt almost obligated to fight the obvious conclusion. Before he could offer a rebuttal, however, Williams went on.

"Now, as hard as that is, I'm afraid that's not the worst of it." He paused a beat, then let out a long sigh. "The FBI has begun a probe into the incident. They're trying to determine *how* the operation was compromised."

Chase straightened, taking an interest. "Good."

He almost added *About time they got off their asses and did something*, but decided against it.

"I'm afraid you don't understand," Williams said.

Chase raised an eyebrow. "What do you mean?"

"Chase . . . it's looking like Michael may have been responsible for the leak."

Chase felt as if he'd just been sucker punched. "What? No way. Not a chance in hell. Michael would never—"

"I can't go into the details," said Williams, cutting him off. "Hell, I don't even *have* all the details, but earlier today, a team of agents from the Bureau showed up at Foggy Bottom with a search warrant and cleaned out Michael's office. My guess is that they'll have done the same at his apartment, and I wouldn't be surprised if they expand it to take in your folks' place since it's *technically* his secondary residence. I'm guessing they'll eventually want to talk to you as well."

Chase was incredulous. "Like I said, no way. There's no chance Michael would leak anything. I know my brother, and that isn't him. They're looking at the wrong guy."

Williams raised his hands. "I'm not the one saying it. I'm only giving you fair warning. I've probably said more than I should have, but . . ." He sighed again. "Some things are more important than following the rules."

Chase nodded. He took a breath to calm himself, then asked, "So how does this end? Are they going to make Michael their scapegoat?"

"It will depend on the outcome of the investigation. But they wouldn't have taken this step if they didn't already have something."

Williams leaned forward and, addressing his driver, said, "Brian, you can take us back."

"So that's it? You won't do anything to help Michael?"

Williams turned back to Chase and his eyes hardened, but only for a moment.

"I'm truly very sorry this is happening," Williams said, squeezing Chase's shoulder. "I really am. But there's nothing else I can do."

Chase was about to reply when Williams's phone rang.

"I need to take this, Chase. Privately."

Chase pursed his lips, doing his best to keep a straight face. He wanted more from Williams. A lot more. He wanted to hear the man promise he would launch his own investigation, that he would help Chase fight off the spurious accusations against his brother, and that he would do everything in his power to find the evidence that would vindicate Michael.

Chase had gotten none of these reassurances. In fact, he'd just been dismissed by Williams, the only man powerful enough to set the wheels in motion.

Seeing Williams was waiting for him to get out of the vehicle before taking the call, Chase nodded his thanks to Williams, then exited the Navigator and started across the parking lot toward his car, his anger boiling somewhere between rage and fury. It was hard enough to lose a brother, but setting him up to take the fall?

Can't let that happen, he told himself.

Williams had given him a heads-up, and at the very least, he appreciated that.

There's nothing else I can do.

"Nothing you can do?" Chase said aloud to nobody as he walked. Then it hit him . . .

Doesn't mean there's nothing I can do, though.

And as he made the long drive back to New York, Chase started thinking about what his next move would be.

CHAPTER THREE

New York

With the wine decanted and breathing, Chase—with an almost military precision—began lining up the ingredients on the counter in the order in which he intended to prepare them: a bulb of purple glazer garlic, a shallot, bunches of flat-leaf parsley, cilantro, fresh oregano leaves, a lemon, a cruet of red wine vinegar, a portion cup containing about a tablespoon of red pepper flakes, and matching salt and pepper mills. The butcher paper–wrapped parcel containing the rib eye sat next to the sink, coming to room temperature—a trick Chef David had taught him—which would not only allow it to cook more quickly and evenly but also keep it juicier.

Chase liked good food, and he enjoyed cooking, but he rarely had the time or inclination to indulge. Four shifts a week at the restaurant, where it was actually in his job description to eat whatever new creation David was making that night in order to come up with a wine pairing, more than sated any gourmet cravings. On his days off, he typically kept things simple, rarely eating anything more elaborate than a grilled cheese sandwich.

But tonight was different.

Tonight, he felt the need to do something Michael would have liked.

SecState Williams's revelation that Michael was now the subject of an investigation had left him rattled. He didn't believe, not even for a microsecond, that his older brother was dirty. Michael was constitutionally incapable of treachery. But that didn't mean he was incapable of making a mistake. An offhand comment overhead by the wrong person, or a bit of spyware accidentally downloaded into his computer.

He did not doubt that an honest and thorough investigation would clear Michael's name. His concern was that the FBI, having already made up their minds about Michael, would begin cherry-picking the evidence to support their foregone conclusions, and with Michael unable to speak up in his own defense, there was little reason to expect an unbiased outcome. If he was going to clear Michael's name, there was only *one* way to make that happen.

He would have to learn the truth about what had happened in Colombia.

But that could wait. At least for another day. Because tonight, he was going to simply remember his brother with good food and good wine.

He began by peeling the garlic, letting the papery outer skin fall into the sink, and exposing the plump, purple cloves beneath. Purple glazer had a mild heat with a sweet, slightly nutty flavor that wouldn't overpower the other ingredients. He broke off three cloves and set them on the large bamboo cutting board and put the rest of the bulb aside. Chase's preferred method for preparing garlic was to smash the cloves with the flat of a chef's knife, which not only made it easy to separate the last layer of skin but also made it easier to mince.

Chase was just reaching for the Shun Classic eight-inch chef's knife in the countertop wood-block knife holder when he heard his phone buzzing. A glance at the upturned screen identified the caller.

David.

With a frown, Chase picked up the phone, thumbed the green Accept button, held the device to his ear, and said a simple "No."

David knew all too well—Chase Burke did *not* pick up extra shifts. He didn't need the money, and he valued his time away from the job. When he was on the clock, Chase gave everything he had, but when he was off . . . that was his time, and he had made that very clear from day one.

That went double for a night like this, but he knew David would still try to sell him on the idea of coming in "just this once," and so he braced himself for the pitch.

What would it be tonight?

He mentally ran through all of David's greatest hits.

Violet is strung out again. You gotta help me, man.

Violet was David's new girlfriend, a former Olympian who had competed in the biathlon, of all things. With her striking features and an athlete's poise, she carried herself with the confidence of someone who was used to being admired. While Chase admitted her marksmanship and endurance were undoubtedly impressive, he found it hard to see how those skills translated to her current gig as one of David's junior sommeliers. While her looks and charm might have dazzled David, Chase wasn't impressed with her wine expertise. Sure, Violet had passed a basic sommelier certification, but to Chase, her grasp of wine seemed superficial at best. Moreover, she often didn't show up for her shifts. Yet, somehow, she had managed to talk her way into being trusted with the key to the wine cellar of a Michelin-starred restaurant.

Or maybe it would be the celebrity VIP with an entourage and money to burn. *You know exactly how to deal with those people, Chase. You're practically one of them.*

Well, David wasn't wrong about that.

David's restaurant relied on high rollers—customers who didn't blink at dropping thousands on dinner and fine wine. Chase knew just how precarious the business was. A few months ago, David had been in a tight spot, struggling to cover payroll after a slower than normal month. Chase had quietly stepped in to help him out, loaning David the money to cover the shortfall. But even with that lifeline, the restaurant was still walking a fine line. The profit margins in fine dining were razor thin, and the sale of a few expensive bottles could mean the difference between breaking even and falling short. To Chase, trusting a junior sommelier like Violet with big spenders felt more like a gamble than a sound business decision.

"Chase," David said, drawing the word out to several syllables, "it's nothing like that, my man."

"Uh-huh. Just calling to shoot the shit, is that it?"

"Nah, man. I mean, I'd be lying if I told you this isn't about me wanting you to come in tonight, but this is more for you than me."

"Is that right? Still, no."

"Now, hold on a second. At least let me tell you the best part."

Chase sighed. David evidently seemed to think that building anticipation would somehow break down his defenses. "Fine."

"That lady congressman you're sweet on? She's got a seven o'clock reservation."

Chase's breath caught in his throat. "Congresswoman Hemsworth?"

Congresswoman Tanya Hemsworth was the recently elected representative for New York's 10th District, which included all Lower Manhattan and several neighborhoods in west Brooklyn. A former detective with the NYPD—twelve years on the job, with three of them deep undercover as part of an investigation into the ruthless Cipriani crime syndicate—she had run on her track record of upholding law and order and a promise to keep up the fight, both at home and across the nation, from the Capitol. She was that rarest of political animals, an unaligned independent who owed nothing to either party and, therefore, put the needs of her constituents ahead of the demands of party leaders. She was also smart, funny, personable, and drop-dead gorgeous.

Chase had not known all of this when she'd come into Chrysalis, back when she was courting donors on the campaign trail. He'd only known that he felt an instant connection with her. When she returned a couple of weeks later, the spark was still there. He felt it when she came to the restaurant to celebrate her victory and again during the handful of other times she came in with one of her aides.

Chase's interest in the congresswoman had not gone unnoticed by Chef David, nor had her interest in the head sommelier. *As much as it pains me to say it,* he'd remarked, *I don't think she's coming back for my risotto Milanese. Just ask her out, man. What's the worst that could happen?*

Chase, a little embarrassed by his schoolboy crush, had dismissed the idea but had nevertheless found himself looking forward to her next visit to Chrysalis.

And, of course, she would pick tonight to come in.

"Party of one," added David, with a conspiratorial undertone. And then, after a significant pause, "But if you can't come in, you can't come in. I'm sure Violet will take good care of her."

"You son of a bitch," muttered Chase, a thin smile creasing his face. "You really know exactly which button to push, don't you?"

Michael, he knew, would have urged him to go for it.

David laughed. "I'm sensing that you're suddenly available to come tonight after all."

Chase checked his watch and let out a dismayed groan. Not because of the time—it was six fifteen, plenty of time to make it to Chrysalis if he left right away—but because of the watch itself, a Vacheron Constantin Patrimony from his father's collection.

After the plane crash, Michael had presented Chase with the elegant Swiss watch, one of their father's favorites. *Dad loved you, Chase. He just didn't know how to say it.*

Yeah, because of Mother, Chase had thought, but not said aloud.

What he had said was, *I'd rather have the Yacht-Master.* He'd been only half joking. The black Rolex Yacht-Master 42 was much more in keeping with his personal sense of style, but he'd never been one for displays of conspicuous consumption. Michael, however, had taken him seriously. *Take them both. I know Dad would want you to have them.*

Chase wanted to believe that was true. *I'll hold on to them,* he allowed. *For now.*

And for the most part, that was what he had done. The only time he wore the Vacheron was when he went out to visit his mother, in hopes that the sight of her deceased husband's luxury timepiece on the wrist of "the second son" might provoke a reaction—any reaction. Today, he'd forgotten he was wearing it.

"Chase," prompted David, "are you coming in or what?"

Chase shook off his reverie. Chrysalis—street level in the historic Chrysler Building at Lexington and 42nd Street—was a thirty-minute walk from his Lenox Hill abode, fifteen if he took the Number Six train, but he rarely took the subway to work. Something about going underground and stuffing himself into a crowded train car just wasn't for him.

He gave a heavy sigh. "I'll be there in half an hour," he said, already putting away the ingredients for his now-delayed dinner.

He ducked into his bedroom and quickly pulled on a periwinkle-blue dress shirt, which added just a touch of class to his faded Levi's. David liked to keep the front of the house "accessible," which was code for unpretentious. Waitstaff in black and white would, he opined, only distract from the gastronomic experience. He wanted his servers to be attentive, tableside when patrons needed them, but otherwise invisible. He thought about keeping the Vacheron, then decided to swap it for the Yacht-Master.

Michael, he thought, *would approve.*

As he grabbed his keys and wallet off the counter, Chase noticed the decanter sitting patiently where he'd left it. A few hours at room temperature wouldn't noticeably affect the Oculus, but he doubted very much that he would feel like grilling the rib eye when he returned home. If he used a vacuum stopper and put it in the fridge, the wine would keep for at least a couple of days. He could try again tomorrow. Or maybe . . .

Maybe I can let Tanya try it.

It was, he realized, the first time he'd thought of her as "Tanya" and not "Congresswoman Hemsworth."

Chase rolled his eyes at his own naivety. Was he trying to convince himself she felt the pull of attraction the same way he did? It sure looked like it. Chef David was right, though.

What's the worst that can happen?

With that thought, Chase grabbed the decanter and put it in his Butterfield Market reusable grocery bag, stuffed in a couple of dish towels for stability, and headed for the door.

That was when he felt his phone vibrating in his pocket.

"Damn it," he muttered. It had to be David, calling to tell him that the congresswoman—that Tanya—had canceled. But when he took out the phone, he saw that the call was coming from Hartford, Connecticut.

Havenwood Retreat.

He could count on one hand the number of times someone from the care facility had reached out to him in the last two years. Not once had they called after business hours.

Had something happened to his mother?

"This is Chase Burke," he said after accepting the call. He almost added, *What's wrong?*

"Mr. Burke, Curtis McGraw here. There's been a . . . well, I guess you could call it a 'breakthrough' with your mother's care."

"A *breakthrough?*" Chase felt his pulse quicken.

"She had an episode this afternoon . . . that's not unusual . . . but when she came around, she asked for you."

The last statement landed on him like a ton of bricks, but Chase resisted the impulse to focus on it. "An episode? What does that mean?"

"As you probably know, people suffering from Alzheimer's are prone to wild mood swings. They can become irrational, paranoid . . . even violent. Here at Havenwood, we have a protocol to minimize physical discomfort and preserve our residents' dignity, but at times, these episodes can be rather intense. She's still quite agitated, but I think if you were to come here, you might be able to help."

Chase looked down at the grocery bag in his left hand. He knew what his priority should be. His mother was asking for *him*, wasn't she? Then again, in his thirty-two years on the planet, had she ever done that?

"Can you put her on the phone? Let me speak to her. See if I can calm her down."

McGraw let out an audible sigh. "Given her present state, I think it's more important that she sees you with her own eyes, as requested."

"Are you sure she's asking for me? Because when I was there earlier, she didn't even recognize me."

"What she said, precisely, was 'I want to speak with my son.' As you are . . . well . . ." Chase knew McGraw was trying to avoid saying *her only son*.

But what Chase knew that McGraw didn't was that his mother had never referred to him as just *my son*. Not ever. No, it was always *My second son, Chase*, or sometimes even just *The other one*.

I want to speak with my son.

If that was indeed what she said, then he knew his mother wasn't really asking for him. She was asking for Michael.

I wish I could talk to him, too, Mother.

Chase took another breath, let it out, then opened the door to his apartment.

"Look, I'm on my way to work. I'll come in first thing in the morning," Chase said, stepping out into the hallway.

"I don't think your—"

Chase ended the call, locked the door, and headed for the elevators, an odd feeling nagging at him.

CHAPTER FOUR

Despite the fact that it was nearly seven o'clock, long past the time when maintenance workers would have clocked out and headed for their favorite watering hole, nobody—not one person strolling down East 42nd Street, coming or going from Grand Central Station—gave a second look at the pair of coverall-clad workmen ascending the ladder affixed to the scaffolding that supported a sidewalk shed above the entrance to the Bowery Savings Bank Building. The structures, ubiquitous throughout Manhattan, were there to protect pedestrians from falling debris related to ongoing renovations to the high-rise buildings they typically surrounded.

Each man made a total of four trips up the ladder, shuttling two large backpacks and six boxes of varying size. When they climbed over the low parapet atop the structure for the final time, they became invisible to the pedestrians and to the passing motor vehicles below.

The two men quickly went to work. They opened the parcels they had brought up the ladder and assembled them into a small, low structure that, when finished, looked like a stack of cardboard shipping boxes. In fact, the structure was made from corrugated cardboard, but the appearance of stacked boxes was a clever illusion. The structure was hollow, with just enough room for the two men to crouch inside, which after a deliberate scan of their surroundings to ensure that nobody happened to be observing them from the upper stories of the adjacent high rises, they did.

Now completely concealed from view, the men unzipped the bags, which contained the tools of their trade. Inside the larger backpack was a Desert Tech Stealth Recon Scout sniper rifle equipped with a Schmidt & Bender scope, a suppressor, and three ten-round magazines. The second backpack held a pair of Glock 17 pistols, six fully loaded seventeen-round magazines, and a Leupold Mark 4 tactical spotting scope. While one man began assembling the rifle, the other opened a small flap in the wall of the carboard structure and positioned the spotting scope so that just an inch or so of it was protruding.

After a moment's observation, the man holding the Leupold said, "Let's call it one hundred and twenty-five meters."

The other man, having completed his task, opened a second flap and, with the suppressed barrel resting atop the reinforced cardboard parapet, peered through his own scope, placing the aiming reticle on the glass doors adorned with stylish gilt letters that read simply CHRYSALIS.

"Looks more like one thirty to me," said the man with the rifle. "But at this range, it hardly matters."

The spotter just grunted and continued peering through his device, intently watching the entrance to the restaurant. The air inside the makeshift structure staled quickly. The two men had endured worse conditions for longer time periods, both in the course of their duties as soldiers in the British Armed Forces and in their post-military career, providing the same services to anyone who could meet their price.

The rifleman was Damien Gray. The spotter was his younger brother, Brad.

Brad, six years Damien's junior, had followed in his brother's footsteps. Both had come up through the ranks and passed the grueling eight-week selection phase to join the elite Special Reconnaissance Regiment. Though they had enjoyed their time with the SRR, Damien and Brad hadn't felt their pay was commensurate with the risks they were asked to take on behalf of their nation. When their mandatory time with the SRR came to an end, they signed their release papers and never looked back.

Honorable discharges in hand, they teamed up with their youngest brother, Nigel—a former cyber information services engineer in the Royal Corps of Signal—to work in the lucrative field of *private security*, a broad euphemism that, in their case at least, included contract killings.

The Ghost Brothers, as they sometimes jokingly called themselves, did not see themselves as cold-blooded, steely-eyed, psychopathic murderers for hire. They were specialists, providing a professional service, no different—at least to their way of thinking—than a doctor, lawyer, or plumber. Damien, the recognized leader of the family team by virtue of both age and experience, insisted on strict adherence to his own ethical code. He would not, for instance, ever accept a contract where children were put at risk, even peripherally. He did not, however, concern himself with normative considerations when accepting a contract any more than a plumber would ask whether it was right or wrong to unclog a drain. Nor did he inquire about the client's motives. The "why" didn't matter.

Little more was said as the two men maintained their vigil on the entrance to the restaurant. Not for the first time since receiving the assignment, Damien silently cursed their client. They were, in his estimation, much too close to the target and, despite their precautions, far too exposed for his liking. Unfortunately, the urban landscape severely limited their options for effective shooting positions. And the egress would be especially tricky.

If it had been up to him, Damien would have chosen a more secluded location and used the high-powered sniper rifle the way it was meant to be used—from about four hundred meters away. But their client had been *very* specific about exactly where and how the job should be carried out. Against his better judgment, rather than refusing the assignment outright, Damien had insisted on a higher-than-usual fee—nearly double their going rate—and the client had agreed.

Now, perched above a busy Manhattan sidewalk, barely the length of a football pitch from the target zone, he wished he'd trusted his instincts and passed on the job.

You're doing this for Allie, he reminded himself.

Allie—short for Alessandra, his seventeen-year-old daughter—was a football prodigy who had a very real shot at going professional. The down payment on this job had allowed him to hire one of the top personal coaches in the UK, someone capable of refining her natural talents to a razor's edge. The goal was to ensure she caught the attention of the scouts who regularly attended school league games in search of promising new talent.

There wasn't anything Damien Gray wouldn't do to make his little girl's dreams come true, and if that meant taking on a little extra risk, then so be it.

Brad's voice suddenly snapped Damien out of his musings.

"Movement! Street level. One hundred meters. Chrysalis's main entrance."

Damien brought his attention back to the view through his scope just as a figure emerged from a dark-colored sedan right in front of the entrance to Chrysalis. Damien applied gentle pressure to the rifle stock, swiveling the weapon just a few degrees to put the aiming reticle squarely on the center of the man's chest.

The man—a stocky fellow with short gray hair wearing a suit that was just a bit too large for his frame—turned a slow circle, looking up and down the block for several seconds.

He's scanning for threats.

Damien wondered if the man was some sort of bodyguard. The vehicle certainly looked like it could belong to the government.

The target package his employer had sent stated that Damien's mark would get to the restaurant by public transport or by taxi. The package had made no mention of a protective detail.

Odds are this ain't her.

Still, Damien continued to observe the man through his scope.

Apparently satisfied whoever was in the vehicle wasn't in immediate danger, the man opened the vehicle's rear passenger door.

A moment later, a brunette woman climbed out from the sedan. For an instant, half of the woman's face was visible. Then she turned away. But it was enough.

Damien swore under his breath. *It's her.*

"Target acquired," Brad said, his tone betraying his own surprise.

Though her face was now hidden, the woman's figure, nicely accentuated by her tailored navy blazer dress, was on full display. Damien made a quiet *tsk* at the thought of what he and his brothers had been hired to do to this woman. Beauty like that was rare, something to be put on a pedestal, not shattered into pieces.

But the brothers had a job to do, and they were going to do it right. They had a reputation to maintain.

They were all too aware that the industry they operated in was cutthroat, with no margin for error. They were fine with that. They understood the game. In Damien's opinion, there were two reasons why their business was thriving.

We don't make false promises, and we deliver on the ones we make.
This job won't be the exception to the rule.

"On target," Damien said, placing the reticle between the woman's shoulder blades, tracking her as she followed her companion to the restaurant door, where a uniformed doorman greeted them.

"Stand by. Stand by," Brad whispered.

Damien, waiting for Brad's go-ahead, adjusted his aim and began to take the slack out of the trigger.

"Get—Hold! Hold!" Brad called out.

Before Damien could inquire what had prompted his brother to stop him from engaging the target, a large group of teenagers walked across his sights.

Bloody hell!

If Brad hadn't been there, Damien would have pressed the trigger. To think that one of his rounds might have hit one of the kids sent a shiver down his spine. As good as his rifle scope was, its field of view was still shit.

Just like looking through an empty toilet paper roll.

Damien watched helplessly as the doorman grasped the oversize brass pull handle and opened the glass door. The bodyguard stepped inside while the woman remained standing outside. Damien willed the teenagers to hurry up and walk away but to no avail. He had no shot. The bodyguard's actions might have seemed ungentlemanly, even a touch rude, but Damien knew the man—most probably a US Capitol Police officer—had done this solely out of concern for his protectee's safety. Having already cleared the street, he was now checking to make sure there were no obvious threats inside the restaurant.

By the time the teenagers had cleared, the woman had already passed through the door and disappeared inside the restaurant.

Damien Gray let out the breath he'd been holding too long and blinked away the eyestrain. "Good spotting, brother," he said, wiping down a bead of sweat from his forehead.

"Yeah," Brad replied without enthusiasm. "Now what?"

"Now we wait."

CHAPTER FIVE

Even if Chase hadn't caught a glimpse of the congresswoman's arrival, the text message from Violet—sent mere moments after Tanya was seated, and no doubt at David's direction—would have made sure he knew. Chase, who was in the midst of a pleasant exchange with a lovely elderly couple celebrating their sixtieth wedding anniversary with a rare night on the town, allowed himself only a glance at the smartly dressed politician sitting by herself at a two-top near the back of the house. She waved at him, which sent his heart racing.

While it was true that the only reason he'd agreed to come in was to see and hopefully have a meaningful exchange with Congresswoman Tanya Hemsworth, he would not put that goal ahead of his duties as the head sommelier of Chrysalis.

When he was finished with the elderly couple, he made his way slowly through the room, checking in with the servers to see if anyone else was requesting his advice, as well as revisiting the patrons who had purchased a specific bottle of wine on his or Violet's recommendation. Only then, when he was satisfied that all other demands upon his time had been addressed, did Chase make his way over to Tanya's table.

"Good evening, Congresswoman," he said, with intentional grandiosity, "and welcome to Chrysalis. I'm Chase, the head sommelier. If you need—"

"I know who you are, Chase," Tanya Hemsworth interrupted, a full-blown smile on her lips.

"Yeah . . . I mean—"

"Oh, I'm sorry," she said, touching his forearm with a brush of her fingertips. "Had you rehearsed a speech for me?"

He had. But he wasn't about to admit it.

During the walk from his apartment, Chase had run through various icebreakers and pickup lines—which would, of course, be used only ironically—and had determined to play things cool. While they had conversed on numerous previous occasions, their exchanges had been limited to wine talk, food, and preferred vacation spots. And despite David's assertion that the feelings Chase was developing for Tanya were reciprocated—she had once asked for Chase's work schedule—he wasn't going to assume anything. Better, he had decided, to start with a blank canvas. He feigned a look of surprise. "Why, no, Congresswoman. Of course not."

"Uh-huh. Call me congresswoman one more time, Chase, and we're going to have a problem."

Chase grinned, happy with how things were starting off between them.

"What would you like me to call you, then?"

"Call me whatever you like," she shot back. Then her voice dropped to a low, husky whisper as she pushed a piece of paper toward him. "As long as *you* call *me*."

Despite her confident smile, the ever-so-faint quaver in her voice betrayed her nervousness, which in turn sent an electric tingle through Chase's entire body. The one thing he hadn't anticipated was Tanya making the first move.

And, she had used his given name twice, a detail that was not lost on him. It was one of the most effective ways to build rapport, a technique that Detective Tanya Hemsworth would surely have employed to win over recalcitrant suspects in the interview room. But it was also one of the most effective ways to foster intimacy and signal affection.

Chase decided to go with the latter explanation.

They remained like that for a long moment, lost in each other's eyes until Chase finally remembered himself. He glanced down at the empty chair across from her. "Didn't I see you come in with someone?"

Her smile slipped, but only a little. "That was Marc."

She turned her head, glancing across the room to the bar where the man who had earlier accompanied her now sat, with what looked like a glass of soda water over ice set before him.

"My babysitter," she added ruefully. "You might have heard that members of the fine old institution I'm now part of aren't universally loved."

"You're kidding," he replied, with just the right amount of facetiousness. Then, he sobered, narrowing his gaze at her. "Marc's part of your security detail."

She nodded.

"Sorry, I know this is a real buzzkill," she said.

Chase waved a dismissive hand. He did not need her to explain, but she went on.

"He's with the Capitol Police. Sometimes, when a threat is specific or credible, they'll assign an officer and a driver to provide close protection."

"Somebody's threatened you?" Chase asked, suddenly feeling very indignant. "Why?"

"Someone is *always* threatening me. It goes with the territory. I can handle it. I don't know if you knew this, but I used to be on the job. A cop, I mean. A detective."

Anyone paying attention to the headlines knew that much, and Chase had done his homework.

"I might have heard that."

"Well, let's just say I made a lot of enemies." She waved her hand again. "But you can't live your life constantly afraid of what might happen. If you let the fear get to you, you'll never leave the house."

"Still, to assign you a bodyguard . . . somebody must consider the threat to be pretty serious, no?"

Tanya shrugged, then placed her hand on the unopened menu. "I'm famished. You do serve food here, don't you?" she asked playfully. "What do you recommend?"

Her nonanswer was answer enough, and the thought of Tanya in mortal danger was not something he could easily shift to the back burner, but for her sake, he made an effort. "I'm just the wine guy, Tanya. I'll get you a proper waiter."

"Something tells me you aren't just a run-of-the-mill 'wine guy.'"

He chuckled. "You're right. Actually, I'm an exceptional wine guy. I got a perfect score on the blind tasting part of the Advanced Sommelier Examination."

"It's your eyes," she went on, ignoring his attempt at sarcastic humor.

Chase again felt the electric tingle surge through his body. "What about my eyes?"

She stared deep into his for a long moment before answering. "They're warm and inviting, but the lines around them . . ." She nodded slowly. "They have a story to tell."

The intensity of her appraisal left Chase feeling almost naked. He broke eye contact, glanced around the house, and then came back to her. "Right back at you, Congresswoman."

Her perfect lips suddenly protruded in a pout. "Are you saying I'm old and wrinkly?"

"Uh, no . . . I just meant—"

Her smile returned. "I'm just messing with you. I believe you were going to tell me about dinner?"

Grateful for the reprieve, he reached out and laid his hand beside hers on the menu cover. "Do you trust me?" Chase asked.

The lingering heat of her gaze told him that his subtext had come through loud and clear. "Yes. I do."

He nodded and slid the menu aside. "I have a Mission Hill Oculus 2019 that's just begging to be enjoyed alongside Chef David's Duck Confit."

"Duck?" She affected a look of mock horror. "Oh, poor Donald."

He shook his head. "No, no. It's Daffy."

"Oh, well then, that's fine."

They both shared a laugh—more so at the poor attempts of covering their nerves with humor than the joke itself.

"I'll get that started for you," Chase said. "Now, if you'll excuse me for a moment, I do have other guests to attend to."

"Yes, yes. Please . . ." Tanya quickly replied, averting her eyes.

"But what about a late lunch tomorrow?" he asked. "I know a place. My treat. If you're free, of course."

Tanya beamed. "I am, and I'd love to."

CHAPTER SIX

I'd love to.

The words stayed with Chase as he tracked down the server assigned to the section where Tanya had been seated and relayed the entrée order, adding an appetizer of fried avocado slices and a glass of champagne—Ruinart Blanc de Blancs.

I'd love to.

Tomorrow couldn't come quickly enough.

Then he had a thought. After their lunch, maybe he and Tanya could catch a show together. He knew people who could get them great last-minute seats, the kind that would make the experience unforgettable. Scanning the restaurant, he thought about asking Violet to cover his shift tomorrow. He'd done this for her enough times before, hadn't he?

She kind of owes me.

But as he looked around, he didn't spot her. She was nowhere in sight.

No matter—I'll ask her after tonight's service.

As Chase began moving about the floor, checking in with tables, answering questions about the wine list, and making recommendations, the fact of Michael's death threatened to cast a shadow over his good mood. What right did he have to be enjoying himself when his brother's life had been violently ended?

He'd been able to keep those dark musings at bay by reminding himself that Michael would not have wanted him to sacrifice a chance at real happiness out of some misguided need to demonstrate his grief through self-denial. He could almost hear Michael's voice in his head, reminding him that "life goes on."

But not for you, Mike, he thought miserably.

With a sigh, he glanced across the floor to Tanya's table just as the server arrived with the champagne and appetizer he'd ordered for her. Catching his eye, Tanya raised the flute of sparkling wine to him in a silent toast and then took a sip.

The gesture brought the smile back to Chase's lips.

It was short-lived.

At exactly that moment, something changed in the atmosphere inside the restaurant. The low, persistent hum of conversation permeating the space did not stop but rather shifted in tone, taking on an almost palpable urgency. It was a subtle change at first, but it immediately set alarm bells ringing in Chase's head. He'd experienced this once before.

In Djibouti.

Right before we were ambushed.

He turned slowly, searching for the source of this strange almost-premonition, and saw Tanya's bodyguard—Marc—running across the restaurant, slaloming around tables, his unwavering gaze fixed on his protectee.

But Marc's actions were not the cause of the disruption. He was merely reacting to it.

Chase followed the gazes of the other patrons who, ignoring the Capitol Police officer, were turning their heads toward the entrance where a series of staccato reports—unmistakably gunfire—shattered the ambient murmur. After a protracted moment of stunned silence, the restaurant's interior was filled with a cacophony of panic.

Some patrons leaped from their chairs, bolting toward the rear of the house in a blind rush to flee whatever was happening outside. Others hit the floor, crawling under their tables. A few remained where they were, frozen in terror at the realization that they were now part of America's new worst nightmare.

An active shooter situation.

Chase remained where he was as well, his heart pounding with a rush of adrenaline, but it was not fear that kept him from moving. The sound of gunfire had awakened a part of him that had mostly gone dormant since the end of his military career. He was in combat mode now. His singular focus was on pinpointing the exact location and nature of the threat because, without knowing who the enemy was or exactly where they were, it was impossible to determine the best course of action.

Another series of reports sounded, closer this time, almost certainly from within the restaurant. Then, through the chaos, he saw them. Two men . . . no, three . . . dressed in black tactical attire, faces hidden behind balaclavas, armed with machine pistols. One of them—Chase thought he must be the leader—was waving his weapon in the air, one handed, loosing bursts into the ceiling as he bellowed an unheard exhortation for people to get out of his way.

Chase looked around for a weapon. He had his wine key in his pocket and an old Swiss Army knife, both of which had small blades that might score superficial damage, but if he was to have a prayer of turning the tables on the trio of attackers, he would need something with a little more penetrative depth.

He spied a steak knife resting on an abandoned plate at a nearby table. The six-inch straight-edged blade was far from ideal, but it was also a hell of a lot better than nothing.

Snapping into action, Chase made the short dash to the table, flipped it over, and ducked behind the concealment it afforded, snatching up the knife like it was a lifeline.

Now what, Chase? What's your next move?

Just like in Djibouti, he was being forced to make a decision in a chaotic environment with incomplete information.

An opportunity will come, he told himself. *When it does, take it!*

Chase spied a flurry of movement off to his right. A young man—presumably one of the restaurant patrons—was on his feet, pointing a handgun in the direction of the assaulters.

"NYPD! Get down! Get down!" the man shouted.

The warning, meant to clear the off-duty cop's line of fire, instead made him the prime target. Before he could get a shot off, a burst from a machine pistol ripped through him, bullets stitching a gruesome pattern across his chest.

Chase's heart sank as he saw the policeman go down. Up until that moment, he had clung to the hope that this was merely a robbery, that the intruders were only after the wallets and jewelry of the restaurant's well-heeled patrons. The casual indifference they had shown in taking a life, however, suggested a different and much darker intent. They were here to kill someone. But who?

Then it hit him.

Tanya!

Her earlier, offhand comment—*Let's just say I made a lot of enemies*—now took on ominous weight.

Fuck.

Chase pivoted toward the back of the house where Tanya, like Chase himself, was crouched down behind an overturned table with her protector beside her. Marc, the Capitol Police officer, had his service weapon out but, unlike the ill-fated off-duty cop, was doing nothing to draw the attention of the gunmen to him and his charge. Chase watched Marc say something into his lapel mic while his eyes darted about the room, fixing the location of the gunmen, searching, perhaps, for an escape route, and likely estimating the odds of survival in a shootout. Marc's attention seemed to fix on the passage into the kitchen.

Chase could almost read the officer's thoughts.

If Marc could get Tanya safely to the kitchen, they could escape out through the back entrance on Lexington Avenue. This had to be the plan Marc communicated to Tanya's driver.

Do it, Chase urged silently. *Get her the fuck out of here.*

But before either of them could make a move in that direction, another black-clad figure emerged from the passage, brandishing his machine pistol and shoving fleeing patrons aside.

Shit.

The preemptive flanking move was proof enough that this was no mere robbery.

Marc, realizing that escape was impossible, grimly took aim at the lone gunman at the back of the house. His weapon barked twice, and the wall behind the intruder erupted in a spray of plaster fragments.

Missed. Damn it.

Or maybe not, Chase amended, for through the settling cloud of dust, he saw a distinctive red splatter on the white wall.

The wounded gunman immediately ducked and veered away before Marc could reacquire him, but the evasive maneuvers proved unnecessary. In the next instant, one of the man's three companions loosened a burst from his weapon that drilled into Marc's body, knocking him to the ground.

Tanya, eyes wide with the horror of what she had just witnessed, started to reach for her fallen protector.

"No!" Chase shouted. "Tanya! Run!"

But the exhortation came too late. In an instant, all four gunmen converged on Tanya. One of them leveled his weapon at Marc's fallen form and pulled the trigger, sending a single round into the Capitol Police officer's skull.

The report seemed to punctuate the assault, and an ominous quiet settled over the dining room. Marc's killer brought his machine pistol up, swept back and forth, and shouted, "Everybody get down! *Now.* And don't anybody get any ideas about playing the hero!"

Almost as one, what was left of the restaurant's clientele dropped to the floor. Chase, feeling the gunman's eyes on him, surreptitiously slid the steak knife up his shirt sleeve before easing down with the others, his movements slow and deliberate. This wasn't the time to stand out. Not yet.

But that moment was coming, and when it did, he'd be ready.

CHAPTER SEVEN

When the black Chevrolet Suburban with blackout-tinted rear windows screeched to a stop right in front of the entrance to Chrysalis, Damien Gray murmured a soft "Now what?"

His mild incredulity turned into alarm when that vehicle disgorged four men in full tactical kit.

"What the bloody hell is this?" he said loud enough for Brad to hear. "Who the fuck are these lads?"

Before Brad could speculate, the SUV pulled away as quickly as it had come, rounding the corner onto Lexington Avenue. The squeal of its tires on the macadam was audible half a block away, as was the report of a machine pistol firing into the air.

"Holy shit!" Brad muttered.

Damien brought the lip mic of his digital radio closer to his mouth, initiating two-way communications with Nigel, who was presently sitting in the back of their hired Ford Transit van four blocks away. "Nige, something weird is going down here. Call the client and patch me in right the fuck now."

"On it. Stand by."

Through his scope, Damien watched as the four gunmen passed through the entrance and were lost from his view, but the staccato pops of their weapons, muted but still audible, continued to paint a picture of an assault in progress. Then he heard a different sound: the trill of an outgoing phone call. A moment later, an electronically distorted voice issued from his earbud.

"What?"

Damien did not know the client's identity, nor did the client know his. All communications between them were completely anonymized thanks to spoofed ISP numbers, a secure and encrypted VPN, and AI-generated voice modulation—Nigel's big contribution to the family business. An unfortunate side effect of bouncing the digital signal from one side of the globe to the other and back again was a slight transmission delay, so Damien waited a couple seconds before replying.

"Something weird is happening here. A bunch of lads with guns just hit the target location. You wouldn't happen to know anything about that, would you?"

The pause that followed was long, much longer than could be explained away by signal delay.

"I have no idea what you're talking about."

Yeah right.

"So, you're saying you didn't send in another team as backup? Or maybe we're the backup for them, and you *accidentally* neglected to tell us about it?"

"Whatever's going on there, it has nothing to do with me."

Damien took advantage of the delay to weigh the significance of this revelation. Assuming that the client was being truthful—and he was reserving judgment on that score—the arrival of the assault team at exactly the moment Damien and his brothers were preparing to carry out their assignment was purely coincidental.

What are the odds of that? Damien wondered.

"Well, be that as it may, I'm going to abort. There's a decent chance that these new guys are going to screw up the entire—"

"Abort?" interrupted the client. "Why?"

Damien counted to three before answering. "That place is going to be crawling with cops in a few minutes. The risk of exposure is too great. We'll try again at another time, depending on the result of whatever is happening here at the moment. But rest assured, if the hit team is here for the same target we are and they take it out, I'll refund the full fee, less our expenses. Again, if the target makes it out unscathed, we'll finish the job in a few days once the heat dies down. You need to—"

"I'm paying you to take care of this *tonight*," snapped the client, the AI voice modulator in no way masking the irritation in their tone. The quickness of the response suggested that they hadn't heard even half of Damien's rationale. "As we planned it. And that's what I expect you to do."

Damien gritted his teeth. "It's not your call—"

A *beep-beep* in his ear signaled the end of the call.

The client had hung up on him.

"Shit," Damien snarled. Every fiber of his being told him to pull the plug and walk away. They would be cutting it close as it was. Once the cops started showing up—they probably had, at best, two minutes before that happened—it would be next to impossible for them to make their egress unnoticed.

On the other hand, he *had* agreed to the client's terms. In the world in which the Ghost Brothers had chosen to live, it didn't pay to renege on an agreement.

"Well?" asked Brad.

Damien drummed his fingers against the stock of his rifle as he weighed their options.

"We're staying," he said a moment later in a tone that invited no debate. "Until the job is done."

CHAPTER EIGHT

Don't anybody get any ideas about playing the hero.

Chase felt as if the warning had been aimed directly at him. He could feel the eyes of the lead gunman on him. One wrong move and he'd be no good to Tanya or anyone else inside Chrysalis.

So, make the right move.

His mind was racing furiously to figure out how to turn the tables on the gunmen. From where he lay, he could just make out the body of the off-duty cop, maybe ten yards away at most. And while he didn't see it, he knew the pistol the man had been holding when he'd been fatally shot was probably somewhere close by.

If I can get my hands on it . . .

From the corner of his eye, he glimpsed a flurry of movement. Tanya, surrounded by the assaulters, had just made a grab for Marc's weapon. Chase glanced ahead just in time to see one of the gunmen lash out with a foot, striking her forearm and sending the pistol flying. Another savage kick caught her in the midriff, curling her into a protective ball.

Chase bristled with rage at the violent assault, but the analytical part of his brain did not fail to note the significance of the attackers' actions. They hadn't killed the congresswoman for resisting, and that meant they weren't interested in killing her.

They want her alive, Chase realized as he slowly reached for the steak knife inside his sleeve. *They want her as a hostage.*

But was it their plan to hold her here, in the restaurant along with everyone else, and negotiate the terms of her release and their exit... or were they planning to abduct her? Remove her to another location? Hold her for ransom?

He got his answer a moment later when one of the gunmen grabbed Tanya by an arm and hauled her to her feet. Still dazed from the kick, she sagged in the man's grip, unable to hold herself up. Her captor didn't bother trying to cajole her into walking on her own but simply began dragging her toward the exit. Two of the gunmen assumed the vanguard position ahead of him, while the fourth—the man Marc had wounded—brought up the rear.

They're taking her.

The gunmen had to know that first responders were already on their way, with precious little time before the cavalry arrived. If they were to have any hope of escaping with their hostage, they would have to move fast. And while they were focused on getting away, Chase would be focused on stopping them.

As the last gunman passed him by, just a couple paces from where he lay, Chase gently brought his hands closer to his body and subtly shifted his feet until his toes were pressing down on the floor.

Almost as if sensing his movement, the man started to turn toward him, and that was when Chase pushed off, springing to his feet in a single dynamic motion right in front of the gunman. Startled by the suddenness of the move, the man fumbled to bring his weapon to bear. But before he could, Chase closed the distance and, with the steak knife held in a reverse grip, drove it down in a hammer blow, burying it to the wooden handle in the side of the man's neck, aiming for the carotid artery. A jet of bright red blood, spurting out in time with the man's heartbeat, signaled he'd found his mark.

As the stricken man's free hand went to his ravaged throat, Chase yanked the knife out and used it to cut deeply into the inside of the man's forearm, its blade tearing through ligaments and tendons alike.

Letting go of the knife, Chase caught the weapon as it fell from the man's suddenly nerveless fingers.

The entire sequence of events had lasted no more than three seconds, but in a fight to the death, three seconds was an eternity. A gush of arterial spray from the man's neck wound splashed across Chase's chest, anointing him in the blood of his victim.

But Chase was barely aware. He was acting on instinct.

As Chase fumbled with the machine pistol—a MAC-10, if he was not mistaken—trying to get his hand around the pistol grip and his finger on the trigger, the man holding Tanya, reacting to the disturbance behind him, turned around, his weapon already extended, the barrel sweeping toward Chase.

Realizing that he wouldn't be able to get a shot off in time, Chase used the MAC-10 to violently cross-check the wounded man across his solar plexus, shoving him toward his comrade. Whether unthinkingly or intentionally, Tanya's captor let fly with a burst that punched into his mortally wounded colleague's back. The impact propelled the man back toward Chase, but he had already dived out of the way.

Chase, who had finally gotten a good hold on the MAC-10, put his sights on the retreating form of Tanya's captor but then hesitated. The machine pistol was an unfamiliar weapon, designed for hosing a target, not pinpoint accuracy, and right now accuracy was what Chase needed most. A single errant round could easily wound or kill Tanya.

That was a chance he wouldn't take.

In the time it had taken him to realize this, one of the two gunmen in the lead turned back to deal with the new threat. Ignoring the muzzle of the man's weapon as it moved in his direction, Chase calmly lined up the sights of his captured weapon with his target's torso and squeezed the trigger. The relatively lightweight MAC-10 bucked wildly in his hand, the muzzle climbing with each round fired. Most of the burst passed over the man's head, shattering the glass windows fronting the street, but the first found its mark, striking him in the forehead.

The gunman pitched over like a toppled tree.

Tanya chose that moment to wrestle free of her captor's grip, bolting for a nearby table. Seeing this, Chase tried to line up a shot on the now-revealed gunman, even as the latter went after Tanya. Before Chase could get off a shot, however, Tanya grabbed a water carafe from the table and then spun around to take a swing at her would-be captor, putting herself once more in Chase's line of fire.

"Shit!" growled Chase. He shifted his weapon onto the other gunman, who was now just a few steps from the exit. Bracing the gun and using a light touch on the hair trigger, Chase fired a short burst that sent the man crashing headlong into the glass door.

In the same instant, the remaining gunman swatted Tanya's attack aside, knocking the carafe from her hand, and then stepped in close, clouting the side of her head with his MAC-10. The blow would have laid her out, but the gunman caught her arm as she started to fall and whipped her around, putting her between himself and Chase. As Chase brought the machine pistol back around, lining up a shot over Tanya's shoulder on the barely exposed sliver of the man's head, the gunman jammed the muzzle of his MAC-10 against Tanya's neck.

"Drop it!" said the man. "Or she's dead."

Chase held his stance, finger ready on the trigger. "If she dies, you die. Drop your weapon."

The gunman spat out a laugh. "I don't think so."

Chase watched helplessly as the gunman, keeping his firearm pressed against Tanya's neck, began shuffling backward, moving toward the exit.

"Stop!" Chase ordered, tracking the man across the floor. "Last chance."

He wasn't bluffing, but he might as well have been. The man's erratic movements brought his head bobbing in and out of view, but never long enough for Chase to pull the trigger. Five shuffling steps brought the gunman to the maître d' station. Three more and they'd be at the exit. Stepping carefully over the body of his fallen comrade, the man put his back against the glass and pushed, opening the door and dragging Tanya after him.

Chase matched him, step for step, never lowering his weapon, praying for the man to make just one mistake. As the door started to swing closed between them, he darted forward, shouldering it open and following the man outside.

After the chaos inside the restaurant, the exterior tableau seemed almost surreal. The concrete was littered with fragments of glass, twinkling like a sea of diamonds, and there was not another soul in either direction. No doubt the shooting had sent pedestrians fleeing, and likely the word was spreading—stay away from Forty-Second and Lex. But just twenty feet away, cars and SUVs continued passing by, the drivers blissfully unaware that they were moving through an urban war zone. Chase kept his weapon trained on Tanya's captor, but the vehicular traffic added a new and dangerous dimension to the situation. If he fired and missed . . .

Then don't miss.

But that wasn't a good answer.

"You've got nowhere to go," he shouted. "Let her go and put down your weapon."

The gunman ignored the ultimatum, backing to the edge of the sidewalk, where he stopped.

"The cops are coming," Chase went on. "You're not walking away from this."

At that exact moment, a big black Suburban rolled past, skidding to a stop a few meters past the gunman. The man didn't glance back at the vehicle, but he did move the muzzle of his MAC-10 away from Tanya's neck.

And pointed it at Chase.

The gunman smiled. "Wanna bet?"

CHAPTER NINE

When the gunman holding the designated target hostage emerged from the restaurant, Damien Gray swore again. The four men the black SUV had dropped off weren't a hit team bent on killing her. They were here to abduct her.

He was going to have to take the shot, after all.

"This just keeps getting better," he snarled, snugging the butt of his rifle into his shoulder and putting the reticle on target, tracking her as her captor moved her away from the restaurant door and toward the street.

"On target," he said.

Come on. Stand still a moment.

To his surprise, the man did stop.

"You're clear to engage," Brad said.

Damien moved his finger to the trigger, took a breath, and started to—

"Hold! Hold!" warned Brad, even as half of Damien's scope was filled with a black SUV. It was the same Suburban that had delivered the assault team to the restaurant.

It occurred to Damien that he had seen four men go in, but only one had come out.

What the hell happened in there?

As the Suburban skidded to a stop past the gunman, Damien reacquired his target.

The Second Son

"On target," he said again.

"I now see two armed men," Brad said. "First one is the hostage taker. Range is one hundred and fifteen meters. Second armed man is at his twelve o'clock. Range is one hundred twenty-five meters. You're clear to engage when you have the shot."

The hostage taker took his machine pistol off his hostage, pointing it at the other shooter standing in front of him, but Damien kept *his* focus on his target, waiting for the clean shot he still didn't have.

It was now or never.

If he didn't take the shot, the lone assaulter would stuff the target into the SUV, and they would both be gone.

Shit.

Damien willed the man to move, but he didn't. He just stood there, firing out the magazine of his weapon at the second shooter. As the hostage taker's weapon ran dry, he took a few steps back toward the Suburban.

If he takes two more steps, I'll lose sight of him.
Time's up.

Damien knew what he had to do. He had one play left. He curled his finger once more around the trigger and squeezed.

Dropping his machine pistol, Chase combat-rolled to his left just as the hostage taker opened fire. Owing to the tendency of the MAC-10 to experience muzzle rise, the rounds passed harmlessly over Chase and everyone else inside.

Then again, killing Chase hadn't been his intent. The man was just trying to buy himself a moment to get his hostage into the SUV. Realizing this, Chase was on his feet as soon as the machine pistol went silent, racing headlong toward Tanya and her captor.

That was when the unthinkable happened.

He heard Tanya cry out as she and her captor tumbled forward, crashing face-first onto the sidewalk.

A single thought shot through Chase's mind with the speed of a bullet.

Sniper!

He threw himself flat, instinctively rolling to his right. The analytical part of his brain, working on autopilot, had taken note of the angle at which Tanya had pitched forward to calculate the approximate position the shot had come from.

Low angle, definitely not a rooftop. Second, or maybe third-story window.

Could the shot have come from the scaffolding across the street?

And why did the sniper take out his own guy?

Was Tanya hit?

There was no time to think it through. The only thing that mattered was to bring Tanya to cover.

But first, he had to get her out of the line of fire.

Chase reversed his roll and then bear-crawled to the fallen pair. He seized one of the gunman's outflung arms, then shoved him unceremoniously off Tanya, who hadn't moved since hitting the ground.

"Tanya?" he shouted.

Movement caught his eye. Chase turned his head in time to see a dark-haired man charging at him with a knife. Chase managed to angle his torso out of the way, but his attacker's knife caught the loose arm of Chase's dress shirt, cutting through the expensive fabric but missing flesh. The man pivoted on his right foot and swung the knife in a vicious arc toward Chase's throat. Chase ducked, came up behind the wild swing, and drove a devastating right hook to his assailant's trachea. The man sank to his knees, his windpipe having been temporarily collapsed by the strength of Chase's blow.

Now that his attacker was out of play, Chase no longer cared about him. His fight with the man had already cost him precious seconds.

Chase scrambled back to Tanya, scooping her up in his arms. Then, offering his back to the sniper, he rushed back inside the restaurant, bracing for the inevitable punch of a bullet in his spine.

Or maybe not even that.

Would the curtain fall so suddenly he would be dead before he knew it?

But a moment later, he and Tanya were back inside Chrysalis, out of the sniper's line of sight—at least for now.

Chase wasted no time celebrating the mere fact of his survival. He glanced at Tanya. Her eyes were still closed. Gently, he lowered her to the ground and rolled her over.

Shit.

There was a dark, ragged hole in the blue fabric of her blazer, about five inches to the left of her spine and just below her collarbone.

Armor-piercing round, he thought. *Had to be to punch through her captor like that.*

He couldn't tell if a vital organ had been hit, but blood was streaming out of the hole.

"No, no, no," Chase murmured. "Stay with me, Tanya! Stay with me!"

Frantic, he tore off his already bloodstained shirt, balled it up, and jammed it against the wound, pressing down hard against the makeshift bandage. The blue fabric almost instantly turned crimson.

"No, damn it," he rasped. "You're not going to die. I won't let you die. Just stay with me," he repeated.

Where in the hell are the paramedics?

Raising his eyes and glancing out into the street, Chase hoped to see the emergency lights of police cars and ambulances responding to the scene. Instead, he saw only the man he had fought with crawl into the black SUV through the passenger door, slowly making his way to the driver's seat.

For a moment, the two men locked eyes. Then, with a squeal of tires, the SUV tore away, leaving Chase alone with the dead and dying.

Overwhelmed, surrounded by the aftermath of the carnage, and still applying pressure to Tanya's chest, Chase knew there was nothing else he could do. Warm blood seeped from beneath his fingers. He pushed harder, willing the bleeding to stop.

First Michael. Now Tanya . . .

As he felt the life slowly drain from her, his thoughts turned to the man he'd seen just seconds before. Chase closed his eyes. He heard cries for help all around him, but all he saw was the face that had been seared into his memory.

The face of the man that he silently swore to find.

And to kill.

PART II
A Promise to Kill

CHAPTER TEN

New York

Because her attention was so focused on the front entrance of the apartment building a block and a half away, NYPD Detective Alice Doyle wasn't fully aware that she had picked up her grande Starbucks cup from the center console until she brought it to her lips and took a sip.

As the lukewarm beverage swirled into her mouth, her face twisted into a sudden expression that approximated the bitterness of the tepid coffee.

Yuck.

She tried to decide whether to spit it back into the cup or force it down her throat. In the end, revulsion won out, and with more conscious determination, she removed the plastic lid, brought the cup back to her lips, and returned the mouthful to it.

From the driver's seat, her partner, Detective James Campbell, gave her a sidelong glance without lowering the monocular bird-watching scope from in front of his face. "Well, that wasn't very ladylike, Alice."

"Fuck you," replied Doyle, good-naturedly. "How's that for ladylike?"

Campbell just chuckled and resumed peering through the monocular.

Doyle replaced the lid and then, after another internal debate about what to do with the cup, came to a decision. "I'm gonna go find a fresh cup," she said. "You want anything?"

"Not this late. If I drink caffeine now, I'll never sleep tonight."

Doyle glanced at the dashboard clock. "It's seven thirty."

"Already?" remarked Campbell dryly, feigning a yawn.

Campbell's sleep habits were a running joke between them. At fifty—fifteen years Doyle's senior—he made no secret of the fact that he liked to be in bed by nine p.m. "Give it a couple years," he would often say. "Then you'll understand."

"You think you're actually going home tonight?" she asked.

"If we're still out here by Ava's bedtime, you can take the blame," Campbell replied.

Doyle's heart tugged at the mention of her eight-year-old daughter, Ava. Right now, the little girl was at home with her favorite babysitter—a necessary expense that devoured most of Doyle's overtime pay.

Campbell made a face, then lowered the monocular.

"Listen, I'm ready to go home right *now*. This is a bust. Either Ethan got his wires crossed, or he was fucking with us. If you want, I'll stop by your place before heading home."

Ava adored Campbell. He had this way of winning people over, especially kids, and Ava had completely fallen under his spell. Every time he stopped by her apartment, he always remembered to bring Ava little gifts—like the stuffed octopus she now took to bed every night—and he proudly displayed her drawings in his cubicle for everyone to see.

"I'm sure she'd like that," she said after a moment.

As for Ethan Sullivan, he was a twenty-six-year-old junior associate at Sovereign Capital, a boutique investment bank headquartered in Midtown Manhattan. Sovereign Capital was on Doyle and Campbell's radar because the bank's managing director, Alexander Blackwell, was suspected of laundering money for extremist groups operating in Europe. When the detectives had caught Sullivan engaging in some minor insider trading, rather than turn him over to the Securities and Exchange Commission for prosecution, they had flipped him, persuading him to become a confidential informant, reporting on Blackwell's activities, both curricular and extracurricular, in hopes of finding the figurative smoking gun that would help them nail the banker . . . or more probably, to help flip *him* to take down the next link in the chain.

That was the thing about international terrorism. There was always another link in the chain.

"Ethan knows better than to lie to us," countered Doyle. "And it's still early. You know Blackwell always works late."

Campbell just grunted.

They'd been sitting in the car for three hours, parked in the bus lane on Second Avenue, watching the front entrance of the Murray Hill Tower Apartments, hoping to catch a glimpse of Blackwell showing up for an intimate rendezvous with one Sofia Benali, a French fashion model of North African descent. Benali—Blackwell's ex-girlfriend—was also a suspected link in the terror-financing chain, though it remained unclear which direction her connection went. Their relationship had, at least so far as anyone could determine, ended more than two years ago, before either was suspected of involvement in financing terror groups. The evidence against both of them was only circumstantial, but it had been obtained independently. Establishing that the two had an ongoing relationship would go a long way toward closing the circle, which was why the two detectives were staking out Benali's building.

If Sullivan's tip suggesting that Blackwell had gotten a booty call from his ex bore fruit, it would be enough for them to get a FISA warrant for electronic surveillance on Blackwell, and *that* would hopefully blow the case wide open.

Or so they were hoping.

Sullivan's tip had come in just as the two detectives were about to call it a day. Since being assigned to the Joint Terrorism Task Force—a collaborative effort led by the FBI but staffed with officers and analysts from local, state, and federal law enforcement and intelligence agencies to thwart terrorist threats, foreign and domestic, aimed at the homeland—Doyle and Campbell rarely worked outside of office hours. Most of the job was done at JTTF headquarters in the Bureau's New York field office in the Jacob K. Javitz Federal Building, where they mostly attended briefings and read and wrote reports.

Yet, despite the seemingly static nature of the work, their investigations were cumulative. Open cases were works in progress—like thousand-piece jigsaw puzzles—slowly taking shape as new pieces were added until, sometimes in surprising fashion, the big picture emerged.

Sovereign Capital, Alexander Blackwell, and Sofia Benali were all pieces of the same puzzle, and if she and Campbell succeeded in obtaining permission to dig deeper into their relationship, Doyle did not doubt that they would indeed find their smoking gun.

Unfortunately, though, there was no way of knowing just how long they would have to watch and wait before Blackwell put in an appearance. As the minutes crept by, Doyle's mind drifted back to home, to Ava, who was probably sitting on her bed, sketching another picture to give to Campbell . . . and to the question that often haunted her.

Am I doing enough as a mother?

She sighed heavily, knowing the answer.

It wasn't just that she had to work long hours, she was also struggling to fill the void Ava's father—an NYC firefighter—had left when he had died on duty three years ago. While everyone had hailed him as a hero, Doyle knew the truth. Beneath the praise and solemn speeches, he'd left her a financial mess to clean up. She'd discovered the mountain of gambling debts, the maxed-out credit cards, and an overdrawn line of credit. His life insurance had covered only half of what he owed, leaving her to shoulder the rest of the burden—a very real and dark shadow that loomed over her every day.

Campbell had been her rock through those dark moments, even paying her rent a couple of times. He'd somehow become a constant presence in Ava's life. Sometimes, Doyle wondered if her daughter loved him more than her.

She took a long look at the half-empty cup and decided that, regardless of her partner's opinion on the effectiveness of their hasty stakeout, she needed coffee. She also *really* wanted to stretch her legs.

Doyle took out her phone and used it to google the nearest Starbucks location, which happened to be just a couple blocks over on Third Avenue.

Perfect.

She turned to Campbell. "Sure you don't want anything? Maybe a nice cup of herbal tea that won't interfere with your beauty sleep?"

Campbell resumed looking through the monocular. "I'm ignoring you."

"Try to keep your eyes open," she said, reaching for the door handle. "Be right—"

The phone in her hand began to vibrate with an incoming call. She glanced down at the screen and saw a name displayed: SSA Whitaker.

"Uh-oh," said Doyle with a frown. "It's the boss."

Campbell lowered the monocular again, and this time, there was nothing playful in his expression.

A call from Supervisory Special Agent Tom Whitaker, the operational leader of New York's JTTF and their boss—at least with respect to their assignment to the task force—was unusual. Whitaker wasn't known for micromanaging his subordinates, preferring to save all questions for the daily briefing.

With a *here goes nothing* raise of the eyebrows, Doyle tapped the screen to accept the call. "Detective Doyle, speaking."

"Doyle. SSA Whitaker, here. Are you still on the Benali stakeout?"

Doyle parsed the question for subtext, trying to determine what tone to take. *Are you still . . . ?* But she sensed no impatience in the senior agent's tone. "Yes, sir. There's been no sign of Blackwell yet, but it's still early."

"You're going to have to put that on the back burner. I need you and your partner back here ASAP."

Doyle glanced over at Campbell. Getting pulled off surveillance when they were so close to having what they needed to get the goods on Blackwell was aggravating, but both detectives knew better than to question the boss. "Back to the FO," Doyle said for her partner's benefit. "Yes, sir. We're on our way."

Campbell raised an eyebrow but then put his optical scope aside and started the car.

"Sir," Doyle went on, "if I may—"

"You may not," said Whitaker, cutting her off. "Put me on speaker. Your partner should hear this."

Doyle did as instructed, then put the phone on the center console. "Go ahead, sir."

Campbell pulled away from the red-painted bus lane and crossed to the leftmost side of the street.

"There's been a mass shooting incident in Midtown about ten minutes ago. Someone shot up a restaurant in the Chrysler Building. A place called Chrysalis."

The name meant nothing to Doyle, but the words *mass shooting* seemed to suck the breath out of her lungs. "How bad is it?"

"All things considered . . . it could have been a lot worse. First responders are reporting six dead at the scene and one critically wounded."

"*Six*," breathed Doyle. "And the shooter?"

"Shooters. Plural. Four of them. If on-the-scene reporting is accurate, they're among the dead."

Doyle and Campbell exchanged a questioning glance. If the killers were dead, then the incident was no longer an active shooter situation. The question was, who had taken the bad guys out?

"Sir, we're five minutes from there," said Doyle. "Do you want us at the scene?"

"Negative. I need you back here to question a witness."

Doyle looked over at Campbell again. The latter shook his head uncertainly. "The witness is at the FO?"

"He's en route now." Whitaker hesitated. "This is where it gets a bit complicated. The witness is connected. Comes from old money. His father was an ambassador. Eyewitness accounts indicate that he almost single-handedly took out the shooters."

"His name wouldn't happen to be Bruce Wayne, would it?" quipped Campbell.

Whitaker evidently didn't get the joke. "No, it's Burke. Chase Burke."

Doyle furrowed her brow. "Sounds like he's the hero. Why are we treating him as a person of interest?"

"Because things don't quite add up. We need to find out why he was there and how he was able to do what he did. So, question him, and then get back to me."

Campbell glanced at Doyle, his expression similarly confused. "Why is the JTTF on this? Shouldn't NYPD be taking point?"

It was a question Doyle should have asked. Although they were both working under the federal umbrella, like all career New York City cops, they had an almost tribal sense of protectiveness when it came to jurisdictional boundaries.

"This wasn't just a random attack," replied Whitaker. "Congresswoman Tanya Hemsworth was among the victims. That makes it federal. And there's reason to believe this incident may be part of a broader terrorist plot. Look, I want you two to dig into this immediately. Go get the full story from Burke and find out if there's more to this than meets the eye."

Doyle and Campbell exchanged a knowing look.

Whitaker had nothing.

He's sending us on a fishing expedition.

As if sensing their shared reticence, Whitaker went on. "This will make a lot more sense once you see Burke's file. I'll brief you when you get here."

Whitaker ended the call without further elaboration, leaving the two detectives with more questions than at the beginning. A mass shooting interrupted by a citizen hero who was now himself a possible suspect in a terror plot?

Campbell turned onto the FDR, flipped on the flashers, and put the pedal down. Federal Plaza was only about five miles away. Hopefully, they would find some answers waiting for them there.

CHAPTER ELEVEN

Chase Burke sat motionless, staring forward, carefully and meticulously taking in every detail of the sterile, clinical interview room.

The space was small, barely large enough to fit the metal table and the three chairs it contained. The walls were a dull, nondescript gray. The air was filled with the faint, lingering scent of disinfectant. A glaring overhead fluorescent light hummed faintly, its too-white illumination casting harsh shadows that made the space feel even more claustrophobic. Behind him, a large mirror covered one wall, which anyone familiar with police procedurals would recognize as one-way glass.

There were no decorative touches. The room was meant to unnerve and intimidate, and it was doing its job well.

Chase had spent more than his share of time in rooms like this, usually—but not always—on the opposite side of the table.

What he couldn't figure out, though, was why *he* was here.

He glanced down at his hands, which were crusted with a thin layer of dried blood.

Tanya's blood.

The realization prompted a wave of anger, and Chase felt his fingers curl into fists.

I should be out there, he told himself. *Looking for him.*

Him, of course, was the SUV driver. Chase closed his eyes and saw the man's face again.

Never should have gotten away.

When the police officers had swarmed over the scene, detaining everyone at gunpoint—standard procedure in such a situation where first responders had no way of telling the good guys from the bad—he had barely registered the blood staining his hands and clothes, too caught up in the chaos and adrenaline of the moment, too concerned for Tanya's survival. But now, sitting alone in the cold, silent room, the reality of the situation was starting to sink in.

He had failed Tanya. He'd let her die.

Chase didn't know the police procedure for dealing with the survivors and eyewitnesses during the aftermath of a mass shooting incident, but he was pretty sure it didn't involve being hustled into the back of a squad car and rushed downtown to the Javitz Building.

They had frisked him, relieving him of his wine tool and Swiss Army knife—*For your own safety*, one officer had explained before guiding him into the isolated rear seating compartment of the police vehicle—and while they hadn't put him in handcuffs, the wary regard they showed him during the ride, and later when he was escorted through a secure entrance and shown into the interview room, told a story that was, only now, becoming clear to him.

Holy shit. They think I had something to do with this.

The door opened, breaking the silence, and two figures in business attire—one male, older and out of shape, one female, younger and definitely in better shape—entered the room and moved to take the seats opposite Chase. Both wore laminated, color-coded ID badges clipped to their lapels, but far more conspicuous were the badge cases, which displayed the distinctive gold shield identifying them both as NYPD detectives.

For several seconds, nobody spoke. The two detectives merely regarded him as if taking his measure or—and he knew this from experience—waiting for him to make the first move. When he did not oblige, the woman finally spoke.

"Mr. Burke," she began, her tone professional but not altogether unsympathetic, "I'm Detective Doyle. This is Detective Campbell. We'd like to ask you some questions about what happened tonight."

"You're NYPD," said Chase. "What are we doing at FBI headquarters?"

The detectives exchanged a look, and then Doyle said, "It's a joint investigation," as if that explained everything.

Chase was pretty sure there was more to it than that but accepted the answer with a nod. "I'll tell you everything I know."

Doyle placed a small digital recording device on the table and touched a button to activate it. "To begin with, I'd like to advise you of your rights."

"Just as a formality," intoned Campbell with a healthy measure of New York sarcasm. "You understand."

Chase's pulse quickened as Doyle recited the all too familiar Miranda statement, which only served to confirm his impression that he was being treated as a suspect. Nevertheless, he kept his expression neutral, acknowledging Doyle's final question—*Do you understand these rights as they have been read to you?*—calmly, with a simple "I do."

"Mr. Burke, we appreciate your cooperation," Doyle said after the briefest pause. "We know tonight has been traumatic, and we just want to get to the bottom of what happened. Can you start by telling us why you were at the restaurant? According to the schedule, you weren't supposed to be working tonight."

"David . . . my boss . . . asked me to cover a shift. It was a last-minute thing."

"You're the . . ." Doyle narrowed her eyes as if consulting a mental notebook. "Sommelier? At Chrysalis?"

Chase nodded. "That's right."

Campbell leaned forward, his eyes narrowing. "So, you just happened to be there on the same night Congresswoman Hemsworth was? That's quite a coincidence."

The male detective's aggression was contagious, and Chase had to fight the impulse to respond in kind. "Not really," he replied, speaking slowly. "When a VIP guest makes a reservation, David likes to have me out front."

Doyle continued in her soothing tone. "Let's talk about what happened tonight. Walk us through it."

Chase took a deep breath, then began recounting the attack, beginning with the moment he saw Tanya's security escort rushing to protect her—he made the conscious decision not to use Marc's name as that would only lead to more uncomfortable questions—and heard the first shots being fired. He described the shooting of both the off-duty policeman and Tanya's bodyguard and the subsequent attempted abduction of the congresswoman.

"Did you recognize any of the gunmen?" asked Doyle.

Chase shook his head. "They wore balaclavas."

Doyle nodded. "Please go on."

Conscious of the recording device and the fact that his next words might be used against him, Chase took another deep breath before continuing. "When I saw that they were there to kidnap Congresswoman Hemsworth, I knew that I had to try and stop them."

Campbell gave a derisive snort. "You stabbed one guy in the neck with a steak knife, took his gun, and used it to kill two more of them. They teach you that in sommelier school?"

"I'm ex-military," said Chase.

"Yeah? Well, so am I," retorted Campbell. "I don't remember learning how to shiv a guy with a steak knife, though."

Maybe you weren't paying attention, Chase wanted to say but thought better of it. "My unit received specialized combative training. They taught us how to use whatever's at hand and how to disarm an opponent." He shrugged. "I just reacted."

"You just . . . *reacted*," said Campbell with an overemphasized shrug of his shoulders. He was layering on the sarcasm.

"Let's talk about your military service," said Doyle. "Or should I say, your record. You were convicted of striking an officer, spent a year at Leavenworth, and received a dishonorable discharge. Do I have that right?"

Chase's jaw tightened involuntarily. "More or less."

"See, to me," explained Campbell, "that suggests a pattern of violent behavior. Criminal behavior."

"So, I should have just hidden under a table like everyone else and let them take her?" The words were past Chase's lips before he could stop himself.

Campbell smiled and leaned back in his chair. "I'm glad you brought that up. Because maybe if you hadn't decided to play hero, the good congresswoman wouldn't be in surgery at NYU right now."

The retort had exactly the opposite effect Campbell intended. Instead of feeling a pang of guilt at the outcome, Chase experienced a surge of hope.

"She's still alive?"

The detectives exchanged a look, then Campbell nodded. "No thanks to you."

Despite everything else, Chase suddenly felt a hundred pounds lighter.

Tanya's alive.

"You see, Mr. Burke," Doyle was saying, "We're having a little trouble reconstructing what happened outside the restaurant. Several of the patrons have corroborated your account of what happened inside, but nobody got a good look at what happened when you followed the last gunman out to the street."

Chase shook his head, recentering himself. "There was an SUV . . . a black Suburban. It pulled up and . . ." He trailed off as the memory of a face appeared in his mind's eye. "I saw the driver's face," he said, suddenly excited. "That prick wasn't wearing a mask."

"We'll get to that," said Doyle. "What happened next?"

"The guy holding Tanya . . . Congresswoman Hemsworth . . . he was using her as a human shield. Before he could pull her in . . ." His head tilted involuntarily with the uncertainty of his memory. "Somebody shot her. Shot them both. A sniper."

"A *sniper*?" echoed Campbell skeptically.

"It had to be." Chase searched his memories. "The shot . . . I saw the hit before I heard the shot. The shooters were wearing body armor, but the round went right through it. Had to be a high-powered, armor-piercing round, fired from . . . no more than a couple hundred yards out."

The detectives looked at each other again, and for the first time since the interrogation began, Chase got the impression that he had just told them something they didn't already know.

Doyle turned to him again. "Let me make sure I understand here. You're saying that someone—some random sniper—killed the fourth gunman and wounded the congresswoman?"

"Yeah."

"Why?" asked Doyle.

Chase spread his hands in a gesture of helplessness. "I have no clue."

Campbell leaned forward, his gaze unrelenting. "See, that's kind of hard for us to believe. You know . . . given your connections."

Chase thought he must have misheard. "My . . . connections?"

Both detectives were staring at him like they had x-ray vision.

"Your story is that you were just an innocent bystander, huh? You're going to stick to that?" sneered Campbell. "You expect us to believe that you have no connections to any criminal organizations?"

Another wave of anger washed over Chase, but he was genuinely confused by the line of questioning. "Criminal organizations? I have no idea what you're talking about."

"Mr. Burke," said Doyle. "I'll remind you that while you have the right to remain silent, lying to us is a crime."

Chase realized, almost too late, that the detectives were trying to rattle him with their vague accusations, get him to admit to something criminal.

But I haven't done anything, he wanted to protest. *I'm not a criminal.*

"I do not," he said slowly, "have any connections with criminals. I never have. I saw something bad happening and I reacted. It's as simple as that."

"No connections," repeated Campbell. "You and your brother weren't close, then?"

"My broth—*Michael*? I don't know what you're getting at, but Michael wasn't a criminal. He was a fed. Former FBI."

"Yeah, sure," said Campbell flatly. "And he was fucking dirty."

"We have the report," Doyle interjected, her tone still "good cop" and sympathetic but full of intensity, "from the special investigators who looked into your brother's death in Colombia. There are some . . . discrepancies."

Campbell seized on this. "Your brother leaked the intel on an operation and got good men killed. He's a traitor. And my guess is that you share a lot in common with him."

Chase's temper flared again. It was getting harder to hold it in. "Why would Michael leak intel? He was *in* one of the choppers that went down."

Campbell smirked. "Was he? Well, I never said the guy was smart."

"Fuck you!" It had slipped out before Chase could contain it. His voice rose, raw emotion breaking through his controlled facade. He looked at Doyle. "You can play good cop all you want. And you"—his eyes flicked to Campbell—"are definitely a *bad cop*, you fat piece of shit. My brother was the best man I've ever known. You're both wrong. About him, about this, about everything."

"Let me tell you what I think." Campbell leaned in, ignoring Chase, his voice low and menacing. "I think you're some sort of deep-cover foreign agent, just like your brother. I think you were working with that sniper to get Congresswoman Hemsworth out in the open so he could shoot her. You're dirty. And I'm gonna fucking prove it."

It took every ounce of restraint that Chase had to not reach across the table and grab the man by the throat.

"We're just trying to understand the full picture, Mr. Burke," said Doyle. "Help us help you. What really happened tonight?"

Chase met her gaze and, with an effort, brought his anger down to a low simmer. "I've already told you what happened. I didn't know what was going to happen. I'm not a part of any criminal conspiracy. I was just in the wrong place at the wrong time."

Doyle crossed her arms and regarded him across the table for a long moment. "Let's start again from the beginning."

CHAPTER TWELVE

Damien Gray pushed the cleaning trolley down the dimly lit corridor of the Shock-Trauma Intensive Care Unit, the wheels squeaking softly on the polished tile floor. He moved with the casual, unhurried pace of someone who belonged there, yet his mind remained sharp and alert, taking in every detail of his surroundings. The faint hum of medical equipment and the occasional beep from a monitor provided background music for his covert infiltration.

In movies, operators like him would just grab a lab coat and a stethoscope and then stroll through a hospital like they owned the place. In the real world, that sort of shoddy business would land you in the nick before you could say "Bob's your uncle." Even in a setting as vast as NYU Langone Health & Tisch Hospital, people knew their coworkers and, more importantly, noticed new faces. A new doctor or nurse strolling the halls would immediately draw the attention of the regular staff, inviting questions and even scrutiny of credentials.

But the cleaning crew? They were practically invisible, their faces a blur to the nurses and doctors who were too busy saving lives to notice the person emptying the refuse.

Even so, he was prepared for the possibility of a challenge, unlikely as it was. He'd been meticulous in crafting his disguise. The work uniform was a perfect fit. His ID badge was not only an exact duplicate of those issued to the support staff, but it even unlocked the security doors separating each section. He'd left his five o'clock shadow and even smeared his forehead with glycerin oil to give it a slightly sweaty, unwashed appearance.

Details mattered. Damien had left nothing to chance. It was why he was the best at what he did.

As he rolled the trolley toward the nurses' station, he saw a middle-aged nurse in scrubs engaged in conversation with an NYPD-uniformed policeman, the latter doubtless posted there to provide additional protection for the hospital's high-profile patient, Congresswoman Tanya Hemsworth. Their conversation trailed off as he approached, the pair evidently mindful of the possibility of being overheard by the night-shift janitor. The constable scrutinized Damien, and Damien, in turn, gave him a nod of acknowledgment as he reached for the waste bin and emptied it into the larger bin on his cart. Neither of the pair noticed the small electronic device, about the size of a pack of gum, that he affixed to the underside of the counter when he returned the bin to its place.

As he moved off, he surreptitiously glanced up at the whiteboard, which listed the surnames of the patients in the unit, confirming that Hemsworth was indeed installed in one of the glassed-in critical care bays. He made a note of the room number, just in case the job required him to pay the congresswoman a visit in person.

He wheeled the trolley down the corridor to the next nurses' station, out of the line of sight of the policeman, and subvocalized into the microphone tucked under the collar of his work shirt. "Are you receiving the signal?"

Nigel's voice came back in his ear bud. "Loud and clear. I'm listening to a man and a woman discussing the target."

"Yeah, it's a nurse and the copper they assigned to protect her. What are they saying?"

Nigel laughed. "They're talking politics. Sounds like they both voted for Hemsworth."

Damien frowned. "We'll that's some useless shite. We need to know if she's going to make it."

"Patience, Big Brother. This is a process. Besides, eavesdropping is only the . . ." Nigel's voice trailed off, only to return a moment later. "Hang on . . . and we're in! The nurse just logged into her terminal."

Damien allowed himself a sigh of both relief and satisfaction. The device he had planted served a dual purpose—in addition to listening in on nearby conversations, it also established Bluetooth connections with compatible electronic devices, which not only included the mobile phones of anyone passing by but also the computer terminal at the nurses' station, which meant that Nigel was now able to see everything displayed on the monitor of that computer.

"Well?" asked Damien after several seconds of silence.

"Hang on. I'm trying to make sense of all this. I'm not a bloody doctor." There was another long pause, and then Nigel's voice crackled in Damien's ear. "All right. It looks like she's on a ventilator. Her vitals have been steady since she came out of surgery. Temperature normal. BP and pulse are low, but O2 is good. Standing med orders . . . Propofol—"

"That's a sedative," said Damien. "They're keeping her in a medically induced coma."

"Norepinephrine. Vancomycin. Meropenem."

"Blood pressure support and antibiotics," Damien supplied. "Okay, sounds like she's stable. Is there a long-term prognosis?"

"Looking." Several more seconds passed. "Not in so many words. Seems like the standing orders are to continue monitoring and reassess in twelve hours."

Damien nodded to himself. "Okay. Let's do the same. Call me right away if there's a change."

"Will do."

Damien continued down the corridor, emptying bins as he went. With his primary mission accomplished, it was imperative to maintain his cover, at least until he was out of the ICU. If he were to abruptly vanish, leaving work undone, it might cause those who had seen him without really seeing him to take notice.

He was just wheeling the trolley onto the lift when Nigel spoke again. "Damien, the client's calling."

Here it comes, thought Damien. "Right," he said aloud. "Half a minute."

He backed the trolley out of the lift car and moved to an out-of-the-way corner, then took out an ordinary mobile phone and held it to his ear so that, to anyone passing by, it would appear that he was simply taking a call, which, in fact, he was.

"All right. Patch it through."

"You're on," said Nigel.

Damien waited a beat, then spoke. "Go ahead."

The electronically distorted voice seemed to fill his head. "What's the situation?"

"The target is in the hospital. Stable, but unconscious at the moment. What do you want me to do?"

He mentally counted down the requisite signal delay and then heard what he had prayed for.

"For now, I want you and your team to stand down. There may be some follow-up work, but the present situation is . . . acceptable."

A rare feeling of relief washed over Damien. "Understood." He tapped his earbud to end the call, then tapped it again. "Nigel, did you copy that?"

"Yeah," came Nigel's incredulous reply. "That's it, then? We're *done*?"

"Appears so."

"This has got to be the strangest job we've ever taken. Shoot, but *don't* kill? Who does that?" asked Nigel.

"As long as they pay, we don't ask," replied Damien. "Listen, do me a favor and put me on the soonest flight to London."

"On it." There was a brief pause. "Okay, there's one leaving at midnight from JFK. It'll be a bit of a push to make it through security, though."

"Book it. I'll head there directly."

"Done."

"Thanks. Listen, just in case the client changes his mind, let's continue monitoring the signal. You can do that from the hotel, right?"

"Until the batteries go dead."

"All right. You and Brad hang there for a couple more days. Enjoy the city. Maybe take in a show. You earned it."

Nigel laughed. "Will do, Big Brother."

Realizing that he still had his mobile in hand, Damien opened the messaging app and tapped out a quick text to his wife:

Conference ended earlier than expected. Leaving soonest. Tell Allie I'll be there for the match.

The prospect of being there in time to watch his daughter play what might very well be the most important game of her life brought a smile to his face.

He hit send, knowing that it would be a couple more hours before Cassie awoke to the message, then wheeled the cleaning trolley into a storage closet. He stripped off the uniform shirt, binned it, and then pulled on a navy-blue polo shirt. A splash of water and a swipe from a paper towel cleaned the glycerin residue from his forehead, after which he stepped out into the hall and made his way back to the lift.

He exited the hospital with the same casual, unhurried pace he had maintained throughout the night and waved down a taxi.

CHAPTER THIRTEEN

Detective Alice Doyle absentmindedly stirred her coffee as she awaited her partner's return. The seating area of the cafeteria was mostly empty, with only a handful of federal employees—likely JTTF staffers pulling an all-nighter—grabbing snacks and drinks to take back to their offices. It was quiet enough that she could hear the audio from the wall-mounted television set, which was tuned to a twenty-four-hour news service and presently carrying almost nonstop coverage of what the media have dubbed the "Midtown Massacre."

Campbell returned a moment later with a can of Coke Zero and settled in across the table from Doyle.

She pointed at the can. "You know that has caffeine, right?"

Campbell's brows drew together. "Nah. The *zero* is for zero caffeine."

"It's for zero sugar," countered Doyle with a smug smile. "Check the label."

Campbell did, his lips moving as he read the ingredients. Then, his face twisted in a frown of disgust. "Shit."

Doyle laughed. The soda contained only about a third of the caffeine in her coffee, but if Campbell was as sensitive to it as he claimed, it might be enough to keep him awake longer than he wanted.

"Well, it's not like I'm getting any sleep tonight," said Campbell, taking a sip.

She gave him a sympathetic smile, watching as he fidgeted with the can. After a moment, he glanced up.

"Hey, did you reach out to Ava's babysitter?" he asked.

Doyle nodded. "Yeah, I did. Thanks for asking, though."

It was a small thing, but she appreciated the gesture. While her partner enjoyed—no, loved—playing the "bad cop" of their partnership, he always looked out for both her and Ava, never needing to be asked.

"So, what do you think?" she asked, shifting the focus back to the case.

"About Burke?" Campbell shrugged. "I think he's hiding something."

Doyle had felt similarly when she'd gotten a look at Chase Burke's file, but after talking to him, she felt less certain of her initial assessment.

Maybe the guy is a hero.

"He seems pretty straightforward to me. His story checks out, and he doesn't strike me as the kind of person to be mixed up in anything shady."

Campbell leaned forward, resting his elbows on the table. "Alice, come on. The guy has a background in PSYOPS. He's *trained* to be convincing. Just because he sounds sincere doesn't mean he's telling the truth. That guy is selling a big pile of shit. Don't tell me you can't smell it."

Doyle ignored the second part of Campbell's comment. "All I'm saying is, we're trained too," she countered, "and our gut instincts count for something, right? Well, my gut's telling me he's not involved in this. At least not the way you seemed to let on when questioning him."

Campbell took another sip of his soda, his eyes narrowing. "Let's just tick the boxes, okay?" He raised a hand and began extending fingers one at a time. "He's a military convict with a dishonorable discharge. He just happened to be at the restaurant on his day off when the congresswoman shows up, and he's right in the thick of it when the shooting starts. Almost like he *knew* it was going to happen."

"Come on, James. The man fought back. What else was he supposed to do?" She sighed. "He wasn't part of it. I just don't see it."

"Okay, say you're right," said Campbell, extending an open palm her way. "Maybe he wasn't involved in the planning, but he must have known it was going to go down. That's why he just *happened* to be there."

Doyle folded her arms across her chest. "How does that make any sense? And even if he did somehow know about it, how does that make him one of the bad guys? What if he heard something was going down and showed up to protect the restaurant? Or maybe—"

"Alice, Alice, Alice . . . ." Campbell said, interrupting her. He shook his head patronizingly. "People talk. Whatever outfit he's part of probably got word that these guys were going to hit the restaurant and kidnap Hemsworth, so they sent Burke in to get her out in the open so that sniper could waste her."

"Okay, but if Burke wanted her dead, why didn't he just let the kidnappers take her?"

Campbell spread his hands. "How should I know? They're criminals. They don't always behave rationally. His brother's a fucking traitor. Let's not leave that part out, all right? Who's to say it doesn't run in the family?"

There it is, thought Doyle. *The brother.*

That, in fact, was the reason Whitaker had saddled the two of them with the job of cracking Chase Burke. Doyle knew that even without it being said in so many words.

The fact is, Burke's brother Michael was a former FBI special agent who had gone on to work for the intelligence division of the US State Department and had, or so it was believed, sold out to a South American criminal syndicate, led his team into a deadly ambush, and quite possibly faked his own death to escape justice. And nobody at the FBI was sure how far Michael's reach in the Bureau extended, which was why SSA Whitaker had turned Chase Burke's interrogation over to the two of them.

But regardless of what Michael Burke had or had not done, Doyle didn't see a clear, sensible line connecting Chase to that conspiracy, nor did she see anything criminal about what Chase had done inside Chrysalis.

"I'm telling you," Campbell went on, breaking her line of thought, "there's something off about this guy. He's too smooth, too composed. Did you notice his watch?"

Doyle shook her head.

"He was wearing a Rolex. What kind of waiter wears a fucking Rolex?"

"It's probably a knockoff. And he's not actually a waiter. He's a sommelier."

Campbell flicked the comment away. "It wasn't a knockoff. Whitaker said he's from old money. So, why's he working at a restaurant? No, there's something fishy about this guy. If he's not involved directly, he knows more than he's letting on."

Doyle looked down at her coffee, swirling the dark liquid in her cup. "So, what do *we* do? We're lucky he hasn't lawyered up, but if we keep him much longer, he's going to."

Campbell shook his head. "All we can do is keep trying to crack him."

Doyle thought he might have more to say on the subject, but Campbell appeared to have run out of ideas. In the long silence that followed, however, the audio from the television set caught her attention.

On-screen, the reporter, Angela Vasquez, was facing the camera, addressing her colleagues at the studio. "Anderson, I'm standing outside the Chrysler Building here in Midtown Manhattan, in front of Chrysalis, one of New York City's premier dining establishments, where a shocking event unfolded earlier this evening. With me is the owner of Chrysalis, Chef David Rousseau, who witnessed the incident firsthand."

The camera pulled back to show the chef—a big man dressed all in white, with a mop of curly black hair—standing alongside the reporter.

"Chef David, can you tell us what happened tonight?" asked Vasquez.

"It was terrible," said the chef, his gravelly voice reminding Doyle of a much younger Harvey Fierstein. "They came out of nowhere. Shooting . . . breaking things. I was in the back, so I didn't see very much of it, but I heard everything. They killed two men . . . policemen, they're saying. And then they tried to kidnap Congresswoman Hemsworth."

"We've heard unconfirmed reports that a member of your staff was involved in the incident," Vasquez pressed. "Can you comment on those claims?"

"Involved?" David shook his head vehemently. "No, no, no. Chase Burke is his name. When everyone else was hiding under their tables, this guy stepped up and took on those shooters. But then, when the police showed up, instead of giving him a medal, they put him in a squad car like some kind of criminal. Chase, if you're seeing this, thank you. We all owe you for what you did tonight. We love you, buddy."

Doyle glanced over at Campbell to judge his reaction as the reporter continued.

"So, you're saying that the man the police have in custody is innocent and in no way connected to what happened?"

"Absolutely, he's innocent," David replied firmly. "Chase is my friend. He's a hero, and I want everyone to know that. I don't know why he was arrested, but all he did was fight back. I probably wouldn't be standing here talking to you if it wasn't for him." The realization of just how close he came to death seemed to hit the man. "Hopefully he'll get released soon."

The reporter seemed a little uncomfortable with David's sensational claims and quickly turned back to the camera. "A stunning twist in tonight's events. Renowned chef David Rousseau claims that the police have arrested an innocent man. We'll continue to follow this story closely as it develops. Back to you, Anderson."

As the broadcast cut back to the studio, Doyle took a deep breath. "Well, this complicates things," she said, turning to Campbell.

Campbell made a dismissive gesture. "It's all hype. Hell, they got half of it wrong. Burke isn't even under arrest."

"Not yet," admitted Doyle. "But now it's going to be a lot harder to make any kind of case against him."

"He's dirty," insisted Campbell. "We just gotta prove it."

Doyle still wasn't buying it. "Say you're right. We're not going to trip him up. He's too cool for that. And I don't see another angle."

Campbell thought for a moment. "Then, let's flip the script. All those people saying Burke is a hero . . . that chef? Let's see if he changes his tune when they hear who Burke really is."

Doyle narrowed her eyes at her partner. Not for the first time, what Campbell was proposing had the potential to backfire spectacularly.

Why does he have such a hard-on for Burke? Doyle wondered.

"The witnesses are just as likely to double down in defending Burke," she argued. "And we'll be opening ourselves up to charges of witness tampering. Any lawyer with half a brain will make hay with that."

But Campbell just shook his head. He tipped back his head and drained the last of his Coke. When it was gone, he squeezed his fist around the can, crushing it in the middle, and slammed it down on the table. "My gut says Burke is dirty."

The words hit Doyle like a slap. Earlier, she had defended the validity of her gut instinct. Now, Campbell was throwing her words back at her.

She nodded slowly. "Okay. We'll do it your way."

CHAPTER FOURTEEN

A light drizzle began falling as Doyle and Campbell drove back up the FDR. The precipitation was barely noticeable until they turned onto 42nd Street and found themselves in a veritable parking lot, because traffic was being detoured around the Chrysler Building.

Campbell muttered a curse as he grudgingly turned on the windshield wipers. The beads of water on the windshield caught and demagnified the red glow of taillights and, as they neared their destination, the flashers of the police cars and ambulances. The effect was a dazzling, if ephemeral, light display that was periodically erased with a scrape of rubber on glass.

Upon seeing the FBI placard on the dashboard of the unmarked sedan, the uniform manning the barricade waved them through, but the situation inside the cordon was almost as congested as the traffic jam they had just left, and they had to park half a block back from the entrance to Chrysalis. This necessitated running a gauntlet past several TV news crews shooting live feeds and B-roll, all of whom quickly focused on the detectives, peppering them with requests for information. Angela Vasquez, standing with her back to the restaurant's entrance to ensure that the yellow crime scene tape was visible in the shot, thrust her microphone in front of Doyle. "Detective," she began, evidently spotting Doyle's shield, "was this a terrorist incident?"

Doyle didn't even break stride as she ducked under the tape.

Beyond the tape, a fifty-foot-long section of sidewalk in front of the restaurant entrance had been roped off, both to facilitate the movement of investigators into the establishment and to preserve the integrity of the scene of the final shooting that had climaxed the event. A large splash of blood marked the spot where Congresswoman Hemsworth and her assailant had fallen, victims of a sniper's bullet, but there were no bodies. Both had been rushed to NYU for treatment; the assailant had been dead on arrival.

Doyle studied the splatter pattern and tried to estimate the path the bullet had traveled. She recalled Chase's comment about the sniper being close—*No more than a couple hundred yards out*—and her gaze wandered down 42nd Street in the direction of Grand Central Station.

What was the sniper doing here?

The question felt much more important than Campbell's irrational quest to implicate Chase Burke, but for the present she saw no alternative but to follow her partner's lead.

Inside the restaurant, the scene was even more intense. Nearly every table had been overturned. China, glassware, and cutlery were scattered about the floor, along with copious amounts of food and drink, all of which was now slowly spoiling with the passage of time. There was, thankfully, very little blood, though five bodies lay sprawled out in full view where they had fallen. Evidence techs were dusting for fingerprints, taking swabs, and meticulously cataloging items. At the back of the restaurant, far away from the worst of the chaos and carnage, FBI agents wearing the distinctive blue windbreakers emblazoned with the Bureau's initials were interviewing patrons and staff members, all of whom looked like shell-shocked refugees.

Campbell caught the eye of one, a colleague from the JTTF. "Special Agent Walton," he called out, making his way toward the man. "Looks like you're pulling an all-nighter."

Walton, who was about Doyle's age, just nodded. "You have no idea. From start to finish, the incident lasted five minutes, but we'll still be picking up the pieces five days from now."

Campbell nodded as if commiserating, then got to the point. "Are you releasing any of the witnesses?"

Walton shook his head. "Not yet. A few of them were taken to the hospital for medical evaluation . . . a lot of 'em reported 'chest pains.'" He made air quotes to indicate his opinion of the self-diagnoses. "Panic attacks, mostly. We'll be holding them there until we get the green light to start letting them go home."

"I'd like to have a word with the guy that runs the place. Chef . . . David Rousseau, I think it is."

"That guy." Walton rolled his eyes. "A real pain in the ass. Insisted on talking to the press."

"You didn't stop him?"

"I tried, and so did his girlfriend, but Rousseau made such a scene that I decided it was easier to just let him have his fifteen minutes of fame. They're around here somewhere. Check the kitchen."

"The girlfriend, she works with him?" Doyle asked.

"Yeah," Walton said, checking his notes. "She's on the list as a junior sommelier, whatever that means. Name's Violet Evans."

Doyle thanked the FBI agent and then, with Campbell in tow, moved through the restaurant to the kitchen, where they found Chef David, a look of profound sorrow on his face as he surveyed the wreckage of his beloved eatery. Pots and pans lay scattered, ingredients spilled, and the smell of burnt food hung in the air. Beside him stood an athletic woman in her late twenties or early thirties. She had auburn hair tied loosely back and wore a fitted white blouse paired with tailored black pants. She was the first to notice Doyle and Campbell. Her brow furrowed.

Doyle couldn't help but feel a pang of sympathy for the chef; the restaurant was clearly more than just a job to him. Doyle nodded to Campbell, letting him know she would take the lead. The "good cop" always made the first move.

"Chef David," Doyle said, stepping forward. "I'm Detective Doyle. This is my partner, Detective Campbell."

David turned toward her, his eyes flickering with exhaustion.

"Right," he said. "This is Violet Evans. My girlfriend. She works with me."

"We'd like to ask you a few questions if you don't mind, sir," Doyle said.

"Again? Why?" Violet asked in a clipped tone. "He's already told the FBI everything. Can't they share their notes with you?"

"Humor us," interjected Campbell, his eyes on David. "After your little performance in front of the camera, we'd like to chat and clear a few things up."

"Told you it was a bad idea," Violet muttered.

"We're just trying to get a clear picture of what happened, Chef," said Doyle, her tone softer than her partner's. "We know you've been through a lot."

David sighed and wiped his hands on his apron. "What do you want to know?"

"Let's start with Chase Burke. In your interview with Angela Vasquez, you called him a friend. I just wanted some clarification on that."

"Chase's an employee," Violet said before David could reply. "He's not really our friend."

David eyed his girlfriend and shook his head. "He's more than an employee, Violet. And you know that." Facing Doyle, he said, "Chase is my friend. And a good one."

"How well do you know Mr. Burke?" Doyle asked.

David cocked his head to the side. "Why do you insist on harassing Chase? He saved lives tonight. You know that, right?"

"He also ended a few," observed Campbell, leaning against the stainless steel counter.

"I know it may seem to you like we're targeting Mr. Burke," Doyle went on. "But when there's an incident like this, we have to be thorough in our investigation. Sometimes, things aren't always what they seem."

"It seemed pretty clear to me tonight," countered David defensively.

"You were in the kitchen when it all went down, love," Violet said, grabbing her boyfriend's arm. "How can you know for sure what actually happened?"

"And what about you, Miss Evans? Did you see anything?" Campbell asked.

"I was in the wine cellar. So, I'm afraid I did not."

"Listen, Chef, this is all part of the process," Doyle said. "The sooner you answer our questions, the sooner we can release Mr. Burke. You want that, right?"

David sighed again. "Chase hasn't done anything wrong. He's the best sommelier I've ever worked with. More importantly, he's a good man."

"How long have you known him?"

"He started here about a year and a half ago."

"And are you friends outside of work?"

David uttered a short, harsh laugh. "I'm the chef of a Michelin-starred restaurant in Manhattan. There is no 'outside of work' for me."

Campbell spoke up. "Don't you think it is a little strange that a rich boy like Burke is working as a waiter?"

"Chase is a sommelier," countered David. "Do you need me to explain the difference?"

Doyle made a dismissive gesture. "He doesn't need the money. So, what we really want to understand is, why is he working here?"

"You're right. He most certainly does *not* need the money." David shrugged. "He actually likes what he does. He loves good wine, and he loves talking about it. It's as simple as that."

"That's a nice story. I've got a better one, though," Campbell said. "He's crooked, and he's using your restaurant as cover for his racket."

"He wouldn't do that. He—"

"Let me ask you something," Campbell said, cutting off David. "Does Burke show you all the expenses he puts on the business credit card? Do you really know where every dollar goes?"

For the first time since the conversation began, Doyle saw a flicker of suspicion cross David's countenance. But then the chef shook his head. "No," he said emphatically. "You're wrong about him. Like I keep saying, Chase is a good man."

"Yet he was here when the attack happened," Campbell pressed. "Pretty convenient, don't you think?"

David's face reddened. "*Convenient?* What the hell is that supposed to mean?"

Campbell shrugged again, slower this time. More exaggerated. "Just trying to see the big picture."

"I asked Chase to come in," David said, a touch of anger seeping into his voice. "I had to beg him, in fact."

"Uh-huh. And why exactly did you do that?" Campbell asked. "Isn't your girlfriend here a sommelier? Why call Chase Burke in? What is it that you're not telling us?"

David hesitated, his eyes darting to the side as he swallowed hard. "It's . . . it's just that when I saw that Congresswoman Hemsworth was coming in, I knew Chase would want to be here for that. Okay?"

Doyle's eyebrows shot up as she stiffened at this revelation.

Damn it! How did Campbell see through Burke's bullshit and I didn't?

"Hold on a second," she said. "Are you saying that Burke chose to come in *because* the congresswoman was going to be here?"

"Yes," David replied quickly, his fingers fidgeting with the edge of his apron.

"Truth is, Chase insisted on being called in," Violet added, but almost as soon as the words left her lips, her expression shifted, as if she realized she might have said too much.

"Insisted? Really?" Campbell said. "How interesting."

Doyle exchanged a quick glance with Campbell, noting the faint smirk tugging at his lips.

"It's not like that," David said.

"Then tell us," Doyle said sharply.

"Look, it's really simple," the chef replied. "Chase likes to attend to our VIP guests personally. *I* like when he attends to them personally. That personal touch is nice. People appreciate it."

"Yeah," said Campbell. "Well, he definitely *attended* to her tonight."

"He was trying to save her!" David's voice rose, impassioned. "He took on those men when nobody else did a fucking thing. He acted when everybody else froze."

"Or maybe he was part of it. Maybe that whole 'hero' act," countered Campbell, throwing air quotes around the word *hero*, "was just him covering his tracks."

David shook his head. "You have no idea what the hell you're talking about! Chase risked his life to protect everyone here. He didn't have to. He chose to because that's the kind of man he is."

"Is that so?" Campbell's tone was skeptical.

"Yes, it is!" David snapped, taking a step toward Campbell. "And if you can't see that, then you're a bigger fool than I thought. Chase is a *hero*, just like I told that reporter, and you're wasting your time trying to pin this on him."

"David, please," Violet said. "This isn't helping."

Doyle stepped between her partner and the chef, trying to cool things down a little. "Chef David, we're not here to accuse anyone. We just need all the facts. Please, help us understand in more detail exactly what happened."

David raised his hands in a defiant gesture. "No. I'm done here. This is a waste of time. You've obviously already made up your minds about Chase. You're wrong, but if you want to head down that road, I can't stop you. Just know that I'm going to tell everyone who will listen that people are still alive tonight because of Chase and that he's a good man who doesn't deserve whatever the hell . . . *this* . . . is."

Doyle sensed Campbell preparing to throw another barb and quickly headed him off. "I'm sure you're right, Chef David. Thank you for your time." She turned away, motioning for her partner to follow suit.

Campbell, however, continued to glower at the chef, throwing out a parting shot. "We're not done with you."

"What the hell, James?" Doyle said when they were back out on the main floor.

Campbell waved the question away. "I was just trying to push his buttons."

"Yeah, well . . . you succeeded at that. I'm not sure what else you accomplished, though."

"Burke is dirty," insisted Campbell.

"Maybe, maybe not, but saying it over and over isn't going to make it true."

"Look, Alice." Campbell stopped walking and looked at his partner. "I've done this job a long time, okay? You have any clue how many pricks I've seen get away with stuff? I'm talking bad stuff. Murder. Rape. You name it. There have been so many times when I knew, I just *knew* someone was guilty, and they walked. Even if we can prove it, it's still not enough sometimes." He sighed, exhaling slowly. "I might be jaded, but Burke is dirty somehow. I can feel it. I can't stomach letting any more bad guys walk free. And remember, a good cop died tonight."

Doyle was sensitive to the fact that Campbell had seen guilty men go free. She'd experienced it, too, and it stung. More than once, she'd questioned if she was even making a difference by being a cop. She believed in justice. That's what kept her going, but even so, some days were harder than others.

Nodding, Doyle softened her approach. "I hear you. Let's just follow the evidence, okay? See where that takes us."

"That's all I'm asking."

"Then we have a deal." She paused a beat. "We're gonna have to cut him loose. You know that as well as I do."

Campbell regarded her for a long moment, then nodded slowly. "You're right. We've been going at this all wrong. We need to drill down on this guy. Find out who he's talking to in his private time. That's the key."

"You want to put a surveillance package on him?" Doyle shook her head. "Good luck getting a warrant for that with what we've got."

But Campbell just gave a cryptic smile. "Who said anything about a warrant?"

CHAPTER FIFTEEN

Brad Gray sank deeper into the plush armchair of his suite at the Langham, the faint hum of Fifth Avenue muffled by the soundproof windows that framed the glittering skyline. He raised his rocks glass—Booker's, neat—and slowly swirled the amber liquid, watching as it glowed in the soft light of the nearby floor lamp. The warmth of the bourbon was already beginning to loosen the tension in his shoulders, its smoky richness familiar, like an old friend returning after a long absence.

Say what you want about how crass Americans are, but they sure know a thing or two about distilling spirits.

The suite itself was an oasis of calm, a stark but welcome contrast to the adrenaline-fueled hours that had just passed. He had felt quite uncomfortable in the sniper's nest he had shared with his brother, but here, every inch of his surroundings whispered luxury—marble floors, polished mahogany furniture, soft Italian linens, and even the plush slippers that now cushioned his feet.

Yet, despite all this comfort, his mind hadn't fully recovered from the events of the night.

They'd barely escaped from their shooting blind outside the Bowery Savings Bank Building ahead of the arriving swarm of emergency vehicles. There hadn't even been time to confirm the kill.

The shot, he corrected himself.

Now that was some bollocks. *Wound the congressman*, their client had insisted when explaining the assignment, *but under no circumstances are you to kill her.*

It was an odd request, even by the standards of the clandestine world they operated in. Usually, their orders were simple and brutal—eliminate the target. But a no-kill order? What was the purpose of that?

Damien had almost refused outright. Wounding without killing was a lot harder than it might seem. Any wound, even a so-called flesh wound, could prove deadly, even if immediate medical attention was given. Add to that the difficulty of placing the shot in a nonvital part of the body without making it look deliberate, and it veered into *Mission: Impossible* territory. But rather than say no, Damien had instead raised the price, and astonishingly, the client had agreed.

Brad had concurred with Damien's reasoning at the time, but looking back, he wondered if maybe his big brother hadn't gotten a little greedy. The assignment had turned into a fiasco with the unexpected arrival of the assault team, but Damien had gone ahead with the plan, taking the shot and almost . . . *almost* killing the target in the process.

"Should have just walked away," he murmured to himself, gazing into the bourbon as if looking for a portent.

But it was Damien's call. He was the boss.

He would always be the boss.

Brad leaned back, letting his thoughts drift. There had been countless operations, each with its own set of risks and challenges. He had followed Damien through them all, never questioning, always executing. But this mission was different, and it bothered him that he couldn't see the bigger picture. Why would their client want Congresswoman Hemsworth alive yet incapacitated? What was the endgame?

His mobile vibrated, pulling him from his reverie. He glanced at the screen, saw Nigel's name, and thumbed the screen to accept the call. "What's up, Nige?"

"The client's calling." Brad thought his younger brother sounded a little flustered. "What should I do?"

"The client?" snorted Brad. "So much for 'stand down.'"

"Should I try to patch it through to Damien?"

Brad glanced at his watch. If there had been no delays, Damien would already be inside the secure terminal, awaiting the boarding call for his flight back to London. "No. I'll handle it. Put it through to me."

There was a long silence over the line. Brad thought it was merely signal delay as Nigel routed the call through his maze of VPNs, and so was both surprised and a little irked when he heard his brother's voice again. "Are you sure? Damien would want—"

"I've got it!" barked Brad. He almost said *Fuck Damien*, but that level of outspokenness would require a lot more than just a few sips of whiskey. He softened his tone. "Damien has his heart set on watching Allie play tomorrow. You know how important that is to him. We can handle this, you and me. The client won't know the difference. And I won't agree to anything without talking to Big Brother first."

Nigel gave a thoughtful hum, then relented. "I guess you're right," he said with a sigh. "Okay, putting it through."

Brad straightened in his chair, assuming a posture of authority, knowing that it would be reflected in his voice, even with the modulator. He'd been craving a chance like this, an opportunity to step out from Damien's shadow and prove that he was every bit as capable. It wasn't that he resented his brother's role as leader. Damien wasn't just the older brother—he was a natural, a born strategist, and a brilliant operator. Under Damien's guidance, the Ghost Brothers had built a solid business and amassed a significant nest egg. But Brad had skills, too, and a burning desire to prove himself as his brother's equal.

He held his breath in anticipation until he heard the client's voice, distorted and detached, in his ear. "I have a new assignment for you."

Brad couldn't help but smile. "I don't think you understand how this works. We finished the job. You don't get to just keep tacking things on and ordering us around."

"You'll be paid, of course," replied the client, unfazed.

"Of course," echoed Brad mordantly. "What's the job?"

"Surveillance. I need you to plant listening devices in a private residence in the Lenox Hill area. I will send you the address. The resident is away at the moment but will be returning soon, so this needs to happen quickly. Can you do it?"

Brad resisted the urge to simply accept and move to the negotiation of price. He needed to confirm with Nigel that they could accomplish the task before committing. "Hold on," he said, then put the caller on mute. Switching lines, he called Nigel.

"You're listening in, right? Can we do this?"

"I don't like being rushed," said Nigel. "We don't know anything about the target. The layout. What kind of security the place has. To do this right, we need at least twenty-four hours to conduct a proper recce."

"But *can* we do it?" pressed Brad. Recalling how Damien had negotiated the original job, he added, "Difficulty just means we can charge more. I just need to know if it's possible."

Nigel sighed. "Is it possible? Yes. We have the equipment in the van and can be in the general location inside of an hour. But Brad . . . this is going to be risky."

"Risky is what we get paid for." Brad ended the connection to Nigel and went back to the client. "All right," he said. "We'll do it. Let's talk compensation."

The client gave a number that was about a tenth of what they had been paid for the original job. It wasn't an unreasonable amount for a surveillance job. Killing someone . . . or wounding them without killing them . . . was inherently more dangerous and, therefore, commanded a bigger paycheck. But Brad knew a lowball offer when he heard one. "Double that number," he said.

"Double?" The weird voice sounded a little put off.

"That's just the first installment," Brad went on. "We get another payment—same amount—when the job is done."

There was a long silence on the line, and when the voice came back, there was a distinctive note of hesitancy. "That's a great deal of money for a simple surveillance job."

"There's nothing *simple* about working for you," countered Brad. "If you want this done fast, it's going to cost you. Take it or leave it."

There was another long pause, and then, "The payment has been transferred to your account."

The client then verbalized the target's name and address, which Brad copied on a piece of hotel stationery.

"Always a pleasure," he said, and then ended the call and sighed deeply.

Finally, he had a chance to show he could do more than simply follow Damien's orders. He downed the rest of his bourbon, savoring the burn, then grabbed his jacket and headed over to Nigel's room.

"It's a go," he said when Nigel opened the door.

"You cleared it with Damien?"

Brad felt a nerve in his cheek twitch. "There's no time. We've got to move on this."

"You promised to clear any decisions with him," Nigel reminded him firmly.

Brad let out a frustrated sigh and took out his mobile, feeling the familiar pang of resentment as he dialed Damien's number.

"Brad." Damien's voice was terse. "What's wrong?"

"Nothing wrong, brother. The client called. We've got a new job. Surveillance. Nigel says it will be a piece of cake."

Nigel shot daggers at him.

"You agreed to this without calling me first?" Damien's irritation was palpable.

"We've got this," Brad insisted. "You're going home to your family. Don't worry, we can handle it."

Damien's growl was audible over the line. "Who's the target?"

"Some guy named Burke."

"*Chase* Burke? That's the man who broke up the assault on the restaurant. It's all over the news."

"Is that right?" Brad feigned nonchalance, though his mind raced to grasp the significance of this new information.

"I don't like this," Damien said after a pause. "I'll meet you. Wait for me."

"We've got this," Brad repeated more forcefully. "Go home. Wish Allie luck for me."

There was a long silence on the other end. Finally, Damien relented. "Fine. But be careful."

"Always," Brad said, then hung up. He looked at Nigel. "Happy?"

"I never said it would be a piece of cake."

"But it will be, won't it? Because you're just that good." He gestured toward the door. "Come on. Let's move out."

Nigel stared back at him for a long moment before finally giving in. "I guess if Damien's okay with it . . ."

Brad forced a grin, though the bitter taste of resentment lingered at the back of his throat. Despite everything, he was still caught in Damien's shadow, still tethered to the need for his older brother's approval. No matter how competent he proved himself, how flawlessly he executed each mission, he would never live up to Damien.

CHAPTER SIXTEEN

Although he had resolved not to behave like a caged animal, after an hour of sitting alone in the interrogation room, Chase had finally risen from his chair and started moving, if only to restore his circulation.

He knew that the two detectives were trying to wear him down—it was standard police procedure. What he couldn't figure out, though, was what they expected him to admit to, and unless he was very much mistaken, they didn't know either.

Their accusations had reeked of desperation. Even the attempt to somehow involve Michael in their conspiracy theory seemed designed more to provoke a reaction from him than anything else.

A psychological op, he thought. *And I fell right into it.*

What irked him the most was that they seemed completely uninterested in the one piece of information that had mattered—the fact that he had gotten a look at the assault team's getaway driver. *That* was the lead they should have been following. They should have put him with a sketch artist or handed him a stack of mug shots to look through, but they hadn't even asked for a description.

Fine. If they're not going to follow up on it, I'll do it myself.

While he wasn't a cop—and had zero interest in being one—he was not without connections.

He took comfort in the knowledge that Tanya was alive. Grievously injured, if Detective Campbell was to be believed, but alive. Now, instead of merely avenging her, he would instead have an opportunity to bring her the head of her would-be abductor—figuratively speaking, of course.

He realized that he had begun pacing the room, acting exactly like the caged animal he had become, and forced himself to return to the chair.

Almost as if that was the cue they had been waiting for, Doyle and Campbell chose that moment to return.

Campbell glared at him for a long moment, then, with a disdainful gesture, said, "You're free to go."

Doyle, standing beside her partner, offered a small, almost apologetic smile. "Thank you for your assistance."

Chase exhaled, feeling some of the tension in his muscles ooze away. He placed his palms on the tabletop and stood up.

"We're gonna be keeping an eye on you," Campbell growled. "You slip up, and we'll come down on you like a ton of bricks. You can count on that."

Doyle shot her partner a look before turning back to Chase. "I'll show you out."

"No need," he replied, eager to be away from the detectives. "Just point me in the right direction."

"I insist," she said, her tone indicating that the matter wasn't up for debate.

Chase shrugged and followed her out of the room. Campbell stayed behind.

Doyle said nothing as she guided him down a hall to a bank of elevators and didn't even look at him as they rode a car down to the ground level. Only when they had exited the secure area did she turn to him.

"Mr. Burke, I know that you must be wondering why we held you as long as we did," she began, her tone conciliatory. "I just want to assure you that our only motivation is to get at the truth. Sometimes, when we don't know where to look, we just have to start digging. It's not fair, but that's the world we live in."

Chase couldn't tell if it was an apology or an excuse, but since he wanted neither, he simply answered with stony silence. If it bothered her, she didn't let it show.

"These are yours." Doyle held out a small plastic bag that contained his wine tool and Swiss Army knife.

He took the bag and shoved it unopened into a pocket, then realized that there was something else in her hand: a business card emblazoned with the logo of the NYPD.

"If you think of anything else," she said, "anything at all, please don't hesitate to call me. Anytime, day or night."

Chase took the card, glancing at the name printed on it—Detective Alice Doyle—before lifting his eyes to meet hers. She stood a few inches shorter than him, but her green eyes, framed by dark lashes, held his gaze with a confidence that made her seem taller.

"You still think I'm involved, don't you?" He shook his head. "You guys have got this—*me*—all wrong."

Doyle's expression softened slightly, but she didn't deny his accusation. "Just call if you think of anything."

Chase jammed the card into the same pocket, then turned and made for the glass exit doors. A light drizzle was falling, which perfectly suited his mood. He paused for a moment, his mind racing with thoughts of what he would need to do next, and then headed to the curb to hail a taxi.

If he was really going to get answers on his own, it was time to get to work.

CHAPTER SEVENTEEN

Brad Gray strolled down East 66th Street, huddled—or so it appeared—under the canopy of a small, telescoping umbrella. The light rain, which cast a shimmering haze in the glow of the streetlights, hardly justified the use of the umbrella, but the rain shield was good camouflage, mostly hiding his face from any curious eyes that might happen to be gazing out from the windows of the upscale townhouses and flats lining the street. Staying dry also served a more practical purpose—when he broke into Chase Burke's residence, he didn't want to leave behind a trail of telltale puddles.

Somewhere overhead, high enough that the mosquito whine of its rotors was all but inaudible, a camera drone, piloted by Nigel, not only monitored his progress but also watched the street in both directions.

"How's it looking?" Brad asked as he neared the steps leading up to the block of flats where Chase Burke made his home.

"I think you're all clear," answered Nigel, his voice crackling with static in Brad's earbud.

"You *think*?"

"There's water on the camera lens. It's obscuring the picture somewhat."

Brad resisted the urge to swear aloud at this apparent technical glitch. Since taking the job had been his idea, he could hardly complain about unforeseen difficulties. "What's your gut telling you?" he pressed.

"I think you're clear," Nigel repeated. "Unless there's somebody hanging out in the blind spot, you should be good to go."

"That's good enough for me." Brad pivoted smoothly onto the walk leading up to the entrance to the six-story building where Burke lived. Burke's flat was on the second floor, so he would not only have to gain entry into the building but also make his way upstairs to Burke's door. Fortunately, there was just one residence per level, so he would only be at risk for exposure in the entrance lobby and in the stairwell.

He shook the rain from his umbrella and then, with a final quick look around to make sure that nobody was watching, bent over the door's ornate entry set and inserted the business end of a lockpicking gun into the lock, working the trigger with practiced ease until he felt the cylinder rotate. He returned the gun to his coat pocket, pulled the door open, and went inside. Behind him, the street remained empty, the cold drizzle continuing its relentless fall.

Bypassing the lift, Brad strode confidently up the stairs as if he had every right to be in the building. As he neared the landing to the second floor, he tugged down the rolled-up ends of the balaclava he'd been wearing like a watch cap, concealing his face, before heading down the hallway to the entrance to Burke's flat.

When he arrived there, he produced a small radio frequency signal detector and ran it along the perimeter of the door, looking for the wireless sensors commonly used in security systems. Finding none, he pocketed the detector and once more went to work with the lockpicking gun, quickly defeating first the deadbolt and then the lock on the door lever, after which he slowly pushed open the door, stepped inside, and closed the door behind him. From the moment he'd reached the landing, the entire process had taken no more than ninety seconds.

"I'm in," he announced, his voice sounding like a shout in the dark interior of the flat. He resisted the urge to activate his electric torch and instead took a moment to let his eyes adjust. Except perhaps for the subterranean depths, true Stygian darkness was a rare thing; there was always light somewhere, and never more so than in a residence with glowing clocks and LED indicators, to say nothing of the light from the street that filtered in through the windows.

Gradually, the gloom receded, revealing the interior to him. He noted the sparse furnishings and the overall simplicity of the decor. It was clear that Burke lived a spartan existence. The lack of clutter gave it an almost sterile feel. The flat looked like it might have been a guest house. Nevertheless, there were a few personal touches.

A gas fireplace dominated one wall of the living room, and on its mantel, a few personal items were displayed. Among them, a framed photo caught his attention. He picked it up and held it so that the subjects were illuminated in the ambient glow from the streetlights. It showed Burke—Nigel had found a picture of him on the internet—standing next to an older man that Brad recognized from news broadcasts on BBC One as US Secretary of State Connor Williams. Brad thought they almost looked like father and son.

"You have some bloody interesting friends, Burke," he murmured.

"What's that?" asked Nigel.

"Nothing." Brad shook his head and returned the photo to its place on the mantel. He affixed one of the tiny surveillance video cameras underneath the mantel, positioning it so that it would cover most of the room. "Camera one is in place."

"Good signal," replied Nigel.

Brad displayed a thumbs-up for the camera and then continued his sweep.

There were two large bedrooms in the flat, but a quick inspection of the closets suggested that only one of them saw regular use. Brad expertly searched the closet of the main bedroom, then riffled through the drawers of the nightstand and dresser. He wasn't looking for anything in particular, just trying to get a better sense of who Chase Burke was. Finding nothing of interest, he installed another camera under the wall-mounted high-def TV opposite the bed. "Camera two, placed."

"Good signal."

He next came to what looked like a library-cum-office. One entire wall was a built-in bookshelf stuffed with hardbound volumes, the titles of which he could not discern in the low-light conditions. Opposite the bookshelf and positioned with an oblique view of an exterior window was a simple desk with a leather office chair. A large-screen black iMac Pro computer dominated one corner of the desktop.

"That's more like it," he murmured. Without knowing more about Burke or his habits, it was impossible to know where the surveillance cameras would be most effective, but common sense dictated that a home office was likely the place where Burke would do and say things of interest to the client.

He positioned camera three on the bookshelf, then moved to the desk, methodically searching the drawers. He found nothing unexpected—sundry office supplies and hanging file folders. On an impulse, he moved the hanging folders out of the way and reached into the back of the big drawer, half expecting to find Burke's stash of booze . . . or maybe even something more illicit, but the drawer held only paper. Nevertheless, the low cut of the drawer box's back wall prompted him to reach up and swipe the underside of the drawer cavity. He wasn't surprised when his searching hand encountered something affixed there. He could tell by the shape that it was a handgun in a molded Kydex holster.

Surmising that it was held in place with a swatch of Velcro, he tugged it loose and brought it out into the low light for inspection. He couldn't make out any manufacturer's marks but recognized it as a 1911. He slid the pistol out of the holster, worked the mag release, and caught the double-stack magazine as it dropped from the pistol grip.

Nine millimeter, he noted absently. *Fifteen rounds and one more in the chamber if he's smart.*

He reseated the magazine, hefted the weapon, then snapped it up as if aiming at an imaginary intruder in the doorway, thumb swiping down the safety, finger caressing the trigger.

Hot damn, he thought to himself, looking down the gun's sights.

Chase Burke had suddenly become a lot more interesting.

From the warm and dry refuge of the surveillance van, Nigel Gray watched his brother's antics with a mixture of amusement and frustration. The camera Brad had placed received infrared light as well as the visible spectrum, so despite the absence of artificial light in the interior of the flat, Brad was fully revealed in the display. Nigel guessed that under the balaclava, Brad was grinning like a rowdy schoolboy.

He thought about chastising his brother, reminding him that this wasn't a game, but decided against it. This was just Brad's way of dealing with the stress of the job.

Besides, he thought, *it wouldn't do any good.*

Nigel glanced at the feed from the drone, which, despite the large, distorted blob in the middle, showed a quiet, nearly empty street. Every few minutes, a car would roll through the neighborhood on its way to somewhere else, but aside from that, there was a decided lack of activity.

On the feed from camera three, he saw Brad holster the pistol and return it to its hiding place in the drawer, after which he delved into his gear satchel and took out one of Nigel's signal-sniffers, just like the one Damien had planted in the ICU to keep tabs on Congresswoman Hemsworth.

"I'm putting a sniffer at his computer desk," said Brad, as if Nigel couldn't already figure that out.

"Copy that," replied Nigel. He clicked on the computer application to sync the sniffer and waited for it to connect. The device wouldn't be able to pull any information from the iMac until Burke logged in, but it would start picking up audio right away.

"Sniffer in place," announced Brad.

On Nigel's screen, the word *connecting* . . . continued to flash.

"Nigel, are you receiving?"

"Bloody hell," Nigel muttered. "The sniffer isn't syncing."

He gritted his teeth and tried closing and restarting the app but to no better effect. "Brad, I need you to reboot the sniffer."

Brad's voice crackled impatiently from the speaker. "Just tell me what to do."

Nigel took a deep breath and began to walk Brad through the process. "There's a reset button on the side of the sniffer. You'll need to use a paper clip or something similar to press it."

"A paper clip?" grumbled Brad. "Hang on. I saw a box of them. Bollocks. I need some light. I can't see shite in this bloody office."

Nigel glanced over at the drone feed. "You're clear for the moment. Do what you need to do."

Burke's library suddenly came alive as Brad activated his handheld torch. The light would be visible to anyone who happened to be looking up at the window, but because the library looked out onto a courtyard behind the building, it was unlikely that anyone would take note.

Several seconds passed, and then Brad spoke again. "Okay, I jammed the wire in the little hole. Now what?"

"You need to press and hold the button for ten seconds."

"Ten seconds? Couldn't you just put in an on-off switch?"

"Short answer? No. Now, just do it."

Brad, nakedly sarcastic, began counting like a small child learning his numbers. When he got to ten, he said, "Can I take the bloody paper clip out of the hole now?"

"Yes. Release the button. It should restart in ten to thirty seconds."

"How will I know if it's working?"

"I'll know," said Nigel. He silently counted to ten, then relaunched the app. The dreaded *connecting* . . . message appeared, but then, after several more tense seconds, a new indicator appeared.

Connected.

"Got it!" Nigel exclaimed. "It's synced."

"About fucking time," Brad muttered. "Anything else?"

"No, that should do it. Get clear." He glanced over at the feed from the drone, and his heart nearly stopped. Instead of the quiet, empty street that he had been watching for the better part of twenty minutes, he now saw a Yellow Cab idling directly in front of the entrance to Burke's building.

"No," he murmured, adjusting the drone's position, trying to find a spot where he could see the taxi more clearly. "No, no, no . . ."

"Nigel, what the hell's happening?" Brad's voice issued from the speakers, urgent and demanding. "Talk to me!"

Nigel squinted, watching as the taxi's rear door opened and someone got out, his face hidden by the smear of water on the camera lens. "No," he whispered.

He tilted the drone to get a better angle on the passenger's face and recognized him right away.

"Brad, get out. *Now!* Burke's home! Get out of there!"

CHAPTER EIGHTEEN

Chase handed the cabbie two twenties and stepped out into the drizzly night. His body ached with fatigue, but his mind, on autopilot, wouldn't slow down, replaying on a loop the evening's events—Chef David's call, the attack at Chrysalis, Tanya's cry as she fell, and the relentless interrogation by the NYPD detectives. And then there were the unresolved questions that kept intruding into his consciousness.

Why did the sniper kill one of his own?
Are the police going to keep coming after me?
Why aren't they looking for the men behind the attack?
Is Tanya going to die?

Finding the answer to those questions was largely out of his hands. He knew he should probably contact a lawyer but was drawing a blank on the name of the firm that his father retained for dealing with family business. His first reflexive thought—*I'll call Michael; he'll know*—brought back the reality of his brother's death like a slap in the face.

Detective Campbell's mocking accusations echoed in his head.
Your brother leaked the intel . . .
Got good men killed . . .
He's a traitor. And so are you.

None of it was true, of course, but did that even matter? The detectives had already made up their minds about him, and now they would spare no effort to find or fabricate the evidence to back up their theory.

So, find the evidence to prove them wrong, he told himself. *Find the real killers.*

A face appeared in his mind's eye, the face of the man who had tried to stab him outside Chrysalis. Every detail was etched into Chase's memory—the dark curly hair, eyes so dark they were almost black, a slightly crooked nose, the almost doughy features of someone who might once have been in fighting shape but was going soft.

Okay, he thought as he slipped his building key into the front-entry lock and pulled open the door. *I've got a face. Now, how do I put a name to it?*

It occurred to him that he might have more than just the man's face to work with. There were also his four dead associates, whom the police would almost certainly soon identify if they had not already. It stood to reason that the man Chase had seen was likely a known associate of at least one of those men, or at the very least, someone who swam in the same murky talent pool from which criminal elements recruited killers. Of course, the detectives weren't likely to share that information with their prime suspect. Chase would need someone with the right connections, someone who could get him the inside information he needed, and he had an idea who might be able to make that happen.

He moved through the entrance foyer, bypassed the elevator as was his habit, then trudged up the stairs, his mind fixed on his next course of action.

Too late to call tonight, he decided. *First thing in the morning.*

He approached the door to his apartment, key in hand, slotted it into the deadbolt, and gave it a twist . . .

A chill went down his spine.

The key had turned, but there had been no resistance, no telltale rasp of the bolt sliding back.

The deadbolt was already unlocked.

Chase stared at the door, his heart beating faster with a fresh jolt of adrenaline. He was certain that he had locked the door before leaving. He *always* locked the door, a habit so ingrained that it might as well have been written into his DNA.

Except . . .

Wasn't it possible that maybe, just maybe, this one time, with so much else on his mind—Michael's death, a chance to connect with Tanya, the call from Curtis McGraw regarding the change in his mother's condition—he might have forgotten to lock up?

No. I didn't forget, he told himself. *I never forget.*

That was the thing about habitual behavior. It was something done automatically, without conscious thought. If anything, deviating from the habit would have registered in his mind and nagged at him throughout the evening.

So why was the door unlocked now?

His pulse still pounding, Chase put his hand on the door lever, working it slowly, quietly, and then pushed against the door.

Also unlocked.

He stood in the open doorway, senses on high alert, studying the situation like a poker player checking his cards. Someone had broken into his apartment, he was certain of that. The police? That was a distinct possibility. He could easily imagine Doyle and Campbell tossing the place, looking for a figurative smoking gun.

There were actually two guns in the apartment—a Wilson Combat EDC X9 and a suppressed SIG Sauer P365 Nitron Micro-Compact—both kept secreted in strategic locations inside the apartment. Because he did not have a permit for them—his military conviction and bad conduct discharge made it all but impossible to clear the permitting process in New York State—the simple fact of his possession of firearms, even for home defense, was a crime, possibly even a felony. While that was immaterial to the case the detectives were trying to make against him, it might give them leverage. But then again, if they had conducted a warrantless search, even a junior public defender could get those charges tossed out.

But what if it wasn't the detectives?

That brought him up short.

Who else would have reason to break into his place?

What if they're still in here?

He now thought about the handguns in a completely different context. The X9 was in a desk drawer in his office, and the SIG was in a disguised lockbox in the bedroom closet—both potentially out of reach, depending on where the intruder was.

Unless the intruder had already found them.

He caught himself, recognizing that he was getting tangled up in hypotheticals. He weighed his options a moment longer, then cautiously moved inside, pulling the door shut behind him. He stopped there, within arm's reach of the door, breath held, looking, listening, *smelling* the air for any sign that he was not alone. Suddenly, his senses were overwhelmed with stimuli—all the little noises and odors that were usually relegated to the background now demanded his attention. Minute details about the way he'd left his living space now seemed in doubt. He could just see the top of a wineglass in the kitchen sink . . .

Didn't I leave that on the counter?

The framed picture on the mantel, the photo of himself with Secretary of State Williams, was reflecting the glow of the streetlights from the big living room window . . .

Has it always done that?

He started to reach for the light switch, but then thought better of it, and instead let out the breath and took a step forward into the apartment. Just then he heard something—a noise as soft as a whisper coming from the hallway—and froze. There wasn't a doubt in his mind that the sound was real, not the product of his runaway imagination.

The intruder was still in his apartment.

Worse, both pistols were out of reach. Unarmed and uncertain who might be inside his home, Chase knew what he had to do. Taking a cautious backward step, he returned to the entrance, eased the door open, and slipped outside. He took out his phone along with Doyle's card and punched in her number.

She picked up on the second ring. "This is Detective Doyle," she said, her tone crisp and professional.

Chase kept his voice to a low whisper. "Detective. It's Chase Burke."

"Burke?" Doyle sounded mildly surprised. "I didn't expect to hear from you again. Certainly not so soon."

"Someone's inside my apartment."

"Is that a problem?" said Doyle wryly.

"Yeah, it's a fucking problem," Chase shot back, as he moved onto the landing and started descending the stairs. "I just got home, and the door was unlocked. Someone is inside right now."

"Are you certain?" asked Doyle, her tone now serious and professional again.

"Yes," Chase gritted. "Now, are you going to send . . ." He trailed off as he glimpsed movement one flight of stairs down—a man wearing a black tracksuit rushing up the stairs.

Chase's first thought was that it might be the man from outside Chrysalis. It wasn't. It was clear that, aside from his dark hair, there wasn't even a slight resemblance. The man was young and lean and . . .

From one flight down, their eyes met, and Chase saw a look of recognition come over the man's face. Then, he saw the pistol in the man's hand.

"Shit," growled Chase.

Fueled by the adrenaline pumping through his veins, he retreated up the stairs, taking them four at a time.

"Burke?" Doyle's voice startled him. He'd forgotten he was still on the line with her.

"Get someone over here. *Fast!*"

Even as he said it, he knew that any help Doyle might send would arrive too late. The man racing up the stairs had to be the intruder's backup, which meant he was now caught between them. He couldn't wait for the cavalry—he needed to act now.

He needed to go on the offensive.

Over the rush of blood roaring in his ears, he could hear Doyle's voice, sounding tinny as it issued from the speaker of his phone, which he still gripped in his left hand. When he reached his floor, he didn't slow but hit his still unlocked front door at a full sprint, bursting into his apartment. If he could somehow sweep past the intruder, reach the bedroom and the SIG, he might just have a chance.

But the doorway was as far as he got.

Standing outside his office door, illuminated by the hallway light, was another man, also clad in a black tracksuit, face covered by a balaclava, aiming Chase's own X9 at his face.

CHAPTER NINETEEN

"Burke!" Doyle shouted into her phone, springing to her feet as if ready for action. "What the hell is going on?"

There was no answer.

Campbell, still seated at his own desk, regarded her from under a raised eyebrow.

After cutting Burke loose, the two of them had returned to their desks in the JTTF common area to write up their reports. Doyle hadn't been exaggerating when she'd told Burke that his call was unexpected. Campbell, fixated on proving that Burke was complicit in the attack on Congresswoman Hemsworth, had played the role of "bad cop" with a little too much enthusiasm.

Meeting his gaze, Doyle switched to speaker mode and set the phone on the desk, but the only sound to issue from the speaker was a rhythmic thump—someone running, perhaps—interspersed with an occasional rasp of someone breathing heavily.

"It's Burke," she said. "Someone broke into his apartment. Call the 19th. Have them send a sector car over there."

Campbell continued to regard her skeptically. "He's fucking with you, Alice."

Doyle blinked, taken aback by her partner's unexpected resistance. "Excuse me?"

"He's just pulling this stunt to cover his ass. Trying to make it look like he's the victim."

Doyle gaped at him, almost too stunned for words, and for a long moment, the only sound to be heard was the thump of Burke's footsteps. Then she snapped.

"What the hell is wrong with you?" she shouted. "A citizen just called in a report of a crime in progress, for God's sake. Call the 19th and have them send a car. Now!"

Campbell brushed her request aside. "He's playing you."

"Son of a bitch," snarled Doyle and picked up her desk phone. Instead of dialing the 19th Precinct, however, she simply hit three numbers.

The call connected almost immediately, and she heard a woman's voice. "911, what's your emergency?"

"This is Detective Alice Doyle with the NYPD, presently assigned to the Joint Terrorism Task Force. This *is* an emergency. I need immediate response to the following location." She supplied Burke's address and then added her badge number so that there would be no question of her bona fides.

The operator did not question her but responded promptly with "Uniforms are on their way."

"Thank you," said Doyle, shooting a death stare at Campbell. "Advise them that I am on my way to the location and will meet them there." She gave the dispatcher her cell phone number, then hung up and grabbed her coat.

"Where the hell are you going?" asked Campbell.

"Where do you think?" Doyle grabbed her cell phone, noting that Burke was still on the line. "Chase, if you can hear me, help is on the way."

"He's messing with you," Campbell reasserted. "You'll see."

Doyle rounded on him. "Maybe he is, but I'm not going to take that chance. Now, are you going to just sit on your ass or come with me and do your fucking job?"

Campbell's face reddened under the verbal assault, but Doyle was already turning away, heading for the door. Then she heard him call out. "Hang on, damn it. I'm coming."

She pulled up short, waiting for Campbell to catch up. "I want to be there to see the look on your face when you realize I'm right," he added when he came abreast of her.

She hesitated, torn between snapping back a reply or jabbing him on the nose, but before she could make up her mind, a voice crackled through the phone's speaker—a voice that didn't belong to Chase Burke.

CHAPTER TWENTY

When Chase saw the masked man and realized that the business end of the matte-black X9 was aimed right at his forehead, his soldier's instincts kicked in.

Instead of freezing in place, he *moved*.

Faster than the intruder could pull the trigger—or at least he hoped so—Chase lunged toward the kitchen and vaulted over the island, dropping down on the opposite side, out of the other man's line of sight. He expected to hear multiple reports, and part of him half expected to feel the punch of a nine-mil, but aside from the commotion of his desperate leap and tumble, all remained quiet in the apartment. Taking a chance, he reached up and grabbed the Shun Classic chef's knife from the counter, then ducked down again, crouching with the eight-inch blade held in a forward grip, ready to strike at the first opportunity.

He was acutely aware of the fact that he was bringing a knife to a gunfight, but as he'd proved once already this night, a knife was better than nothing.

Here we go.

He strained to catch the sound of any movement from the intruder, trying to anticipate from which direction the attack might come, but for several seconds, all was quiet.

Then the other man spoke. "Burke? Chase Burke, is it?"

Chase caught just a hint of an accent. British, maybe?

What the hell? he thought but didn't answer.

"Listen, mate," the gunman went on. "I know you probably aren't going to believe this, but I'm not here to hurt you."

Definitely a Brit.

Still, Chase held his tongue. If he answered, the man would be able to pinpoint his exact location.

Then he heard footsteps at the entrance. He peeked around the corner just as the gunman he'd seen out on the street stepped inside the apartment.

"He's in the kitchen," warned the first gunman. "Careful. He might be armed."

Chase figured there was nothing to gain with continued silence, so he called out, "I am armed. Come any closer, and I'll drop you like I did your buddies in the restaurant."

"Chase," replied the first intruder. "Mate. Those lads at the restaurant . . . they weren't with us."

"Bullshit!"

"It's true, Chase. Listen, let's just talk this out, all right? Nobody needs to get hurt. We aren't the bloody bad guys."

Chase strained to detect any change in the man's pitch or volume, anything that might indicate that he was moving as he spoke. He sensed that the gunman was trying to lull him into complacency, perhaps to give his buddy cover to make a move.

"Good guys usually don't break into someone's home carrying guns," Chase retorted, his hand tightening on the pakkawood handle of the chef's knife, ready to react if and when the intruders made their move.

"Now that's a fair point. But after the stunt you pulled at the restaurant, can you blame us for being a little . . . proactive? We don't know whose side you're on."

The significance of the accusation surprised Chase.

Who are these fucking guys? What do they want from me?

"So, you were there?"

"Look," said the man irritably. "This is getting tired. We've got the advantage here, so why don't you put down your weapon and slowly come out from behind there? Then, maybe we'll talk it—"

"That's not going to happen," interrupted Chase. "I called the police. They'll be here any minute. If I were you, I'd get out now while you still can."

"You don't strike me as the type of man who calls the cops."

"He might be telling the truth," the second man interjected, breaking his silence. "He was on his mobile when I came up. Maybe we should—"

Suddenly, another voice rang out from near the entrance, "Police! Drop the gun!"

A second later, all hell broke loose.

CHAPTER TWENTY-ONE

The unmasked gunman spun around, raising his pistol, only to stagger back, simultaneous with the sound of multiple reports. Blood erupted from his torso as rounds tore through his body. Somehow, the wounded man stayed on his feet a few seconds longer, sidestepping toward the kitchen in a belated attempt to remove himself from the line of fire, only to collapse near Chase's feet.

Two uniformed police officers swept into the apartment, guns drawn, ready to reengage with the wounded suspect, unaware that there was a second intruder.

"Get down!" Chase shouted, but his warning came too late.

The apartment was suddenly filled with the thunder of gunfire as the masked intruder opened up with the X9.

Both officers went down.

Through the ringing in his ears, Chase heard the masked intruder yell, "Nigel! Hang on, brother. I'm coming."

Almost too late, Chase grasped the man's intent. He spun around just as the masked gunman stepped into the kitchen from the opposite side. Their eyes met, and then the smoking barrel of the X9 swung in Chase's direction.

Chase had nowhere to go, and no time to get there, so he did the only thing he could. He flung the Shun Classic at the intruder's masked face.

In an action movie, the blade would have stuck right between the man's eyes, buried to the hilt in his skull, but Chase knew better than to expect that outcome. Even in the hands of a skilled knife thrower, scoring a deadly strike with the kitchen blade would have required a monumental stroke of luck. The Shun wasn't designed as a throwing weapon, wasn't balanced to fly true, and wasn't heavy enough to penetrate even in the unlikely event that it struck point-first.

Never mind that Chase was hardly a skilled knife thrower. He was merely hoping to spoil the gunman's aim and maybe buy himself a split second to make his escape.

As it turned out, however, for the first time that night, luck was on Chase's side.

His throw was off target, the blade veering left and dropping just before impact, but amazingly, it struck point-first, slicing into the fleshy part of the gunman's upper right arm before ricocheting away to clatter on the floor. The masked man let out a cry, probably more of dismay than pain, and shrank back, leaving a trail of quarter-sized blood drops on the floor.

At almost the same instant, another uniformed officer swept into the apartment, firing his pistol at the masked man. The interior of the dwelling filled with smoke and dust as rounds punched into walls and cabinets, chasing the intruder as he fled down the hall.

Chase threw himself flat on the kitchen floor, and though he didn't see the mortally wounded unmasked intruder raise his pistol and fire at the unsuspecting officer, he heard things play out in a matter of seconds.

He jumped at the sound of the close report and looked up just as the uniformed policeman went down. Without thinking, Chase threw himself onto the bloodied gunman and seized his wrist, slamming the hand that held the pistol against the floor until the weapon fell from nerveless fingers. Only then did Chase realize the gunman had slipped into unconsciousness.

All too aware of the fact that there was still one more armed intruder to deal with, Chase picked up the pistol, spun around, and, staying low, fast-crawled through the kitchen, following the blood trail like a stalking hound. As he rounded the end of the island, he saw the wounded masked gunman crouched at the near end of the hallway, clutching his right shoulder. Chase lined up the front sights of his pistol at the man's center mass. The man looked down, and Chase saw the X9, which had fallen from the intruder's grasp and now lay at his feet.

Their eyes locked, and Chase hesitated, unsure about what to do now that the intruder no longer held a gun. In that moment, the masked man exploded into motion, surging forward at astonishing speed and covering the short distance between them in a flash. The man, ducking low to avoid the pistol's aim, slammed his shoulder into Chase's midsection. The impact knocked the wind out of Chase and sent him stumbling backward against the wall.

Before Chase could recover, the intruder grabbed his gun hand with a crushing grip and brutally wrenched his wrist. Pain flared in Chase's forearm, and the pistol slipped from his fingers, clattering to the floor and spinning out of reach as the gunman kicked it away.

Okay, this guy knows what he's doing.

But so did Chase.

Chase twisted his body to the left and drove his elbow into the man's face with all the force he could muster. The elbow connected with a satisfying crunch, but Chase wasn't done. Exploiting the opening, he delivered a powerful punch into the gunman's left kidney with the full weight of his body behind it. The intruder let out a sharp, involuntary grunt as the punch landed, and a flicker of shock crossed his eyes. He staggered but remained upright, as if his muscles had seized.

Chase saw the pistol lying a few feet away and dove for it. Getting both hands on the weapon, he rolled over and aimed at the intruder, using the front sight post of the pistol. Realizing that all was lost, the masked man pivoted away, rushed out of the hallway, and hurled himself at the big living room window, smashing through the blinds and the windowpane.

What the hell?

Chase scrambled to his feet and hurried to the window, arriving just in time to see the man execute a textbook parachute landing fall—rolling to the side as soon as his feet made contact to distribute the energy of the impact and reduce the likelihood of injury—on the sidewalk one story below. A moment later, the man was up and running, though clearly with some difficulty, down the street. His escape route took him past a pair of NYPD patrol vehicles parked outside the entrance, their flashers casting red and blue light up and down the street.

Chase put his sights on the retreating man's back and his finger on the trigger, but he didn't fire.

It was the police cars that stopped him.

Self-defense was one thing, but shooting a man in the back—even someone who had invaded his home—wasn't so easy to defend.

"Dammit!" he snarled, watching the figure disappear into the night.

He turned back to the scene of chaos inside his apartment, everything shot to hell, three police officers down—two of them shot with *his* unlicensed pistol—along with one intruder, and he had no idea why any of it was happening.

Focus, Chase, he told himself.

He hurried over to the nearest policeman, ready to offer whatever aid he could, but immediately saw that the officer was beyond help. A hollow-point 9mm round from the X9 had caught him in the forehead, killing him instantly. The other two uniforms had caught headshots as well—their NYPD-issue ballistic body armor hadn't done them a bit of good against a pair of trained killers.

Then Chase heard a groan from the kitchen. A word weakly uttered.

It was a name.

"Brad . . ."

Chase approached cautiously, leading with his pistol, until he saw that the unmasked gunman, who now lay in a spreading pool of his own blood, posed no threat. It was a wonder that he was still clinging to life.

Chase knelt beside him. "Who are you?"

The man's glassy eyes seemed to look right past him. "Brad?"

"Brad's gone." Chase searched his memory, recalling what the masked man had said after the shooting had started. "Nigel? Are you Nigel? Brad's your brother?"

The man's lips moved, but no sound came out.

"Why did you come here?" pressed Chase. "What do you want from me?"

"Hems . . . Hemsworth—"

"You're part of the crew who tried to kill her, aren't you, asshole? Aren't you? Why? Why do you want her dead?"

"It . . . wasn't . . ." He trailed off, a final breath slipping past his bloodstained lips as he passed into oblivion.

In the silence that followed, Chase could hear the sound of distant sirens growing louder.

"Shit!" he shouted.

He knew how this would look. Detective Campbell already believed that he was complicit in the attack on Tanya Hemsworth and wouldn't hesitate to implicate Chase in the deaths of the three policemen. And even if Chase somehow managed to escape prosecution, he wouldn't be able to run down the only lead he had—and find whoever was really responsible for all the killings—if he was in custody.

There was only one choice left to him.

I can't stay here.

But what did he know about being a fugitive?

His mind was already racing to cover all his bases. The police would undoubtedly flag his phone and credit cards. His likeness would be circulated to law enforcement agencies throughout the city. Surveillance cameras would be checked against facial recognition software. There were ways to get around all of that. Criminals and secret agents did it all the time, but he was neither. He didn't have any established aliases. No stash of fake passports and credit cards. No *Mission: Impossible*–style makeup kit to change his facial features.

Yet, he wasn't completely without resources. His PSYOPS training had taught him the essentials of social engineering, as well as the ability to improvise.

Think, Chase.

First step . . . always have a plan.

An old Yogi Berra quote popped into his head. *If you don't know where you are going, you might wind up someplace else.*

He couldn't afford to simply run blindly into the night. He needed a destination, a place not merely to seek refuge but to begin his own investigation into the assassination attempt on Tanya. Somewhere the cops might not think to look.

His gaze fell on the mantel and the picture of him standing alongside Connor Williams.

Of course.

He had been planning to reach out to Williams anyway, for help in identifying the man he'd fought outside the restaurant.

A deep background check might uncover his relationship with the Secretary of State, but Connor's name wouldn't be high on the list of known associates.

He grabbed the photo off the mantel.

No sense leaving them a hint.

A quick frisk of the dead intruder turned up a key fob emblazoned with the Ford logo and a cell phone—a Samsung Galaxy A14. Overcome with curiosity, he positioned it in front of the dead man's face. He waited, but the phone didn't unlock. For a moment, he debated giving up, but then his gaze fell on the power button, which he knew also functioned as a fingerprint scanner on some phones. Almost as an afterthought, he pressed the man's thumb to it. The screen lit up, granting Chase access. A quick check of the phone's contents turned up only a call history going back less than twenty-four hours. He doubted the information would lead anywhere but took a screenshot of the call history and then texted it to his own number. Pocketing both the phone and the key fob, he moved into his bedroom and opened his lock box.

The little fireproof safe was where he kept important documents: his passport and social security card; a copy of his birth certificate; his college transcripts and sommelier certification; and, for better or worse, his DD214 and copies of all his military records.

It was also where he kept the SIG, two boxes of Federal HST nine-mil Luger hollow points, and $5,000 in cash, just in case.

He shoved all of it into a black gym bag, along with the X9 and the photo with Connor Williams, then grabbed a clean shirt and a fresh pair of jeans and stuffed those in as well.

As he was about to leave, an idea struck him. He dug out his phone, realizing only then that he still had Doyle on the line.

Had she heard everything?

Detective Campbell might have already made up his mind, but his partner, Doyle, seemed at least willing to hear reason.

He almost asked if she was still there but then decided that could wait and instead ended the call. There was a better way to make contact with the detective.

He took out Doyle's card, scribbled a series of digits on it, and then placed it face up on the kitchen counter. Then, he stuffed the cell phone and the Ford key fob he'd taken off Nigel in between the cushions of his couch and, with that final task complete, stepped over the bodies in the doorway and, after one last look at his apartment, headed out.

CHAPTER TWENTY-TWO

Brad Gray huddled in the shadows, clutching the gash in his shoulder caused by the knife Chase Burke had thrown at him. Despite applying constant pressure to the wound, blood continued to seep through his fingers, soaking the sleeve of his track jacket, which was already saturated from the constant drizzle. Thankfully, the black fabric concealed the bloodstain, and the fat drops of diluted blood that dripped onto the rain-slick sidewalk were quickly washed away.

But as painful as the knife wound was, it had been Chase's punch to his kidney that had ended the fight. The impact had sent a stabbing shock deep into his core. Even now, it felt as though his insides had been crushed. With every breath he took, the agony in his side intensified. It was taking all his willpower to remain standing.

After a quick stop at the van to acquire a few pieces of essential gear, he'd run . . . hobbled, really . . . in the opposite direction from the approaching sirens. Nigel had left the van locked, so Brad had been forced to smash his way in—another delay, but a necessary one. He'd grabbed Nigel's laptop and the go-bag that held everything he would need to survive a couple of days on his own and then tossed an incendiary grenade into the vehicle to destroy everything that remained.

Several blocks over, he'd found a city park—completely deserted, thanks to the rain—and hunkered down to assess his situation. Things at Burke's apartment had spiraled out of control so quickly he could hardly believe it. He'd been mere moments from making his exit when Nigel had called to warn him of Burke's arrival. Another sixty seconds and he would have gotten away clean.

Now, everything was falling apart.

He sat on the path with his back pressed against a low concrete wall and fought the urge to vomit.

Even though he was starting to shiver, he pulled off the soaked jacket to expose the wound. In the gloom where he hid, the cut was just a dark line, maybe two inches long, drawn across his pale flesh. Watching the blood dribble from the gash, he couldn't help but think about Nigel and the fact that he'd abandoned his brother.

But what else could I have done?

Nigel had gone down hard, taking several rounds to the gut. Brad knew that if Nigel was to have any hope of surviving, he would need immediate medical care, and that wasn't something Brad could give him, not while running for their lives. When the police arrived on the scene, they would see to it that Nigel was taken to a hospital.

It was a sound rationale, but it did little to assuage his guilt.

He fished out an Israeli dressing from his go-bag and slapped it over the wound. The cloth pad was impregnated with a hemostatic gel to stop the bleeding and, unlike earlier versions of the compound, produced only a mild sting as it came in contact with the wound. He pressed it down and then wrapped the fabric tails around his upper arm to both hold the pad in place and put direct pressure on the wound. That would do for a while, but he would need to find somewhere warm and dry to stitch it up.

Going back to the hotel was a definite nonstarter. While it would take a while for the police to determine Nigel's identity—or rather, the cover identity under which he was traveling—they would eventually get it, and from there, it would be an easy thing to connect the dots to both Brad and Damien.

I have to tell Damien, he thought with a groan.

It was critical that Damien be advised that his cover was compromised. He would have to quickly initiate damage control measures to create a false trail that wouldn't lead the authorities back to anyone with the last name Gray.

So much for spending the day with Allie.

The worst of it, though, would be telling him about Nigel.

"Nothing for it," he muttered, taking a burner phone from his go-bag. He powered it up and punched in the number of the phone Damien was presently using. The call went immediately to voicemail.

"Fuck!"

Damien was probably already in the air on his way to London.

I am so fucked.

Panic set in, generating a swirl of dire possibilities. His heart began to race, and his shoulder throbbed in time with his pulse.

Pull it together, Gray. Do something. Even if it's the wrong thing, do something.

He shook off the panic and brought his focus into the moment. Inertia was the enemy now. He needed to find somewhere safe, somewhere warm and dry.

He needed help.

But who could he turn to?

He could only think of one person.

After doing his best to wring some of the moisture out of the jacket, he pulled it on over the bandaged wound and then got to his feet and started moving again.

A couple blocks over, he came to a multi-story car park. The entrance was monitored by CCTV cameras, so he did his best to keep his head down as he made his way inside, ascending the stairs to the first floor where he began walking down the row of parked cars, looking for a quiet corner where he could set up Nigel's laptop.

Although he was—*had been*—the family's computer expert, Nigel had taught his brothers the basics of using his anonymized global communications system, and so it took all of a minute for Brad to place the call. The line trilled with the outgoing send, and then the electronically distorted voice came over the line.

"Is it done?"

Brad had to fight the urge to cackle like a maniac. "No, it's not fucking done. Burke came home early, and now everything's gone to shite."

The client took a moment to process this. "Then what the hell are you calling me for?"

"Because I . . ." Brad faltered a moment, then uttered three impossible words. "I need help."

"Help? You must be joking."

"No, mate. I'm hurt. My bro . . ." He caught himself. "My teammate is injured, maybe dead. The coppers will be after us soon if they aren't already. We've got to do some damage control."

"Why on earth do you think I would help you with that?" The electronic masking couldn't hide a note of incredulity.

"Because if you don't, I'll have to turn myself in. No other choice. And you better believe, I'll sing."

There was a long pause. "You can't implicate me. You don't know who I am."

"Is that what you think, mate?" Brad let the implication hang in the air. It was a bluff, but the client didn't know that.

There was an odd sound on the line, an electronic sigh. "What about Burke?"

"What about him?"

"Did you kill him?"

"No," said Brad, and then, to cover his failure, added, "I figured if you'd wanted him dead, you wouldn't have paid me to put him under surveillance."

The client took a moment to consider this. "All right. I'm going to give you the address of a safe house. One of my representatives will meet you there for a debrief. I think it goes without saying that the present contract is forfeit, but there may be a chance for you to redeem yourself."

Brad had to fight the urge to tell the client to fuck off.

"Just give me the bloody address."

CHAPTER TWENTY-THREE

A couple blocks from Chase Burke's building, Doyle and Campbell passed a pair of fire engines with their flashers going and saw half a dozen firefighters in turnout gear, hosing down the still-smoking shell of what had once been a large utility van.

"Rough neighborhood," Campbell remarked dryly.

Doyle didn't respond, but her detective instincts told her the vehicle fire, so close to the battleground that was Burke's apartment, could not be a coincidence.

She was still processing everything they'd heard coming over the open line: Burke confronting the intruder; the man's insistence that he wasn't part of the Chrysalis shooting as well as his tacit admission to having been somehow present; the arrival of another intruder, warning that the police might be en route; and then . . . absolute mayhem.

Burke's line had exploded with the sound of gunfire, followed by a far more ominous silence. Someone had called out a 10-13 over the radio—the code for officers need assistance—and then the radio had gone ominously quiet. Burke's phone, however, had transmitted a second volley of gunfire. Then, in the stillness that followed, Burke's voice had been audible, questioning someone, almost certainly one of the intruders. Doyle had heard two names—Nigel and Brad—but the man's voice had trailed off, and not long thereafter, the call ended.

Minutes later, a small army of uniforms had arrived in response to the 10-13 and found three dead police officers and one dead suspect, but no Chase Burke.

Doyle couldn't help but feel a measure of responsibility for the death of the three officers. If she had taken Chase's call more seriously from the start and warned them about what they would be walking into, maybe things would have turned out differently. What troubled her most, however, was the question of Chase Burke's involvement.

"I told you Burke was bad news," said Campbell.

"You heard what happened," Doyle countered. "He was defending himself."

Campbell snorted. "Yeah, sure. Seems like that happens to him a lot."

Doyle was growing frustrated with her partner and his insistence on Burke having had a hand in whatever went down at the restaurant.

But was she being too hard on him?

Maybe.

Whereas Doyle had a thirst for chasing the truth no matter where it led or how much work was required, Campbell had always seemed to favor the path with the least amount of resistance.

Alice, when you'll have as many years on the job as I do, you'll understand that the simplest explanation is usually the most likely to be correct, her partner liked to say.

Despite her reservations, she had to admit that, more often than not, he was right on the money. She'd experienced it numerous times. Campbell—claiming his "experience told him plenty"—would form a theory early on into a new case, whereas she would let the evidence guide her, allowing the truth to shape her theory as they went. They had different approaches, and yet—though she wasn't exactly sure how it happened—Campbell's theory was usually correct. The evidence would later confirm what he seemed to know from the start.

What does he see that I don't? She wondered. *What am I missing?*

Doyle took a breath to settle herself, then said, "Okay, let's say you're right about Burke. How do you explain what we just heard?"

"Simple. Classic turf war. A falling out among rival criminal gangs. And now we've got three dead cops. We need to lock him up, Alice." Then Campbell added, "Or put him down."

Doyle just shook her head. She hoped it wouldn't come to that.

Burke's building was a buzzing hive of activity, with police cars and CSU vans crowding the street. They parked and made their way up the stairs to Burke's second-floor apartment, which was now cordoned off with yellow tape. Carefully stepping around the blood splatter at the entrance, Doyle and Campbell entered the apartment. Inside, CSU techs were busy marking evidence and taking photographs. Between the shooting at Chrysalis and this, it was proving to be a busy night for the Crime Scene Unit.

The bodies of the slain officers had already been removed. It was an unwritten rule in the NYPD that first responders weren't dead until a doctor at a hospital made that determination, not because no effort would be spared in attempting to resuscitate them—and miracles did sometimes happen—but rather to avoid leaving the bodies of the fallen at the scene for hours awaiting the arrival of the medical examiner.

The dead shooter, however, was a different story.

"That must be Nigel," Doyle remarked, looking down at the figure sprawled out in a pool of blood on the kitchen floor. The man looked to be in his mid-thirties, fit, clean-shaven, with close-cropped dark hair.

Campbell didn't answer but knelt beside the man, pulled on a nitrile glove, and did a quick search. "Nothing," he grunted.

"CSU probably beat you to it," said Doyle.

"Or Burke did. Covering his tracks."

Rather than continuing to argue with her partner, Doyle turned to the nearest technician and showed her credentials. "Detective Doyle with JTTF. Did you remove any personal effects from the body?"

The young woman shook her head but then cocked it to the side. "Did you say Doyle? Alice Doyle?"

"That's right."

The tech glanced around the room nervously and then came back to Doyle. "I didn't log it as evidence, but there's a card on the counter with your name on it."

"I gave it to the building's resident. We questioned him earlier in connection with another investigation. He called me just before all of this happened."

The woman nodded in understanding. "Do you want it entered into evidence?"

Doyle thought she understood what the tech was getting at. In the days to follow, when every aspect of this incident was put under the microscope, the mere fact that Doyle's card was found at the scene would likely come back to bite her on the ass, even though there was a perfectly straightforward explanation.

"Where is it?"

The tech pointed to the counter, which was littered with chunks of wall plaster and a fine layer of dust. The card, curiously, was clean, sitting atop the debris. Doyle picked it up and saw that her phone number had been crossed out with a pen. She turned it over and saw a different number, handwritten, along with a four-digit extension.

"Burke left you a love note?" asked Campbell.

"Sure," she replied dryly. "If your idea of romance involves crossed-out phone numbers and voicemail extensions."

Doyle took out her phone and called the number. She thought it would probably connect to an attorney's office, and so was mildly surprised when a recorded electronic voice instructed her to enter the PIN to access a voicemail box. She tapped in the four-digit number and heard Chase Burke's voice in her ear.

"Detective Doyle," he began, sounding a little breathless as if recording the message while on the move. "Sorry to run, but I think we both know that if I stuck around, your partner would haul my ass off to jail without giving me a chance to explain. Well, here's my explanation. I know this looks bad, but I swear, I had nothing to do with it. There were two guys . . . Brad and Nigel . . . I'm pretty sure they're British, and I think they're brothers. Brad was the one in my apartment. He was wearing a mask, so I didn't get a look at his face, but the other one, Nigel . . . he's the one that got shot by the first two cops that showed up."

Burke's message was rambling, as if he was trying to process what had happened, even as he verbally reviewed the events.

"Brad shot them," he went on. "I fought with him, but he jumped out the window and took off. He's hurt, though . . ."

He trailed off for a second as if collecting his thoughts. "I'm going to figure out what's really going on . . . who's really behind all this. I know your partner has already decided that I'm guilty, so you'll forgive me for not turning myself in. I hope I'm not wrong in thinking I can trust you.

"I took a phone and a car key from Nigel and stashed them under the couch cushion. There wasn't much on the phone, but you can use the key to track down their ride. Maybe there will be something in it that will help you figure out who these guys are.

"I'm going to be tossing this phone after I hang up, so you won't be able to call me . . . or track me . . . but if you want to get in contact, call my number and leave a message in this mailbox. If I come up with anything, I'll do the same."

There was a soft rush of air as if Burke had just blown out a breath. "Okay. That's it, I guess."

A double beep signaled the end of the message.

Doyle lowered her phone and realized that Campbell was staring at her.

"Well?"

She narrowed her eyes, considering whether to share with her partner what Burke had just revealed. Everything Burke had said in the call aligned with what they had overheard and seemed to exonerate him, but she doubted Campbell would see it that way.

She decided to split the difference. "Burke left me a voicemail message. He said that he stashed some stuff he took off one of the bodies."

"Why the hell did he do that? We would have found the stuff anyway."

"A good-faith gesture," she replied, evading the question. She turned toward the living room, spotting the couch, and moved toward it. "He said it's under the couch cushions."

She pulled on a pair of gloves and lifted one of the cushions. Doyle lifted another, revealing the items Burke had described.

"Hello," he said, scooping up the phone. He played with it for a moment, then raised his eyes to Doyle. "Locked. Maybe one of the FBI techs can crack it."

"It's evidence," countered Doyle. "We need to log it."

"We do that and we might never get access to it. Certainly not before Burke or somebody can get to it remotely and wipe the memory."

"Burke's the one who gave it to us."

Campbell shrugged. "Sure. He wants you to think he's cooperating." He gestured to the key. "What do you want to bet that belongs to that car-b-que we passed on our way here? Covering their tracks."

Campbell looked around the apartment as if seeing it for the first time, then returned his attention to Doyle. "I think we're done here. We need to get back downtown and get the ball rolling."

"I'm sorry, and what ball would that be?"

Campbell stared back at her as if the answer was obvious. "The search for Chase Burke."

CHAPTER TWENTY-FOUR

Falls Church, Virginia

Secretary of State Connor Williams was jolted awake by the insistent buzzing of one of the phones on the nightstand. He had two—one for official use and an unpublished private line reserved for family and close acquaintances. All calls to the official line were screened by a staffer at Foggy Bottom before being routed through and, unless the call concerned some major international incident, weren't typically put through after hours. Anyone with the number for the private line would know better than to reach out to him so late, so a call at this hour—*What time is it, anyway?*—to either line, could only mean bad news.

He stared at the ceiling for a brief moment, trying to bring himself to full awareness, then swung his legs off the bed and looked down at the nightstand.

The screen of his private phone was lit up, displaying *UNKNOWN CALLER*. Because his own number was unpublished, he rarely received spam calls, though it did happen on rare occasions. The likelier conclusion, however, stirred a sense of unease in his gut as he thumbed the screen to accept the call.

"Yes?" he said, eschewing his standard greeting and self-identification.

"Do you know who this is?"

Williams's blood ran cold. He recognized the voice instantly. "I do."

"I'm texting you a number. Call me back when you can." Then the call ended.

Williams sat still, staring at the phone that now displayed the message: "Call ended."

Damn it, he thought.

The cryptic statement needed no interpretation. While his personal phone was notionally private, provided he did not discuss official business, his status as a public servant meant that he could be required to hand over his call records for review. There were some calls for which, even with the expectation of privacy, there could be no record whatsoever. This was one of them.

Rising slowly from the bed, he pulled on a robe and then padded from the room, moving to his study and the wall safe concealed behind a reproduction of Vermeer's lost masterpiece *Woman Eating Oysters and Pouring Out Wine*. From the safe, he took out a prepaid cellular phone, one of a dozen he kept for just such a purpose, and then stepped over to the credenza and decanted three fingers of Laphroaig into a rocks glass. Phone in one hand and Scotch in the other, he stepped out onto the balcony, which commanded a spectacular view of the Washington, DC, skyline, and took a seat at the outdoor café table.

After fortifying himself with a sip of whisky, he activated the burner phone and then punched in the number he'd been given. The line didn't even ring twice.

"Thanks for calling me back."

"My God, Chase," Williams moaned. "You're all over the news. What the fuck have you gotten yourself mixed up in?"

Hours earlier, Williams had gone to bed with the news reports of the shooting in New York City and the FBI's announcement that Chase Burke, a person of interest in the case, had also been involved in a fatal shooting incident in which three NYPD officers had been killed. Williams did not believe for even a second that Chase was complicit in either incident, but nonetheless, he was a "person of interest"—one step removed from "suspect"—and that did not bode well. The fact that Chase was evidently refusing to surrender to the authorities only made matters worse.

And now he's calling me.

"I didn't do any of the shit they said I did, sir," said Chase. "I didn't kill those cops, and what happened at Chrysalis was self-defense."

"Then you've got no reason not to turn yourself in. Running just makes you look guilty. You're smart enough to know that. The optics are bad right now. And I don't even—"

"It's not that simple," interrupted Chase. "There's a lot more going on here than anyone realizes. I tried to explain that to the cops, but they blew me off."

Williams drained his Scotch and took a deep breath. "All right, let's hear it. What do you *think* is going on?"

There was a pause on the line. "It's not like you to be patronizing."

Williams felt his cheeks go hot with the rebuke. "You're right. I'm sorry." He took another deep breath. "Go on, I'm listening."

"The guys who hit Chrysalis were trying to abduct Congresswoman Hemsworth."

"That's what all the news reports are saying."

"Right. Well, whoever shot her wasn't working with the kidnappers. I don't think the cops realize that."

"Okay." Williams pondered this for a moment. "How do you explain that?"

"I can't—at least not *yet*—but when I got home tonight, there was a guy in my apartment waiting for me. He claimed he wasn't working with the kidnappers, but I'm pretty sure he was the sniper who actually shot her."

Chase's cadence had grown increasingly frantic with the need to unburden himself, so Williams let him talk.

"I *know* he's the one who killed two of those cops," Chase went on. "His brother killed the other one . . . their names are Brad and Nigel. They're British . . . at least, I think they are. They both had an accent . . . Nigel's dead, but Brad got away."

When Chase paused for a breath, Williams changed the subject. "Where are you now?" There was a suspiciously long pause, prompting Williams to add, "You can trust me, Chase. I'm just concerned about you."

"I'm on the train."

Williams frowned, not at the vagueness of the reply but rather because he knew exactly what train Chase was talking about and where he was going. "That's probably not the best place for you to be right now."

"I'm not going home if that's what you think. I'm sure that's the first place they'll look for me."

"Then I don't understand."

"It doesn't matter. I need your help, Connor."

William pursed his lips, not because Chase had used his first name—he'd known Chase and Michael since they were teenagers—but because getting involved in this mess was the last thing he needed right now.

"For God's sake, you know I can't get involved in this. Call Phil Sterling. Your father trusted him. He can walk you through—"

"I don't need a lawyer."

"I beg to differ."

"A lawyer will only be interested in proving my innocence. And the cops will only care about proving my guilt. I'm trying to find out what's really going on . . . who tried to kill Tanya. Look, those people are still out there, and if I don't stop them, they're going to finish the job."

Williams did not fail to notice Chase's use of the familiar when referring to the congresswoman. "You're not an investigator, Chase."

"There's no one else." Chase took an audible breath. "I need your help." He paused a beat, then added, "And you owe me one. For Jerry."

Williams bristled. "That's low."

"Yeah," agreed Chase, "but I have nowhere else to turn."

"Fine." Williams realized he had clenched his fists. With a conscious effort, he uncurled his fingers. "All right. What do you need?"

CHAPTER TWENTY-FIVE

New York City

Despite the agony coursing through his body, Brad Gray somehow remained upright, each step down to the underground platform feeling like a battle against gravity. The searing pain in his kidney had escalated and was now sending fierce, electric jolts through his spine and into his legs. At least his arm, which was caked with dried blood, was no longer bleeding, thanks to the hemostatic gel.

Pain was something he could deal with—it wasn't the first time he'd been wounded—but between the blood he'd lost, the hit to his kidney, and the fact that he was still losing body heat due to his wet clothes, "dealing with it" was taking a toll. He was exhausted, barely able to keep his eyes open.

I need rest.

But rest was a luxury that would have to wait. Now more than ever, he needed to keep his wits about him.

He leaned against a pillar, surreptitiously making a 360-degree check of his surroundings, wary of anyone who might be paying him a little too much attention. In his disheveled state, he expected a few second looks, but the handful of late-night commuters with whom he shared the platform seemed lost in their own worlds, their faces reflecting a blend of fatigue and indifference as they stared at the screens of their mobile phones.

His biggest concern was being noticed by the ever-watchful eyes of CCTV cameras. He knew he had passed several, and despite his best efforts to look away without being too obvious, it was almost a certainty that his likeness had been captured. Nevertheless, the underground—*the subway,* he corrected himself—remained the best way for him to get to the safe house without attracting too much attention.

A rush of warm air preceded the arrival of the subway train. The doors hissed open, and he staggered inside the nearly empty car, collapsing onto the molded plastic seat. A moment later, the train jolted forward, and his view of the brightly lit platform was replaced by the darkness of the tunnels.

As the train moved from station to station, each one looking more rundown than the last, Brad's thoughts kept returning to Nigel. He couldn't shake the image of his brother bleeding out on the floor of Burke's kitchen or the guilt he felt at having left Nigel behind. As necessary as his decision had been at the moment, no amount of rationalization would ever ease his conscience.

When the automated voice came over the loudspeaker, announcing "Next stop, 14th Street-Union Square," he struggled to his feet and shuffled closer to the door so that he could make it off the train during the too-brief stop.

In contrast to the other stations he'd seen, Union Square was a bustling hive of activity, with commuters hurriedly moving between lines and buskers and panhandlers looking for handouts. Brad clenched his jaw against the pain and exhaustion, then ventured out into the labyrinth. He'd plotted the route using the city's trip-planner app, but the simple instructions to "Transfer at 14th Street-Union Square to the L train" had not prepared him for how much walking he would have to do, how many stairs he would have to go up and down. When he finally descended the stairs to the platform for the L train, it took every ounce of will he possessed to simply stay on his feet long enough to board the train when it arrived five minutes later.

From his route, he knew that the L train would take him out of Manhattan, under the East River, to the borough of Brooklyn, where he would need to make another transfer to reach the general vicinity of the safe house. Worried that he might not be able to survive another long walk, he grabbed a bottle of water from his go-bag, along with some caffeine pills and a couple of packets of extra-strength aspirin. He'd been reluctant to take the pain meds for fear that their anticoagulant properties could cause his shoulder wound to start bleeding again, but he also knew that without them, his ability to move and—if necessary—react might be fatally compromised.

When the train finally emerged from the tunnel onto an elevated track and he saw the lights of Brooklyn passing by outside the window, Brad felt as if he'd been transported to a different world. Feeling somewhat revitalized, he made the next transfer at Broadway Station, descending once more below the surface to board the A train for the last leg of the journey.

Fifteen minutes later, he exited the Rockaway Avenue station, stepping out onto Fulton Street, and took a moment to orient himself. He'd studied a street map and memorized the route from the station to the safe house, but the problem with a map recce was that the map didn't reflect the territory. The rundown buildings and the graffiti that covered nearly every available surface were a stark contrast to the gentrified affluence of Manhattan's Upper East Side where Burke lived. This neighborhood had a palpable sense of neglect, and it made him uneasy. Most of the storefronts were closed, their shutters down and locked, the facades of the buildings crumbling and darkened by years of grime.

At least the rain had let up.

Keeping his head down, trying to appear inconspicuous while simultaneously staying alert, he made his way down Fulton Street. The distant sound of a siren added to his growing sense of paranoia. He cursed himself for having left all his weapons behind, letting them burn along with everything else in the van.

Following his mental route map, he took a right turn, moving away from Fulton and deeper into the grid of side streets lined with long blocks of row houses. Here, the streetlights were fewer, and the shadows seemed to grow darker and more menacing. His unease intensified. He couldn't shake the feeling that he was being watched. Followed. The safe house was only two blocks away, but his instincts screamed at him that something was wrong.

On an impulse he took a left at the next intersection, crossing the street and moving away from the safe house. With the change in direction, he saw someone in the periphery of his vision coming up the same sidewalk he had been walking on before making the turn. The person seemed to hesitate just a moment but then continued on as if pursuing some other destination.

Brad's heart rate spiked with a fresh adrenaline dump. He *was being* followed. But was this someone who knew who he was or merely a local predator who saw him as a target of opportunity? The latter seemed more likely in the rough neighborhood.

Brad continued along his new course, turning left at the end of the block, and risked another glance back. There was no sign of the trailing figure. Either his shadow had abandoned the pursuit after realizing that he'd been spotted, or he was racing ahead to circle the block and outflank him. Brad did an abrupt about-face and backtracked to his original course, moving as quickly as his aching body would permit. When he reached the street he'd originally been walking down, he saw only empty sidewalks in both directions.

The safe house location was in a row house, sharing a common wall with the houses to either side. The client had advised him to bypass the front entrance and continue down to the end of the row, where a narrow alley afforded access to the rear of the building. Still wary of being followed, Brad ducked into the alley, then immediately retreated into the shadows, pressing himself against the rough brick wall, watching and waiting, listening intently for any sound, any hint that his shadow was still out there.

He waited thirty seconds . . . a minute . . .

Nothing.

Breathing a sigh of relief, he pushed away from the wall and turned in to the alley—and then he was suddenly knocked back by two sharp blows to the chest.

He lay there on the wet pavement, stunned, the breath knocked out of him and his mind reeling with the knowledge of what had just happened.

I've been shot! Twice!

He'd heard the first report, the distinctive clap of a suppressed handgun, loud enough to get the attention of anyone nearby but just as easily dismissed because it didn't sound anything like a gunshot in a movie.

Some part of him knew that he had to get back on his feet, to either flee or fight, but his body refused to comply.

He detected movement, then saw a face hover into view above him. In the gloom, he couldn't make out much in the way of detail, but when she spoke, her voice confirmed his suspicion that his assailant was female. "You had one simple job, and you fucked it up."

Brad's mouth moved, trying to form words. "Who . . . who . . ."

She shook her head sadly. "I expected better, given your outrageous fee."

The face dipped out of view as the woman knelt beside him and began patting him down. He felt his mobile phone sliding from his pocket, felt the strap of the go-bag coming off his shoulder. Then the face reappeared.

"This probably doesn't need saying, but . . ." She shrugged. "You're fired."

Brad saw the dark outline of her suppressed weapon swing into view above him. There was a minuscule flash of light, and then his world went dark forever.

CHAPTER TWENTY-SIX

Detective Alice Doyle sat at her desk at JTTF headquarters, staring into Chase Burke's eyes—or, more accurately, the eyes in the photo of Burke presently displayed on her computer monitor—as if he might start talking to her.

In her present state, if he had, she wouldn't have thought it the least bit unusual.

She had managed to get home for about four hours, but sleep had proved elusive. Her regular prescription for staving off fatigue—*More coffee, please*—had left her feeling wired, but the caffeine had done little to clear away the mental fog. She rubbed her temples and tried to focus on the task at hand.

Before leaving the previous night, she had disseminated Burke's picture to law enforcement agencies throughout the greater Metro New York area. Every port, every transit stop, every place he might try to flee the city had been alerted. Now, she was buried in the noise that such an alert typically generated. Erroneous reports, mistaken identities, suspicious activity completely unrelated to the manhunt, but not one solid lead.

Burke had simply vanished.

A knock on her desk broke her concentration. She looked up to see Campbell standing there with two grande cups from Starbucks. He sat one down in front of her with a sympathetic smile. "Thought you might need this."

Doyle figured that if she imbibed any more caffeine, her veins might literally explode, but nonetheless managed a grateful smile. "Thanks."

"So, how goes the search?"

"A big fat zero. We're at plus-seven hours. If he made it out of the city, he could be halfway to anywhere."

Campbell made an equivocal gesture. "My money's on him trying to make it back to the family home in Southampton. He's a spoiled rich kid. He'll run home to hide under mommy's skirts."

"His mother is in a private Alzheimer's treatment facility in Connecticut," replied Doyle, wondering how her partner had missed that. "But we've got the Southampton PD watching the place anyway."

Campbell just nodded. "Mark my words. That's where we'll get him."

"I'm not so sure. Burke's nothing like our typical suspect. He's smart, resourceful. He knew to ditch his phone. He hasn't used credit cards."

"So the asshole watched a Jason Bourne movie. It doesn't mean anything. He'll slip up. They always do. It's just a matter of time."

Doyle returned her gaze to the photo on her computer screen. "What if we're wrong about this?"

"*Wrong?* He ran. That's what guilty people do."

"That's what *scared* people do," countered Doyle.

"Did he seem scared to you?"

Doyle accepted this with a slight nod. In the voicemail he'd left her, Burke had sounded a little rattled but definitely not *scared*. "I've just got this gut feeling that we're chasing the wrong rabbit."

"You're talking about the British guy? We've only got Burke's say-so that he even exists."

"C'mon, James. You heard the call. There were two different voices in that apartment with Burke. Two guys with British accents."

Campbell raised his hands in a show of surrender. "And we're following up on it. But it's gonna take time to ID the stiff from Burke's apartment, and we've got nothing on the other guy. Burke is the devil we know."

Doyle shook her head. Campbell was like a dog with a bone, and the bone was Chase Burke. "Yeah," she finally said and then gestured to her computer. "I've got to get organized for the presser."

The press conference, where she would lay out the response of the JTTF to the shooting at Chrysalis and the subsequent investigation, including the hunt for Chase Burke, was scheduled for 0730, giving her just forty-odd minutes to get all her ducks in a row.

Campbell chuckled. "Good luck with that. Talking to reporters ranks right up there with going to the dentist and talking to my ex on my list of things to avoid."

"Hey, you're going to be standing right next to me."

"Yeah. Keeping my big mouth shut to make you look good."

It was Doyle's turn to laugh. "Well, you're not wrong."

As if that was the signal he'd been waiting for, Campbell settled into his own desk and woke up his computer. Doyle, feeling somewhat reenergized by the conversation, began scrolling through her emails, reviewing the latest updates from the tip line.

Nothing . . . nothing . . . nothing . . . wait!

An email from Matthew Kim, the digital forensics specialist to whom she'd given the phone recovered from Burke's apartment, requested that she call him back. She'd asked Kim to contact her—and only her—directly with the results of his analysis.

She closed the email app and pushed away from her desk. To Campbell's questioning glance, she merely replied, "Gonna use the restroom and freshen up."

Her decision to keep this one branch of the investigation to herself had been a spur-of-the-moment one. Maybe it was Campbell's insistence on Burke's guilt—and Burke had been the one to provide them with the phone—or the fact that Campbell had made the unilateral decision to hold the phone back, but she felt like this was a lead she wanted to pursue on her own, without Campbell's one-note commentary.

She found Kim in his lab in the digital forensics department, up to his elbows in partially disassembled electronic devices. "Looks like you've been having fun," Doyle remarked, looking over the array, trying to identify the Samsung she'd handed over to him late the previous night.

Kim returned a bemused stare, then followed her gaze. "This? This is just for practice." He picked up a freshly sealed plastic evidence bag containing the phone, completely intact and looking exactly as it had when Campbell had plucked it from Burke's couch. "Here you go."

"You were able to unlock it?"

Kim shrugged. "I'm surprised you weren't. It's got a biometric lock. Fingerprint scanner. I just took it to the morgue and placed your dead suspect's index finger on the power button."

"I guess we should have thought of that," replied Doyle.

Why didn't we think of that? she wondered and then answered her own question. *Because Campbell said it was locked, and I just took his word for it.*

"Unfortunately, I'm afraid there's not much there," Kim went on. "The call log only goes back about a day, as you would expect from a burner, and all the numbers it was used to call have been deactivated."

"So, it's a dead end."

Kim shrugged.

Doyle sighed. "Thanks, Matt. I appreciate the quick turnaround."

"Anytime, Detective."

If Campbell noticed the length of her supposed restroom visit, he didn't comment. "Good news," he announced upon her return. "We've got an ID on one of the stiffs from the restaurant. Vinnie Moretti."

"Moretti?" The revelation was unexpected but hardly a surprise. "There's a name I haven't heard in a while."

"Like ten to fifteen, eight with good behavior. Moretti went down with the rest of the Cipriani Syndicate."

"And Tanya Hemsworth was the one who put him away. Now we've got our motive. What do you want to bet the rest of the slabs turn out to be Cipriani muscle?"

"That is a bet that I would not take," replied Campbell, grinning.

"That explains the attack at the restaurant, but it doesn't explain the two Brits at Burke's place."

"Or how Burke is involved."

Doyle had to fight the urge to roll her eyes.

A dog with a bone.

CHAPTER TWENTY-SEVEN

West Babylon, New York

Chase sat in the corner booth, nursing a bottomless cup of coffee and picking at his stack of pancakes, trying to will himself to take a bite. His long odyssey from the city had been mentally grueling, and exhaustion weighed heavily on him. He needed a nap, not breakfast, but he knew that aside from actual sleep, food was the next best thing. Hence the pancakes.

Even so, he was too anxious to eat.

After fleeing his apartment, he had left a voice message for Detective Doyle, hoping she would understand the significance of the numbers he'd left on her card. Then, he made his way to a Duane Reade that was open all night, paying cash for a couple of prepaid phones and a few other items with which he planned to alter his appearance and, hopefully, elude the net cast by the police. From there, he headed on foot to Penn Station and boarded the Montauk Line of the Long Island Railroad.

Knowing the police would likely have the family home under surveillance, he left the train in Lindenhurst, ducking into a wooded area where he spent the remainder of the night in a futile effort to get a little rest. Sleeping in the open didn't bother him, but his mind, alert to the possibility that someone might have seen him wandering through the neighborhood and called it into the local cops, kept him wide awake and ready to move, even when it was obvious that his late-night jaunt had gone completely unnoticed. With the first hint of twilight in the sky, he gave up on the idea of sleep and made his way to a nearby IHOP, hoping that breakfast and coffee would recharge his batteries a little.

Now, as he sat in the booth, he used one of the prepaid phones to call his voicemail box. There were three new messages, all from Chef David.

The first one was brief, and the worry in David's voice was barely masked. "Chase, it's David. Just checking in. Call me when you can."

The second had come in a few hours later. "Chase, I don't know what's going on, but we're hearing things. Violet and I saw something on the news, and your name came up. Call me. Please."

The third message was less than thirty minutes old. "You need to let us know where you are, Chase. Whatever's happening, we'll figure it out, but you can't just disappear, man. Call me."

Chase lowered the phone. Calling David back wasn't a priority, not right now.

A TV mounted high on the wall in the corner of the restaurant, tuned to a twenty-four-hour news station, was currently broadcasting a press conference from the New York Federal Building. The volume was turned down too low to be heard, but the captions were on, allowing Chase to follow along.

The familiar face of Alice Doyle came onto the screen as she took the podium. Chase leaned forward, intently focused on the black text bar.

As you are no doubt aware, last night, a group of armed men attacked a restaurant in Midtown Manhattan, where Congresswoman Tanya Hemsworth was dining.

Chase followed along as Doyle recounted the incident he had barely survived, her manner clinical and detached as she took viewers through the investigation.

I'm pleased to be able to announce that we have made some progress. We've identified one of the assailants as a known figure in New York's organized crime community, Doyle continued. *We believe it was their intention to abduct the congresswoman but were unable to accomplish that objective due to the timely interference of restaurant staff and patrons.*

Chase did not fail to note the vague characterization of his "timely interference" as part of a group effort, but he was more interested in what Doyle had revealed about the identity of the attackers.

A known figure in organized crime?

That squared with what Tanya herself had said about having enemies, but it didn't explain the sniper at the restaurant, nor did it account for the men who had invaded his home. There was more going on than Doyle, or anyone else in the JTTF, realized, but nobody seemed to be worried about it.

However, Doyle went on, *in the ensuing chaos, Congresswoman Hemsworth was critically wounded and is presently being treated for her injuries.*

The suspects were heavily armed and demonstrated a high level of coordination, Doyle continued. *Our investigation is ongoing, and we are exploring all possible leads to determine the full extent of their motives and connections.* She paused a beat, then turned to someone off screen. *Can we put up the picture?*

A moment later, the image on the screen changed to show a photograph of a person Chase immediately recognized. It was a face he saw every day, looking back at him in the mirror.

Oh shit.

He shot a surreptitious look around the restaurant, certain that all eyes would now be on him, fingers pointing in disbelief as they realized that the man being shown on the news was sitting in their midst, but no one seemed to have noticed him, not even among those who were actively watching the press conference.

He allowed himself a small sigh of relief. The measures he had taken to alter his appearance—buzzing all his hair off with a beard trimmer he'd purchased at the Duane Reade and the addition of low-magnification reading glasses—appeared to be working.

This is Chase Burke, read the caption at the bottom of the screen. *We have reason to believe that Mr. Burke may have information critical to this investigation. He is not a suspect at this time. However, anyone with knowledge of his whereabouts is urged to contact our tip line immediately.*

"Everything okay, hon?" asked his waitress.

Chase looked up, mirroring her friendly smile. "I could stand a warm-up," he said, sliding the mostly full coffee mug toward her. With a look of mild bemusement, she decanted a couple tablespoonsful into the mug and then moved off, leaving him to his business. On the television screen, a toll-free phone number was being displayed, along with his picture and a description of his physical attributes.

We are committed to finding those responsible for this attack and bringing them to justice, read the caption. *We urge anyone with information to come forward.*

Chase took a sip from the mug, then checked his watch. He still had a few minutes to go before keeping his next appointment but decided that if he loitered any longer over a plate of uneaten pancakes, the friendly server might decide to take a closer look at him. He left some cash on the table, then stood up and headed to the restroom.

His reflection surprised him. His new look would take some getting used to. He took a deep breath and turned his back on the mirror, leaned against the sink, and after checking to make sure that the door was locked, took out the burner phone he'd used to call his voicemail box.

He'd been disappointed when Doyle hadn't left him a voicemail to respond to his message, but judging by her comments at the press conference, it was clear that his appeal to her hadn't made much of an impression.

Chase dialed the number for Havenwood Retreat and asked for Curtis McGraw. He held his breath until McGraw picked up. "It's Chase Burke," he said.

"Chase? My God, are you all right?"

I guess he's heard, thought Chase, wondering if the call had been a mistake. "Not really," he said. "How's my mother doing?"

"Not well," replied McGraw gravely. "She saw you on the news just now. She's having a full-blown panic attack."

Chase felt his heartbeat quicken. "She recognized me?"

"I . . . I guess so."

"Can you put her on? I'd like to talk to her."

"Weren't you listening? She's having an episode. We may have to sedate her."

Still reeling from the revelation, Chase didn't know what to say. After a moment's pause, McGraw spoke again. "Chase . . . I know that you're . . . not able to move about freely."

Of course, McGraw would know that. He'd been a cop in London before coming over to manage Havenwood.

"We don't care about any of that," he went on. "All we care about is your mother's health. I think it would help immensely if you could come see her. We can be very . . . discreet about it."

Chase's first impulse was to reject the offer out of hand. McGraw's promises notwithstanding, the FBI would surely be watching Havenwood Retreat, just on the off chance that he might put in an appearance.

And yet . . .

She recognized me?

"I'll . . . see what I can do."

Curtis sighed. "I understand, Chase." Then he added, "Be careful."

Chase ended the call and stripped the phone down, removing the SIM card and battery, dropping the former in the toilet and the latter into a pocket. He crushed the rest under his heel and dropped the pieces into the trash can, then flushed and headed out.

He walked briskly through the restaurant, turning over this latest development. Now that Michael was gone, his mother was his only family, and despite their problematic history, he would always feel something for her. It wasn't quite love—too much had happened for that—but it was close.

And she had recognized him, hadn't she?

But what could he do for her now? Worse, what good would he be to her if Doyle and Campbell ran him to ground and locked him away?

No, he had to keep his priorities straight: Find out who was behind the attack on Tanya Hemsworth; clear his name; then, and only then, would he be in a position to help his mother.

Outside in the parking lot, he breathed in the brisk morning air. It invigorated him in a way that caffeine and carbs had not, but he knew the effect would be short-lived.

A moment later, a black, late-model Toyota 4Runner drove into the lot. Chase watched as the SUV pulled into a slot near the turn-in. A fit-looking, well-dressed man got out and glanced around. His eyes found Chase's, lingering there for just a second or two, and then moved on without any sign of recognition. Then, the man knelt beside the front tire and tied his shoe.

When he was done, he stood up again and took out his phone, staring at the display until, just a couple minutes later, a blue Honda Civic with a rideshare sticker in a corner of the windshield pulled into the lot. The man waved the car over, got in, and then both were gone.

Chase watched the Civic disappear down the road and then turned his attention to the 4Runner. After a quick look around to make sure that the strange episode had not attracted any undue attention, he strode over to the vehicle, mimicked tying his shoe, just as the Toyota's driver had, and deftly retrieved the key fob the other man had left behind.

He unlocked it, slid inside, and started it up.

After a night on the run, slinking in the shadows, hiding in the woods, and looking over his shoulder, just sitting behind the wheel of the SUV gave him a much-needed sense of being in control of his life.

A cell phone, left in the center console by the vehicle's previous occupant, chimed with an incoming call. The phone was connected via Bluetooth to the 4Runner's onboard entertainment system, and Chase tapped the screen to accept the call in hands-free mode.

"Jerry's looking good," he said. "He's beefed up a little since I last saw him."

The voice of Secretary Connor Williams filled the vehicle's interior. "Success agrees with him," he said pensively. "I'll be honest, Chase, I'm not at all comfortable involving him in this business, but he insisted. He seems to think he owes you some kind of life debt."

Chase didn't reply. What could he say? The truth was, Jerry and Williams *did* owe Chase for saving the younger man's life, along with the rest of his Ranger team, in Djibouti, and for fronting him a portion of the money he had used to get his tech start-up off the ground. Chase prided himself on not being the sort of person to call in a debt like that, but desperate times called for desperate measures.

"Tell him we're square," he finally said.

"Oh, I did. Be sure of it." Williams paused a beat. "I'm sending you the address of a vacation rental house where you can crash for a while, but I wouldn't advise staying there too long."

An incoming text message flashed on the center screen—an address in Deer Park. Chase tapped the screen again to send the directions to the onboard GPS.

"Thank you, sir. I really appreciate this."

The Secretary made a disapproving noise. "I'm going out on a limb here, Chase. If this blows up in my face . . ."

"I know," said Chase. "If there were another way, I'd take it."

Williams sighed. "What's the next step?"

"Did you catch the press conference?"

"I did. Seeing your picture on a nationally televised broadcast is doing wonderful things for my ulcer."

"They identified one of the shooters from the restaurant. He's connected to the mob. I'm guessing the rest of them will be as well."

"Okay. How does that help you?"

"I saw the face of one of the guys that got away. I'd be able to pick him out of a photo lineup. If you can get me access to the police database, I think I could put a name to the face."

"Chase, the number of people with known mob associations must run into the hundreds . . . thousands, even."

"I think we'll be able to refine that list down quite a bit. These guys were hitters. That's going to narrow the field. And I'm betting they all knew each other. Once the police get IDs on the rest of them, it shouldn't be too hard to cross-reference their known associates."

Williams gave a thoughtful hum. "This isn't normally what we do at State, but I think I can arrange access to the Organized Crime Task Force records section through INR."

"Michael's department?"

"That's right. INR routinely requests information on organized crime activities. That's our in."

The mere mention of Michael's name caused an upwelling of emotions, not the least of which was guilt. With everything going on, Michael's death had receded from Chase's awareness like an outgoing tide. Yet, the fact that he would be utilizing the same resources Michael once had felt like a sort of sign as if his big brother was looking out for him from the great beyond.

Williams was still talking. "Give me a couple of hours to set this up. I'll have to tread carefully. On the upside, that will give the FBI time to identify the other shooters. That should speed things up a little."

"Good plan," said Chase past the lump that had risen in his throat. "And Connor, I can't say it enough. Thank you. I'll owe you one when this is all said and done."

"Well . . ." The Secretary seemed at a loss for words. Finally, he murmured, "Let's just call it even."

CHAPTER TWENTY-EIGHT

Brooklyn, New York

"So, they found a stiff in a Brooklyn back alley," remarked Detective James Campbell as the unmarked car rolled down Atlantic Avenue. "Imagine that."

Doyle understood his cynicism even if she didn't share his viewpoint. It was easy to judge a place and the people that lived there based solely on appearances—and by that metric, they were unquestionably in a rough part of town—but such judgments weren't just simplistic, they were manifestly unfair. For every reprobate, corner dealer, street hustler, or tagger, there were at least a hundred good people just struggling to keep their heads above water. People who needed a helping hand, not a judgmental stare.

Those were the people she had sworn to protect and serve.

But if reports from the scene were to be believed, this crime was *not* per the norm. "It's not just any stiff," she said.

"You really think it's Burke?"

Doyle shrugged equivocally. "The officer on the scene thought it was possible. Hard to say since half his face is missing."

"I don't think it's him. He wouldn't have come out here. This isn't his kind of place."

Doyle noted that her partner said it as if he was speaking in absolutes. As if his mind was already made up.

Again.

Still, Doyle wasn't so sure.

She shrugged again, her mind running through every imaginable scenario. If she was being honest, part of her was inclined to agree with her partner. Still, a third shooting incident in less than twenty-four hours warranted a second look, if only to rule it out as being somehow connected.

Campbell took a left onto Utica and then a right on Fulton. The view outside remained depressingly bleak until they turned north on Howard Avenue and entered a more residential part of the neighborhood, with tree-lined sidewalks fronting charming old brick row houses.

What a difference a block can make, thought Doyle.

Then Campbell made another turn, revealing a street blocked off by barricades and a cluster of NYPD patrol cars, and was snapped back to reality.

They showed their creds to the uniform manning the barricade and then made their way up to the crime scene. Although a bullet hole—right above the bridge of his nose—had disfigured the face of the man sprawled out on the ground at an alley entrance, one look confirmed that it wasn't Chase Burke.

That one look was also enough for Doyle to decide that the trip had not been wasted.

"Two to the chest, one to the face," supplied the detective leading the investigation. "Kinda looks like a pro job to me."

Doyle agreed but did not say it aloud. She took a picture of the dead man's face, then pointed to his shoulder. "There's something under his jacket there. What is that?"

"Some kind of bandage."

Doyle slipped on a pair of nitrile gloves, then knelt beside the man, carefully pulling aside his track jacket to expose the bandage and then moving the blood-soaked pad away as well, revealing a nearly two-inch gash that, although still fresh, did not appear to have been actively bleeding at the time of death.

"This is a pressure bandage," she observed. "Probably treated with QuikClot or something similar."

"Like in our BTKs?" asked the detective. BTKs—belt-worn trauma kits—were a standard issue to NYPD officers and meant to provide rapid lifesaving intervention in the event of a serious injury, such as from a gunshot. "This guy's a cop?"

Doyle shook her head. "The dressings are a standard part of combat medical kits. He could be a former soldier, or maybe whoever patched him up was."

"Maybe whoever stuck him caught up to him and decided to finish the job."

Doyle returned the bandage to its place and stood. "Looks that way," she said. "This isn't the guy we were looking for, but as soon as you can pull a name, send it to us. It could be something."

"Will do," said the detective.

―――

"That tracksuit looked familiar," remarked Campbell as they headed back to their car.

"Noticed that?" she answered with a wry smile. "Burke said there were two intruders. Brad and Nigel. My gut says we just met Brad."

"You think maybe Burke hunted him down and finished the job?"

Doyle gave him a sidelong glance. "Would that be rich, pampered Chase Burke? Or Chase Burke, the stone killer?"

"Hey, we already know he's a killer. I'm just saying he's also from money."

"If Burke was planning to hunt Brad down, why would he leave that message?" Doyle asked. "These guys had British accents. Burke said he thought they were brothers."

"So?"

"So, let's assume that they're British citizens. We run their pictures against Customs records for the last couple of weeks and see if anything shakes out."

To his credit, Campbell did not reject the idea out of hand. "Maybe check with hotels too."

Doyle nodded approvingly. "Now you're getting it."

The search soon bore fruit, though not entirely as expected. A review of UK passport holders coming through Customs did not yield anyone named Nigel or Brad, and the only males with the same last name were part of a family—a father and two adolescent sons on holiday from Manchester.

They had better luck reaching out to the city's hotels. Their outreach turned up a positive match on both men, presently booked into rooms at the Langham on Fifth Avenue, staying under the names Charles Kensington and Edward Fairfax—Nigel and Brad, respectively. The two men had arrived in New York on separate flights, but a cross-check with the British consulate confirmed Doyle's suspicion that the names were aliases, the passports evident forgeries.

"Now that's some James Bond shit," Campbell had remarked as they examined the photographs of the passports. "I think we're looking at a couple of international hit men."

Doyle, recalling what Chase had said in his message, nodded slowly. "Two different groups of hitters, both targeting Congresswoman Hemsworth. The first group was trying to abduct her while these two were trying to kill her."

"Which side was Burke on?"

Doyle gave him a sidelong look. "You still can't accept that he might have just been in the wrong place at the wrong time?"

Campbell seemed not to hear. "He obviously wasn't working with the kidnappers. He whacked three of 'em. I'll bet he was working with

Brad and Nigel, and they had a falling out. Maybe Burke was a loose end they wanted to tie up."

Doyle knew it was a waste of breath to challenge Campbell's assumptions. "Let's get over to the Langham. Maybe we'll find something that will tell us who these guys were working for."

The opulence of the Langham, with its polished marble floors and modern art pieces, was quite a change from the grim streets of Brooklyn where they'd found the body of the suspected hit man.

They were greeted in the lobby by the front desk manager, a clean-shaven, well-coiffed thirtyish man in a tailored suit who introduced himself as Marcus.

"Thank you for talking to us," said Doyle after she and Campbell presented their credentials. "As I said on the phone, we're looking for information about two men who we believe were guests here. Charles Kensington and Edward Fairfax."

"Yes, that's correct." Marcus seemed just a touch pensive. "Am I to understand that both of them are . . ." He grimaced, unwilling to finish the thought.

"Deceased? It's looking that way." Doyle held out her phone, showing him the picture she'd taken earlier that day.

Marcus glanced at it, then looked away, visibly pale. "Yes, that looks like Mr. Fairfax."

Doyle flipped to a photo of Nigel, taken at Burke's apartment. "How about this one?"

Marcus steeled himself and studied the picture, which, owing to the location of Nigel's wounds, was not quite as gruesome. "That's Mr. Kensington."

Doyle nodded. "Could we have a look at their rooms, please?"

"Certainly. Right this way."

Marcus led them to the elevator lobby and onto a waiting car, which bore them to the nineteenth floor. Doyle noted that the manager did not have to consult the computer to get the room number—evidently, that information was now permanently inked in his brain.

When Marcus opened the door to admit them, Campbell let out a low whistle. "Holy shit," he murmured. "I'm in the wrong business."

The room—or rather the suite—was huge, looking more like a luxury residence than a place to spend a night. The front room had a plush sectional and a modern-looking octagonal coffee table, but its most commanding feature was the floor-to-ceiling window looking out at the Empire State Building. Yet, there was little trace of the room's occupants. A quick check of the bedroom and bath turned up nothing—no luggage, no toothbrush by the sink, no trash in the wastebasket.

Doyle turned to Marcus. "Did you already turn the room over?"

Marcus shook his head. "I had no reason to. Mr. Kensington has the suite booked for two more days."

Edward Fairfax's suite on the twentieth floor was much the same.

Trying to hide her disappointment, Doyle turned to Marcus again. "I'd like to talk to any of your employees who might have been on duty when they were here, and especially whoever was on duty last night and might have seen them leave."

"Of course. I can arrange that. As it happens, I was at the desk last night."

"You saw them leave?" asked Campbell. "Were they together?"

"Yes."

"When was this?"

"The first time was at . . ." Marcus looked at the ceiling for a moment. "Around five. It was after ten when they returned. And then they left again not long after that."

Doyle glanced over at her partner. "Right about the time we cut Burke loose."

Campbell nodded. "Can you remember anything about them? Were they acting weird, or did anything seem suspicious?"

Marcus shook his head. "No, nothing like that. I would have guessed they were heading out to a party or something."

"It was a party, all right," said Campbell.

Doyle folded her arms across her chest and rolled back onto her heels. "You seem like a smart guy, Marcus. Must have a lot of interactions with people throughout the day. Think hard. *Nothing* about these guys seemed off to you?"

Marcus tilted his head to the side. "Well, maybe one thing," he said. "But I don't know if it's even worth mentioning."

"It can't hurt," prompted Doyle.

"Maybe this is stupid, I don't know, but . . . well, I just remember thinking that it was a little strange that Mr. Turner didn't come back with the other two."

Doyle and Campbell exchanged a confused look, and then both spoke at the same time.

"Who's Mr. Turner?"

CHAPTER TWENTY-NINE

London, England

The blond girl's ponytail whipped wildly about her head as she dashed toward the ball, quickly closing in on her opponent near the halfway line. Timing it perfectly, she extended her foot to poke the ball away, stealing possession with a clean touch. The girl kept the ball close to her feet as she weaved through a couple of defenders, then put on a sudden burst of speed, cutting inside the penalty area. She faked a shot with her left foot, forcing the goalkeeper to commit early, then calmly slotted the ball in the bottom right corner of the net with her right foot.

The crowd gathered along the touchline at the edge of the pitch erupted into cheers, and Damien Gray, caught up in the excitement, joined in, pumping his fist in the air and shouting, "Allie! Allie!"

He felt a gentle pressure on his arm and turned to see Cassie nodding her head toward the man they suspected of being a scout for the England women's national team. Scout or not, he was holding his mobile up, recording every moment of the game. Damien took his wife's hand and gave it an enthusiastic squeeze.

Allie was having the game of her life. Her training and hard work, not to mention the support Damien had provided, was about to pay off, and he couldn't be prouder.

Yet, as the ball was moved to the center ring and the players resumed play, Damien's excitement ebbed, supplanted by the sense of dread he'd been feeling ever since leaving New York the previous night.

He hadn't at all liked how things had gone down across the pond. Everything about the job had been just a bit off, and the fact that he hadn't been there to oversee the last-minute surveillance job Brad had agreed to only deepened his sense of unease. He kept telling himself that he was worrying about nothing. Brad and Nigel were certainly capable of running a surveillance op without him, weren't they? His anxiety about it had more to do with his tendency toward being overly controlling rather than any deficiency on the part of his brothers.

But why haven't they called to check in?

He looked over at Cassie again, trying to find his way back into the moment, but a glimpse of Meg's face sucked him right back into the quicksand of dread.

Meg—Nigel's wife, Allie's aunt and godmother—had no idea what her husband did for a living, any more than Cassie suspected Damien's true profession. As far as the wives were concerned, they were international security consultants, advising corporate clients on best practices—ninjas in the boardroom, maybe, but definitely not literal assassins.

What would she do if she knew that Nigel risked his life every time we left for a job? What would she think if she knew that I was the one who put him in danger?

He shook his head, appalled at where his thoughts had gone. Nigel wasn't in any danger. It was a surveillance job, not a hit. The biggest risk they faced was getting caught on a CCTV camera and having their cover blown.

Is that what happened? Is that why they haven't checked in?

One thing was certain. Until he resolved his doubts, he wasn't going to be able to enjoy Allie's moment of glory.

He leaned close to Cassie and gave her a peck on the cheek. "I'm just going to use the loo."

She returned a smile. "Hurry back."

He pushed through the small crowd, bypassing the facilities, and crossed over to the car park where he would have both quiet and privacy.

Another check of his mobile showed no missed calls and no new messages. He dialed Brad's number. Nigel had set them up with a VoIP that could be easily synced to any mobile device, so no matter how many burner phones they went through, the brothers could always stay in contact.

Unless, of course, they'd tossed their last phone.

The call rang out and went straight to voicemail. He ended the call and tried Nigel's number. Again, no answer.

"Bollocks."

Something had gone wrong. He was certain of it. But why hadn't they called in?

He swiped over to a news app and navigated to the latest headlines from the USA. If Brad or Nigel had been caught and arrested after breaking into the flat of the man who had disrupted the shooting at the restaurant, it might rate a headline. Not surprisingly, the "assassination attempt" on Congresswoman Tanya Hemsworth was still the lead story.

The phrasing elicited a snort of derision.

If they only knew, he thought, *I probably saved her life with that shot.*

Then he spotted another headline.

Hero Waiter Chase Burke Named Person of Interest by the FBI After Shooting Leaves Three Cops Dead

Three cops?

Earlier reports had mentioned two plainclothes officers killed in the shootout at Chrysalis. Had there been another?

He tapped on the link to read the article, and his heart sank. The shooting referenced in the headline had occurred at Burke's flat, where Brad and Nigel were supposed to be conducting their surveillance op.

It wasn't hard to imagine what had happened. Burke had probably come home unexpectedly, caught Brad in his flat, and called the police, and Brad, in a monumental display of poor judgment, had tried to shoot his way out.

No wonder he's not taking my calls.

Then Damien read something the headline hadn't prepared him for.

"Chase Burke has been named a person of interest by the FBI after a shootout in his home left four dead, three of them NYPD officers."

Four dead.

Damien suddenly felt weak in the knees. He staggered back, falling against the fence surrounding the car park, leaning against it to steady himself.

Four dead, three of them coppers. Who's the fourth? Brad or Nige?

A flash of blue light in the periphery snapped him back into the moment. He looked up just as a line of police cars rolled down the drop-off lane between the car park and the stadium, their emergency flashers strobing, and knew instantly that they had come for him.

He looked back toward the stadium where, judging by the sudden crescendo of cheers, someone had just scored another goal. Was it Allie?

He needed to think . . . no, he needed to *act* quickly.

Losing himself in the crowd wouldn't work; the police would just lock down the venue, and then they would have him. No, he had to get away now while they were focused on containing him inside the stadium.

He stayed perfectly still as the police vehicles screeched to a stop, disgorging a small army of uniformed constables who quickly formed into a picket line, sweeping toward the stadium.

Taking a deep breath, he looked around for an escape route. Using a shell company, the brothers had purchased a flat in Kensington where they kept weapons and electronics; if he could reach it, he'd be safe, at least for a while, but getting there might be a problem. He didn't dare take his own car. They would already be on the lookout for that.

Steal a car?

That might give him a short head start, but once the stolen vehicle was identified, they'd use CCTV cameras to pinpoint his location, and then they would have him.

On foot, then, at least until he could hire a cab.

Before he could make a move, a disturbance at the stadium entrance stopped him in his tracks. The constables were coming back out, and they weren't alone. Cassie and Meg were with them. The women weren't handcuffed, but judging by their agitated expressions, they weren't going along happily.

His stomach churned. Cassie wouldn't be able to tell them anything substantive about his operations, but that was little comfort. He'd done everything possible to insulate her from his world, but now she had been pulled in. What would they tell her? What would they call him?

What would Allie think when they told her that her beloved father was an assassin for hire? And what about her chances of being picked up by the scout?

Two men in business suits, clearly plainclothes detectives, followed a few steps behind the police procession, scanning the street outside, looking for someone . . . looking for him.

He clenched his fists, fighting the urge to rush over and intervene. There was nothing he could do that wouldn't end with his capture and arrest. Or worse.

"Fuck." He turned away abruptly, unable to bear another moment of watching, only to slam into someone—a stocky young man on his way from the car park to the stadium with his girlfriend in tow.

"Oi," snarled the man, shoving back. "Watch where you're fucking going, mate."

Damien's instincts kicked in before he even had time to process what was happening. He reacted without thinking. His hand shot out, and he caught one of the man's wrists, twisting it with such ferocity that the man was instantly debilitated with pain. But Damien wasn't finished. He drove his knee up into the man's crotch, doubling him over.

The girlfriend's shrill scream filled the air like a fireworks display. A second later, Damien was off and running.

CHAPTER THIRTY

New York

Despite the burden still weighing on his shoulders, Chase felt revitalized as he held the wheel of the 4Runner steady, going with the flow of traffic on the Long Island Expressway. A hot shower and a couple hours of sleep in an actual bed had done wonders, and now he almost felt ready to take on the world.

Almost.

He knew he had an uphill battle ahead of him. So far, there had been no word from Secretary Williams regarding access to the law enforcement records that, he hoped, would put a name to the face of the man he'd struggled with outside Chrysalis. But even if that lead bore fruit, he would still have to find the man, while somehow avoiding the dragnet Doyle and Campbell had cast to catch him.

Speaking of Doyle . . .

He took the exit to Little Neck and pulled into a comfortable-looking neighborhood a block over from the parkway, where he used his remaining burner phone to check the voicemail box. If the FBI was able to somehow backtrace his location, all they would learn was that he was in Queens, and he would be long gone before they could act on that information. He was surprised to find a message from the detective.

Chase, this is Detective Doyle. I thought you should know we've made a significant breakthrough in our investigation, which seems to support your account of what happened last night. I urge you to come in. We just need you to answer a few questions, and then I feel certain you'll be able to put all of this behind you. Please, get in touch as soon as you can.

Chase played the message a second time, listening for the lie. Doyle could say whatever she wanted, making promises she knew she didn't have to keep. Why did she imagine he would believe her?

Still, the thought of getting out from under the shroud of suspicion was tempting.

Instead of playing voicemail tag, he decided to give Doyle a call. There was some risk involved, but he would be rid of the burner and long gone before she could pinpoint his exact location.

"What kind of breakthrough?" he said as soon as she picked up.

Doyle drew in a breath. "Chase. It's good to hear from you."

"Answer the question or I'm hanging up."

"Okay."

She was speaking slowly . . . stalling? Chase's finger hovered over the red button.

"We identified the man who was killed in your apartment."

Chase moved his finger away. "Nigel?"

"His full name is Nigel Gray. He's a former British soldier who works . . . or *worked*, I should say, as a private security consultant."

"Security consultant. In other words, he was a hit man."

There was a brief pause, then Doyle said, "I'd say that's a fair characterization."

"What about his brother? Brad?"

"They were in business together. And Chase . . ." She hesitated again, but it seemed to Chase more like she was trying to decide how much to tell him rather than attempting to drag the conversation out so that her partner could trace the call. "We found Brad too."

Chase felt an unexpected wave of relief. That must have been the "breakthrough" Doyle had promised. "Then you know this has nothing to do with me."

"That's just it, Chase. They were in your apartment. Clearly, it has *something* to do with you. Come in, and we can talk about it."

"*I* don't know why they were there. Why don't you ask Brad?"

"We can't."

"Why the hell not?"

"I think you already know why, Chase."

He frowned and almost disconnected the call. "You're just fucking with me. I'm hanging up."

"Fucking with you?" she said incredulously. "You're fucking with us. Brad's dead. Don't act like you didn't already know that."

The revelation jolted him. *"Dead?"* He swallowed. "I mean, hold on a second. I wounded him, but it was barely a scratch. I can't believe he would have bled out."

"Wounded him?"

"In the shoulder. I threw a knife at him. It was self-defense."

"Was it also self-defense when you cornered him in that alley and shot him in the fucking face?" said a familiar male voice.

And there's Detective Campbell.

Still, Chase was shocked.

Someone took him out too. Why?

"I don't know what you're talking about," Chase said, "but we're done here."

He thumbed the button to end the call, realizing only after he'd done so that he'd failed to ask the obvious question.

Who was the gunman that shot Brad Gray?

Doyle and Campbell thought he had done it, so obviously, they didn't know.

Who did that leave?

The call had left him with more questions than answers, but he had at least added two more pieces to the puzzle.

Nigel and Brad Gray. Contract killers.

Professional assassins hired to take out Tanya Hemsworth, and on the very night that a gang of mob soldiers had attempted to abduct her. The timing was too perfect to be a coincidence.

But who had killed Brad?

Chase couldn't shake the feeling that he was being dragged into something far bigger than a simple hit job—this had all the signs of an organized crime turf war. Somehow, he'd landed right in the middle of it. He made a mental note to ask Connor Williams to look into the Gray brothers.

He stared down at the phone, knowing that he should strip it and destroy it immediately, but then he remembered that there was one other call he wanted to make before tossing the phone. He dialed the number, put it on speaker, and when the receptionist answered, he asked to speak with Curtis McGraw.

The transfer took only a moment. "This is Curtis McGraw."

"It's Chase Burke. I just wanted to check in again."

"Chase?" McGraw sounded tentative, leaving Chase to wonder if the FBI net had fallen over Havenwood Retreat. But then McGraw went on. "Your mother is doing better. I think . . ." He hesitated again. "It would do wonders if you could come out here for a visit, but I don't suppose you'll be wanting to do that."

"It's probably not a good idea right now."

"I think . . . she might be able to handle a phone call."

Chase felt his pulse quicken. The thought of talking to his mother . . . not just addressing the empty shell of the person she had become, as he had been doing on a weekly basis for months now, but actually talking *to* her filled him with both hope and trepidation. Hope that this moment of lucidity might presage a positive development in her treatment. Trepidation that it might be simply a fluke, a door that, while open now, might soon close forever. If that were true, this might be his last chance to say the things he needed to say to her. He cursed the circumstances that prevented him from simply rushing to her side.

"Yes," he managed, suddenly feeling a little lightheaded. "I'd . . . really like that."

"All right, give me just a moment." Canned background music replaced McGraw's voice, but the interlude was brief. A woman's voice, but not his mother's, came over the line, "Mr. Burke?"

"Yes?"

"It's Lucy. Lucy Noonan. We met yesterday?"

Chase almost laughed aloud. Yesterday seemed like a million years ago. Then he remembered her—Lucy Noonan was his mother's new nurse. "Yes, I remember."

"I'm going to give you to Henrietta now."

There was a faint shuffling sound over the line, and then Henrietta's voice rang like a clarion in his ear. "Chase? Are you there?"

Chase tried to respond, but the words wouldn't pass the lump that had welled up in his throat.

"Chase?"

"I'm here," he managed to croak. "I'm here, Mother."

"Oh, Chase. It's so good to hear your voice." Was that a quaver of emotion rippling through her impeccable mid-Atlantic accent? "It's been too long."

"I know. I'm sorry." He didn't know what else to say.

For the first time since hearing Michael had died, Chase suddenly didn't feel all alone in the world. He knew the moment wouldn't last forever. It simply couldn't. Not with her condition. But right now—all he wanted was to see his mother and give her a hug.

"I saw you on the television. They're saying you were involved in a shooting. It's not true, is it?"

His heart sank.

"It's . . . it's all a misunderstanding. I haven't done anything wrong, Mother. I promise."

"I know it is. Must be. Just be careful, Chase. Ask Michael to help you out. Have you heard from him?"

Michael . . .

The mention of Michael was an indicator that his mother wasn't as lucid as he had hoped. Still, though, she had told him to be careful. That had to mean something, right?

Careful.

Then again, careful would be hanging up, destroying the phone, and getting as far from where he was as possible.

But he couldn't bring himself to sever the connection. Not now. Not when she was lucid.

"I miss you, son."

The unexpected admission sent a twinge through him, akin to biting on a piece of foil. He couldn't remember her *ever* saying the words.

Suddenly, he knew what he had to do. "I'm going to come there to see you," he declared. "I'll be there in a couple of hours, okay?"

Her long silence—when he had expected only an enthusiastic affirmative—was ominous.

"Mother?"

"Do you really think that's a good idea?" she said, sounding irritated.

"I'll be careful."

"I mean, with all the trouble you've already caused. Now, you want to come here, and make even more trouble? Do you ever stop and think about how your actions will affect others?"

Every word felt like a skewer through his heart. It was as if a switch had been thrown, sending an electrical current into the dormant creature that was the real Henrietta Enfield Burke, and now, fully roused, she had thrown off the illusion of motherly affection, unleashing months of pent-up disapproval.

"Michael would never do anything like this to me," she went on. "He's a good son. Nothing like you. Put Michael on. I want to talk to him. I want to talk to my boy."

"Michael is dead, Mother," said Chase flatly. "He's not coming back."

"You don't believe that. *I* don't believe that!"

Chase thumbed the button to end the call, squeezing the phone in his fist until he heard the screen crack.

But the initial hurt he'd felt was already ebbing away. So was the anger. He couldn't blame his mother for her reaction. She was like the scorpion in the fable, unable to resist her venomous nature, even to her own detriment.

Now, he felt only pity for her.

He took a breath, then began methodically disassembling the phone, removing the SIM card and battery, and then breaking the rest into pieces, which he tossed out the window before driving away.

CHAPTER THIRTY-ONE

Detective Alice Doyle mentally reviewed her conversation with Chase Burke and wished, not for the first time, that her partner had kept his trap shut. Maybe Burke wasn't ready to come in yet, but the fact that he had called was a hopeful sign.

Or at least it had been until Campbell spooked him.

Back to square one.

Burke hadn't sounded like a guilty man on the run for his life. His surprise at learning of Brad Gray's death had seemed genuine, as had his insistence that he didn't know why the Grays had made a move on him.

Maybe that's the question we should be asking.

Campbell already thought he had the answer—a falling out among coconspirators—but to Doyle, it just didn't add up. Nor did it seem likely that the Grays had targeted Burke because of his interference in their assassination attempt; professional contract killers didn't operate that way.

So why were they there?

"Got a location ping on Burke's cell," Campbell announced, breaking her train of thought. "He's in Queens. Just a couple blocks from the LIE."

Doyle shrugged. "He'll have already destroyed that phone and moved on. We're not going to find him."

"I'll start pulling traffic camera footage from the area. Maybe we'll get lucky."

"Maybe," agreed Doyle, thinking *And then what? If Burke doesn't have any answers, we're just wasting our time looking for him.*

Her instincts told her that Chase Burke was innocent. A victim of circumstance—wrong place, wrong time. More than that, he was a maligned hero. Going after him was a waste of time and resources and could very well backfire into a public relations nightmare.

They already knew who the real bad guys were. Fingerprints had yielded IDs on the men who had died during the attack on Chrysalis, mob muscle recruited from the organizations that had once comprised the Cipriani Syndicate. No doubt, the mastermind of the abduction plot was someone higher up in the criminal underworld.

Brad and Nigel Gray, the men responsible for killing three NYPD officers, were dead, but whether they had played a role in the attempt on Congresswoman Hemsworth's life, as Campbell seemed to think, was not yet clear. Determining how they figured into the big picture was where she and Campbell should be focusing their attention instead of wasting time going after Chase Burke.

Hopefully, the London Metro Police would soon have the third Gray brother in custody. Maybe then they would be able to get some answers.

After Marcus, the desk manager at the Langham, had provided them with the name of a third man working with the Gray brothers—a man with a UK passport issued to Alec Turner—they had passed the information along to the London Metropolitan Police, who not only confirmed that the passport was a forgery but were also able to put a name to the face.

Damien Gray.

The Gray brothers, all military veterans, ran a corporate security consulting outfit that, until now, had never been associated with any criminal activity. Two of the brothers—Damien, the oldest, and Nigel, the youngest—were married, and Damien had a teenage daughter whom, by all reports, he doted on. In fact, he had returned home to London for the sole purpose of attending his daughter's soccer game. Not the sort of behavior one typically associated with steely-eyed hitmen. But rather than taking this as an indicator that the Grays had simply made a bad decision, Doyle took the absence of any suspicious behavior as a sign the Grays were very good at their *real* job—contract killing. So good, in fact, that it was doubtful forensic investigators would be able to follow a money trail back to whomever had hired them, which was why it was imperative that Damien Gray be taken alive and compelled to talk.

Figuring out what the Gray brothers were doing in New York was the key to unlocking everything. Doyle was sure of it.

She mentally reviewed the sparse evidence they had collected. Nigel Gray's cell phone was a dead end, offering no useful information. Ballistics tests on the pistol they had found at the scene indicated that it had been used to kill only one of the three responding officers, but beyond that, the weapon had proved untraceable and couldn't even definitively be tied to either of the Grays. The only other item they had was the key fob, presumably for the van that had been torched a couple of blocks from Burke's apartment.

Given the intensity of the fire, it seemed unlikely that the wreckage would yield any evidence, but in the interest of turning over every stone, it was probably worth a look.

She logged into the NYPD evidence management system and scrolled down to see what the CSU techs had turned up but found no listings for anything recovered from the van and no information about the van itself.

Maybe they haven't processed it yet.

"James—" She caught herself, realizing he would probably just shoot down the idea.

But Campbell had heard her. "Yeah?"

She shook her head. "Never mind. Crazy idea."

He shrugged, then checked his watch. "Not too late for a cup of tea," he said. "You want one?"

"Sure. Thanks."

As he moved off, she took out her phone and called the 19th Precinct, asking for the head of the Evidence Collection Team assigned to Burke's apartment. After a few moments on hold, she was connected with Sergeant Mark Feinblum.

"Sergeant Feinblum, it's Detective Doyle, assigned to JTTF. I was wondering if there's a time frame for processing the van that burned up a few blocks from the scene of last night's shooting?"

Feinblum seemed confused by the question. "I'm not sure what you're talking about, Detective."

Doyle frowned. "There was a van on fire when we arrived on the scene. There's a good chance it belonged to the shooters. It was supposed to be processed."

"I know the van you're talking about. But nobody put in a request to have it entered as evidence. Detective Campbell told us it was unrelated."

Doyle felt an unexpected chill shoot down her spine.

Detective Campbell told you that?

But she didn't say that. "Oh, you're right. My mistake. Wires crossed." She paused a beat, then went on. "Just out of curiosity, where did the van end up?"

"We send all our impounds to Erie Basin. There wasn't anyone inside, so unless it pops as stolen, it'll be a while before anyone gets around to taking a look at it."

"All right, thanks for your help, Sergeant," Doyle said and rang off.

She stared at her phone, thoughts racing, stomach churning.

Campbell had kept Nigel's phone out of evidence, and now he'd done the same with the van.

She had known Campbell for years. He was a good cop, a good detective, and had always had her back. The idea that he might be deliberately sabotaging their investigation was ludicrous. But what else was she supposed to think?

She wanted to believe there was a rational explanation, needed to believe it, but she just couldn't see it. She took a deep breath, trying to calm the storm inside her. Regardless of what Campbell was up to, she needed to follow this lead. Tonight, after the end of the shift, she would go out to Erie Basin and examine the van herself.

And, for the first time since they'd been partners, she wouldn't tell Campbell a thing.

CHAPTER THIRTY-TWO

Chase left the 4Runner in a parking garage on East 40th Street and walked the rest of the way to his destination. He kept his head up as if daring passersby to recognize him. Judging by the indifferent expressions of all who might have seen him, nobody gave him a glance, much less a second one. Still, out of an abundance of caution, he gave a wide berth to the tourists taking selfies in front of the iconic stone lions that guarded the steps to the entrance of the Stephen A. Schwarzman Building, known to most New Yorkers simply as "the library."

It had been a few years since his last visit, and Chase took a moment to appreciate the grand beaux arts architecture and the statuary figures that adorned the facade, symbolizing the Contemplation of Justice and the Authority of Law. The significance of this was not lost on him. He was here in pursuit of one of those ideals while actively fleeing the other.

The brief phone conversation with his mother had left him more rattled than he cared to admit. He had long ago come to terms with her relegating him to the role of "second son," but her sudden admission of love dissolved the scar tissue, opening that hurt afresh. Her subsequent turnabout felt like salt poured into the wound. He shook his head, pushing the thoughts away, trying to focus on the task at hand.

He went inside, passing through the grand lobby, and ascended the stairs to the third floor, where he made his way to the magnificent Main Reading Room and logged into one of the public computers using his personal library account. There was some risk in doing this, but he didn't think it was very likely that the authorities would have flagged his library card. Then he went to work.

Secretary Williams had texted him a remote login that would allow him to browse the Organized Crime Task Force database, a collection of all the intelligence gathered on known or suspected members of criminal organizations. The volume of information was considerable, encompassing not only the usual bad actors like the Sicilian Mafia or the Russian Bratva but also more recent entries on the stage—street gangs and white-power groups. Fortunately, the identity of the Chrysalis shooters, which had been released earlier that day, allowed Chase to narrow the field down to merely a few hundred possibilities.

He could have reviewed the files using the phone Williams had given him but figured that he would have a harder time matching a face to a photograph on a screen the size of a playing card.

The process was tedious, each face blending into the next. He flagged several possible hits—mobsters, it seemed, had a certain look—but none of the faces in the photographs were quite like the image in his mind's eye. Then, he clicked on the file of a man named Antoni Bonetti.

Just a glance at Bonetti's picture—a passport photo rather than a mug shot—sent an electric surge through his body, transporting him back to that fateful moment outside Chrysalis when he had almost . . . *almost* saved Tanya.

The thrust of a knife . . . his own desperate pivot and counterstrike . . . Tanya bleeding out in his embrace while the dark-haired man crawled into the Suburban . . . their eyes meeting in a moment, frozen forever in his memory.

Those same eyes now stared back at him from the computer screen. The eyes of the man he had sworn to hunt down and kill.

But first, they were going to have a long talk.

CHAPTER THIRTY-THREE

London, England

Damien Gray sat in the darkened interior of the Kensington flat, with his Heckler & Koch USP resting in his lap and a tumbler of Laphroaig on the side table in easy reach, wondering how, despite all his precautions, everything in his world had turned to shite.

His eyes were fixed on the door, waiting for it to burst open in a storm of flash-bang grenades and policemen in full tactical kits shouting for him to get down.

He still hadn't decided how he would react when that moment came. Should he go out with guns blazing? Or should he surrender, resigning himself to a life behind bars, forever cut off from Cassie and Allie?

After an hour, and a couple more splashes of Scotch, he began to think that maybe the police weren't coming for him after all. Improbable as it seemed, he had somehow managed to elude the watchful electronic eyes of the surveillance state the United Kingdom had become and preserve the secrecy of his off-the-books sanctuary.

This realization did not greatly improve his mood.

Regardless of whether they caught up to him, he was fucked. Full stop.

He could never go back to his life. Never again would he hold Cassie's hand or watch Allie play football. For all practical purposes, he was already dead.

What troubled him the most was how they would regard him in the days, months, and years to come. Would they find it in their hearts to forgive him? Or would they find his duplicity irredeemable? Live or die, he could not imagine a worse fate than that.

If only I could explain it to them.

There was a way, of course. Nigel had taught him how to use a virtual private network and end-to-end encryption to access his personal mobile phone account, either with a burner or directly from a computer. He could simply give Cassie a call. The police might be monitoring her phone, but they would never—*probably never*—be able to backtrace to his location.

But it wasn't fear of capture that caused him to hesitate. The truth of it was that he was too afraid of what she might say.

Eventually, however, the agony of not knowing simply became too great. He went into the study and used a pristine laptop computer to connect to the VPN. As soon as he connected to his mobile account, notifications began popping up. Missed calls. Frantic text messages from both his wife and daughter, variations on a theme:

Where are you?
What the hell is going on?

The most recent, from forty-five minutes ago, was a video message. Hands trembling with both anticipation and dread, he clicked on the file.

Cassie's face appeared, looking worn and tear-streaked. He didn't recognize the room behind her; she was probably still in police custody. Her voice was thick with emotion as she began to speak.

Damien, please, if you're seeing this, you need to come in. I'm so scared right now. They're saying that you . . . she broke off, overcome with emotion, but after a deep breath, she resumed. *I'm frightened, and Allie . . . Allie keeps asking where you are. I don't know what to tell her. Just come in, Damien. Do it for Allie. Whatever happens, we'll get through this, I promise. We can figure this out together. I love you. Please, just come in.*

Damien felt utterly gutted. He sat back, the pistol feeling heavier in his lap, the last traces of resistance crumbling under the weight of Cassie's pleas.

He would do it. Turn himself in. It was the only possible way to salvage something from the wreckage of his life.

But there was something he had to do first.

He logged out of the mobile account, switched over to the business line, and called the client.

The line rang several times before the connection was established, and after a moment, the client's electronically modulated voice issued from the speaker. "Well, this is an unpleasant surprise." Then, before Damien could respond, the client added, "Mr. Gray."

Damien was momentarily dumbfounded.

How does he know my name?

But, of course, he already knew the answer to that question.

The same way the police knew.

"What happened in New York?"

"What *happened*?" said the client. "What happened is that your brothers fucked up. I gave them a simple job, and they ended up in a shootout with the police."

"Are they . . ."

Damien couldn't bring himself to finish the question, but after the momentary signal delay, the client did. "Dead?" There was another pause. "What do you think?"

Though he had already known his brothers were gone, the confirmation still stung.

"How did it happen?"

The silence that followed seemed to go on forever. Finally, the client replied, "Your brother Nigel was killed by the police."

Damien's heart skipped a beat. *Nigel . . . dead?*

But the client wasn't finished. "Brad was . . . Chase Burke hunted Brad down and tortured him before finally putting a bullet in his head."

The knuckles of the hand gripping the pistol went white as Damien struggled to control an unexpected surge of rage. "Burke did that?"

"He did." There was another long pause, and then the client spoke again, this time with something that, even with the robotic quality of the voice modulator, almost sounded like sympathy. "Burke is still out there. The police can't find him. But maybe . . ."

"Maybe what?"

"Maybe it takes a killer to hunt a killer. How do you feel about getting a little payback?"

The prospect immediately ignited a fire in Damien's heart, but it did not blind him to the practical considerations. "It's no bloody good. I can't leave London."

"If I could arrange to get you back here, under the radar . . . could you really do it? Hunt down Chase Burke?"

Cassie's plea echoed in his thoughts.

Whatever happens, we'll get through this, I promise. We can figure this out together. I love you. Please, just come in.

But so did the client's grim assessment. *Chase Burke hunted Brad down and tortured him before finally putting a bullet in his head.*

Really, what choice did he have?

"Just get me there," he said, surrendering to the fire. "And I'll put a bloody end to Chase Burke."

CHAPTER THIRTY-FOUR

New York

Antonio Bonetti wasn't a convicted felon but rather a former officer with the San Marco Marine Brigade of the Italian Navy. After retiring from service, Bonetti had relocated to Manhattan where he had quickly appeared on law enforcement's radar owing to his employment as a driver in a limo company operated by Jack Ruffino of the Ruffino crime family.

As a foreign national living in the USA on a work visa, Bonetti's home of record—an apartment in Lower Manhattan—was on file, which was why, a little more than two hours after learning the man's identity, Chase was in a Grand Street pizzeria a couple blocks from the building where Bonetti lived. As he waited for his order—one large pepperoni pie, to go—Chase idly sipped a Coke and used the phone Williams had given him to review the Organized Crime Task Force's extensive dossier on the myriad criminal affairs of the Ruffino family.

He skipped the early history of the Family, which went back more than five decades, focusing on more recent developments, notably the Family's inclusion in the Cipriani Syndicate. The leader of the Syndicate, one Judah Stine, had unified several of the city's ethnic mobs—the Mafia, the Irish, and even the Russians—transforming them into a veritable multinational corporation of crime. Stine was currently serving multiple life sentences in ADX Florence, owing in no small part to former NYPD detective, now Congresswoman Tanya Hemsworth's undercover operation.

It wasn't a huge leap of logic to imagine that the abduction plot was an attempt by the remnants of the Syndicate, or perhaps even Judah Stine himself, to get a little payback against the woman who had brought them down. If Stine or one of his successors was ultimately responsible for the attack on Tanya, they would join Bonetti on Chase's vendetta list.

But that still didn't answer the question of who had hired the Gray brothers.

One thing at a time, Chase told himself.

He picked up his pizza and carried the warm takeout box directly to the entrance to Bonetti's building, where he rang the bell for the man's apartment. The pizza was just a form of camouflage, a prop to explain his presence in the lobby. In the age of the gig economy, people making food deliveries were so commonplace as to be invisible. He didn't expect Bonetti to buzz him in, no questions asked, but that was beside the point. Chase was just trying to establish whether his quarry was at home. If Bonetti answered on the intercom, Chase would simply pretend that he'd gotten the wrong apartment and then move to the next phase of his plan. After a minute of no response, he tried again, more insistently.

Still nothing.

Chase figured that Bonetti either was not at home or was pretending to be out, lying low after the previous night's events.

He was just about to try hitting buzzers at random in hopes of being let in when one of Bonetti's neighbors, on her way out, held the door for him.

And who says New Yorkers are rude, thought Chase, thanking the woman profusely.

When he reached Bonetti's floor, instead of going directly to the man's apartment, Chase first knocked at the doors of his nearest neighbors, ready with his "wrong address" excuse just in case someone answered, but his aggressive pounding failed to bring any response either from the tenants or from any other residents responding to the noisy disturbance. Satisfied that he had the floor to himself, Chase approached Bonetti's door.

Breaking and entering techniques were not something Chase had been taught in the course of his Army career, but he had a natural aptitude for skill acquisition, and after some internet searches and a couple of very instructive YouTube videos, he had determined that the quickest way to gain entry into Bonetti's apartment—aside from finding the man at home—was with a bump key.

Unlike lockpicking tools, which were not readily available except through online vendors, a bump key was easy to make and easy to use. It consisted of nothing more than an ordinary key blank, which could be purchased at any hardware store, cut in a zigzag tooth pattern. When inserted in a lock and then struck with a small hammer while under slight tension, the vibration would force the pins inside the lock to align momentarily, ultimately allowing the lock cylinder to turn. Since most residential locks utilized either the KW-1 or SC-1 keyway, Chase purchased one of each, in both the five- and six-pin configuration, along with a rubber mallet.

Bonetti's lock turned out to be the ubiquitous KW-1 five-pin variety. Working quickly, Chase slid his bump key into the deadbolt cylinder, applying gentle but constant pressure, and began tapping it with the mallet. The noise was no louder than his earlier knocking, and after about fifteen seconds of banging away at it, he felt the key turn. He repeated the process with the lock in the doorknob until it, too, yielded.

With a final look up and down the hall, Chase drew his SIG and then, standing to the side of the doorway, turned the knob and pushed the door open. After a quick peek around the jamb to ensure that Bonetti wasn't waiting to ambush him, he went inside, pulling the door shut behind him.

He immediately noted the apartment's tidy appearance—no dishes in the sink, no overflowing ashtrays, everything in its place. The living room was sparsely decorated. The bed in the bedroom was made with military precision. The apartment felt more like a hotel room than a personal residence.

Chase moved into the bathroom and noted that the towel hanging on the rack by the shower was dry, as was the shower itself. Everything was dry—the sink, the bar of soap, the toothbrush in the holder. While these were not perfect gauges of the passage of time, Chase reckoned that at least twenty-four hours had passed since the bathroom had seen any use. Bonetti hadn't come home after the assault on Chrysalis, and unless Chase was very much mistaken, he had no plans to do so in the near future.

While unfortunate, Bonetti's absence was not entirely unexpected. Bonetti would have known that it was only a matter of time before the police began looking for him, especially with an eyewitness able to identify him, and so he had gone into hiding. No doubt, someone in the Ruffino family was giving him sanctuary. Figuring out who and where was going to be a needle-and-haystack challenge.

Anticipating this possibility, Chase had plumbed the depths of the OCTF dossier on the Ruffino operation, looking for rental properties and budget motels where mob operatives might find refuge for extended periods without leaving a paper trail. While the list was neither short nor comprehensive, it was a place to start. Ranking the list in terms of probability, one location floated to the top of the list.

Following Judah Stine's imprisonment and the presumed end of the Syndicate, the Ruffinos, under the guiding hand of Giacomo "Jack" Ruffino, had returned to more traditional criminal enterprises, racketeering, and illegal gambling. One of their more profitable endeavors was a quiet partnership with a shady real estate developer named Vincent Marasco. Marasco was notorious for his cozy relationship with city officials and his use of lawsuits to challenge zoning laws, yet he somehow managed to avoid doing anything obviously illegal. Jack Ruffino had invested heavily in Marasco's developments, the latest of which was the transformation of a derelict waterfront property in Red Hook into "luxury lofts." The project was behind schedule and over budget, at least on paper, which translated into a sizable tax write-off for all involved, but according to police surveillance reports, the fully furnished model unit was sometimes used by family members and friends for romantic trysts and other illicit activities.

It was time to pay a visit to Red Hook.

CHAPTER THIRTY-FIVE

With the identification of the four dead Chrysalis shooters as members of New York City's criminal underworld, the focus of the JTTF investigation began to shift away from the ongoing manhunt for "person of interest" Chase Burke. Therefore, when Detective Alice Doyle announced, at six in the evening of the day following the shooting, that she was going home to recharge her batteries and to see her daughter, nobody gave her so much as a sideways glance.

Doyle, however, did not go directly home.

On her way out, she pulled out her phone and dialed Ava's sitter. She picked up on the second ring.

"Hey Alice," she said, her voice warm amid the background sounds of chopping and clinking dishes. "Everything okay?"

Doyle felt a pang of guilt as she imagined her daughter's sitter in the small kitchen, preparing Ava's dinner.

"Yes, of course," Doyle said, keeping her tone light despite the storm in her head. "Just calling to let you know I'll be a couple more hours. Something came up at work."

The sitter reassured her not to worry about it and that she had already started dinner, and that Ava was helping set up the table.

After ending the call, and instead of heading west through Tribeca and then north up the Henry Hudson Parkway to her apartment in Morningside Heights, Doyle went the opposite direction, driving her 2019 Mazda 3 across the Brooklyn Bridge and then taking the Brooklyn-Queens

Expressway south toward Red Hook—a route that coincidentally took her, quite unknowingly, less than a quarter mile from where Chase Burke was covertly surveilling the converted warehouse owned by Vinnie Marasco.

The Erie Basin Auto Pound, one of the NYPD's many vehicle-evidence storage facilities, was situated on a U-shaped man-made breakwater that extended out into Gowanus Bay and formed the protected harbor, reclaimed from marshland, known as Erie Basin. The auto pound was a sprawling, open-air lot, enclosed by a chain-link fence and, for the most part, unapproachable except from the water. A single road led past the main gate out to the main lot, where vehicles recovered from crime scenes and potentially containing evidence were kept for a minimum of thirty years.

Doyle presented her credentials to the bored-looking officer at the main gate. "I'm looking for a vehicle that was brought in late last night. A burned-out van."

The officer consulted a tablet computer and, after a few swipes, nodded. "Yeah, we've got it." He finally met her gaze. "You been here before?"

Doyle shook her head. "First time."

The officer nodded. "I'll take you to it."

He opened the gate and then surprised Doyle by climbing into a waiting patrol car.

"Oh," she murmured. "I guess we're driving."

She followed him out into the main lot, down a seemingly endless row of derelict vehicles, many of them damaged beyond any hope of repair. Finally, about half a mile from the entrance, the patrol car's brake lights flashed on. Doyle did not need the officer to tell her that they had arrived. One look at the carbonized remains of the van told her that.

"Well, that's it," said the officer. "Not much left of it."

"I'd like to take a closer look at it if that's okay."

He shrugged. "Knock yourself out. I'm going to head back to the gate. If you get lost trying to leave, just call dispatch."

Doyle wasn't sure if the last part was a joke but nodded and thanked him. As he drove away, she turned her full attention to the wreckage.

The intense heat of the fire had warped the metal and reduced much of the interior to ash. The smell of burnt plastic hanging about the wreckage was almost overpowering. Nevertheless, Doyle activated her flashlight and did a slow walk around the van, playing the beam into the shadowy crevices of the interior. The damage was so extensive that it seemed doubtful she would find anything of consequence. Yet, the mere fact that her partner had gone out of his way to ensure that the van was not included in the evidence collected from the shooting at Burke's apartment compelled her to keep looking. She tried not to think about the broader significance of Campbell's omission.

After her initial walkaround, she pulled on a pair of nitrile gloves and moved in for a closer look. Gently probing the debris, she brushed away the top layer, hoping to uncover whatever it was that had prompted someone to want to so thoroughly destroy the vehicle.

She found it behind the passenger's seat.

Her pulse quickened as a layer of ash flaked away, revealing the upper receiver of a rifle, its metal warped and partly melted by the fire's intense heat. Given its condition, she was hesitant to even touch it, much less attempt to identify it—this was a job best left to the evidence techs—but there was not a doubt in her mind that she was looking at the rifle that had been used in the assassination attempt on Congresswoman Hemsworth, the missing piece that connected the Gray brothers to the shooting.

Yet, it was not the discovery itself that left her reeling. She had already suspected the Grays' role in the previous night's events—the rifle only confirmed it. The question that burned in her like acid was why Campbell had gone to such lengths to hide it.

Is James dirty?

Doyle felt a tightening in her chest. Could Campbell—the man she trusted with her life, the man she had left alone with Ava countless times—really be a dirty cop? The thought slashed through her mind like a knife. She could almost believe Campbell's obsession with pinning the crimes on Chase Burke had prompted him to conceal some minor evidence to push the case in his favor.

But this—this was different.

This was beyond merely "forgetting" to log a cell phone into evidence or writing a questionable report. This was deliberate. There was no other explanation, and that made her feel sick. James Campbell was hiding something far worse than just a bias.

Another thought was also creeping up from the pit of her gut: How was this going to reflect on her? She was his partner. For how long had she turned a blind eye, missed the signs, given him the benefit of the doubt? Could she have stopped him sooner?

The wave of confusion was paralyzing.

Why was it that the men in her life always seemed to betray her? First her ex-husband, Ava's father, with his gambling problem. She'd never seen it, never suspected it. And now, Campbell . . . her partner, her rock, the one constant she thought she could rely on. Was she really going to turn on him?

How did I miss that too?

Her heart pounded as she tried to absorb the possibility that Campbell was dirty. She was at a crossroads, forced to make a decision that would change everything. The weight of it pressed down on her chest.

Shit!

Am I really gonna turn on him?

Her head buzzed with the possibilities and the endless consequences waiting for her on the other side of her choice. A small voice whispered in her mind, urging her to reconsider, to think it over.

You've missed something. Look at it again. It's probably just a misunderstanding.

Just ask him. You owe him that much.

You owe Ava that much.

For a moment, she thought she might throw up. She swallowed the bile rising in her throat, the bitterness of what felt like his betrayal thick on her tongue.

She had to do what was right, no matter how much it tore her apart. She would call SSA Whitaker rather than take it to NYPD internal affairs. If Campbell was trying to cover up or destroy evidence implicating the Gray brothers, then it stood to reason that he was somehow involved in the assassination attempt, and that put his actions squarely in the domain of the federal investigation.

She took a deep breath, trying to steel herself for what had to come next. Her hand shook as she pulled out her phone. Scrolling through her contacts, she found Whitaker's number. Doyle stared at it, her thumb hovering over the screen, her heart pounding in her ears.

Could she really do this? Go behind his back?

Could she betray her partner?

The answer, she realized, was that he had betrayed her first.

And with that, she made her decision.

No turning back now, she told herself. *Please forgive—*

But before she could finish her thought, much less actually hit the call button on her phone, something hard and heavy crashed into the back of her head, and everything went dark.

CHAPTER THIRTY-SIX

Red Hook—so named for its red clay soil and its protrusion into the Upper New York Bay—had the reputation of being one of the roughest places in the city. A major shipping hub in the mid-nineteenth century, the area was occupied by dockworkers living in boarding houses and shantytowns. Poverty and crime soon took root like weeds, impossible to eradicate. Efforts to address the systemic poverty through public housing projects backfired, leaving residents caught in an inescapable cycle of escalating misery and violence, such that by the late twentieth century, in the throes of the crack cocaine epidemic, Red Hook earned the dubious distinction of being one of *Life* magazine's "worst" neighborhoods in the country. The devastation wrought on the low-lying area by Hurricane Sandy in 2012 hadn't done the area any favors.

But Red Hook had one thing going for it. Waterfront property was always in demand, and slowly but surely, gentrification was transforming the landscape. While it was debatable whether this was a net positive for local residents, it was certainly a boon for developers like Vinnie Marasco, who snatched up derelict properties, gave them a mostly cosmetic makeover, and then either sold them at a 1,000 percent markup or, as was the case with the property Chase had been observing for the last hour, left them unfinished and unsold, to claim the tax write-off.

Not much had happened during that hour. The area was quiet, the streets all but deserted as the afternoon gave way to dusk. Chase's eyes never left the old brick building, the lower floor of which was concealed behind a fence wrapped in construction banners promising "Luxury Lofts—Coming Soon," but no one came or went from the site, and there was no sign of movement inside. Although the upper-story windows were all covered with paper, the building didn't look like an active construction site.

The lack of activity bothered him, making him wonder if this was just another dead end. He considered leaving but decided he needed to be certain. The thought of Bonetti slipping through his fingers was too much to bear.

With his bump keys in his pocket and still using the pizza box—now a couple slices lighter—for cover, Chase got out and made his way down the block to the narrow opening in the fence that led up to the front entrance. He was a little surprised to see a video doorbell mounted beside the doorbell. Careful not to look directly at it and holding the pizza box up for display, he pressed the button.

A few seconds later, a gruff voice issued from the device. "Yeah?"

Chase felt a flush of anticipation. *Maybe not a dead end after all.* "Pizza delivery," he said.

"I didn't order a pizza." The man sounded suspicious, but there was something else in his speech pattern . . . a distinctive emphasis on the syllables.

An accent? An Italian accent?

Chase shrugged. "I don't know. I'm just the delivery guy." He pretended to study a receipt. His original plan had always been to feign ignorance, realizing that he had the wrong address, but a sudden impulse prompted him to abandon that plan. "Some guy named Jack ordered it. Said to bring it here."

There was a long silence, and Chase began to worry that he had overplayed his hand. Was Bonetti . . . or whoever was inside the place . . . calling Jack Ruffino to see if the delivery was legit? And if they realized it wasn't, what then?

Still using the pizza box for cover, Chase dropped one hand to his side, letting it drift closer to the SIG nestled in his waistband at the small of his back.

Then the voice spoke again, this time without the earlier hint of suspicion. "Yeah, okay. Bring it inside. Up the stairs to the second floor, first door on the right. It's open."

Chase felt a familiar tingle of adrenaline, the same feeling he'd experienced during deployments when venturing into potentially hostile territory. This wasn't like at Chrysalis or even the confrontation with the Gray brothers at his apartment. He wasn't reacting to contact this time, he was *initiating* it.

There was a click as the entrance lock disengaged, and as he pushed through, he drew the SIG, keeping it hidden under the pizza box. The foyer had been repurposed as the reception lobby for the sales office, but just past the desk, a flight of stairs rose up to the second floor. Chase purposefully ascended the steps, going directly to the designated door, then turned the handle and pushed it open.

If Bonetti was wise to his deception, there was a very good chance that he would be greeted with a bullet, but Chase didn't think that would happen. His gut told him that the initiative was still his, and he fully intended to use it. Careful to keep his expression neutral in order to maintain his cover to the last possible moment, he stepped through the open doorway and entered the apartment.

In that first second, he took in every detail—noting all the blind corners, the layout of the furniture, what might present a tripping hazard or be used as a concealed firing position.

The front door opened into a spacious open-plan living room and dining room feeding into the kitchen and a flight of stairs rising to the upper level where, presumably, the bedrooms were located. The living room sported an L-shaped sectional wrapped around two corners of a large coffee table and facing an enormous HD television on the same wall as the door through which Chase had just entered. Sprawled out on the sectional, glued to the soccer game on the big screen, was the man Chase had come for—Antonio Bonetti.

But Bonetti was not alone.

A second man sat on the opposite leg of the sectional. His attention was also fixed on the game, but he threw a momentary glance in Chase's direction. Chase, who was already adapting his plan to this new development, returned a nodding acknowledgment, even as the man looked away.

The presence of the second man changed the odds, but the element of surprise was still on Chase's side.

But how do I play this?

He could cover both men with the SIG, provided he kept a good standoff distance, but if either one of them made a move, Chase would have no choice but to fire. That would be unfortunate because he had some questions for Bonetti, but the thought of shooting them did not trouble him in the least. These men, whether directly or in a support role, had participated in the attack on Chrysalis, a place that felt almost like a second home to him.

And they tried to harm Tanya.

In military terms, and in Chase's mind, that was enough to make them legitimate targets.

Then he noticed something else. Sitting atop the coffee table, along with a depleted bowl of chips and three empty wineglasses, was a matte-black pistol. It was closer to Bonetti than to the other man but just out of reach unless he leaned forward.

With his attention momentarily on the pistol, Chase didn't realize that Bonetti was looking at him until he heard the man's voice. "Just put it on the table over there. Then piss off, will ya?"

Chase's gaze flicked up to Bonetti's, and in the instant their eyes met, recognition flared in the other man's face.

Shit.

Moving faster than Chase would have believed, Bonetti hurled himself forward and made a grab for the pistol. Chase flipped the pizza box out of the way and brought his left hand forward to brace the SIG, taking aim, not at Bonetti but at the pistol on the coffee table, and squeezed off two shots.

The first bullet punched a hole in the table, six inches from the pistol. The second struck Bonetti's arm just above the wrist, the hollow-point round nearly severing the appendage. Bonetti's momentum carried him forward anyway, but when his extended hand made contact with the butt of the pistol, his fingers simply flopped uselessly, unable to grasp it.

With Bonetti out of the fight, Chase pivoted to the other man just as he made a grab for a weapon concealed in a shoulder holster under his jacket.

"Don't," Chase warned.

The man ignored him, hauling out a big revolver. Chase fired twice, center mass. The man jolted as if he'd just received an electric shock, flopping backward onto the sectional. Chase held his aim on the man a moment longer, just in case there was still a little fight in him—there wasn't—then switched back to Bonetti, who was now clutching his wounded arm and whimpering. Chase didn't care. He needed answers.

"I've got some—" he started, but movement from the staircase cut him off.

He raised his eyes just in time to see a man leap from the staircase, hurtling through the air, one hand stretched out ahead of him, the point of a stiletto protruding from it like the tip of a spear.

Chase brought the SIG up, but he was half a second too late to get a shot off. Instead, he succeeded only in deflecting the blade before the man crashed into him. The SIG flew from Chase's hands as the force of the impact sent him staggering back. The knife wielder landed catlike and sprang at him again, slashing with the stiletto.

Chase barely managed to dodge the attack, the blade slicing the air mere inches from his face. When the next attack came, however, he was ready. He sidestepped, grabbing the man's wrist with both hands, locking it down with a grip fueled by adrenaline. Chase threw an elbow into the man's jaw, stunning him, but not enough to cause him to relinquish his hold on the knife.

Stay on him. Don't give him room.

The man twisted violently, trying to free himself from Chase's grasp. He was strong, and he managed to drag Chase sideways. But rather than fight it, Chase flowed with the motion and used the shift in his momentum to drive his knee up into the man's midsection. The blow landed hard, doubling the man over and knocking the wind out of him. A second knee strike, this one connecting with the man's chin, snapped his head back. His adversary staggered away, the stiletto still clenched in his fist, wild desperation glinting in his eyes. Chase knew another wave of attacks was coming his way.

I have to finish this.

As if on cue, the man let out a guttural roar and surged forward, slashing the stiletto in a frenzy. Chase threw himself to the side, narrowly dodging the blade as it whistled past him, and dove toward his SIG. The instant his fingers closed around the grip, Chase rolled onto his back and brought up the pistol. The man lunged again, the point of the stiletto gleaming as it came straight for Chase. He squeezed the trigger twice, putting two rounds into the man's face before he could close the distance.

Getting to his feet, and careful not to repeat his rookie mistake of losing situational awareness, Chase kept his head on a swivel and scanned his surroundings as he closed with Bonetti. Before the other man could offer a protest or plea, Chase brought the butt of his SIG crashing down on the top of Bonetti's skull.

CHAPTER THIRTY-SEVEN

Pain jolted Doyle back from the darkness—a sharp ache that stabbed through her cranium, throbbing in time with her pulse like the mother of all migraines. She tried to shift position, desperate to find some kind of relief, but her body refused to respond. It wasn't just discomfort, it was a chilling, almost total immobility. Her limbs felt heavy, leaden, as if bound by invisible weights. A surge of panic shot through her, sharper than the pain. Something was horribly, dreadfully wrong.

What happened?

She searched her memory, trying to recall. She remembered finding the rifle in the wreckage of the burned van, then coming to the gut-wrenching realization that Campbell was dirty, then . . .

Then somebody hit me.

She tried to move again and, this time, felt the bite of the restraints that held her wrists together behind her back. *Flex-cuffs,* she guessed. This alone did not account for her immobility, however. With her awareness returning, she realized that she was lying on her left side in an almost fetal curl, with her cheek resting on something rough but slightly yielding.

A carpeted floor?

The faint vibration humming through the surface upon which she lay provided the final clue she needed to fully grasp her situation. She was in a moving vehicle, crammed into the confined, suffocating space of a trunk.

A few agonizing seconds later, she felt the slight change in inertia as the vehicle braked to a stop. There was a subtle increase in the level of ambient noise—a window lowering—and then she heard an all too familiar voice. "I'll be back to pick up my car, but I was never here. Got it?"

Doyle's blood ran cold. It was Campbell. She had trusted him, let him in.

Son of a bitch.

But her rage wasn't solely for him. Some of it was aimed squarely at herself. She'd misjudged him. Badly.

"Never saw you." The second voice, barely audible, belonged to the officer who had escorted her out to the wreck.

The noise level changed again as the window was raised, and then Doyle felt the vehicle accelerate. She tested her bonds again. The fingers of her left hand had gone numb due to lack of circulation, not from the restraints but because she was lying on her left arm. Her right hand, however, was still working, and she was able to curl her fingers down to make contact with her bindings, confirming her suspicion that Campbell had used flex-cuffs—disposable plastic handcuffs that were basically double-loop heavy-duty zip ties.

Flex-cuffs had a vulnerability. Once tightened, the one-way ratchet that kept the loops from slipping could be loosened or broken by forcing the bound hands apart with a sudden, violent motion. Unfortunately, her present body position did not allow her the freedom of movement to take that action.

Still, the mere possibility that she might be able to free herself was a ray of hope shining in the darkness.

She tried moving again, twisting her body to reawaken her numb left arm. The attempt was only partly successful. Her arm remained pinned under her body, but she was able to move her bound hands a little, enough to ascertain that Campbell had taken her sidearm and phone.

But maybe he didn't get everything.

Extending her arms as far as she could and bringing her knees toward her chest to the extent the close confines allowed, she strained to reach the ankle holster where she kept a little Glock 43. The effort sent fresh waves of pain throbbing in her skull, but she kept trying . . . stretching . . . reaching . . . until her fingers brushed the empty holster.

She slumped in disappointment. Of course, Campbell would have known to check her for an ankle carry.

As she lay there, breathing heavily, waiting for the pain to subside so that she could try something else, she heard Campbell's voice again. "Call C. M."

With an effort, she brought her breathing under control and cocked her head, listening. Her hopes that he would go hands-free were quickly dashed. There was no outgoing ring tone. Her only clue that the call had gone out came when she heard Campbell say, "It's me."

There was a pause, then, in an angry voice, Campbell said, "No, everything's *not* all right. Your boys did a piss-poor job of cleaning up after themselves, and now I've got to take care of it. You promised me it wouldn't come to that."

Your boys?

The significance of those words hit Doyle like a gut punch as the pieces fell into place.

Campbell was speaking to the person who had hired the Gray brothers to assassinate Congresswoman Hemsworth. And now he was doing damage control—because of her. She'd give anything to hear what the person at the other end of the line was saying.

"I tried, damn it!" Campbell went on. "She just wouldn't let it go . . . no, it's fine . . . I've got a better idea. I'll pin it on Chase Burke. Win-win, right?"

A pause. "Well, thank you, Curt. It's nice to feel appreciated," Campbell said, but Doyle could tell he was being sarcastic.

"Fuck! Fuck! Fuck!" shouted Campbell as she heard him slam his palm against the steering wheel again and again.

It was fleeting, maybe even a bit naive for her to think so, but Doyle thought she heard it—a glimpse of the conflict within him.

He doesn't want to do this. He's trapped, forced by someone who wields power over him.

Whoever they were, they had their hooks deep into Campbell. He was someone's puppet.

A puppet too weak to cut his own strings.

Doyle remained perfectly still, waiting for more, but when Campbell spoke again, it wasn't to the person on the other end of a phone line. "I guess you heard that?"

He's talking to me, thought Doyle. She didn't respond, biting back a retort.

"Whatever," Campbell went on with a derisive snort. "It'll be over soon enough. It's too bad, really. You're a good detective, Alice. Too good for your own good."

Realization set in, and Doyle's mind raced faster.

Oh God. He's going to do it.

"Why didn't you just follow my lead? If you had, you'd be home with Ava instead of in the trunk of your Mazda. And now, I have to finish this."

He's going to do it, Doyle thought again. *He's really going to kill me!*

"For Ava's sake," said Campbell, his voice flat, emotionless. "I'll make this quick. And I'll make sure Chase Burke pays for everything that's happened."

CHAPTER THIRTY-EIGHT

With Bonetti down for the count, Chase quickly checked the rest of the loft to ensure that there were no more surprises waiting for him, then set about binding the man's wound. After the trouble he'd gone to in making sure that he didn't kill Bonetti, it would have been a shame for him to bleed out before he could answer a few questions.

Once the bleeding was under control, Chase used electrical cords to lash Bonetti's arms and ankles to a dining chair. When he was satisfied that the man was bound fast, he slapped his face a few times until he came around.

A low moan escaped Bonetti's lips before he was fully conscious. Then, as the pain of his nearly severed hand registered, a torrent of guttural Italian spewed forth. *"Cazzo. Figlio di puttana . . . il mio braccio!"*

"That sounds bad," remarked Chase, leaning back just enough to avoid a potential headbutt.

Bonetti's eyes blazed with murder. "You son of a whore. I'll tear your fucking head off."

"Hmm. That'll be quite a trick with just one hand. And trust me, if you don't get to a hospital soon, you're going to lose that hand. Maybe everything below the elbow. But don't worry, I'll call an ambulance . . . after you tell me what I want to know."

Bonetti let out a bark of laughter that quickly dissolved into a curse as the pain reasserted itself. "You'll call an ambulance? Sure.

And after that you'll tuck me into bed and read me a bedtime story? Go to hell."

Chase backhanded Bonetti in the face hard enough to make the chair creak.

"Wrong answer. Pay attention, Tony."

Bonetti glared at him, the pain making his eyes water. *"Che cazzo vuoi?"*

"English."

"What the fuck do you want?"

"I told you. I want to talk. Specifically, I want to talk about who hired you to kidnap Congresswoman Hemsworth."

"I don't know what you're talking about."

Chase shook his head. "We both know you were at Chrysalis last night. You saw me, I saw you. So, let's skip the part where you play dumb and move on to the part where you tell me who's pulling your strings. Because right now, you're wasting time, Tony. And time isn't something you have a lot of. Not if you want to keep that hand of yours."

Bonetti's resolve appeared to waver, but he remained defiant. "Forget it. I lose a hand, I lose a hand. I talk to you, and I lose my life."

"You've got that backward. Just ask your buddy there." Chase gestured to the body occupying the other side of the sectional. "Answering my questions is the only chance you've got to walk away from this."

"You'll kill me anyway," Bonetti muttered.

Chase tilted his head to one side and said, "Tony, Tony . . . I'm a sommelier, not a hit man. I don't kill people for fun. I pair wines with meals, for crying out loud. This?" He gestured around the bloodied apartment. "This is just me trying to have a conversation. But if you don't start talking, I'm going to have to get . . . creative."

"A sommelier? What kind of fucking sommelier does this?" Bonetti asked, his eyes darting around the room.

"The kind with a bad temper," Chase replied, deadpan, pressing the tip of his pistol against Bonetti's left knee. "You're losing your knee in three, two . . ."

"Wait! Wait! Fuck!"

Chase kept the pistol poised, but his finger had stopped pulling the slack in the trigger.

"Talk. Fast," Chase barked.

"I was there, okay? We were supposed to grab the woman."

"Why? For ransom?"

"Ransom? That bitch is worth more dead."

"Who wants her dead? Give me a name."

Bonetti eyed the gun a moment before relenting. "Stine."

"Judah Stine? He's rotting in a federal prison."

"You think that changes anything? He's as powerful there as he ever was. He's still calling the shots."

"So why didn't he just have you kill her in the restaurant? Would have been easier."

"He doesn't just want her dead. He wants her to suffer. On camera. *Voleva fare di lei un esempio.* He wants to send a message, make her an example. This is what happens to the people who come after him."

Bonetti hadn't told Chase anything new but merely confirmed what everyone already suspected. "What about the sniper? Was that backup in case you screwed up?"

Bonetti shook his head. "I don't know anything about that."

Chase studied him for a long moment, searching for any flicker of deception. There was none. Having broken, Bonetti had no reason to lie.

Which left him right back at square one.

"All right, Tony. It's your lucky day. I'm going to call a friend of mine. Here's how this works. You tell her everything you told me, and she'll make sure that you're taken care of. She might even protect you from Judah Stine."

He took out one of the new burner phones he'd purchased earlier and punched in Doyle's number.

The line rang and rang, and then he heard "You've reached Detective Alice Doyle. I'm not able to take your call at the moment . . ."

"Looks like this might take a bit longer than I thought," Chase said, ending the call. "Good thing I brought pizza."

Bonetti just glared at him.

CHAPTER THIRTY-NINE

James Campbell gripped the wheel of Doyle's Mazda, his knuckles pale against the dark leather.

"Such a nice neighborhood," he muttered, scanning the streets of Morningside Heights as he drove through the familiar, tree-lined blocks.

And he meant it too. The neighborhood, home to numerous religious and educational institutions, most notably the Cathedral of St. John the Divine and Columbia University, with historic brownstones standing shoulder to shoulder with modern apartment buildings, was an oasis of urban serenity.

Parking sucks, though.

It was his third orbit around the block in search of a spot close enough to Doyle's building to make logical sense for the scene he planned to stage. It didn't have to be perfect, but it did have to make sense.

He finally got lucky, spotting someone getting into a car just around the corner from Doyle's building. He stopped short, and when, after what felt like an interminable delay, the car pulled out, he slid the Mazda into the vacant spot and turned off the engine.

Campbell closed his eyes. He didn't want to do this. Not to Alice. Especially not to Alice. But he was in too deep. Too many secrets, too many favors owed. He'd tried to push back, had even considered turning himself in, but then they'd said her name.

Ava.

That threat had broken him, twisting him into submission. If he didn't bring this investigation to a close in a way that would satisfy his masters, they would go after Ava.

And that was something he couldn't live with.

He took a few deep breaths to calm his nerves.

"How you doing back there, Alice?"

As with all his previous attempts to engage her during the long drive up, Doyle did not answer. He'd given her a pretty good thump back at the auto pound lot, so it was possible that she was still out cold or even dead. But the more likely explanation was that she was playing possum, maybe hoping that he would leave her for dead or that she could even somehow turn the tables on him. He didn't expect her to make it easy. Alice was a fighter, and he respected that, but part of him almost hoped she wouldn't wake up at all. It would make what he had to do easier. Less . . . personal.

Sitting in the driver's seat of the parked vehicle, Campbell watched the flow of the neighborhood—joggers, people walking their dogs, students hurrying back to their dorms—gradually decrease as dusk deepened. When at last both street and sidewalk were clear, he got out and went around to the back, holding Doyle's little Glock 43 low but ready. He hit the button on the key fob to open the rear hatch.

Doyle lay exactly as he had left her, curled up on the carpeted floor of the Mazda, her back to the opening, her wrists bound with flex-cuffs. In the glow of the interior light, he could see a crust of blood matted in her hair.

"Huh," he murmured. "Maybe I *did* hit you a little too hard."

That wouldn't really complicate things too much. His plan was to make it look as if Doyle had been killed after getting out of her car. It hardly mattered whether it was a bullet that killed her or blunt force trauma. Still, depending on how critically the CSU tech read the scene, there might be questions about the sequence of events—questions that would challenge his easy interpretation, that Chase Burke had lain in wait and ambushed Doyle.

Keeping the Glock trained on her, he cautiously reached out, brushing the hair away from her neck and pressing two fingers against her exposed throat.

Pulse strong, he thought. *Still alive.*

He glanced up and down the block. Still clear, but that could change at any moment. He needed to get this done. But the thought of Ava lingered in his mind. Alice was her whole world now that her shit-for-a-dad had got himself killed in a fire. Though he couldn't be sure, Campbell had always believed Ava's father knew he had no way out of his gambling debts and had decided to end it once and for all, by dying a hero's death.

Campbell didn't fail to notice the irony of the situation. Just like Ava's dad, he was also in too deep.

Would it change anything if I were to swallow my own gun?

He'd do it in an instant if he thought it would save Ava, but Alice was like a dog with a bone. She wouldn't let go.

And then, they would come for her daughter.

No, if he didn't follow through, they would hurt Ava in unimaginable ways. They had him trapped, and Alice's life was the ransom.

"I know you're awake, Alice. And I bet you're just dying to know why I'm doing this, am I right? This is your chance to find out."

He hoped her natural curiosity would overpower her impulse toward self-preservation. But Doyle remained motionless.

The sudden buzz of a phone in his pocket startled him. It was Doyle's phone. He took a step back and drew out the device. "It's for you," he said, glancing at the illuminated screen. "Unknown number. I'll bet it's your friend Burke. Want me to answer it?"

Doyle did not stir.

Campbell continued staring at the phone, wondering whether to take the call. If it *was* Burke, this might be a way to lure him into the area, maybe even putting him at the scene of Doyle's murder. On the other hand, talking to Burke might do just the opposite, inadvertently giving him an alibi.

The phone went silent before he could make up his mind.

Well, I guess that takes care of that, he thought, returning his attention to Doyle.

He reached down to pull her out of the trunk, then saw that her hands were no longer bound together.

He froze. She didn't.

She struck like a rattlesnake, twisting around, delivering a quick jab aimed at his groin. Something flashed—light glinting off a steel edge—and then he felt the impact against his right thigh. He flinched, trying to retreat, but she struck again, and this time, the steel was red with his blood.

He whipped the pistol at her head. The blow landed with a satisfying crack, and Doyle went down. Her blade—a little T-handled push knife that he must have missed in his initial search—flew from her grasp.

He leaped back, his pant leg already damped with blood, and brought the Glock up.

"Hey! What's going on?"

The voice yanked him back to the moment. He spun around toward the voice and saw a young man, shirtless, wearing running shorts, coming up the sidewalk behind them. "Fuck," he rasped and almost shot the jogger. Instead, he grabbed his badge case, displaying his shield. "Police business. Fuck off."

The kid balked, though whether at the sight of the badge or the pistol, it was impossible to say, then began backing away. Campbell turned just in time to see Doyle duck around the side of the Mazda.

"Shit!" He started after her, but the sudden movement sent waves of pain radiating from the wounds in his thigh, and he fell against the side of the Mazda, leaning against it to stay on his feet. He was starting to feel lightheaded, darkness closing in at the edges of his vision.

"Alice, listen to me," he shouted. "It's . . . it's not what you think."

He tried to hang on to consciousness for just a few more seconds, but it was an impossible task.

She must have nicked my femoral artery.

Suddenly, he was falling, and as he went down, he felt a knee dig into his back. As his breath went out in a whoosh, Doyle seized the hand that held the Glock in both of hers and slammed his arm down hard on the pavement. He tried to hang onto the weapon, tried to push Doyle away, but he was too slow, too weak.

His last thought, as consciousness faded, was that he'd failed—failed to protect Ava.

I'm sorry.

CHAPTER FORTY

Doyle snatched up the Glock and aimed it at Campbell, backpedaling a few feet to create some standoff distance. "Give it up, James."

Campbell didn't reply, didn't even move. He just lay there, his eyes closed, panting, the fight seemingly gone out of him. Doyle swiped a hand across her face, smearing away the blood that was streaming from a gash in her forehead and getting in her eyes, and then began slowly easing forward, ready to put Campbell down for good if he so much as twitched. But her partner . . . the man who had tried to kill her . . . didn't move.

She grabbed the handcuffs from his belt case, expertly snapping them around his wrists. Even with his hands bound, she remained vigilant, frisking him one-handed, removing his pistol, his backup, searching his belt for a hidden blade like the one she had used to cut her flex-cuffs and turn the tables on him, and taking both of their phones from his pocket. Only when she was certain that he posed no threat did she relax her guard. Head throbbing, emotionally and physically drained, she sagged against the Mazda and used her phone to call 911.

She gave the dispatcher her name and badge number and requested paramedics and a federal law enforcement response. Based on what had happened at the impound yard, she didn't know who in the NYPD could be trusted. She knew she ought to also call SSA Whitaker, get him involved, if only to cover her own ass, but her need for answers was more urgent.

She checked Campbell's injuries. Her knife had made two deep cuts in his thigh; though he was losing a lot of blood, it wasn't spurting out, which indicated that the blade had missed his femoral artery—or at least hadn't severed it completely.

He would live, if the ambulance got there quickly.

She wasn't sure how she felt about that.

"Why did you do this to me? I don't understand, James. Who in the hell are you working for? Who's calling the shots?"

Campbell opened his eyes. He stared back at her, eyes full of feral rage.

"You . . . you have no idea—"

"I heard that call you made," she said, cutting him off. "You've been covering for the Gray brothers. Hiding evidence." She searched her memory for more details from the overheard phone call. "Who's C. M.?"

Campbell gave no answer.

"You know you're going away for this. How long is up to you. Do yourself a favor. Get out ahead of it." She leaned back, regarding him. "Well, I guess you do have the right to remain silent."

Then she held his phone in front of his face. "Smile."

Campbell's brow furrowed in confusion, then his eyes widened when he saw the home screen light up, but Doyle was already scrolling through Campbell's contact list. She found the listing for C. M. There was no other information, but there was a picture—a slightly younger Campbell and a middle-aged white guy, side-hugging for the camera.

She took a picture of the screen with her own phone and then showed it to Campbell. "Is that C. M.? Looks like you two are pretty close. Who is he? Someone on the job? Is he a cop?"

Campbell had closed his eyes again.

"I'm going to find out who he is, James. It's just a matter of time. The longer you wait to cooperate, the less leverage you're going to have."

Campbell remained stonily silent.

Doyle leaned back against the Mazda. So what if Campbell didn't talk? She would find C. M. without his help. In fact, it was better if he didn't cooperate.

But that was something she would worry about tomorrow. Right now, she just needed something to make the pain go away.

Where are those paramedics?

She strained her ears, listening for the sound of approaching sirens, but instead heard only the buzz of an incoming call on her phone.

Unknown number.

She recalled Campbell's earlier taunt. *I'll bet it's your friend Burke.*

What if it was Burke?

She hit the button to accept the call.

CHAPTER FORTY-ONE

"Detective. It's Chase Burke."

Chase heard a noise, like a faint gasp, and then Doyle's voice came over the line. "Burke. Are you ready to come in?"

Despite the bravado underpinning the question, there was an unmistakable note of strain in Doyle's voice. Chase decided to ignore the question. "I thought you should know, I found one of the hitters that tried to abduct Tanya. He was taking his orders from Judah Stine. If you had worked with me instead of trying to put me away, we all could have saved ourselves a lot of trouble."

"Burke . . . Chase, just hold on a second." There was a rustling sound as if Doyle was changing positions. "Okay, start from the beginning."

"Remember how I told you I saw one of the guys outside the restaurant? Saw his face? Well, his name is Antonio Bonetti. He's a driver for Jack Ruffino. I don't know if Ruffino is the go-between with Stine or not. That's something you can ask Bonetti."

"Chase, you're not making any sense. Just slow down and tell me what's going on. No, better yet just tell me where you are, and I'll come to you."

Chase gave a snort of derision. "Sure. Let's meet for coffee."

"Just listen for a minute, will you? Things have changed here. I know that you're not a part of this. We can clear everything up, but you've got to trust me, okay?"

"Trust you? Right. Because you're the good cop."

"Chase . . ."

He cut her off. "Save it. I didn't call to negotiate." He glanced over at his prisoner, who still glared at him with barely contained hatred. "Like I said, I tracked down Bonetti. He's ready to flip on Stine if you're willing to make a deal. He's at a loft in Red Hook." He gave the address, even though he suspected Doyle and her partner were probably already pinning down his location from the call data. "By the way," he added, "you're welcome."

He was about to end the call, but Doyle's plea reached out across the distance. "Chase, listen to me. Campbell's dirty. He was working with whoever hired the Gray brothers and was trying to frame you. I know that you're innocent. You don't have to keep running."

Chase stared at the phone, his mind reeling from the revelation. Was she telling the truth? Was Campbell really working with the assassins?

It sounded too crazy to be anything but true.

But that didn't mean he could trust her.

He ended the call without another word and immediately began stripping the phone. When it was reduced to its constituent parts, he turned to Bonetti. "Looks like it's your lucky day, Tony. You get to live. In a little while, a lady cop is going to pay you a visit. Tell her what you told me and ask her to put you in the witness protection program."

"Go fuck yourself."

Chase just shrugged and headed out.

Less than ten minutes later, a trio of US government–issued SUVs, bearing a small contingent of US Marshals, rolled up in front of the loft and swarmed the building.

It took a little longer for Doyle to get there.

Ignoring the advice of the EMT who, after assessing her injuries, strongly recommended she be taken to the nearest emergency room for a full traumatic brain injury assessment, Doyle stayed on the scene, awaiting the arrival of Supervisory Special Agent Whitaker and a team of agents from the JTTF. She knew her boss would have a lot of questions and felt that staying put and preserving the crime scene was the right call. Because, until she could find hard evidence to link Campbell to the mysterious C. M., she had only hearsay—literally—to connect her partner to the assassination conspiracy. If one of Campbell's fellow corrupt cops found a way to erase all the forensic evidence implicating him in the assault on her, then it would be his word against hers.

Not surprisingly, her accusations against Campbell were initially received with skepticism, but after she walked SSA Whitaker through the details of what had happened, he grudgingly admitted that her story seemed consistent with the evidence.

"And I'll have agents keeping an eye on your place and Ava's school," Whitaker said. "Just in case."

But, notwithstanding that allowance, after taking her statement, he ordered her aboard the waiting ambulance and verbally placed her on administrative leave pending the outcome of the investigation.

Then she told him about her conversation with Chase Burke.

Now, half an hour later, she was following Whitaker up the stairs to the loft where Burke had located and subdued a suspect identified as Antonio Bonetti.

"He needs to go to the ER," reported the lead marshal, "but he's refusing medical attention until he can talk to, and I quote, 'the lady cop.'"

Whitaker shot a glance at Doyle. "Refusing medical treatment seems to be a common theme tonight." He then looked past the marshal to the carnage in the loft's front room. His eyes widened as he took in the scene—two dead men and a wounded suspect tied to a chair. "Burke did this?"

Doyle shook her head uncertainly. "I really couldn't say, sir. He just told me to come here."

"He's a menace," Whitaker declared. "I want him brought in."

"Yes, sir. I'm working on it."

"Not anymore, you aren't. You're off the case." He raised a hand to forestall any protest. "I believe you, Alice, and I'm sure the investigation will clear you of any wrongdoing, but until it's official, you can't be a part of this."

"I understand, sir. But Burke *is* willing to talk to me. We wouldn't be here otherwise."

Whitaker frowned. "I'll take it under advisement. Now, let's see what our . . ." He glanced over at the bound man. ". . . subject has to say."

As if on cue, Bonetti looked over at them, focusing on Doyle. "Give me a deal, or you don't get anything."

Doyle and Whitaker exchanged a glance, then the FBI man took the lead. "Mr. . . . Bonetti, is it?"

Bonetti shook his head. "Deal first."

"All right. Assuming that you have something worth dealing for . . . what do you want?"

"Put me in . . . what do you call it? Witness protection. And I'll tell you everything."

Whitaker regarded him for a long moment. "I'm not authorized to make that deal, but I can probably convince the attorney general to sign off on it. But you've got to give me something before I make that call."

"I'll tell you what I told the other guy. Judah Stine ordered us to kidnap the congresswoman. Give me a deal, and I'll say it in court. Otherwise, forget it."

"Kidnap? Not kill?"

Bonetti bared his teeth in a grimace. "Make your call, policeman."

Whitaker gave him a hard stare for a moment, then took out his phone and stepped away. Doyle waited until her boss was out of earshot, then addressed Bonetti. "Did Stine hire Brad and Nigel Gray?"

Bonetti looked like he might just snarl at her, but then he replied, "I don't know them."

"What about C. M.? You know who that is?"

Bonetti gave a little head shake.

Doyle frowned. With Bonetti's testimony, they would probably be able to have Judah Stine transferred to a dark hole in the ground for the rest of his natural life, but it still left half the mystery unsolved.

Who is C. M.?

Whitaker returned just then. "All right, Bonetti. You've got your deal. Once you get that hand looked at, the marshals will transfer you to a safe house for debriefing."

"Good," said Bonetti. "Now, get me to a fucking hospital."

From the back seat of his borrowed 4Runner, Chase watched as a procession of federal agents, clustered around the two medics wheeling an ambulance gurney bearing Bonetti, filed out of the building. Alice Doyle, looking somewhat the worse for wear, was part of the group, but Detective Campbell was conspicuously absent.

If Doyle was telling the truth about Campbell being a dirty cop, then she was probably being truthful about his involvement with the Gray brothers, and that meant she was a step ahead of him in finding the identity of the person responsible for the attempt on Tanya's life.

He knew he could probably leave it there, let the feds do the rest, but his mind kept returning to the previous night, to Tanya bleeding out in his arms and to the promise he had made to kill the man responsible for it all. At the time, his righteous fury had been aimed at one man—Bonetti—but now he knew that Bonetti had merely been a pawn in Judah Stine's game, just as Brad and Nigel Gray, and for that matter Detective Campbell, had been someone else's pawns.

Unfortunately, he didn't have the first clue who was behind it all.

But Alice Doyle did. And just as he had led her to Bonetti and, ultimately, Judah Stine, she was going to lead him to the unknown mastermind.

As the vehicles pulled away, flashers illuminated, Chase started the 4Runner and trailed after them.

CHAPTER FORTY-TWO

London, England

The sleek black Mercedes-Benz S-Class, its windows tinted to an impenetrable darkness, looked a little too much like a hearse for Damien's liking, but when it rolled up in front of the safe house, he climbed in anyway. If the client's offer was genuine, then this was his best chance—maybe his only chance—to get back across the pond so he could avenge his brother's death.

But what if it was a deception? A betrayal?

Well, it isn't like I have much choice in the matter, is it?

The car bore him through the night, along the banks of the Thames, out to the London City Airport, through a security gate, and directly onto the tarmac to a waiting Gulfstream V.

As he stepped onto the airstair leading to the posh cabin of the aircraft, a flight attendant stood waiting for him at the top, her smile warm but professional.

"Welcome aboard, sir. You're the last one to arrive, so if you could—"

"The last one?" he interrupted, a flash of tension tightening his muscles.

"Yes, sir. As I was saying, if you could just find a seat and fasten your seatbelt, we'll be taking off shortly."

Before he could challenge her once more, a gravelly voice with a Scottish brogue bellowed, "Well, well. Look who decided to join the party."

Damien, startled, turned his head toward the three hard men already seated at the very back of the cabin. Then he did a double take on one of them. "Mac?"

Ian "Mac" McAllister, a burly Scot with a shaved head, had been a demolitions expert in Damien's SRR unit and, like Damien, had taken his skills into the private sector as a contractor after leaving the military.

"Well, don't just stand there like a daftie," Mac said. "Sit yersel' down so we can get this show on the road."

With his heart rate already returning to normal, Damien settled into one of the plush leather seats while the flight attendant closed the door in preparation for takeoff. When he was buckled in, he faced his old comrade-in-arms. "Mac, you rogue. What are you doing here?"

"Babysitting you." He nodded to the other two men. "These are my mates. That's Nate." He indicated a dark-haired, wiry figure who looked like he was on the verge of falling asleep in his chair. "He's my long gunner. And that young punk over there"—he thrust his chin at the other passenger, a stocky young man with curly red hair and a baby face—"that's Ollie."

Ollie nodded perfunctorily but then added, "Brad was my mate. I'm so sorry."

"We're all sorry, Damien," added Mac. "That's why we're here."

As much as he appreciated their condolences, Damien remained confused. "How did you hear about Brad? I only just found out myself a few hours ago."

"Got a call. Strange bloke, using a voice changer. Told us you might need an assist in hunting down the scum who killed Brad. Wasn't sure I believed him until the money showed up in our account. And here we are."

Damien's mind boggled at this revelation. He had known that the client was wealthy and likely connected, but to put such an operation together in a matter of hours indicated not only wealth and power but organization on a scale approaching the capabilities of a nation-state.

Who is this bloody client, anyway?

Mac was still talking, going on about how his team had been kitting up to "take care of some business for His Majesty"—shorthand for a government contract—when the call from the client came in. Damien just nodded along, his mind already moving forward in time, resetting the game board. When he'd taken up the gauntlet, setting his sights on the murderer Chase Burke, he'd expected that it would be a singleton operation—finding Burke, stalking him, waiting for the right moment to pounce. It was a dangerous way to operate, especially as Burke had revealed himself to be something more than just an everyday wine steward. In a one-on-one matchup, the roles of hunter and hunted could easily be reversed. But now, with the support of Mac and his mates, it would be a very different game. They would box Burke in and then close around him like a fist.

And then what?

The thought came to him from out of the blue.

After you get your revenge, then what?

He would never be able to return home, never be able to hold Cassie in his arms, never be able to openly cheer for Allie. He could always reinvent himself, adopt a new identity, continue to ply his deadly trade as ever before . . . maybe even sign on with Mac's outfit. But that was just work. And work was what you did so that you could live.

As the jet accelerated down the tarmac, he gazed out the porthole, watching as the city lights flashed by and then quickly fell away below, and felt a profound sense of loss. He hadn't just lost his brothers, he had lost his family too. His life as he knew it was over.

Worry about that later, he told himself. *After Chase Burke is dead.*

CHAPTER FORTY-THREE

New York

Doyle had barely made it through the door before Ava came bounding toward her, arms outstretched.

"Mommy!"

Doyle smiled, her daughter's voice a balm on her soul after what she'd been forced to endure. She hugged Ava tight, breathing in the familiar scent of her shampoo.

"Thanks for everything," Doyle said to the sitter. "You're a lifesaver."

"Always a pleasure. Should I sleep over? I can take her to school in the morning if you want?"

"No, we'll be fine. I'll drop her off. Colleagues of mine will pick her up after school, but I'd like you to be here when she gets back."

———

The next morning, Doyle was in the kitchen preparing breakfast when Ava walked in with her small backpack.

"Hey, sweetie," Doyle said. "Scrambled eggs and toast?"

"With a side of apples!" Ava piped up with a grin. "And extra cinnamon on the toast!"

"Extra cinnamon, coming right up!"

As she worked, she stole glances at Ava, who sat at the kitchen table, swinging her legs and humming a tune. Doyle hated how her schedule kept her from Ava, but Ava seemed to take it in stride. Still, she worried about what Ava's reaction would be once she realized "Uncle" James wasn't coming over anymore.

As if on cue, Ava looked up from her half-eaten plate of eggs and fumbled for something inside her backpack. "Here, Mommy. Can you give it to Uncle James?" she asked, her voice hopeful. "Do you think he'll like it?"

Doyle's heart skipped as she took in the drawing. Ava had drawn herself and Campbell standing together, smiling under a bright yellow sun. Campbell's stick figure had a badge drawn on his chest in blue crayon and a little heart above his head.

Doyle forced a smile, pushing down the knot in her stomach. "I'm sure he will, sweetheart. It's beautiful, just like you."

After breakfast, Doyle hailed a taxi to take Ava to school. Doyle's Mazda 3 was now a crime scene and, ironically, had been towed to Erie Basin, where it would stay until the disposition of the case against Campbell, which probably wouldn't happen any time soon. They shared a joyful ride, Ava nestled against her, talking animatedly about her favorite teacher. Doyle listened, trying to soak up every word, knowing it would be hours before she could see Ava again.

On her way back to her apartment, Doyle's thoughts returned to Campbell. Last she heard he was still in surgery. The good news was that Bonetti was singing like a jay, and the federal prosecutor was already moving quickly to roll up all the little fish involved in the actual execution of the attempted abduction in order to bolster the case against Judah Stine and his senior lieutenants in the New York criminal underworld. And despite the fact that Chase Burke had done most of the actual legwork, as far as SSA Whitaker was concerned, Doyle had been the one to bring Bonetti in, which not only was a feather in her cap but made the JTTF look good too. That would hopefully absorb some of the blowback that would come from having a dirty cop on the payroll.

A few blocks away from her apartment, she asked the cab driver to head down to the Westside Market on Broadway and 110th Street. She needed to stock up on some supplies.

She grabbed a basket and made her way to the produce section while her mind continued to churn over the details of the case. Bonetti claimed no knowledge of the sniper who had fired the bullet that had nearly killed the congresswoman, but that didn't mean the order hadn't come from someone higher up the food chain.

Maybe even the mysterious C. M.

I hope Campbell will flip, she thought, picking up a bunch of still-green bananas and setting them in her basket. *He knows who's calling the shots.*

"Good morning, Detective."

Doyle was too much the professional to be startled, but her pulse still quickened when she recognized the voice coming from behind her. "Hello, Chase," she said, turning slowly to face him. Burke was wearing a ballcap, but she could tell that he'd cut his hair since their last meeting—no doubt one of the reasons he'd managed to avoid detection. "How the hell did you find me?"

He ignored the question. "Congrats on the arrest. You're the hero of the hour."

She narrowed her gaze at him. "Bringing you in would be like the cherry on top of that sundae. Care to give me a good reason why I shouldn't put you in handcuffs right now?"

His mouth curled into a half smile. "Is that really what you want?"

"More than anything."

His smile broadened. "I guess that could be fun."

The unexpected entendre caught her off guard. "Wait, that's not what I meant."

"Let's cut the crap, okay? You're not going to arrest me. You know I'm innocent. So, enough posturing. Let's just have a nice conversation, okay?"

"When I said you were innocent, that was before I learned that you killed those two men at Bonetti's place. Or are you going to claim that was self-defense too?"

Burke waved the question away. "Tell me what you know about Brad and Nigel Gray."

"You're nuts, Burke. Why would I tell you anything?"

"Because you owe me. I gave you Bonetti. I practically gift wrapped him."

Doyle frowned. "Maybe this hasn't sunk in yet. I'm a cop. You're not. So, while I appreciate you doing your duty as a *concerned citizen*"—she made a point of rolling her eyes—"and providing a tip that led to the arrest of a suspect, we're not partners. This isn't a give-and-take. So, instead of playing vigilante, why don't you get out of the way and let us do our job. Before you get in *real* trouble."

"Those men came to my place. *My place.* And your partner was trying to pin all of this on me. So, this isn't just me 'playing vigilante.' Somehow, I'm mixed up in this, and I want to know why. And I think you know more than you're telling me."

Doyle frowned. Burke was right.

Damn him.

And as much as her professional instincts told her it was a bad idea to share privileged information with a civilian, her gut told her that giving Burke a sniff might just be the thing to crack the case wide open. "Who's C. M.?"

Burke's only reaction was a slight upward eye movement, a response typically indicative of a memory search. "Why don't you tell me?"

"Campbell called C. M. last night. Right before he tried to kill me. I think C. M. hired the Gray brothers to assassinate the congresswoman."

"Your partner tried to kill you? I guess that explains all the . . ." He gestured to his face. "Bruises."

"Yeah," replied Doyle, unselfconsciously. "But I still kicked his ass."

Burke shrugged. "C. M. doesn't ring any bells for me. I take it Campbell isn't talking?"

"No." She gave him a hard stare. "Are you sure you don't know who C. M. is? Anyone with those initials? I got the distinct impression that he knows you. Or at least knows who you are. I think he's the one who sent Brad and Nigel over to your place."

Burke's eyes reflected a glimmer of curiosity. "What exactly did he say?"

"I could only hear Campbell's side of it." She searched her memory, trying to recall the conversation. "He said, 'Your boys left a mess.' Something like that. I think he was talking about the Gray brothers leaving evidence at your place."

"What evidence?"

"That key you left me. It belonged to a van. Somebody . . . probably Brad, tried to torch it to destroy any evidence, but it didn't get everything. I found a rifle in the wreck, which I'm betting is what they used to shoot the congresswoman. Campbell was actively trying to hide it. Right after I found the rifle, he jumped me."

"He say anything else?"

"He said that he would have to take care of the mess, which I assumed meant me. He was going to kill me outside my place and then try to pin it on you. The way he talked about it made me think that C. M. knew who you were." The *something else* came back to her. "Curt."

Burke's head snapped up. "What?"

"Campbell said . . ." She paused again, trying to remember exactly what she had heard. "He said, 'Thank you, Curt.' The *C* in C. M. is for Curt."

She could tell that a chord had been struck. Burke visibly paled. "That means something to you, doesn't it?"

"I'm . . ." Burke's head twitched from side to side. "I'm not sure."

"Oh, wait," said Doyle. "I just remembered. I've got a picture."

She took out her phone, brought up the picture she'd taken of Campbell's contact list, and then showed it to him. "This is C. M."

Burke's gaze locked on the image, and in that instant, Doyle saw total recognition. "You know him, don't you? Who is he, Chase?"

Burke didn't reply, but his body language was all the answer she needed. He took an uncertain step back, as if stunned by what he had just seen, but then his expression hardened. Without a word, he turned and walked away, his strides long and purposeful.

"Chase, wait! Who is he?"

Burke didn't look back.

Doyle set the basket down and went after him, but in the moment it had taken her to realize what he was doing, his pace had quickened, and she had to break into a run just to keep him in sight. Walking, but at a pace faster than some people could run, Burke leaped over the chain blocking an unused checkout lane and bounded through the exit doors.

Doyle thought she was only a few steps behind him, but when she burst through the doors and out onto the sidewalk, Burke was gone. She searched the street in both directions, hoping to glimpse his retreating back, but there was no sign of him. It was as if Chase Burke had vanished off the face of the earth.

CHAPTER FORTY-FOUR

You know him, don't you? Who is he, Chase?

Doyle's words echoed in his head like an accusation.

Who's C. M.?

Some part of him had known . . . even before the picture . . . when all Doyle could give him were those two initials . . . he *had* known.

C. M.

Curt M.

Curtis McGraw.

Reeling from the revelation, his mind clouded in a fugue state, he had driven ten miles past Yonkers before realizing he was heading north—toward Hartford.

Curtis McGraw, the director of Havenwood Retreat, the man responsible for the care of Chase's mother, was also the man who had hired the Gray brothers to assassinate Tanya Hemsworth and then sent them to *his* apartment.

How was it possible? Why?

Chase felt like he'd slipped into a parallel universe where black was white, up was down, and chaos had replaced logic.

Except he knew better. There *was* a logical explanation. He just didn't have all the pieces yet. Maybe that was why his internal autopilot had put him on the road to Hartford, even while his conscious mind groped for a connection. But as much as he wanted to storm into McGraw's office at Havenwood Retreat, hold the man at gunpoint, and demand answers—

Why did you order Tanya's death? Why did you send those assassins to my home?

Who in the hell are you?

—he knew he would need a better plan.

He realized, much to his chagrin, that he had made the classic mistake of conflating a professional relationship with a personal one, thinking of McGraw as a friend and confidant when, in reality, he knew very little about the man, aside from the fact that he had left a career with the London Metropolitan Police to take the management position at Havenwood.

He was a cop. A dirty cop? Like Campbell?

He recalled the picture Doyle had shown him of the two men together. Was that the connection?

It was *a* connection, but it wasn't *the* connection. McGraw wasn't some New York crime boss. He was the managing director of a residential care facility—the same care facility where Chase's mother resided. That was *the* connection—Chase just couldn't see how the piece fit into the puzzle. That was something he would have to ask McGraw about.

Yet, as much as he wanted answers, there was a far more compelling reason to get to Hartford with all haste.

Does he know about Campbell's arrest? Does he know that I know what he is?

Without taking his eyes off the road, he activated one of his burner phones and dialed the number for Havenwood Retreat.

"Can you put me through to Henrietta Burke's room, please?" he said when the receptionist answered.

This was the moment of truth. Based on past experience, there was a good chance the call would go directly to McGraw. He steeled himself for a possible verbal showdown with the man.

You wouldn't want anything to happen to your mother now, would you?

He was surprised when he heard a female voice come over the line—his mother's nurse. "Henrietta Burke's room."

Chase searched his memory, trying to recall the woman's name. *Lucy. Lucy Noonan.* "Lucy, this is . . ." He hesitated, remembering that as far as the world was concerned, he was still a fugitive. "This is Henrietta's son. Can you put her on, please?"

There was a long pause—ominously long—and when Lucy spoke again, her voice was as taut as a garotte. "She's resting right now."

"Can you wake her? It's urgent."

"I'm afraid I can't do that."

Chase's scalp began to tingle with dread. *It's already happened. Curtis is making his move.*

But then Lucy continued. "I'm really very sorry, but Henrietta gave me explicit instructions not to disturb her for any reason. The last couple of days have been very . . . challenging for her. She needs rest."

Chase strained to catch some hint of duplicity in her voice, but if she was lying, she was damn good at it. "I guess that makes sense."

"I'll tell her that you called."

"Thank you. I appreciate that." If Lucy was being truthful, then his mother wasn't in immediate danger. He knew he should probably let it go at that but decided he had to know for certain. "Can you transfer me to Mr. McGraw?"

"Umm, I think he's off site today. The front desk might be able to put you through to his cell phone."

Off site? Was McGraw already in the wind? "That's okay. I'll try him later."

He ended the call, feeling only marginally relieved, and gazed into the near distance. Hartford was still a good two hours away.

A lot could happen in two hours.

PART III
A Brother's Vengeance

CHAPTER FORTY-FIVE

West Hartford, Connecticut

At the prompt from the onboard GPS, Damien Gray turned off the highway onto a gravel service road that plunged into the forested environs of the Talcott Reservoir flood-control dam. The dam was part of the West Hartford Reservoir recreation area, situated between greater Hartford and the suburbs and farm communities to the west. The route, preloaded into the GPS of the Ford Explorer that had been waiting for him at Hartford-Brainard Airport when the flight had arrived early that morning, showed the destination about half a mile farther up the primitive road. The lush greenery reminded him of his early days as a soldier, rucking through the wilds of Wales and Scotland on long training exercises—quite a change from the deserts and urban landscapes where he had subsequently spent most of his time, either with the Regiment or doing contract work. It had been a long time since he'd gone hunting in the woods.

Mac, sitting in the passenger seat beside him, had been in a pensive mood since landing, or more accurately, since they'd received a call from the client directing them to the waiting Explorer. In the SUV's boot, they discovered duffel bags containing encrypted radios, an assortment of weapons, and the ammunition to go with them.

Mac, uncharacteristically, had looked at the open bags like they were full of venomous snakes. "Something feels off about this, Damien."

"Off?"

"I don't know how you're used to operating, mate. But this isn't how we do it."

Damien understood the cause of Mac's apprehension. Typically, the client's involvement in an operation was limited to two things—supplying the target and transferring money into an offshore bank account. The contractor took care of all logistic considerations, from arranging transport for the team to procuring untraceable weapons and to determining the best method for executing. There was a very simple reason for this: Clients couldn't be trusted.

"I didn't hear you complaining on the flight over," replied Damien.

Mac shrugged. "Well, I admit. That beat the hell out of flying commercial. But this . . . ?" He gestured at the guns. "The client chooses the weapons. The vehicle. And all we're told is to drive out to the middle of nowhere and wait for further instructions." He shook his head. "I don't like being on a short lead."

"I hear you. I don't usually work this way either. But this job is different. We have a narrow window of opportunity. There's just not enough time to do things the way we usually do."

"But that's what I'm talking about. If your client can put all this together in less than twenty-four hours, what does he need us for?"

"He probably doesn't need us," admitted Damien, "but this isn't an ordinary job. It's personal. Burke made it personal."

Mac was unconvinced. "I don't like it," he repeated. "This feels like it could be a setup."

"Mac, you sound like an old man. Let me worry about it." But the simple truth of the matter was that Mac was right. It *was* a setup. When Chase Burke died, there wouldn't be any doubt that Damien Gray, driven by the desire to avenge his brother's torture and murder, had done the deed. The authorities wouldn't look any deeper than that. But now that his secret life had been exposed, what difference did it make? He would take the heat, while Mac and his shooters would be able to simply fade into the background.

When the GPS finally signaled that they had arrived, Damien pulled off the gravel road and called the client. "We're at the coordinates. What's the plan?"

"Five hundred meters east of your present location, you'll find the fence line of a private care facility called Havenwood Retreat. Chase Burke's mother is a patient there. He'll be paying her a visit sometime in the next few hours, but he's probably not going to come in through the front door. Deploy your team in the woods and wait for him."

"That's it?"

"Are you unclear on the assignment?"

"No, I understand what we need to do. But what if Burke slips past us? Do we go in after him?"

There was a long silence as the client seemed to consider the question. "Do what you must to get the job done. Once you take care of Burke, you're on your own."

And then, before Damien could ask any further questions, the line went dead. He stuffed the phone in his pocket and then used the Explorer's GPS to access a satellite map of the surrounding area.

Havenwood Retreat occupied six acres of woodland sandwiched between the Talcott Reservoir area and the residential communities of West Hartford. The facility was fenced on all sides, presumably to keep patients from wandering off into the woods, and accessible only through the main gate at the end of a long, meandering road that wended back to the main highway.

"We'll establish observation posts at the corners of the property," Damien explained. "That should give us visual coverage in all directions. Nate, I want you on the east side and the main gate. I don't think Burke will try to come in that way, but just in case, I want you covering it with the sniper rifle. I'll take the west, watching the approach from the forest. Mac, you and Ollie can flip for the north and south."

"What do you want us to do if we spot him?" asked Ollie.

"If he's on foot, radio in right away. I'll come for him. If he's in a vehicle, or it looks like he might get away, do whatever you have to do to disable him. Shoot out his tires or shoot him in the foot . . . I don't give a fuck how you do it. Just don't kill him." He paused a beat and then, more to reassure himself than the others, added, "Chase Burke is mine."

CHAPTER FORTY-SIX

After entrusting his ailing wife to the care of the staff at Havenwood Retreat, a grateful Robert Burke had made a point of sending a Christmas card, along with a not-insignificant monetary gift, to the facility's director, Curtis McGraw. Following their father's death, Michael and Chase had agreed to do the same the following year, which was why Chase had no difficulty locating McGraw's condominium in downtown Hartford.

His plan was to locate McGraw's car—a black Lexus 500 LC, which Chase usually saw parked in a reserved spot at Havenwood—and then lay in ambush, drawing the man out by calling to request an in-person meeting at the Retreat. When McGraw came out to his car, Chase would spring his trap, confront McGraw at gunpoint, and demand answers.

Unfortunately, two trips around the block and a top-to-bottom inspection of the building's parking garage had failed to yield a sighting of the luxury coupe. McGraw wasn't home. And he wasn't at work.

Where the hell is this guy?

Chase's worst fear was that McGraw, anticipating his wrath, had gone on the run, perhaps even fleeing the country for safer climes, but McGraw didn't seem like the sort of person to run from a fight. If anything, he would be the one trying to bait Chase into a trap.

Well, two can play that game.

Rather than going out to find McGraw, he would wait for McGraw to come to him. The Havenwood director would have to come home sometime, and when he did, Chase would be waiting.

He hunkered down behind a thick concrete support pillar near the bottom of the ramp down to the first level. As long as he stayed alert, he could keep the pillar between himself and anyone walking or driving by while still keeping an eye on the entrance to the garage.

With nothing to occupy mind or body, the wait was interminable. The first ten minutes felt like an hour. After thirty, he began questioning the decision to loiter in the garage. Perhaps there was a better place to confront McGraw or, at the very least, keep watch.

He reminded himself that patience was key, recalling his Army training and the mental techniques to stay sharp and focused in situations exactly like this. He practiced controlled breathing, visualizing each inhale and exhale. He began paying attention to the sensory inputs—not just the sights and sounds but the smells of the city and the feel of the concrete beneath him—and gradually, his perception of the flow of time began to change.

Then, not quite two hours after his vigil began, Chase's patience was rewarded. McGraw's Lexus rolled down the ramp, turned the corner, and headed for the second level. He waited until the coupe passed out of view before stepping out into the open. Keeping to the shadows, with one hand hovering near the butt of the SIG tucked in his waistband, he descended the ramp, rounding the corner just in time to see the Lexus turning the next. Advancing in this fashion, he moved from corner to corner, level to level, until he finally saw the vehicle pull into an empty slot, whereupon he ducked behind another support pillar and drew his pistol. A hundred feet away, Curtis McGraw stepped out of his vehicle.

Unaware that he was being observed and oblivious to the imminent showdown, McGraw's face and body language radiated anxiety. Chase thought he looked as if he hadn't slept in days.

During the long drive up to Hartford, Chase had thought about what approach to take. How would he get McGraw to talk? Should he go hard, push McGraw's buttons, and demand the truth at gunpoint? The thought of simply brandishing his gun and forcing McGraw's hand was tempting. It would be quick—direct. But quick wasn't always the best solution. Too much aggression might backfire by making McGraw clam up entirely. Chase couldn't afford that.

Still, being nice wouldn't do it either. The man was slippery, that much Chase had learned. So what was left? What was the middle ground?

Show force, but don't overplay it. Split the difference, he decided.

A tightrope act, for sure. He would have to use just enough pressure to rattle McGraw without sending him over the edge.

Chase took a deep breath, then stepped out into the open, putting himself directly in McGraw's path. He raised the pistol to the low-ready position, not pointing it directly at McGraw. McGraw's eyes flicked up briefly, registering the mere fact of his presence without immediately grasping its significance. Then he looked again, saw the gun, and froze.

"Hello, Curtis," said Chase. "You and I need to have a little chat."

McGraw stared back, speechless for a moment, and then slowly raised his hands. "Chase? What are you doing here? And . . . my God, is that a gun?"

"Let's skip the part where you pretend like you don't know what's going on. I just need to know one thing: Are you calling the shots, or is there someone above you?"

"Someone above? *What?* Chase, I don't—"

Pfft! Pfft!

The muffled but distinctive reports of two suppressed pistol shots cut McGraw off in mid-sentence. His body jolted as if hit by an invisible hammer, and for a split second, disbelief clouded his features as if his brain hadn't yet processed what had just happened. Then his knees gave way, and he fell in a heap.

For a single, horrified second, Chase thought he had somehow fired the shot, a reflex action, his subconscious desire for revenge overriding his priorities . . . but no, his finger wasn't even on the trigger.

Someone else shot him . . .

He flung himself sideways, out of the line of fire from the shooter who had to be right behind him, and dove behind a parked car, hitting the ground hard. His breath came in short, sharp bursts as he pressed his back against the vehicle.

Two more reports came in quick succession, followed almost simultaneously by the noise of the rounds striking a nearby concrete wall. Chase dared to raise his head for a brief instant, his eyes searching for any sign of the shooter.

There—a shadow moved.

The gunman was hiding behind the very same concrete column Chase had used for concealment just before confronting McGraw. He brought the SIG around, trying to acquire the barely glimpsed target, but before he could, two more shots creased the air above him, forcing him to seek the partial cover the car offered. Chase moved to the front of the car, wanting to use the engine block between himself and the assassin. From the corner of his eye, he saw McGraw's crumpled body, face down on the concrete floor of the underground garage, unmoving, and with a crimson pool spreading beneath him.

Shit!

It occurred to him that he'd at least gotten one answer to his questions. McGraw hadn't been the one calling the shots. He was just another pawn in the game.

Just like Brad, Nigel, and Campbell.

Taken off the board to keep me from learning the truth.

But who's playing the fucking game?

Chase slid forward. Leaning around the front bumper of the vehicle, he fired twice at the concrete pillar before drawing back just as quickly. Wanting to change his firing position, he moved quickly to the rear of the vehicle, coming to rest in a prone shooting position.

From his new vantage, he could see the gunman's left shoulder and part of his face, which was hidden behind a dark balaclava. Chase didn't hesitate. But even as he began to squeeze the trigger, the gunman moved, turning toward him as if sensing his presence. As Chase's pistol bucked in his hand, the assassin threw himself back, disappearing from view.

Chase cursed his luck. The gunman wouldn't make the same mistake twice, that much was certain. The smart play for Chase was to stay put, let the assassin make the next move. But that idea grated against every instinct Chase had. Reacting wasn't his style. Whether in the ring or in combat, he had always thrived on being the one dictating the action, pressing the attack.

But as he began to formulate what to do next, a small, dark cylinder about the size of the suppressor attached to the end of his SIG bounced erratically across the concrete floor before skidding to a stop a few feet from him.

Chase had just enough time to think *flash-bang* before his world turned upside down.

CHAPTER FORTY-SEVEN

Detective Alice Doyle had not gotten to where she was in life or at work by cutting corners or ignoring procedures, but she also hadn't done it by ignoring her gut. And right now, her gut was screaming to her that, one way or another, Chase Burke held the key to breaking the case wide open.

Burke had recognized C. M.'s photograph, she was certain of that, just as certain as she was of the fact that Burke was probably already on his way to confront the man. So, instead of reporting her contact with Burke and initiating a full-scale manhunt, she took a different tack.

She began with a call to Matthew Kim, the FBI's digital forensics technician who had unlocked Nigel Gray's burner phone. Without mentioning that she was on administrative leave, she asked Kim to get a location on the phone associated with the number Campbell had assigned to C. M. The number had a 917 area code—Manhattan—so Doyle was a little surprised when Kim called back to let her know that, while the number had stopped pinging cellular towers earlier in the day, it had almost never left the Hartford area.

Chase Burke's mother was in a care facility in Hartford, was she not?

Doyle didn't think that was a coincidence, especially not after witnessing Burke's reaction, but she couldn't see how the pieces fit together.

I need to get to Hartford.

With her Mazda out of commission, she walked to the nearest car rental agency.

"I'm sorry, but we have no budget cars left," the clerk said. "The only available option is a black BMW 760i."

Doyle glanced at the price on the screen.

Holy shit!

It would burn a hole in her bank account. She could already tell she would have to fight with her insurance company to cover the extra cost.

But with precious time slipping away, and with Burke's lead growing with every second she stood there doing nothing, what other choice did she have?

A few minutes later, she was headed north toward Hartford, comfortably seated behind the wheel of the BMW. As she settled into the drive, she got Kim to search the employment records of Havenwood Retreat. It didn't take him long to match C. M. to the facility's director, Curtis McGraw.

And just like that, her entire perception of things changed.

Chase Burke was no longer merely an innocent bystander caught up in events beyond his control. Somehow, in a way she couldn't yet fathom, Chase Burke was connected to what had happened. Ironically, Campbell had been right about that, but then, of course, he already knew what that connection was.

Campbell had said something else too. Something about Burke's brother being a foreign agent, leaking intel about classified operations. Was that the connection? Or had that been misdirection on Campbell's part?

Doyle's next call was to McGraw's place of work. Posing as a potential client interested in the exclusive retreat for her aging mother, Doyle had worked her charm and subtle probing into the conversation. It had paid off. The receptionist had let it slip that McGraw wasn't on the premises but likely at home.

"I'll reach out to him and see if he can swing by Havenwood," she'd said. "He only lives a short drive away."

Armed with this new information, Doyle once again called Matthew Kim. This time, she asked him to search for known addresses for all the Curtis McGraws in the Hartford region. There were three, but only one was close enough to the Havenwood Retreat to make sense.

With the address in hand, she sped up, praying she would get there before Burke did something stupid. How exactly she'd stop him—with no badge, service weapon, or official standing—was something she hadn't quite figured out yet.

She followed the onboard GPS navigation to McGraw's downtown apartment, pulling into a spot just around the corner from the front entrance. Now that she was here, the question of what to do next required an answer. Arresting McGraw would have been her first choice, but because she was on administrative leave, she couldn't even approach him as a representative of a law enforcement agency. She could warn McGraw that Chase Burke was coming after him, but it would tip him off that he was under investigation. That left her with only one valid option: to intercept Burke before he triggered a violent confrontation with McGraw. She would have to reason with him, provided, of course, she wasn't already too late.

With most local residents out living their daily routines, the streets were quiet—too quiet for Doyle, who was used to the constant noise and energy of Manhattan. Just as she was about to round the corner to the front of the building, a loud bang reverberated in the air around her, taking her instantly to a heightened alert status.

Doyle knew the difference between a car's exhaust backfire and the crack of a gunshot. This was neither—this sounded more like a small explosion. Not the kind that leveled buildings but more like some sort of grenade. Her hand shot instinctively to her hip, only to remember she didn't have her gun. She retreated to the cover of her vehicle and took out her phone to call 911.

Just then, a man rounded the corner of the building at a brisk jog. Her cop brain kicked in immediately, cataloging the man's details: thirties, white, dark brown hair and beard, above average height, athletic build. He wore denim jeans and a loose-fitting windbreaker—the kind a person might wear to hide a concealed weapon. She quickly opened the camera app on her phone, but before she could snap a picture of the man, he ducked down behind a Toyota 4Runner parked across the street.

Ducking for cover? wondered Doyle, bracing herself for another, more powerful explosion.

A moment later, however, he was up again and running down the block. She followed him with the phone, recording him as he ran, but he never looked her way. He disappeared around the next corner without showing his face a second time.

The suddenness of the man's appearance and subsequent departure felt surreal, and the apparent absence of any sort of emergency response to the explosion made her question her original assessment. Had she misheard and then let her imagination run away from her?

Shit!

Then, she noticed Chase Burke walking around the front of the building, and all her doubts were wiped away.

CHAPTER FORTY-EIGHT

Producing an intense burst of light and a deafening 170-decibel explosion—equivalent to standing next to a jet engine—the stun grenade, more commonly known as a flash-bang, was designed to create sensory overload, disorienting anyone close to the detonation, leaving them vulnerable to a follow-on attack. Although Chase had managed to close his eyes and open his mouth a fraction of a second before the stun grenade went off, the blinding light still burned his retina, and the concussive wave ripped through him, shredding his equilibrium and sending him reeling like a drunkard. The world around him spun violently out of control, his sense of up and down dissolving in a maelstrom of deafening sound and blinding white.

Chase fully expected to die.

He dropped to his knees, not to stabilize himself but because his legs could no longer support him. With sheer instinct, he brought his pistol up—not in defense but in defiance. Maybe, just maybe, if the gunman's next shot didn't kill him outright, he would get off one last lucky shot.

But the killing shot never came.

As the haze receded and the world came into focus, Chase realized that the assassin, having completed his primary objective by silencing Curtis McGraw, had fled the scene, using the flash-bang to cover his own escape.

Why the man had not killed him as well, he could only guess, but he was certain that it was not merely a matter of luck. The unknown master of the game had some other fate in store for him.

Perhaps I'm meant to take the rap for McGraw's death.

But why?

Why are they targeting me for all of this?

Chase silently wished he could call Michael or their father. They'd both know what to do. How to handle things. The fact that he couldn't turn to them now brought on another wave of grief.

I'm not them, he told himself.

No sooner had the thought formed than another realization came to him. He wasn't his brother or his father because he was still alive. Michael. His father. Curtis McGraw. Even his mother's former nurse, Shana. They were all dead.

His family was in the eye of a death storm and had been for months.

Why didn't I see it sooner?

Rising to his feet, he shambled forward, passing McGraw's corpse, clearing the pillar where the assassin had been hiding, and started up the ramp. His head felt like it was stuffed with cotton, and his ears continued to ring, but the effects of the flash-bang continued to diminish with each passing second until he was able to increase his pace to a jog.

There were still a few pieces of the puzzle that didn't seem to fit. Why had McGraw sent the Gray brothers after Tanya Hemsworth? But for Nigel's dying admission, Chase almost would have believed that *he* had been the sniper's target. But then again, Detective Campbell had moved quickly to point the finger at Chase.

Had that been the plan all along? Shoot Tanya and then implicate Chase in the conspiracy? Was that why Brad Gray had broken into his apartment? Had he gone there to plant evidence of Chase's collusion in the plot?

Then Chase remembered the three messages Chef David had left on his voicemail box.

Was David part of it too? Was that why he had called Chase back to work? Chase dismissed the thought. David wouldn't betray him, not after what Chase had done for him.

Or would he? Were David's financial troubles even real?

Shit.

And then there was Violet. Chase had never fully trusted her. She had always seemed shallow, as if she was playing a role. In his mind Chase replayed the exact words David had used in one of his messages.

You need to let us know where you are, Chase.

Us. David and Violet.

Had they been forced to make contact with him? Why would they both need to know where he was? They weren't exactly a team, not outside of work anyway.

None of it added up. None of it.

Chase wondered what anyone could possibly gain by involving him. Why would anyone go to such lengths to frame him for a crime he didn't commit? What did he know that was so dangerous?

Nothing. And that was the truth.

So, if it's not about me, then who?

Then it hit him.

It's Mother.

Her husband. Her firstborn son. Her nurse. The director of the facility where she was essentially imprisoned. All were dead, and Henrietta Enfield Burke was the thread that connected them all.

Did it go even deeper than that?

It wasn't beyond the realm of possibility that McGraw or someone in his employ at Havenwood had become aware of information she may have in her possession. Perhaps something she said during a rare lucid moment? Maybe she knew more details about his father's death. Or Michael's.

They were all killed because they knew too much.

The thought sent a shiver down Chase's spine. If that was the case—admittedly, a big *if*—then it meant that either Michael or their father had uncovered something worth killing for to keep hidden. And if that was true—yet another big *if*—then it was possible that Henrietta had come to learn from them whatever it was that got them killed.

As far-fetched as his theory seemed, it worked. If Michael or their father had some kind of damaging or sensitive info, and there was even a chance that Henrietta knew about it, then that meant her life was in danger too.

Only they can't get to her.

Even if someone inside Havenwood Retreat had reason to believe Henrietta had incriminating information, there were far too many eyes, not to mention security cameras, to make a move on her. And with Secretary Williams dropping by on occasion, the risks were too high.

So, what can they do?

And that was when it all made sense.

If they couldn't kill her outright, the next best play was to tie up the final loose end, tighten the circle of people who cared for Henrietta so tight that even if she started shouting sensitive information from her bed, they could keep a lid on it. Eventually, she would die of natural causes, taking those secrets with her.

I'm the last loose end . . .

They killed her husband. They killed her first son. And now, someone was trying to frame her second son for murder and conspiracy. Even if they couldn't kill Chase, or hadn't been able to yet, they could slap attempted murder charges on him as a way to discredit what was left of her family.

Just me and Mother. We're all that's left.

Chase shook his head and quickened his pace. The *why* didn't matter anymore. All that mattered was getting to his mother and keeping her safe.

As he exited the garage, he glanced up and down the street, looking for the retreating assassin. Not seeing him, Chase shoved the SIG into his waistband and headed for the 4Runner.

Realizing he couldn't trust anyone at Havenwood, Chase wondered who the real mastermind was behind things. If McGraw wasn't the one calling the shots, who was? Could it be someone else at Havenwood?

He thought about Henrietta's former nurse, Shana. Had she figured out what McGraw was doing? Was that why she had been killed? Had McGraw or someone else ordered her death? And what about the new nurse, Lucy? Was she part of the conspiracy or another potential victim?

His first glimpse of the waiting Toyota brought him up short. Something about it didn't look quite right, but it took him a moment to realize what it was. The SUV was canted at an odd angle, almost as if . . .

Damn it!

Both passenger side wheels were sitting on their rims. Someone, doubtless the assassin, had slashed his tires.

Frustration welled up in Chase's chest like a volcano about to explode. To have endured so much . . . survived so much . . . only to be stopped by a pair of flats.

"Need a ride?"

Chase looked across the street and saw a familiar face sitting behind the steering wheel of a parked black BMW sedan.

It was Detective Doyle.

CHAPTER FORTY-NINE

Doyle felt a twinge of pleasure at seeing Chase Burke frozen in place, a deer caught in the headlights, but when his eyes began to dart left to right, searching for an escape route, she realized that she was mere moments away from losing him again.

"Chase," she said, "just get in. I'm not going to arrest you."

His eyes narrowed. "How did you find me?"

"I'm a detective, Chase. It's kind of what I do." Sensing that Burke would need a better answer than that, she went on. "If you must know, I figured out that C. M. is Curtis McGraw, and since I knew you were coming for him, I thought maybe I could head you off. Keep you from doing something stupid."

Burke's only reaction was a slight flaring of the nostrils. "Curtis is dead."

The declaration was like an injection of ice water into Doyle's veins. "Did you . . . ?"

"No. I didn't get the chance."

"Was it the guy that slashed your tires?"

"You saw him?"

"Yeah. Less than two minutes ago. I didn't get a very good look at him, though." She paused a beat. "Are you just going to stand there, or are we gonna go after him?"

Burke continued to regard her with suspicion. "Whose side are you on, Detective?"

"Whose side?" She shrugged. "I don't even know what the sides are, Chase. I guess I'm on the side of the angels. Law and order. Truth, justice, and the American way. What side are you on?"

This gave Burke pause. "I guess I'm trying to figure it out too."

"Then let me help you."

Burke seemed to consider the offer a moment longer, then walked over to the 4Runner, opened a door, and reached inside to retrieve a small gym bag. Then he went around the BMW and slid into the passenger seat. "I have to get to Havenwood Retreat," he said. "I think my mother is in danger."

Doyle didn't immediately question this. It was enough to get him in the car. "Tell me how to get there."

He gestured forward. "That way. Take the next left, then keep going until you hit Main Street. Then take a right and follow it for three or four miles."

Doyle nodded and let off the brake. Without looking over at him, she asked, "What's in the bag?"

He gave her a sidelong glance. "You sure you want to know?"

"No. But tell me anyway."

"Some cash. A couple of phones." He paused a beat before adding. "A Wilson Combat EDC X9."

Doyle kept her reaction neutral. "I figured it would be something like that."

"It's mine," he went on. "But it's also the gun Brad Gray used to shoot those cops at my place."

That was a bigger pill to swallow. "Chase . . . you should have left that at the scene."

"And give your partner one more thing to hold over me?" He shook his head. "I don't think so."

Doyle pursed her lips together, then decided to circle back to the more immediate question. "Why do you think your mother's in danger?"

"If you figured out who Curtis McGraw is, then you already know the answer. Somehow, it all connects to Havenwood Retreat. And

Havenwood connects to me through Henrietta." He shook his head. "I was hoping Curtis would give me some answers, but I never got a chance to ask him."

"You must have some idea. I mean, it's your mother we're talking about."

"I really don't." Burke gazed out the window. "We've never exactly been . . . close. And the last few years, she didn't even know who I was. But now I'm wondering if . . ."

His voice trailed off, and Doyle figured he was trying to decide how much of his theory to share with her.

"What are you thinking?"

Chase sighed. "This is going to sound crazy."

"Try me."

"What if my dad and brother were killed because they found, I don't know . . . *something*."

"Like what?"

"That's the thing, I really don't know," Chase replied, rubbing the back of his neck. "But if someone killed them to shut them up, then there's a chance that my mother stumbled on it too. Or maybe she has evidence. Something incriminating."

Doyle kicked that idea around in her head. "Okay, let's say you're right. Your mom knows something that got your dad and brother killed. Why not just put a bullet in her and call it a day?"

"I haven't figured that part out yet," said Chase. "Maybe they can't get to her. Or maybe they're not sure if she has anything on them. She has late-stage dementia. She won't last much longer anyway."

Doyle wasn't ready to say it out loud, but the logic tracked. It was far-fetched, to be sure, and something she wouldn't have believed a week ago, but now, after all that she'd seen, she couldn't outright dismiss that Chase was on to something.

"Why bring you into this mess, Chase? Explain their—whoever *they* are—reasoning for coming after you."

"Maybe they think I'm the loose end."

But you're alive.

"You tie up loose ends permanently. You don't go after them for attempted murder."

"Yeah, I thought that too. Like I said, I don't know. I just can't quite see it."

"What if," stated Doyle. "Can't believe I'm going to embrace this conspiracy theory . . . what if you're right about your mom, dad, and brother? Your mom has dementia, so it's not like you can interrogate her to get the info out of her. So maybe they're worried about some sort of fail-safe."

"A fail-safe?"

"Yeah, in the movies, that would be the part where the person who knows where all the bodies are buried has a plan to release what they know to the media in the event of their untimely demise. Something like that."

Chase frowned. "I can't quite see her putting all that together in her current state."

"Maybe your father did it to protect her." Doyle shrugged. "I'm just spitballing here, but it might explain why whoever is behind this would rather discredit you . . . make you and your family look fucking nuts instead of just killing you." When Chase didn't respond, Doyle added, "Sorry to put it so bluntly."

"No, you could be right. I hadn't even thought about that."

Doyle held off on her follow-up questions until she made the turn onto Main Street. "Level with me, Chase. If any of what we're talking about is true, you must have some idea about what your brother or your father might have stumbled onto."

Burke was silent for a long moment. "The only thing I keep coming back to is something your partner said when he was talking about Michael . . . he more or less accused him of being a spy and being dirty. That's bullshit, though. Michael was a good man."

"And your dad?"

"My dad came from old family money. He worked a few years as an investment banker at a big firm, then spent the rest of his life in the foreign service. He was about to become the US ambassador to the Czech Republic."

And now they're both dead. Doyle didn't say that part out loud. "So, what's your plan? Head over to Havenwood and storm the place? Wave your gun around like you did with Bonetti?"

"If I have to." Burke glanced over at her. "Or you could just flash your badge."

Doyle grimaced. "Yeah, about that."

CHAPTER FIFTY

From his perch in the branches of a beech tree, Damien Gray scanned the fence line, hoping . . . *praying* . . . that Chase Burke would try to sneak past him.

The thought of what that bastard had done to Brad churned in his gut.

He knew that avenging his brother's death would only bring temporary satisfaction, but it was all he had. He'd given up everything else. His marriage was effectively over. It was unlikely that he would ever see Allie again. He could still access his offshore bank accounts, but what good was money to him now? Revenge was all he had left.

And after that?

After that, he had no idea what would become of him. The thought of living each day with the knowledge of what he'd lost, drowning his sorrows in alcohol, felt unbearable.

Better to just eat a bullet, he thought. *But first . . . Burke.*

There was a crackle of static in his ear and then a voice. "Nate here. I've got a vehicle coming up the drive. Black sedan. Looks like a high-end BMW."

This was not the first vehicle to come down the long drive to Havenwood Retreat's front gate since they'd begun their vigil, but Damien nevertheless tensed in anticipation.

There was a brief pause, then Nate went on. "Female driver. I don't see any passengers."

Damien frowned. Could Burke have found an accomplice? "Keep an eye on it," he advised.

His eyes flicked back to the tree line, searching for any hint of movement. He didn't really expect Burke to take the direct approach. The front gate would be too obvious, too exposed, for someone as smart and resourceful as Burke was turning out to be. Damien felt certain Burke would try to sneak in from the woods.

Nate's voice came over the line again. "Got another one. Silver SUV. Male driver." A pause. "Doesn't look like the picture you showed us, but it's hard to say. He's got a beard, and he's wearing a ballcap."

"Any passengers?"

"Negative. He's alone."

Beard and a ballcap. Damien frowned. Burke had managed to elude federal authorities for nearly two days. It stood to reason that he might be utilizing a disguise or otherwise changing his appearance to avoid being identified.

Could be nothing, he thought. *Or it could be everything.*

"Keep monitoring your sectors. I'm going to move in and check this guy out."

CHAPTER FIFTY-ONE

Doyle did not give the parking valet so much as a glance as she exited the luxury sedan and made her way to the covered entrance. This level of rudeness did not come naturally to her, but it was in keeping with the persona she was trying to project. As a detective, she was always looking to build rapport, whether talking to a witness or a suspect, but as Burke had explained, she would need a different approach when interacting with the staff at Havenwood Retreat.

"They cater to a certain clientele," Burke had explained during the drive out. "Namely, the ridiculously wealthy. If this is going to work, you're going to have to unleash your inner diva."

"In other words, I have to treat 'the help' like total shit?"

Chase nodded. "Pretty much, yeah. Otherwise, they'll smell a rat."

"Got it."

Burke had not been wrong about Havenwood. Everything about the place, from the perfectly manicured landscaping to the Georgian Revival architecture, exuded an air of exclusivity. This wasn't merely a long-term care facility—it was a resort.

They sure know how to live, though.

Doyle wasn't comfortable in situations like this, where every little detail screamed affluence, where even the young woman behind the reception desk looked like she had stepped from the pages of a fashion magazine. Doyle could feel the weight of the woman's stare upon her, assessing her . . . no, *appraising* her as she crossed the polished marble floor toward the desk.

Treat the help like shit, she reminded herself.

Squaring her shoulders and putting on her best *don't fuck with me* face, she marched up to the desk. "Alice Kennedy," she announced haughtily. "Yes, of *those* Kennedys. You can tell Mr. McGraw that I'm here. Now."

The receptionist blinked, clearly a little rattled by the forcefulness of Doyle's affect. She hesitated for a moment before replying, "I'm sorry, Ms. Kennedy, but Mr. McGraw is out at the moment."

"Maybe you didn't hear me," snapped Doyle. "I said, 'Tell Mr. McGraw that I'm here.' Which part of that didn't you understand? He's supposed to give me a tour." She snapped her fingers in the woman's face. "Go. I don't have all day."

"I . . . um . . . I'm sorry. As I said, Mr. McGraw isn't here right now. And there's no tour on the schedule."

Doyle cut her off, her tone sharpening. "I didn't ask what's on your schedule. I'm here to see Mr. McGraw. All you need to do right now is get him for me."

The receptionist swallowed nervously and reached for her phone. "Let me just—"

"*No,*" Doyle snapped, leaning over the counter slightly, her voice rising. "You are not going to call him. You are going to march back there to Mr. McGraw's office and tell him to come out here. *Now.*"

Sensing an opportunity to escape the confrontation, the receptionist nodded quickly and all but scurried out from behind the desk, disappearing down a corridor into Havenwood's administrative warren.

As soon as the woman was lost to view, Doyle took out her phone, checked to make sure the line was still open, and then, in a low voice, said, "All clear."

Chase Burke, once sure the valet had left the parking area, emerged from the trunk of the BMW. Twenty meters away was the side entrance to the recreational building. Curtis McGraw had once mentioned an underground tunnel that connected this building to the main lobby.

Chase slipped through the side entrance and was immediately greeted by a warm, welcoming atmosphere. The large space was a lively hub of activity. A dozen elderly patients were gathered around tables, playing cards, while others watched a nature documentary on a gigantic flat screen on the wall. Chase couldn't help but notice the smiles lighting up their faces as the vibrant images flickered across the screen. Three nurses in pastel scrubs moved between them, offering blankets. One of the nurses greeted Chase with a nod but immediately returned her attention to her patients.

Chase scanned the room, looking for his mother. She wasn't there.

He took note of the layout, and his gaze fell on a side hallway at the back that led deeper into the building. As he entered the hallway, he noticed that the walls were lined with framed photographs of smiling patients and staff. His mother wasn't among these, which didn't surprise him.

Getting Mother to smile is a herculean task.

Near the end of the corridor, he spotted what he was looking for. On a small, neatly placed sign on the wall, it read **SERVICE TUNNEL—STAFF ONLY**, accompanied by a wheelchair-accessible symbol. An arrow pointed toward a wide door at the hall's end, which was fitted with a push-button automatic door opener.

Chase approached and pressed the button. The door opened smoothly, revealing a well-lit ramp that led down to the tunnel. The lights overhead were bright, and the white-tiled walls glistened under their glow. The entire passage was well maintained, which, unfortunately for him, meant it was frequently used by the staff.

Chase made it halfway through the tunnel when a figure appeared around the bend ahead—a nurse pushing a supply cart. She slowed when she saw him, and for a moment their gazes met. Chase saw her confusion. She hadn't expected to see anyone like him in the tunnel. Chase maintained his neutral expression and didn't break stride. The nurse averted her eyes and quickened her pace. But a few steps later, Chase heard the unmistakable crackle of a walkie-talkie.

"Hey, Karl? It's Sophie," the nurse said, her voice hushed but just loud enough to carry through the tunnel. "I've got someone in the service tunnel. Not staff. Could you check him out?"

Chase cursed under his breath. Of all the people to be contacted, it had to be Karl. He knew Karl. He was one of the orderlies who worked at the facility, a kind, always super-friendly and helpful, but by-the-book man. A man who had the trust of Curtis McGraw.

Precisely the sort of person who wouldn't hesitate to ask questions. Questions Chase didn't want to answer.

He quickened his pace. He had to get out before Karl showed up.

And he almost made it. But luck wasn't on his side. Just as he was about to reach the exit, the door opened and Karl stepped into the tunnel. The broad-shouldered orderly froze; a confused, concerned expression flashed across his face.

"Chase, what are you doing here, my man?" he asked. "You're not supposed to be down here. You know that."

Chase could tell Karl wasn't being aggressive, just curious. A problem, nonetheless.

"Yeah, I'm sorry. I got lost."

"But you're not in the books for today, Chase," Karl said, his brow furrowing. "Let me reach out to Mr. McGraw."

Chase could see the questions forming in the orderly's eyes. When Karl reached for the walkie-talkie clipped to his belt, Chase moved. He stepped forward, grabbed Karl's wrist, and twisted it to disarm him of his radio.

"Chase, wait—" Karl yelped, but Chase couldn't wait. He had to end this quickly.

Chase swept Karl's legs out from under him, forcing him off balance and crashing to the floor.

"I'm sorry," Chase muttered as he flipped Karl onto his stomach.

"What . . . what are you doing?" Karl grunted, trying to twist free.

Chase wrapped his arm around the man's neck from behind and applied pressure, cutting off the blood flow to his brain. A few moments later, Karl's body went limp. Chase carefully lowered Karl's head to the ground. The orderly wouldn't be out long; Chase needed to make sure he wouldn't follow him or sound the alarm once he woke up.

Working quickly, Chase unbuckled Karl's belt and looped it around his ankles, pulling it snug. Then, he unlaced the man's shoes, pulled the laces free, and used them to tie Karl's wrists behind his back. The knots were tight, but not painfully so. At least Chase hoped they weren't. He didn't want to hurt the man, just immobilize him.

Chase opened the door leading out of the tunnel, pausing just long enough to cast one last glance at Karl, who had already started moving again, then headed to the lobby.

Chase reached the lobby a minute later, and without acknowledging Doyle, he slipped past her and headed straight down a separate hallway that led to the residential wing.

Chase was familiar with this section of the Havenwood Retreat. Even though McGraw or some other senior staff member had always walked with him to his mother's room, he could have found his way blindfolded. The fact that he was now moving unescorted through the facility did not go unnoticed by the handful of nurses he passed along the way, but his determined stride and laser focus gave them little chance to interdict. One called after him, tentatively shouting "You're not supposed to be in here," but he ignored her completely.

He figured he had a minute or two, at best, before someone realized that they ought to summon an orderly, but that was more than enough time to get his mother.

Chase pushed the door to his mother's room open, and as he stepped inside, he was immediately greeted by the sunlight filtering through the three large windows that framed a view of the meticulously kept garden outside. The room was somewhat elegant, far from the sterile, institutional feel of most care facilities. Plush armchairs upholstered in rich fabric flanked the windows, and a small, polished walnut coffee table sat between them, adorned with fresh flowers in a crystal vase. Against the far wall stood a cherrywood armoire with gold-colored handles. Even the bed, draped with a cashmere throw across the foot of the mattress, was more like something from a luxury hotel than an assisted living facility.

Despite the lavish surroundings, something was off.

Henrietta wasn't in her room.

"Damn it," he muttered, glancing toward the bathroom where the light was off.

A voice belonging to an orderly in an immaculate white uniform reached out to him from farther down the hall. "What are you doing here? You need to go back to the main lobby, sir."

"Sure thing. My mistake," Chase said, turning away and backtracking.

If Henrietta wasn't in her room, then she was most likely either in the dining facility or at the Memory Garden.

Unless they've already moved her somewhere else. Or . . .

He pushed the thought away and veered into an adjacent hallway, heading for the door that led outside and opened directly onto the paved path out to the Memory Garden. The sprawling park, which occupied an area roughly the size of a football field, was designed to be serene yet practical. Because its open layout allowed clear lines of sight, making it easier for staff to monitor the residents, Chase didn't need to venture too far from the residence building to see the entirety of the green space.

Despite the peaceful surroundings, his anxiety spiked as he scanned the benches, fountains, and gazebos. There were more than a dozen people scattered throughout the Memory Garden, but Henrietta wasn't among them. A cold knot of fear twisted in his gut as he went back inside, running, not walking, through the corridors to the dining room.

Henrietta wasn't there either.

Where the hell is she?

For a moment, Chase stood frozen at the entrance to the dining facility, feeling as if hope was slipping away. His mother was gone, and he had no idea if she was still alive.

This isn't over, he told himself. *Someone here knows where she is. And I am going to make them tell me.*

He turned back in to the residential wing, quickly spotting the familiar door that led to Havenwood's administrative center. McGraw had often used this door when he needed to bring Chase to his office. Unfortunately, the door was secured with an electronic lock. Chase was contemplating whether to try battering it down or shooting the lock with his gun when he heard footsteps behind him.

Chase turned in time to see the orderly with the immaculate uniform barreling down the hallway, his breath labored, but his eyes locked on him. The man had clearly been pursuing Chase through the residential wing, and this time he wasn't interested in words.

Karl had probably wiggled free of his restraints by now and had surely called for help.

The orderly's hands shot out, aiming to grab Chase and end the pursuit with force. Chase moved on instinct, sidestepping the initial grab. The orderly, thrown off balance by the near miss, stumbled, but recovered quickly. He launched himself at Chase again. Chase ducked low, driving his shoulder into the man's midsection. The man's weight forced Chase back a step, but he used the momentum to shift his opponent, twisting the man's arm and locking him into a tight grip. The man, although out of breath, was stronger than he looked and fought back, elbowing Chase's ribs a few times in desperation. Pain flared through Chase's side, but he held on and angled the man into a choke hold. The orderly thrashed wildly, clawing at Chase's arm, but Chase's hold was unyielding. A few seconds later, the man's attempts to pry himself free faded into sluggish movements. When his fingers finally slipped from Chase's arm, and his body went limp, Chase lowered him to the floor and relieved him of his key card.

Chase swiped the key card across the electronic sensor pad beside the door and waited for the telltale click of the electronic lock mechanism disengaging. He pulled the door open, the SIG now in hand, and slipped inside, keeping the pistol low and unobtrusive.

From the far end of the hallway, he could hear Doyle in the front lobby going full diva, demanding the one thing that nobody, except for a psychic medium, could give her, namely an audience with Curtis McGraw. Chase wondered how much longer she could maintain the ruse but then decided that it didn't matter because in about thirty seconds Doyle's "Karen" act would be the least of the worries in the offices of Havenwood Retreat.

From his earlier visits, Chase had familiarized himself with the names of those occupying the offices lining the main corridor, though he had only ever met a handful of them in person. With McGraw out of the picture, operational matters would likely fall to his assistant, Mary Anne Hendricks. Whether her role extended to include the illegal detention of his mother remained to be seen, it was a place to start. Bypassing several doors, more than a few of them propped open, Chase homed in on the assistant's office like a laser-guided missile. But as he passed the door to McGraw's office, he froze in his tracks.

That door was also open.

By itself, this detail was merely incongruous. There might have been any number of reasons for McGraw to keep his office door open when he was not on the premises. But that wasn't what had brought Chase up short.

He'd heard something. Someone. A voice from McGraw's office asked a question.

"What the hell is going on out there?"

He blinked, unable . . . unwilling to believe his ears.

It . . . it can't be . . .

"Curtis scheduled a tour for a prospective client," came the answer, though Chase barely heard it through the roar of blood rushing to his head. "Only he didn't tell anyone before he left. Mary Anne is handling it."

"Since when does Curtis play tour guide?"

No, Chase told himself, his reality suddenly shattered. *It can't be true.*

His head spinning, Chase was frozen in shock for what felt like an eternity. Unable to blink or breathe or move, his vision narrowed, and he was acutely aware of the sound of his own muffled heartbeat, which filled his ears and threatened to drown out everything else. Swallowing, he placed a hand on the wall to steady himself as he tried desperately to make sense of it all. But no matter how hard he tried, his brain seemed to be unable to register what was happening.

It can't be true, he told himself again.

And yet, some part of him knew that it was. The second utterance confirmed it, and with the addition of that single piece, the puzzle, while still incomplete, suddenly made sense.

He thumbed open the phone and tapped the only number in his contact list. As the outgoing tone sounded, Doyle's tirade abruptly halted, and in the silence that followed, he could hear the chime of her phone.

"Excuse me," said Doyle, retaining a bit of her imperious tone. "I have to take this."

Then Chase heard her voice in his ear. "Do you have her?"

Chase started to reply but then realized he didn't know what to say. He shook his head and then whispered, "We had it all wrong. I know what's really going on here. I know who's really running the place."

CHAPTER FIFTY-TWO

How did I not see this?

But Chase knew the answer.

I didn't want to see it.

Maybe if I had, Dad and Michael would still be alive.

The thought came out of nowhere and hit like a gut punch because he knew it was the absolute truth. This was the secret that had cost him his family.

It ends today.

Right. Fucking. Now.

He moved his right hand—the hand holding the SIG—behind his back and then walked through the doorway into McGraw's office. Two wide windows framed the back wall, not floor-to-ceiling but large enough to flood the office with natural light. Beyond them, the dense forest stretched out.

As the overheard conversation had indicated, there were two people in the office—two women. One of them was seated behind McGraw's sleek Scandinavian-design desk. The other slouched in a guest chair on the opposite side.

Although she was facing away from him, Chase recognized the latter as Lucy Noonan, his mother's new nurse.

He had an unrestricted view of the other woman, the one sitting at the desk.

It was his mother, Henrietta Burke.

Both women looked up in surprise, and then both spoke at once, their voices overlapping, jumbling together.

"Mr. Burke," said Lucy, jumping to her feet guiltily as if she'd been caught in the middle of some indiscreet act. "This is unexpected. I didn't know you were coming today."

Henrietta, meanwhile, had taken on a hard expression. "Lucy, who is this man? You know I don't see anyone without an appointment."

And then Lucy was talking again, speaking in a low, conspiratorial stage whisper. "This is something we do for her sometimes. Let her think she's part of the management staff. Mr. McGraw lets us use his office."

"Well, young man," barked Henrietta. "You're here. You might as well introduce yourself."

Chase matched her stare and held it for a long moment.

Lucy spoke again. "Mr. Burke, today has been a difficult—"

"Sit your ass back down and shut up," Chase said, pointing his gun at her. "I need to speak with my mother."

Lucy visibly blanched as her eyes lit on the gun, then her gaze flicked to Henrietta. The look lasted less than the blink of an eye, but Chase caught it.

The nurse raised her hands in a show of compliance and sat.

"You think I'm your mother?" gasped Henrietta, her voice rising two octaves. "What the hell is this man talking about? I'm not anyone's mother." She faced Chase again. "You obviously have mistaken me for someone else, young man, and frankly, I'm not comfortable with the idea of being around you."

"It's going to be all right, Mrs. Enfield," Lucy said.

"But I don't know this man," wailed Henrietta.

Chase ignored her, keeping his attention on Lucy. Her use of Henrietta's maiden name hadn't escaped Chase.

Chase closed the door and locked it.

Henrietta shrank back in the chair, her eyes darting between the desk, Lucy, and Chase as if trying to remember something that eluded her. Her hand trembled slightly as she clutched the armrest, her expression a mix of confusion and fear. "I really don't know you, young man," she said, her rich mid-Atlantic accent giving her speech a dramatic quaver. "You should leave before I call someone to have you removed."

Chase studied his mother closely, noting the minute shifts in her expression—the nervous tics, the quivering lip—and a shadow of doubt darkened his certitude.

"Please, Mr. Burke," Lucy said, her eyes pleading. "I'm not sure what's going on, but I'd . . . I'd really like to leave. Please."

Chase swallowed hard.

If I'm wrong about this . . .

But he wasn't wrong.

"You can drop the act, Mother," he said quietly but firmly. "And you, too, Lucy, if that's even your real name. I know what's going on here."

"Why . . . why do you keep calling me that?" Henrietta's voice spiked again. She looked as if she was about to burst into tears.

"You don't have to pretend anymore. I heard you talking to Lucy before I came in. I've got to give credit where credit is due—it was an impressive performance. Both of you. Bravo."

She clamped her hands over her ears. "Why are you saying these horrible things?"

Chase felt his own emotions rising. "For God's sake, just *stop*." He shook his head. "And to think I actually came here to save you."

The comment elicited a brief but measurable pause in Henrietta's histrionic outpouring, but then she cried, "Save me? Why are you saying these things? I don't even know who you are."

"It's over, Mother. Curtis is dead."

Lucy straightened in her chair at the revelation, but Henrietta froze, transfixed by his words.

Chase filled the silence. "I thought that the person who killed him was coming after you next. But then when I heard you talking . . . when I realized that all of this . . ." He waved a hand in a sweeping gesture.

"All this bullshit is just a put-on . . . that's when everything suddenly made sense. Your sudden *decline*. Dad's death. And then Michael's. And the accusations that he was a traitor. It's you. You're the traitor."

Henrietta just stared back at him, eyes wide, astonished.

"How long have you been selling out your country?" Chase pressed. "Your family? I'm guessing it goes back years. Maybe before you even met Dad. Was marrying him part of the assignment?"

Chase didn't expect an answer and didn't wait for one. "I'm guessing someone figured it all out a couple of years ago. You knew you were about to get burned, but instead of running, you started faking symptoms of Alzheimer's disease. That was genius, really. Any suspicious behavior could be dismissed as an episode of dementia. And then you got Dad to send you here to this . . . *resort*." He spat the word out like a bad taste. "What happened then? Did he figure out that you were playing him? Playing us all? Did he see through your little act?" He paused a beat before setting the hook. "Is that why you killed him?"

"You think I killed someone?" shrieked Henrietta. "You're mad."

"Obviously you didn't do it yourself, but you might as well have. And then, when Michael figured it out, you did the same thing to him. Not only that, but you tried to make it look like *he* was the traitor." Chase paused a beat. "First your husband, then your firstborn son. You are one unbelievably coldhearted bitch."

He searched her face for a tell . . . a twitch . . . anything to confirm his accusations. He was certain that she was faking her dementia, certain that she was deeply involved in some sort of criminal conspiracy, but the rest? The rest was conjecture. Little more than a gut feeling.

But he trusted his gut and continued.

"And then you ordered the death of Tanya Hemsworth," he said. "I'm still trying to figure out why. Was she introducing some new bill that would have shut your operation down?" He shrugged. "What I really want to know is whether it was always your plan to hang that on me, or was I just in the wrong place at the wrong time, and you decided to take advantage of it?" He shook his head. "You know, I'm grateful for one thing. I think this would be a lot harder to bear if you had ever even pretended to love me."

Henrietta winced as if the words had physical weight, but then her expression changed. She straightened her back, then met and held his gaze for the first time. Her lips curled slowly into a smile. She leaned back in the office chair and brought her hands together in a slow clap.

"Congratulations, Chase. I guess you're not a complete idiot after all."

CHAPTER FIFTY-THREE

Until that moment, some part of Chase desperately hoped to be proven wrong. Henrietta's mocking laughter removed all doubt.

He felt like throwing up.

"You got most of it wrong, of course," she went on, "but you saw through my little charade. I'll give you credit for that. Ah," Henrietta sighed, "do you know how annoying it is to have to play dumb? To bring myself down to your level? I thought I was going to actually lose my fucking mind. I knew Robert or Michael would have figured it out at some point. That's why I needed them gone. But you? *You?* Never."

It took a moment for Chase to grasp the significance of this admission.

Had his mother just confessed to killing her husband and firstborn?

But Henrietta didn't give him the opportunity to follow up. "For what it's worth, I knew it was your night off. You weren't supposed to be at the restaurant. And I had no idea Judah Stine was also planning to make a move on her." She shook her head. "But you showed up anyway. Just had to be the fucking hero, didn't you? God, what a pain in the ass you turned out to be."

Chase was so accustomed to his mother's contempt that her harsh words served only to ground him, drawing him back from the brink of despair.

"I was thinking the same thing about you," he shot back. "You know, if you'd ever really bothered to get to know me, you would have known that I don't back down from a fight. You should have just left it alone. If you hadn't sent those killers after me, I probably would have just let it go."

Henrietta hissed through her teeth. "Those incompetent assholes were just supposed to bug your apartment, not go on a killing spree. What can I say?" she said with a maniacal smile. "Good help is hard to find."

Chase cocked his head to the side. "Bug my place? Why?"

She raised an eyebrow. "You really don't know? Can you believe that, Lucy? It seems we've been worried about nothing."

The nurse just shrugged.

Chase wanted to pursue his line of questioning but sensed that Henrietta wasn't going to simply volunteer the information.

But why bug my place? Keep her talking . . .

He changed tack. "And then you asked Curtis to put that dirty cop on me . . . set me up for murder."

"Oh please, you were born to play the part, Chase. A pathetic loser with no respect for authority. I guess it's no surprise that you managed to elude the police. Being a lowlife is the only thing you seem to have a knack for. Well, that and getting kicked out of the military."

"Fuck you," snapped Chase, unthinkingly, instantly regretting the lapse in self-control. Henrietta had gotten under his skin, just like she always did.

There was so much he wanted to ask her, so many questions he wanted answered, but getting those answers out of a woman who was willing to feign dementia for two years wasn't going to be easy. Just like in the boxing ring, he would need to keep her off balance, distract her with feints, fool her into overcommitting. "You killed Shana, didn't you? Did she see through your act?"

Henrietta rolled her eyes. "Please, Chase. Now you're just embarrassing yourself."

"No, of course not," he went on, putting it together on the fly. "She would have had to be in on it all along. But she screwed up somehow. Let something slip. So, you had to arrange an 'accident.'" He saw the truth of it in her eyes and switched gears again. "The one thing I can't figure out is why you slashed my tires?"

The jab had the intended effect. His mother's face registered incomprehension. Nevertheless, she kept her guard up. "I don't know what you're talking about."

"Sure you do," said Chase. "I thought you were done playing dumb. Maybe you're just too used to the role to stop now."

Very slowly Henrietta leaned forward and put her arms on the table while looking Chase dead in the eye. "I don't give a shit about slashing tires. I have throats slashed, not rubber. Tires are a little below my pay grade, you smug little prick."

The coldness of his mother's response sent a shiver up Chase's spine. *She's telling the truth,* he realized. *She really is heartless.*

"Maybe you should have told your hired killer that," said Chase, trying to regain the upper hand in the back-and-forth game being played out. "He had me dead to rights after he killed Curtis."

Henrietta's eyes widened with surprise as she shot Lucy a worried glance.

"You mean *you* didn't kill him?" Henrietta asked, her shield finally slipping.

Chase realized he'd made a serious miscalculation.

She hadn't ordered Curtis's death. That makes no sense. So then who killed him?

But then Henrietta's face changed again, understanding dawning in her eyes.

She knows. She knows who killed him.
She has an enemy.
And the enemy of my enemy is . . .

"You think I've been working with him," Chase said, thinking out loud. "That's why you wanted to bug my apartment."

"I gave you too much credit. That was my only mistake." She shook her head, not a denial but a dismissal. "You're in over your head, Chase. This is so much bigger than your little brain can comprehend. Just walk away, like you always do."

Channeling three decades of pent-up frustration, years of yearning for love from a woman incapable of giving it, Chase's gaze locked onto her, into a sharp, laser-like focus.

Even now, with her life in my hands, she can't bring herself to pretend.

He brought the SIG up and aimed it at her chest. "It's over, Mother. It's done. *You're* done."

She spat a contemptuous laugh. "You think you get to decide when this is over, Chase? You think you're going to turn me in and that will be the end of it?" She wagged her head. "You have no idea how deep this goes. You think James Campbell is the only policeman working for us? It's not over. Not even close. We are just getting started."

Chase stabbed the SIG at her. "Then maybe I won't turn you—"

He froze as movement flickered at the edge of his vision.

Lucy, he thought, realizing too late that his mother's grandiose posturing had been nothing but a distraction.

Lucy's chair screeched against the floor as she lunged, a letter opener gleaming in her hand. Chase spun, too slow to totally avoid the first strike. He felt a hot sting as the blade slashed across his forearm, slicing through fabric and skin. He slammed his arm down hard, trying to knock the weapon from her grasp, but Lucy was fast—much faster than he expected—and he only caught air. She swung the letter opener at him again, this time at his throat. He ducked, the blade whistling just over his head, and he snapped off a shot that hit the nurse center mass.

She stumbled back, eyes wide with shock, but still on her feet. Time seemed to slow as Lucy, defying all logic, raised the letter opener once more.

"Drop it!" Chase yelled, his finger on the trigger.

With a guttural cry, Lucy hurled the letter opener at him. Chase fired, his round ripping through her skull, but not before the letter opener had already sailed through the air, spinning end over end. Chase watched, helpless for a split second, as the steel blade hurtled toward him. He jerked his head at the last moment, feeling the air part as the edge grazed by, just inches from his face.

Chase pivoted back to Henrietta, his instincts kicking in—too late. He found himself staring down the barrel of a small, polished revolver. His heart dropped. Henrietta's hands were steady—and perfectly manicured, Chase noted—and held the weapon with unnerving calm.

His pulse quickened as he took in the revolver. The hammer already cocked back, and Henrietta's finger rested on the trigger. He wouldn't have time to raise his own weapon, not fast enough anyway. It would be over before he could even blink. His mind raced, calculating, but no plan materialized.

She had him dead to rights.

He still had so many questions for her.

Had she really orchestrated all this? The deaths of her husband and oldest son—had she planned it all along? Why did she want Tanya dead? Who did she think he was working with?

And now, he would never know the truth. His own mother was about to kill him in cold blood.

This can't be real.

Nobody is this heartless.

But deep down, Chase knew the truth.

She's going to do it.

Chase's breath hitched, his voice barely above a whisper.

"Mother, don't. Please—"

"You're no son of mine," she sneered. "I should have smothered you in your sleep the day I brought you home."

Then, a single bullet struck Henrietta Enfield Burke's still-glamorous face, killing her instantly.

CHAPTER FIFTY-FOUR

Even though she had been listening in on Chase's confrontation with his mother over the open phone line, the eruption of violence came as a surprise to Doyle. Nevertheless, her cop instincts kicked in instantaneously.

She hauled out the pistol Chase had loaned her—*Just in case*—and pushed past the pair of women who had been trying, unsuccessfully, to appease her. The sound of gunfire had startled them, but the sight of the demanding and entitled "Ms. Kennedy" brandishing a firearm sent them fleeing in terror.

Doyle moved quickly but cautiously toward the door leading back into the offices, peeking around the frame before committing herself. Heart pounding, nerves taut as a garrote, she eased around the corner, her weapon raised and ready. She was pretty sure that the two shots, which had been fired less than ten seconds ago, had come from inside one of the offices lining the hallway.

She had taken only a few steps when doors creaked open and people began stepping into the hallway, faces painted with a mix of confusion and curiosity, unaware of the danger.

Damn lookie-loos, thought Doyle.

"Police! Get back!" she shouted, her voice slicing through the growing murmurs.

The warning had the desired effect. The clueless onlookers scurried back into their offices, but her voice had also announced her presence to any bad guys, sacrificing the element of surprise.

Too late to worry about that now.

A third report split the air, and Doyle reflexively dropped into a crouch. In the next heartbeat, she heard a loud thud—as if a body had hit the ground—followed by heavy footsteps from the office to her left. Keeping her pistol steady, she moved toward the open doorway where the sounds had come from.

"Police!" she shouted, stepping into the office.

Her eyes swept the room like she was solving a hidden-object puzzle, focusing on one thing—finding a gun. Everything else faded into the background.

But there was no gun. No shooter.

Just the still body of a woman in scrubs, the name Lucy stitched onto the chest.

Henrietta Burke's nurse?

The scrubs' fabric was turning red from the blood spreading from a stomach wound. Doyle's eyes trailed upward and locked onto what seemed to be a bullet hole above the nurse's left eye.

What the hell?

"Chase?"

For a long moment, there was only silence, but then she heard a choked reply from behind the desk. "Here."

Still wary of a threat and bracing herself for the possibility that Chase might have caught one of those bullets, she kept her pistol at the ready as she stepped around the desk.

Chase was kneeling on the floor, hunched over the body of his mother, cradling her head in his hands. His back was to her, partially blocking the woman's face from view, but the blood trailing down Chase's thighs told her all she needed to know—Henrietta Enfield Burke was dead.

"God, Chase," she breathed. "What happened?"

He looked up, his eyes were vacant. His lips were moving, but it was as if he couldn't form the words.

"Did you . . . ?" she couldn't help asking, the question slipping out before she could stop herself.

Chase shook his head and managed a reply. "Someone outside."

Doyle's eyes snapped to the window. There, clear as day, was the bullet hole.

"Shit!" She dropped down beside Chase, lowering her profile. "The shooter's still out there?"

"I . . ." Chase seemed to be wrestling with the concept. "I'm not the target."

"What?"

"He wasn't here for us. For me." His eyes dropped to his mother's lifeless form. "He got what he came for."

It took a moment for the significance of this to hit home.

"Chase, do you know who did this?"

Chase didn't answer right away. Instead, he closed his eyes for a moment, his expression shifting as he took a deep breath. Gently, he laid his mother's body onto the floor.

When he turned to face her, his voice was once again steady.

"No, but it's time I found out."

CHAPTER FIFTY-FIVE

Damien was just approaching the cultivated park area—known to Havenwood Retreat's residents as the Memory Garden—when he heard two gunshots coming from inside the building.

His instincts had been spot on. Chase Burke *had* been in one of the vehicles Nate had spotted, and now he was inside the grounds, doing God only knew what.

He keyed his radio mic. "It's Burke. He's inside. Mac, Ollie, close in on the main residence. Nate, stay where you are and provide cover for us. And if anyone tries to leave, stop them. Do whatever it takes, but don't kill Burke. I'm the one who gets to end his life, understood?"

The three mercenaries had just sent back their acknowledgments when a third gunshot rang out. Damien didn't flinch; his focus was now entirely on reaching the residential building, finding Burke, and making him pay for what he'd done to Brad. Nevertheless, the part of him that had survived countless missions—both in the service of his country and in pursuit of private wealth—recognized that the third shot had been fired by a different weapon than the first two he'd heard. He was heading into danger, of that there was no doubt.

There was an active shooter situation inside Havenwood Retreat. Maybe Burke was shooting the place up, or maybe someone was shooting at him. Either way, Damien knew he might very well be walking into live fire.

Won't be the first time, he thought, pulling his balaclava down to cover his face before charging out into the open.

All across the Memory Garden, residents and staff members, already on heightened alert after the gunshots, turned to look at him as he trespassed in their Edenic sanctuary. Whether it was the Heckler & Koch MP5SD he carried at the low ready or merely the fact that a masked intruder was sprinting through their midst, cries of alarm rose up all around him. Men and women scurried out of his way, diving for cover behind benches and tree trunks.

Ignoring them, sweeping the grounds for any sign of movement, he continued forward. He was within reach of the rear entrance to the facility when he heard the scritch of someone breaking squelch on the radio.

"Nate here. I've got eyes on a lone bloke, armed with a rifle. He's moving fast toward the vehicles. I've got the shot. What's the word?"

Damien came to a full stop. "Is it him? Is it Burke?"

"It's the bearded fella from the silver SUV," replied Nate. Then, with more certainty, he added, "Shall I take the shot? Doesn't have to be lethal."

The question hung over Damien like the blade of a guillotine. Was the bearded man Chase Burke? If it was indeed him, this whole thing could end now with a single trigger pull from Nate. Burke would be down, and Damien could move in to finish the job.

But what if it wasn't him?

Damien didn't care. The man was armed, wasn't he? He was fair game.

"Shall I take the shot?" repeated Nate. "I need an answer. Now! I can only see one-half of the lot, and I'm about to lose sight of him."

The client's words echoed in Damien's head.

Chase Burke hunted Brad down and tortured him before finally putting a bullet in his head.

He hadn't come all this way to let someone else end Burke. "Do not engage. I say again, do not engage. If he tries to leave, disable his vehicle."

The silence from Nate stretched on longer than Damien liked.

"Nate," he snapped, "did you copy my last?"

When the reply finally came, it was cold, sharper than Damien expected. "Yeah, I heard. But this is bollocks, and you bloody well know it."

Damien's jaw clenched, and for a moment, he felt the urge to fire back. But he needed Nate on his side, focused on the objective, not tangled in an argument.

"Mac, Ollie, what's your status?" he asked.

Mac answered first, slightly breathless, his voice rising and falling as he spoke while moving. "I'm coming in from the north side. Fifty meters out."

As soon as Mac's transmission ended, Ollie signaled that he was almost to the south end of the building.

"Good copy. Rally on the car park," said Damien. "Stop Burke from leaving, but *do not* kill him unless he's firing directly at you. Shoot his legs if you must, but keep him bloody alive."

He veered away from the rear door and began moving parallel to the building, quickening his pace to a full sprint. The most direct route would have been *through* the building, but the potential for delays navigating an unfamiliar layout, stopping to open doors, and dealing with patients and staff favored taking the longer but quicker route around the building. He wouldn't reach the parking area first—Mac and Ollie would almost certainly arrive ahead of him—but it would be close.

He ran as if the winged Furies—the ancient spirits of vengeance—were bearing him forward. Every step brought him closer to his prey. Every breath he took was a reminder of why he was there. He had sacrificed everything for this moment, and now it was within reach. Chase Burke would pay for what he had done to Brad.

And then it would be over.

CHAPTER FIFTY-SIX

Chase could feel Doyle's big green eyes on him.

"What?" he asked, glancing over.

Doyle blinked. "You want us to leave? Are you insane? Chase, this is a crime scene. We can't leave. We have to wait for the police."

Chase shook his head, Henrietta's warning still ringing in his ears. *You think James Campbell is the only policeman working for us?*

"No. We can't trust the police. We don't know *who* we can trust right now. My mother as much as said that there are more dirty cops working for them."

"'Them,' Chase? Who's '*them*'?"

This is so much bigger than your little brain can comprehend.

Chase shook his head. "I don't know, but if we don't get out of here right now, they'll make sure we never find out. We can deal with the police later. Trust me, Alice. Please."

Doyle stared back at him, frowning, but then her expression hardened. "If Campbell hadn't tried to kill me last night, I'd say you were paranoid." She sighed. "I'm probably going to regret this, but . . ." She waved a hand toward the exit. "Let's go."

Chase nodded and then headed through the doorway, stepping over Lucy's body on his way out. Despite his outward show of stoicism and determination, Chase felt as if he was drowning.

Henrietta Enfield Burke was dead.

The woman whose contempt had loomed over him like a thunderhead, whose neglect . . . whose unabashed *hatred* had ironically forged him into the man he was . . . his mother . . . was gone.

For as long as he could remember, he had clung to the admittedly naive hope that she would change, that she would shed her spiteful, calculating persona and emerge as someone capable of loving him. When she had begun showing symptoms of dementia—*But of course, that was a lie, wasn't it?*—he had prayed for one lucid moment in which she might redeem herself. But the truth, the horrifying truth, was that she had been involved in something so dark, so malevolent, that he realized that he had never truly known her at all.

What had she been part of? Why had she done it?

The fact that he would never really have an answer was a crushing weight on his shoulders, a burden he would carry for the rest of his days. Whatever she had been involved in, it had consumed her, and now it threatened to consume him too.

Stepping through the lobby exit was like stepping through a portal to another planet. The clear blue sky and peaceful surroundings contrasted the chaos he had just left behind.

Not surprisingly, the parking attendant had deserted his post—a small wooden kiosk covered with a slanted canvas awning. Behind the counter, a pegboard held half a dozen keys, and Chase's eyes quickly landed on the BMW's fob.

"Shit, what a mess. I don't know how we're even going to begin to unfuck this," Doyle said, catching the fob Chase had lobbed at her.

"We'll figure it out," said Chase. "Right now, we just have to get out of here before—"

He broke off as he glimpsed movement off to their left. Fifty yards away, a figure was emerging from the woods, moving toward the parking lot at a brisk run.

Chase did a double take, and his eyes widened.

This wasn't just any figure. The man's face was covered by a dark balaclava, and he was carrying a suppressed submachine gun, though Chase was too far away to identify the model.

That must be the man who took out my mother.
And he's still on the premises. Guess I was wrong about that too.
Shit!

He was about to shout a warning to Doyle when the running man skidded to a halt, staring directly at them. And then, the business end of his gun began swinging toward them.

"Get down, Alice!" Chase shouted as he brought the SIG up.

Because his pistol was easier to maneuver than the man's weapon, Chase was able to snap off two shots before the man could get him—or Doyle—in his sights. The man, though, was beyond the accurate range of the pistol, and both of Chase's rounds missed their mark. But his shots hadn't been in vain, either, as they had the desired effect of discouraging the gunman from standing in the open and returning immediate fire. Instead, the man dropped to the ground, assuming a prone firing position.

The shooter's weapon was almost silent, and with no telltale muzzle flash to give him away, Chase didn't even realize the man was firing back at them until bullets started zipping over his head and cracking into the facade of the building behind them.

Doyle, who was now crouched five feet to Chase's left, fired several times in the man's direction. The rounds missed, but they must have come close because the shooter rolled twice to his right, then sprang to his feet and sprinted toward a tall tree.

Chase knew he and Doyle could not afford to stay in the open. They needed to find cover. And fast.

"Head for the parking lot! I'll cover you!" he shouted.

As Doyle got up and dashed toward the parking lot, Chase steadied his aim and squeezed the trigger five times, each bullet slamming into the tree trunk where the shooter had taken cover. As the man peeked around the edge of the tree, Chase fired another round. This time, the shooter flinched back. Chase couldn't be sure, but he thought his last round might have clipped the man.

"Go!" yelled Doyle, who had taken refuge behind a Volvo SUV.

The moment the detective started firing, Chase ran toward the parking lot at a full sprint, covering the distance in record speed and throwing himself down next to her.

"I thought you said this guy wasn't after you," said Doyle.

"Yeah, I'm aware," he grunted back, inserting a fresh magazine into the SIG.

"So, who the hell is *he*?" Doyle asked.

"No clue." Chase shook his head. "Every time I think I have it figured out, someone throws another curveball."

"Well, it's two against one, and I like those odds."

Chase couldn't help but smirk at her confidence. It was misplaced but, somehow, oddly moving. From the moment this whole mess had begun in the dining room of Chrysalis, with him taking on multiple gunmen with nothing but a steak knife, he'd been on his own. A one-man act with no one watching his back. Now, finally, the equation had changed.

But we're still outgunned. What I'd give for an M4 right now.

"How do you want to do this?" she asked.

Chase considered the question. "I say we make a go for your rental," he said. "It's close by."

"Agreed. Cover me."

Never one to let someone else face danger in his place, Chase was about to suggest they reverse those roles, but Doyle didn't give him a chance. Squaring her shoulders, she readied herself for action. "On three. One . . . two . . ."

Chase quickly snapped his focus toward the location where he had last seen the shooter, and when Doyle said "Three," he edged around the rear end of the Volvo and aimed his pistol at the tree trunk.

Even though he didn't see the shooter, Chase squeezed off two rounds, hoping it would be enough to keep the shooter pinned down.

Had the man moved? Was it possible he had changed location?

Damn it!

Chase twisted around, scanning left, then right. And that's when he saw him.

Shit!

"Doyle! Contact right!"

A masked figure—this one much taller than the other—was approaching from the north side of the building, a suppressed MP5SD aimed straight toward the parking lot.

So much for two against one.

Chase barely had the time to raise his pistol before the gunman opened fire. Chase backpedaled, darting to the opposite side of the Volvo just as a rain of metal tore into the vehicle, splintering the fiberglass and shattering the windows. Over the deafening noise, he thought he heard the muffled report of Doyle's weapon.

Chase watched as the man continued to close in, low in a combat crouch, delivering accurate fire at both of their positions. The shooter dropped his empty magazine and slammed in a fresh one, then brought his weapon back up with unnerving speed as he directed a blistering wave of fire at Doyle. Chase didn't hesitate and leaned out from cover. He began firing round after round, not bothering to aim, as he tried to draw the man's attention away from Doyle.

But the shooter kept coming, relentless, pushing forward through the cross fire, his rifle far more accurate than their pistols. Chase ducked as more bullets sprayed the side of the Volvo.

A sharp pain shot across his face as shards of metal sliced his right cheek and forehead.

Fuck!

Pushing the pain out of his mind, Chase fired again, but the man kept coming, advancing with deadly precision. Chase knew he had only a few rounds left in his magazine.

What about Doyle? How many rounds had she left?

Then, the gunman staggered, his body twisting as if hit by an invisible punch. Chase couldn't tell if it was one of his rounds or Doyle's, but the impact made the shooter falter. This time, with no rounds coming his way, Chase took an extra moment to aim.

The shooter, now injured, tried to break contact, but his window of opportunity had already closed. He flinched as Chase's next round found his right leg and then pitched back when Doyle shot him in the throat.

"Chase!" Doyle's shout cut through the sudden quiet. "Let's go!"

Chase blinked, realizing that he was still aiming at the dead shooter. He turned toward the detective. She was gesturing emphatically toward her rented BMW, but her left arm was drenched in blood, the deep red soaking through her sleeve and dripping down onto the pavement.

"Alice, your arm—" he began.

"I know," she cut him off. "I'm fine. We've got to move."

She was anything but fine, but he nodded and rose to his feet.

CHAPTER FIFTY-SEVEN

Damien rounded the end of the main residence building just in time to see Mac go down in the cross fire. Nate, still holding position at the exit gate more than two hundred meters away, was screaming in his ear.

"Ollie is hit! A round nicked his neck! He's bleeding out!"

Damien cursed out loud.

Chase Burke had just taken out two more of his brothers-in-arms. Yet, as much as Damien wanted to make Burke pay, he knew their deaths were on him. He had led them into this nightmare and had tied their hands by his insistence that they leave Burke alive.

And now, Mac and Ollie were either dead or dying.

Damien was still trying to figure out how it had happened. Nate had initially been tracking the man from the SUV with the assumption that it was Burke, but then Ollie had called in reporting confirmation that Burke was exiting the residence building along with an unknown female.

So, who was the guy in the SUV?

Before he could answer that question, the shooting had started, and just like that, Ollie and Mac were out of the game.

He heard Nate's voice again. "They're in a car. A black BMW. They're going to get away. I'm repositioning, and I'll engage as soon as I have a shot. I'm done fucking around."

Damien saw the BMW accelerating through the car park. He brought up his MP5SD and fired several controlled bursts, his rounds striking the rear windshield and bumper. Then the BMW vanished around the corner, its taillights blinking once, as if mocking him.

The BMW's tires screeched as Doyle took the corner hard, flooring the accelerator. Chase gripped the armrest out of reflex but otherwise showed no reaction. They weren't out of this yet—the shattered back window told him that much. There was at least one more shooter to deal with.

Chase stole a glance at the NYPD detective. Her face was pale, and every time she moved her left arm, he caught the faint wince she tried to hide. Her eyes, though, were still sharp. But the moment they were out of this mess, he would take the wheel and drive straight to the hospital.

"Private security," Chase muttered, more to himself than to Doyle. "Curtis must have hired them for extra protection. Or maybe Henrietta did."

"Protection from *what*? It's a nursing home, for God's sake."

Before Chase could answer, a loud crack reverberated through the vehicle as something struck the hood of the sedan mere inches from the windshield. He ducked, intuitively recognizing the impact for what it was—a bullet.

"Incoming!"

Doyle, who was already hunching down in her seat to reduce her profile, cranked the wheel to the left, trying to swerve out of the line of fire, even as a second round struck the windshield and ripped through her seat. Before either of them could react, two more bullets tore through the interior of the BMW, one of them grazing Chase's seat. Several shots hit the front of the vehicle, triggering a series of warning lights across the instrument panel as the engine whined in protest.

Another round blew out a front tire in a violent pop, and the BMW began to jerk uncontrollably, its ruined tire shredding against the asphalt.

"Hang on!" shouted Doyle.

In a desperate attempt to regain control, she overcompensated, pulling the wheel too sharply. The BMW veered off the road, and Chase was thrown against the door, knocking his head against the window. An instant later, the now out-of-control BMW slammed into a large concrete flower bed.

In that moment, everything seemed to slow down. The world outside the vehicle blurred—a dizzying swirl of blue sky, green lawn, and black asphalt.

The car flipped over—and Chase heard the screeching of metal and the crunching of glass shattering in a rain of glittering diamonds, but it felt distant, as if he was watching it happen to someone else. His hands scrambled for anything to grab as he and Doyle were tossed violently from side to side as the BMW corkscrewed twice before finally slamming into a tree and coming to a stop.

Chase blinked, waiting for everything to stop spinning. When it finally did, the world still looked off kilter, and it took a moment longer for him to realize why. Everything was upside down—the car, his view, his body, his thoughts. The sedan had come to rest on its roof, and he was hanging in the seat belt. He turned his head to see Doyle in a similar state, eyes fluttering open, her face streaked with blood and dirt.

"You okay?" he managed.

"My . . . left arm," moaned Doyle. "I . . . I can't . . . feel it. Seat belt release . . . can't reach it."

"Let . . . let me help you," Chase said, ignoring the throbbing pain radiating through his entire body.

He fumbled with his seat belt, his fingers numb and clumsy, until the latch finally gave way. He dropped hard onto the headliner but managed to twist mid-fall to protect his head. Still, the impact sent a fresh wave of agony through him. But he pushed past it. Chase crawled toward the shattered window, the jagged edges scratching at his skin as he dragged himself out of the wreckage. Flopping down on the torn-up grass beside the overturned BMW, he gasped for breath, trying to gather his bearings.

That was when he saw the masked figure looming over him.

CHAPTER FIFTY-EIGHT

Chase reacted instantly, flipping back onto his stomach and pressing his hands into the grass, trying to push himself toward the wreck. His SIG was somewhere in that mess—if he could just reach it. It was a Hail Mary, and he knew it, but he had come through too much to simply give up and die.

Yet, as fast as Chase was, the gunman was faster.

In a blur, the man closed the gap and sent a brutal kick right between Chase's legs. The blow landed with precision, sending a wave of white-hot pain through his entire being and forcing the air out of his lungs in a strangled gasp. Before Chase could recover, a heavy boot crashed down onto his spine, pinning him to the ground. Then, Chase felt the business end of a submachine gun—the still-warm steel of its suppressor to be exact—pressing hard against the back of his neck.

"How the bloody hell did you walk away from that crash, Burke?" the man asked. "Not that I'm complaining, mind you."

There was something familiar about the man's voice—

No, not his voice, Chase realized. *His accent.*

But what really caught Chase's attention was the fact that the man hadn't just executed him on the spot.

Why am I still alive?

Could this be the man who had killed Curtis McGraw in the parking garage? The same guy who had subsequently escaped without killing Chase, even when he had the chance?

No. It can't be.

If McGraw's killer had wanted Chase dead, he could have easily finished him off in the garage after incapacitating him with the stun grenade.

This wasn't him. Chase was sure of it. He was also convinced that McGraw's assassin was the same man who had shot Henrietta through McGraw's office window.

No, the man standing over him was someone else, and Chase had the sinking feeling that the reason why the man hadn't put a bullet through his skull had nothing to do with mercy.

"I made a promise that I would look you in the eye when I pulled the trigger," said the man, as if reading Chase's thoughts. "I wanted you to know exactly who's killing you. Now turn around. Slowly."

Chase felt the pressure leave his back and, from the corner of his eye, saw the gunman take a step back. He weighed the odds of being able to make a move before the man could get off a shot but decided against it. His assailant was fast, strong, and already committed to the idea of murder.

Keep him talking, he thought. *Maybe he'll make a mistake.*

"All right, I'm going to turn over."

Chase slowly rolled to the left until he was on his back, looking up at the gunman who had moved back a few steps and had his suppressed rifle trained on his head.

"Who are you?" Chase asked.

"You don't know?" The man uttered a short bark of laughter, then reached up with his left hand and tore the balaclava away. "You're a clever bloke. Go on, figure it out."

Chase didn't recognize the man, but there was something familiar about his face. That, coupled with the accent, was enough for him to make an educated guess. "This is about Nigel and Brad Gray, isn't it?"

The man's expression darkened at the mention of the names, and Chase knew he'd hit close to the mark. "You're their brother . . . Damien."

The man gave a satisfied smile, and Chase realized that this little bit of recognition was the only thing Damien had been waiting for before killing him. As if on cue, Gray's finger moved toward the trigger.

Think of something!

"Nigel said something before he died," Chase blurted out, desperate. "A message he wanted me to pass on to you."

Chase's words had the desired effect. Gray's finger moved back to the trigger guard.

"I was with Nigel when he died. I held his hand," Chase continued, pushing the lie. "He didn't die alone."

"You're lying," Gray growled, his eyes filled with hate.

Chase was indeed lying, but he hoped Gray's curiosity would buy him some more time to think of an escape.

"I'm not lying! I swear! Look, I'm sorry about what happened to them, but they broke into my apartment. I was just defending myself."

"Defending? You were *defending* yourself when you tortured my brother to death?"

"Torture? I didn't torture anyone. I'm a sommelier, for God's sake! A cop shot Nigel. Brad got away."

Chase recalled Doyle telling him that Brad's body had turned up in Brooklyn but decided to keep that to himself.

"I have no idea what happened to him, but I didn't torture him, and I sure as hell didn't kill him."

Chase could see that his testimony had failed to sway the eldest Gray brother.

"Do you want to know what Nigel said or not?"

Chase could see the hesitation on Gray's face. If Gray could only lower his gun, Chase would roll out of the way, then launch himself at him and maybe, with a lot of luck, reunite him with his brothers.

Chase's heart sank when Gray, who must have realized he was too close to Chase, took a few steps back.

Just when Chase thought everything was lost, Doyle's voice rang out.

"Damien Gray! Drop your weapon!"

Gray's attention snapped to Doyle, and the muzzle of the MP5SD shifted away from Chase. Doyle, who was standing on the opposite side of the overturned vehicle, had her pistol trained on Gray across the BMW's undercarriage. But Gray just as quickly returned both his gaze and his weapon to Chase, a smile creasing his face.

"You look pale, Detective," Gray said. "And your hand is shaking. I'm guessing you won't be able to hold that gun for much longer."

"Chase didn't kill Brad," Doyle said quickly. "I can prove it."

Gray didn't react. His weapon remained trained on Chase, the muzzle steady and unwavering.

For fuck's sake, Alice, thought Chase. *Just shoot him.*

But he didn't say it aloud. The fact that Gray hadn't pulled the trigger meant Doyle's words had at least given him pause.

"The man who hired your brothers to bug Chase's apartment . . . he's the one who killed Brad," Doyle went on. "Tying up loose ends."

"Why should I believe you?" Gray shot back. "You'd say anything to save his sorry arse."

Doyle shook her head. "Like I said, I can prove it. Curtis McGraw is the name. That's who killed Brad. Or at least ordered his death. I overheard a phone call between McGraw and my ex-partner, a dirty cop named James Campbell, talking about it. McGraw is dead and Campbell is in custody. He's not talking, and right now the case against him isn't exactly airtight." She paused a beat, letting it sink in, then continued. "You were lied to. I'm guessing that the people who hired you to kill Chase are the same ones who paid you to kill Congresswoman Hemsworth."

Gray gave a slight head shake. "You have it all wrong. We weren't hired to kill her. We were told to wound her."

Wound her? thought Chase. *That doesn't make any sense.*

"It doesn't matter. These people set you up," Doyle said. "Don't make it worse by killing an innocent man."

Gray shook his head again. "This man isn't innocent, Detective," he muttered. "And for me, it's already too late."

"It's not!" pressed Doyle. "Think about it. You can make a deal. Testify against them. I can't guarantee immunity, but you *will* live to see your family. Your wife. Your daughter, Alessandra. Think about them, Damien. Don't turn your back on them. Don't throw it all away. You're a father. There's still a chance you can have a life with them."

Chase could see the doubt creeping into Gray's eyes. His grip on the submachine gun faltered, his hands no longer rock steady. Chase hesitated. Should he let Doyle keep talking or spring into action?

"If you pull that trigger, I'll kill you, and you'll have died for nothing," Doyle said. "Take a second to think, Damien. What will your daughter think of you once she learns you murdered an innocent man in cold blood? That's the memory she'll be left with. You'll ruin her life too!"

Gray seemed to consider Doyle's words, and Chase noted that the submachine gun was dipping slightly and that Gray's hands were no longer rock steady.

Gray blinked, then he nodded. "All right. I'm going to lower my weapon."

Chase got to his feet and snatched Gray's MP5SD from his grasp.

He breathed a sigh of relief.

But the moment did not last.

"The fuck you doing, mate?" The shout came from another masked figure, approaching from the drive, a scoped assault rifle at the high ready, aimed at Doyle's chest.

Doyle swung toward the newcomer, but the advantage was his.

"Drop it!" he yelled at her.

Doyle let go of her gun just as Chase raised the submachine gun.

"No! Enough!" shouted Gray, putting himself between Chase and the gunman.

"Move out of the way!" the man yelled.

"I said enough! It's over, Nate," Gray said, walking toward the masked man, his hands raised high. "Burke didn't kill Brad. It wasn't him."

"Well, he fucking killed Mac and Ollie now, didn't he?"

"It was a mistake. We were set up. I'm not going to kill that copper, or Burke for that matter."

"Then let me take care of it," retorted Nate, sidestepping to aim around Gray.

Chase was moving, too, trying to get an angle on Nate, but Gray was still in his line of fire.

"No, Nate. Just walk away while you still can. I'll take the heat for this."

"Fuck that," snarled Nate, stabbing Gray in the chest with the muzzle of his sniper rifle. "Move or I'll kill you too."

The crack of a gunshot cut the threat short. Nate's head snapped to the side, a halo of red floating above him as he crumpled to the ground.

Chase ducked instinctively, expecting more incoming rounds any second.

Shit!

But the rounds never came.

"Alice! Are you hit?" Chase shouted.

"No. You?"

"I'm good."

In front of him, Gray had dropped to his knees, burying Nate's head in his hands. "Damn it, no."

For a long second, Chase thought Gray might go for the sniper rifle, but he didn't. He just sobbed quietly, mourning yet another brother-in-arms lost to a lie.

Although Chase hadn't seen who had fired the shot or where it had come from, he knew another shooter had joined the party. Staying low, the MP5SD gripped tightly in his hands, he rushed to Doyle's side.

Damn.

Gray hadn't lied. She didn't look good. Doyle was slumped against the side of the wrecked BMW, her face glistening with sweat. Her left arm hung limp at her side, and there was blood streaked across her face. Though she forced a smile, the tightness around her eyes told Chase she was in a lot of pain. Despite everything, she had recovered her pistol and was now holding it in her right hand.

She needs medical assistance. Soon.

Chase grabbed the pair of handcuffs Doyle kept in a pouch clipped to her belt and used them to secure Gray's hands behind his back. To Chase's surprise, the man didn't resist. He just sat there looking at his dead colleague.

Chase spotted a small tactical medical pouch rigged to Gray's vest by Velcro and yanked it free. He dropped to his knees next to Alice, unzipped the kit, and peeled back the fabric of her sleeve. About two inches above her elbow, a bullet had ripped through her flesh.

"It's not pretty, but you're gonna be fine," he said, wrapping a pressure bandage around the wound.

Alice grimaced but nodded.

"I'm gonna get you to a hospital," Chase said as he tightened the bandage, "but I first need to make sure whoever fired the last shot isn't about to—"

"Look," Doyle said, cutting him off.

He followed her gaze, and that was when he saw a bearded man wearing a ballcap and sporting sunglasses walking toward a silver Ford Explorer that was idling on the main drive. There was a rifle in the man's hands, but it wasn't aimed at any of them.

"Who's that?" Doyle asked.

Chase didn't have a clue. He was just as confused as she was.

Did Williams send someone?

Nothing else makes sense.

Chase got to his feet and started walking toward the Explorer.

"Hey! Wait!" he shouted.

But the man didn't stop. When he reached the SUV, he opened the front passenger door and set his rifle down.

Chase, jogging now, winced with each step.

"Chase, wait!" he heard Doyle call out behind him.

He ignored her, focused on the man who had just saved them from the hired killer.

As he drew near, the man spoke, still not looking back.

"I can't stay."

His voice was low and hoarse, like someone who had suffered a throat injury.

"That was you in the parking garage," said Chase. "You killed Curtis McGraw."

"He would have killed you if I hadn't."

"Maybe. Maybe not," countered Chase. "If I had been able to question him, we could have avoided all of this."

"Is that what you think? You don't know how these people operate. He would have lied to you, right up until the moment you let your guard down, and then he would have killed you."

"I'm done chatting. Turn around so that I can see your face."

"Not a good idea. For your sake," the man replied.

"Show me your face," Chase repeated, angry. "I want to know who killed my mother."

The man scoffed.

"You think this is about you?" he asked. "It's not. So let it go, Chase Burke. Let *me* go. Get back to your life. I've heard you're quite a good sommelier."

"You killed Henrietta Burke," Chase said. "Why?"

"I had to," replied the man. "She was about to kill you."

"She wouldn't . . ." Chase's voice faltered. "Maybe if I had talked to her . . ."

"Do you really think that would have stopped her? Believe me, it wouldn't have. I know."

"How the fuck would you know any—"

"You! Show me your hands!" Doyle interrupted as she came up behind Chase, the pistol in her left hand leveled at the man with the ballcap.

"Chase . . . who's this?" she asked.

"Someone Williams sent," he replied. "Am I right?"

The man hesitated, then gave a slight nod, still not turning.

"Enough of this shit," Doyle said. "Turn around, slowly."

"If I do this, neither of you will be safe. The less you know about me, the better. Let me be on my way. If you don't, it will only get worse for all of us. Trust me on this."

Chase had just about enough. Temper rising, he closed in on the man, intent on bringing him down if that was what it took.

The man must have sensed Chase's presence, because he said, "All right. Have it your way."

With a sigh, the man surrendered to the inevitable. Slowly he raised his arms, then turned to face Chase.

Chase's world seemed to stop as the man removed his ballcap, then his sunglasses.

It can't be. It's not possible, Chase thought, feeling the blood drain from his face.

He wanted to say something, anything, but he couldn't find the words. He swallowed hard, replaying what the man had said to him seconds before.

Do you really think that would have stopped her? Believe me, it wouldn't have. I know.

Seconds ticked by with nobody moving.

It's not possible, Chase told himself again while gesturing for Doyle to lower her gun.

When Chase was finally able to talk, only one word came out of his mouth.

"Michael."

CHAPTER FIFTY-NINE

Lightheaded from the blood loss caused by the gunshot wound to her left arm, Alice Doyle felt a chill as she stared at the man standing before her. There was something unsettling about him. She'd seen plenty of men like him in her career—hard, quiet, dangerous. But something about this one held her gaze longer.

"This man is . . . Michael Burke?" asked Doyle, her voice raising an octave.

She barely saw a resemblance.

Well . . . maybe around the eyes. The beard made it hard to tell.

Chase nodded. "Yeah. My brother." It was evident he was as stunned as she was.

"But . . . I thought you were dead?" The words came out before she could stop herself.

Michael turned slightly toward her. His quiet confidence—the aura of someone who didn't care what she thought—was infuriating and . . . oddly magnetic.

"I should have known," Chase muttered next to her.

Doyle didn't buy it. "How? How could you have known?" she asked.

"When I told my mother about Curtis, the look she gave me . . ." Chase shook his head. "I think she suspected you"—he chinned toward Michael—"were still alive and that we were working together. That's why she sent Brad and Nigel Gray to search my apartment. That look from her . . . yeah, I should have known. I just couldn't figure out how all the pieces fit together."

Doyle remained silent, her eyes darting between the brothers.

"I tried to keep you out of this, Chase," Michael said, stepping closer. "When I slashed your tires, I was hoping you'd take the hint and stand down."

"A warning, huh?" Chase said. There was a sudden bitterness to his tone. "Or did you think I was part of it too?"

Doyle noticed the faintest flicker of guilt cross Michael's face.

"I didn't think you were, Chase. I'd hoped you weren't," Michael replied, "but I had to be sure. Now I know. You're still the man I thought you were."

"Can you say the same about *yourself?*" cut in Doyle, facing Michael, her pistol still at the low ready. "Are you one of the good guys? A lot of bodies are piling up here, Michael. And from where I stand, most of the blood is on your hands."

Michael's face darkened. "There's a reason for all of that. It's a long story."

"No shit," she snapped, refusing to give him an inch. "Make it short."

Michael glanced at Chase, then nodded. "Short version? There's a global criminal organization called FATHOM that pretty much runs the world, and Henrietta Enfield Burke was on their board of directors."

"FATHOM?" countered Doyle. "Never heard of it. Sounds like a bogeyman tale."

"It's not. Their tentacles reach into governments, corporations, terrorist organizations . . . they can force a sitting president to set aside his reelection campaign or set up an assassination attempt on a former president in broad daylight with a single shooter on the nearest fucking sloped rooftop. That's child's play for them. You name it, they're calling the shots."

Doyle thought about Damien Gray's admission.

We weren't hired to kill her. Just wound her.

Still, it was a lot to process.

Chase spoke up in his brother's defense. "Mother said they were just getting started."

"Yeah, well, that's the one thing she wasn't lying about. FATHOM has a plan. I don't know what it is exactly, at least not yet, but I'm going to find out. And I'm gonna stop them."

"So, you faked your own death to bring her down?" asked Doyle.

"Not by plan, no. She tried to kill me. I just got lucky, and once everyone thought I was dead, well . . . staying dead seemed the best of my limited options."

"I wish you would have trusted me enough to reach out," Chase said.

Then, taking Doyle by surprise, Michael crossed the distance to his brother and pulled him into an embrace. Doyle looked at the brothers, feeling like an outsider. Beneath Chase's stoic composure, she saw the hurt he carried—the betrayal, the shock of losing his brother and finding him again, all in the same heartbeat. As for Michael . . . for all his gruff exterior, he clung to Chase like a man who'd been adrift and who had finally found his anchor.

"Guys, you need to go," Doyle said after a moment, then added, "You could have told your side of the story, you know? And you still can, Michael. Let me help you."

Michael shook his head. "No offense, but when your own mother tries to kill you, it doesn't exactly inspire a trusting—"

"You can trust *me*," said Chase.

Michael took a deep breath. "I know. But this isn't your—"

"Don't you dare say it isn't my fight. It is now."

Michael gave his younger brother a hard look, but then cocked his head to one side as if straining to hear something. Then he turned his attention back to Chase. "Your friend is right. I have to go."

"Then I'm coming with you."

"Chase . . ."

"I'm part of this now, Michael. Whether you like it or not."

Michael pursed his lips together as if trying to come up with an irrefutable argument against Chase's decision.

Doyle looked from brother to brother, then made up her own mind.

"Chase is right," she said. "He knows too much. When the police get here, they're going to take him into custody. If FATHOM really is as powerful as you say they are, then it will only be a matter of time before he has a fatal accident or 'hangs' himself in his cell." She handed the pistol—Chase's own Wilson EDC X9—over to its rightful owner. "Get out of here, both of you. I'll handle this."

"Come with us," Chase said. "You need to see a doctor, Alice."

"I'm not leaving," she replied. "In any case, the paramedics will be here before you two can get me to a hospital."

"Alice—" started Chase, but Doyle cut him off.

"I said no. Go! Go before I change my mind."

She could see Chase's gratitude shine in his eyes, and as he moved around the Ford's front end, she called after them.

"I'm in this too," she said. "When you get to wherever it is you're going, you damn well better give me a call. I think I've earned that."

"I'll be in touch. Count on it," Chase said.

Michael met her gaze, and for a moment, something flickered in his eyes. Was it surprise, admiration even? It was hard to tell. He hadn't spoken a word, or even smiled, but he'd given her the kind of look that told her she'd just made an impression.

She wasn't sure why that mattered to her—but it did.

CHAPTER SIXTY

The officers from the West Hartford Police Department, along with two fire trucks and three ambulances, arrived at Havenwood Retreat eight minutes later. Anticipating an active shooter situation, the cops were surprised when an injured woman, identifying herself as a federal agent, met them at the gate. While the paramedics worked on her, Detective Alice Doyle, NYPD, assigned to the Joint Terrorism Task Force, informed the on-scene commander the immediate threat had been neutralized and that a suspect, Damien Gray, was in custody. She also advised him to limit West Hartford Police Department's activities as the federal government would be claiming jurisdiction.

The fact that Detective Doyle was unable to present credentials posed a problem, so the on-scene commander put a call in to the New York office of the JTTF, asking for verification. When he mentioned Doyle's name, the call was quickly routed to the director of the office, Supervisory Special Agent Whitaker, who confirmed that the crime scene would be under federal jurisdiction and then advised him to immediately take Doyle into custody and to drive her to the nearest hospital where FBI special agents would be waiting for them. At least she'd been given a few minutes to arrange care for her daughter. Doyle's parents, who lived in Jersey City, thankfully didn't ask too many questions when she'd asked them to look after Ava for a few days.

To be honest, Doyle had expected nothing less from Whitaker. In helping Chase Burke, she had gone so far out on a limb that she couldn't even see the tree. The only thing she had going for her was the fact that she had brought in Damien Gray—who had confessed to shooting Congresswoman Tanya Hemsworth—but even that counted for little against the laundry list of laws, statutes, and police procedures she had violated. It didn't help that, after spending two days at the hospital, she had demanded—as was her right—to speak with her police union representative instead of answering the FBI's questions.

She knew that her career in law enforcement was over. Prison time was even a possibility. But her instincts told her that if she so much as whispered the word FATHOM, or the name Michael Burke, her future career prospects would be the least of her worries.

Then everything changed.

Instead of being taken from her cell in lockup to the interview room, where she had spent the better part of the preceding seventy-two hours, she was escorted to Whitaker's private office. There, her manacles were removed and she was invited—invited, *not* ordered—by the supervisory special agent to have a seat.

Whitaker's face was expressionless, but she sensed nothing welcoming in his demeanor and braced herself for some new harangue. Instead, after appraising her for an uncomfortably long moment, Whitaker leaned forward and slid a thick manila envelope across the desktop toward her.

Doyle regarded the offering with a raised eyebrow. "What's this?"

"Your creds and your weapon," said Whitaker, making no effort to disguise his contempt. "You're cleared to return to duty, once your health has improved, of course."

Still wary, Doyle took the envelope. She could tell by its heft that Whitaker wasn't deceiving her about the contents. "That's it?"

Whitaker frowned. "This decision was made well above my pay grade. It seems that, despite your"—he paused, eyes narrowed as if searching for the right word—"unorthodox approach to this investigation, the AG prefers to take the win. You brought in Congresswoman Hemsworth's would-be assassin and identified a mole inside our agency, and it's the opinion of the higher-ups that subjecting you to disciplinary action would weaken the criminal case." He leaned back in his chair. "That said, you're no longer attached to JTTF."

"I don't understand. Are you firing me?"

"You're being reassigned. That's all I know." He motioned toward the door. "Good day, Detective Doyle."

Reassigned?

The word hung over Doyle like a Damoclean sword.

Reassigned where?

Judging from Whitaker's reaction, while she had been officially absolved of any wrongdoing, unofficially she was now a pariah. And unofficially, there were innumerable ways to punish a police officer for going rogue and upsetting the status quo.

Maybe they would put her on night duty at the Erie Basin impound yard.

That would be fitting.

Still, she had her badge and her freedom, and that was more than she'd started the day with. And maybe her new schedule would allow her to spend more time with Ava?

When her personal effects were returned to her, she found that the battery on her phone was completely dead. Unable to check her messages or call into her home precinct for an update, she decided to go home to her parents and Ava.

Which was why she didn't see the text message until it was almost too late.

Chrysalis. 6 pm. My treat. CB

Owing to traffic delays, Doyle's cab didn't arrive at the Chrysler Building until 6:08. The sidewalk in front of Chrysalis, which had been an active crime scene the last time she had been there, bore no residue of the violence that had occurred the week prior. The same could not be said for the restaurant's front entrance. Several of the large windows looking out from the dining room were boarded over with sheets of plywood. A large sign affixed to the front door promised that the establishment would be reopening soon.

Doyle frowned. Had Chase gotten his wires crossed?

Then, a darker possibility occurred to her.

What if that message wasn't from Chase?

This paranoid moment proved fleeting, for a few seconds later, the restaurant door opened to reveal Chase Burke, looking a good deal better than the last time she'd seen him. "Detective. You made it."

"After everything we've been through," said Doyle with a smile, "I think it's okay if you just call me Alice."

He inclined his head in a slight bow. "Alice, it is. Please, come inside." Noticing her glance at the sign on the door, he added, "It's okay. I know the owner."

She followed him inside and was relieved to see that, just as with the exterior, all traces of the violent incident had been wiped away. But for the absence of any staff, the establishment appeared ready for dinner service.

"Looks like they'll be open again soon," remarked Doyle.

"David wants to wait a couple of weeks before reopening," said Chase. "Just long enough for the Chrysalis Massacre to drop off the news cycle."

"So, if you didn't bring me here for dinner, why am I here?"

"Oh, there's dinner," replied Chase, laughing. "But if you've got your heart set on gourmet cuisine, I'm afraid you're in for a disappointment."

He led her through the bar seating area and into the main dining room, where she was surprised to see two men seated at one of the tables. One of them was Michael Burke. The other, an older, distinguished gentleman, looked very familiar. Both men stood as Chase brought her over and made introductions.

"Alice, you've already met my brother, Michael. And this is Secretary of State Connor Williams."

Doyle hid her surprise, accepting Williams's handclasp with a smile. "I thought you looked familiar."

"Secretary Williams is an old friend," explained Chase.

"He's also my boss," added Michael. "After I crawled out of the jungle in Colombia, he helped me get back stateside and has been supporting my off-the-books investigation into FATHOM."

"There will be plenty of time to talk shop later," Williams broke in, turning to Chase. "I believe you mentioned something about dinner?"

Dinner turned out to be takeout from an Italian restaurant down the street. While not exactly Michelin-star-worthy fare, Doyle found the baked ziti bolognese, garlic knots, and Caesar salad a definite upgrade from the food she'd been served during her time in federal custody. The wine, selected by Chase from Chrysalis's cellar, probably had something to do with that assessment.

As the meal progressed, Michael recounted the tale of his long and mostly solitary battle with the mysterious entity known as FATHOM under the aegis of the State Department's Office of Analysis for Terrorism, Narcotics, and Crime. "Early on," he explained, "I was just gathering intelligence. Reading interviews. Analyzing data. Crunching numbers and looking for patterns, trying to identify the key players. Certain names kept popping up, some of them being diplomats in the foreign service whose travel patterns overlapped FATHOM's activities, others were people close to me. I made a list. Initially, there were over twenty names on it, but as my investigation progressed, it became shorter until there were only five names left."

"And your mother's and brother's names were among them," said Doyle.

"Actually, at first, I thought it was my father." He glanced at Chase. "Our father. I didn't want to believe it, of course, but based on the data, it had to be either him or Henrietta, and by then she was already exhibiting signs of Alzheimer's. So, I added Chase to the list."

"Henrietta must have realized you were closing in on her and used the dementia diagnosis as a shield," Doyle said.

Michael nodded. "She didn't just hide behind the diagnosis. She turned Havenwood Retreat into FATHOM's new Northeastern headquarters, bringing Curtis McGraw—an ex–London cop who had been in FATHOM's pocket for most of his career—on as director. I fell for her act along with everyone else." His expression hardened. "And then she tried to kill me."

Michael recounted how he'd been maneuvered into joining the hostage rescue mission in Colombia, how they had been led into an ambush, and how his helicopter had been shot down over the rainforest.

"I'm really not sure how I survived," he went on. "I must have been thrown clear of the wreckage. At that point, I didn't know who to trust, so when the rescue team arrived on the scene, I hid out. Eventually, I was able to make my way to civilization and contact Connor."

"But you decided to let everyone think you were dead," said Doyle.

"It seemed like a good idea." He looked over at Chase again. "I'm sorry I put you through that."

Chase just shrugged.

"I couldn't go poking around Havenwood," Michael went on, "so I did the next best thing and started watching Curtis McGraw. I bugged his place, hoping he would let something slip. Then you showed up, and things . . . escalated."

"I think that's where I came in," said Doyle. She downed the last of the wine in her glass in a gulp, then leaned back and regarded Michael. "So, what's next?"

"Actually, that's why we've asked you here," said Connor Williams. "The fight against FATHOM isn't over."

Doyle raised an eyebrow. "I thought Henrietta Burke *was* FATHOM?"

"From what we've been able to unpack, Henrietta Burke oversaw FATHOM's East Coast financial empire—money laundering on a global scale. Losing her will be a setback for the organization, but not a death blow." He glanced over at Chase and Michael. "If you'll pardon the expression."

Michael waved the apology away. "I'm not shedding any tears for her."

Chase just looked back impassively, but Doyle wondered if he shared his brother's antipathy for their mother.

"Why?" Chase finally asked. "Why did she do it? Why did she join FATHOM?"

Michael's expression hardened. "I don't know the reason behind her decision, or exactly when it started, but I don't think she ever truly loved our father."

Chase frowned. "What do you mean?"

"I think she was already working for FATHOM when they met," Michael said. "She married him because she was ordered to."

"Because of his position in the foreign service?" Doyle asked, leaning forward now.

Michael nodded. "And because of his connections. Dad was on a first-name basis with some very powerful people."

"Access FATHOM wanted," Chase murmured.

"Or needed," added Williams. "The point is, we have an opportunity to go on the offensive."

Doyle shook her head. "No offense, but we got lucky this time. If FATHOM is as powerful as you say, then it's going to take a lot more than just"—she glanced at Michael—"a rogue agent who is officially still 'dead' and"—she nodded to Chase—"a badass sommelier who's still a person of interest in an ongoing federal investigation. You're going to need an army."

"You're not wrong," replied Williams. "We're already working on building that army. I'm establishing a small task force to go after FATHOM. Michael will be heading up operations. I'd like you to join us."

"Me?" Doyle shook her head. "As much as I'd love to, I'm not with the JTTF anymore. I've been reassigned."

"I know," said Williams. "I'm the one who requested your reassignment. If you want the job, that is."

Doyle was taken aback. "That was your doing?"

"Like you said the other day," Michael put in, "you've earned it."

"And for what it's worth," Williams went on, "Michael is now officially back among the living, and Chase has been cleared as well."

"You're on board too?" Doyle asked, glancing over at Chase.

Chase nodded. "Never been one to walk away from a fight."

Doyle laughed. "I noticed that about you."

Chase rose and topped everyone's wineglasses, then raised his. "To putting FATHOM out of business."

"Hear, hear," said Williams.

After glasses were clinked and the toast drunk, Chase set his glass down. "On that note, I'm afraid I'm going to have to leave you."

"And right when things were getting interesting," remarked Doyle with a smile. "Hot date?"

Chase offered a wan smile. "We'll see. David will come by to lock up later."

"You trust him?" she asked, then added, "I guess you do, if we're here of all places."

Chase sighed. "I did wonder if he or Violet were somehow involved, but Connor confirmed they weren't."

After Chase was gone, Doyle turned to Michael. "So, I guess you're my boss now. What's the plan? How are we going to put FATHOM out of business?"

"Simple," said Michael as he placed his hands flat on the table and leaned toward her. "First, we're going to figure out who they are."

"Sure," said Doyle. "The whole makin' a list and checking it twice. Even Santa does that. But then, what's our play?"

His response wasn't as jolly.

"Then we're going to burn them down to the fucking ground."

CHAPTER SIXTY-ONE

New York

Chase stepped out of Chrysalis and paused, letting the crisp evening air settle over him, grounding him. The city's familiar sounds—honking taxis, the hum of traffic, the occasional laughter filtering through the din—were a reminder of a world that felt both close and achingly far away. How long had it been since he'd truly savored these sounds?

It feels like a lifetime.

It was hard to believe that it had only been a few days since his old life had effectively ended. So much had happened. So much had changed.

His quest to find Tanya's attackers, to deliver justice on his own terms, had taken him down a rabbit hole so deep that he wasn't sure he would ever find his way back to daylight.

He had never wanted to be a cop . . . or whatever the hell he was now. All his life, he had prided himself on choosing his own path. Whether it was boxing or joining the Army or becoming a sommelier, he'd followed his heart. Now, all of it seemed pieces from someone else's life, fragments from a past that no longer fit.

A sommelier? He shook his head at the absurdity of it now. He wasn't that man anymore, and he knew it. His world had shifted. He was leaving behind everything he knew, everything he had built, to face an unknown future. A future where he would be up against a powerful criminal organization. A future that offered no guarantees.

Henrietta's doing, he thought bitterly. Even dead, she was still exerting her spiteful influence.

It took him about twenty minutes to make the walk, first heading east along 42nd Street and then south on First Avenue. He passed the Field of Lights and made a silent promise to come back one day when he could take the time to enjoy it.

He entered the hospital and checked in at the main reception desk and then headed for the elevator. When the doors slid open, he stepped off and went to the nurses' station, where a uniformed policeman sat, watching his approach with undisguised wariness.

"I'm Chase Burke. I called ahead."

The change in the officer's demeanor was instantaneous. A broad smile broke his stern expression. He jumped to his feet and extended his hand. "Mr. Burke. It's a pleasure to meet you, sir. You're a real hero."

Such praise would have made him uncomfortable under the best of circumstances, but at that moment, it was the last thing he wanted to deal with. Nevertheless, he managed a polite "Thanks" and accepted the handclasp, then gestured down the hallway. "Can I go in?"

"Sure thing."

Chase took a breath and let it out slowly, gathering his courage, and headed for the patient's room.

He had no idea how this was going to go.

So much had happened.

So much had changed.

Tanya.

Her name alone sent a surge of conflicting emotions through him. How would she react? Would she be happy to see him? Or would she resent his presence, a reminder of everything she'd endured? He'd rehearsed this moment in his mind, thought of a dozen things he might say, yet he felt utterly unprepared.

Her door was open, but from the doorway, he could only see the foot of the bed. Uncertain of what to do, he rapped his knuckles on the door. "Hello?"

"Come on in."

Swallowing down the lump of nerves in his throat, he complied.

Congresswoman Tanya Hemsworth was sitting up in her hospital bed. She wore no makeup, her hair was pulled back in a ponytail, and her smart business suit had been replaced by an unflattering hospital gown. Her face was pale, and an assortment of tubes and wires connected her to monitors and IV pumps. She'd been totally stripped of the polished appearance he was used to seeing. She looked vulnerable . . . and beautiful.

Her eyes met his and he thought he saw a flicker of surprise, or was it relief? He couldn't be sure. Then, her lips curved into a faint, but genuine, smile—a fragile reassurance that maybe, just maybe, everything was going to be all right.

EPILOGUE

Tehran, Iran

The forty-minute ride from Imam Khomeini International Airport to the Pasteur Street headquarters of the Ministry of Intelligence was by far the shortest leg of Ali Reza's long homeward odyssey, but it felt like the longest.

This was due partly to cumulative travel fatigue. Rather than spending a few days at his Istanbul apartment to backstop his cover identity—he had traveled from New York as Mehmet Demir, a Turkish software engineer—he had, after a brief layover, transferred to a Tehran-bound flight. Fourteen hours spent either on a plane or waiting for one was a drain.

But jet lag was something he could tolerate. What really made the drive into the heart of Tehran seem to take forever was his eagerness to report to Minister Khatib personally. Like the proverbial watched pot, time seemed to slow in direct proportion to the importance of the information he carried, information that was far too sensitive to pass along in a phone call or email concerning the most audacious covert operation ever launched by the Ministry against the Great Satan, America.

Eventually, however, the ride ended. The Tara arrived at the front gate to an unassuming compound comprised of nondescript buildings assigned to fictitious government agencies, and after an ID check, the driver pulled into the compound and deposited Reza in front of one of the buildings.

Reza was quickly ushered into an office where he found the head of the Ministry, attired in his customary cleric's robes and black turban, seated behind a desk. Khatib regarded him with a disdainful expression, which Reza mistakenly assumed to be a response to his neatly trimmed beard, uncovered head, and Western clothes. "Forgive my appearance, Minister. I came directly from New York, where I was operating undercover."

Khatib made a dismissive gesture. "I've heard about your operation in New York. You took a great risk."

Reza hid his surprise at Khatib's tone. "I took great care to ensure that there is nothing to connect us to the operation."

"I'm not talking about the risk of exposure. You gambled with our most valuable asset and very nearly lost."

While outsourcing the project had masked any connection to the Islamic Republic of Iran and thus ensured the long-term viability of the project, it had meant giving up direct control of the operation. If it had gone wrong, Reza would have borne full responsibility, regardless of whether the mistakes had been made by the hired contractors.

But it had not gone wrong.

Reza inclined his head in a show of submission. "Respectfully, Minister, I did not lose."

"Yes, that is true. Allah has blessed your efforts." Khatib sat back in his chair. "What is the current status of the asset?"

"It is just as I predicted. The Americans love a hero. Congresswoman Hemsworth will make a full recovery from her injuries. She's up nearly ten percent in the polls, and pundits are already talking about her viability as a candidate for the vice presidency. We may proceed with the next stage of Project XIII."

"Indeed," said Khatib. "Proceed as planned, Reza."

A thin smile stretched across Reza's face.

This is only the beginning . . .

ABOUT THE AUTHORS

Photo © 2024 Lisane Paquette © *Ryan Steck*

Simon Gervais is a former infantry officer and federal agent specializing in counterterrorism who served in the Royal Canadian Mounted Police, safeguarding dignitaries like Queen Elizabeth II and President Barack Obama. Now a bestselling thriller writer, Gervais is the author of *The Elias Network* and *The Elias Enigma*, as well as the Clayton White and Pierce Hunt series—all optioned for TV. He also penned *The Blackbriar Genesis* for the Robert Ludlum estate. Learn more at http://SimonGervaisBooks.com.

Ryan Steck is the author of *Fields of Fire*, *Lethal Range*, *Redd Christmas*, *Out for Blood*, and *Ted Bell's Monarch*, an Alex Hawke thriller. He's also the founder and editor in chief of The Real Book Spy website and an official Amazon Influencer. Praised as "one of the hardest-working and fairest reviewers out there" (author Lisa Scottoline), Steck is considered by some as "the authority on mysteries and thrillers" (author A. J. Tata). Steck's fourth Matthew Redd novel, *Gone Dark*, is due out in 2025.